DAVID ...
T...

A man returns home to his ... hoping to breathe new life into the twisted architecture of his childhood home. But when his wife and daughter go missing, the only clues are a cellar full of milk and a whispering old woman....

CLIVE BARKER—
The Book of Blood

The dead walk across thousands of miles of highways and byways. The intersections of these highways create a thin veil between their world and ours. One boy thinks he can interpret their incessant chatter and finds out too late the dead don't take kindly to lies....

DAVID GERROLD—
... And Eight Rabid Pigs

What if there was a bad thing for every good? What if Santa Claus had an alter ego? What if there was a Santa Claus with greasy gray hair, a beard full of slimy things, and an appetite for bad little children? What would happen if people believed in him?

NIGHT SCREAMS

NIGHT SCREAMS

EDITED BY

Ed Gorman and
Martin H. Greenberg

A ROC BOOK

ROC
Published by the Penguin Group
Penguin Books USA Inc., 375 Hudson Street,
New York, New York 10014, U.S.A.
Penguin Books Ltd, 27 Wrights Lane,
London W8 5TZ, England
Penguin Books Australia Ltd, Ringwood,
Victoria, Australia
Penguin Books Canada Ltd, 10 Alcorn Avenue,
Toronto, Ontario, Canada M4V 3B2
Penguin Books (N.Z.) Ltd, 182–190 Wairau Road,
Auckland 10, New Zealand

Penguin Books Ltd, Registered Offices:
Harmondsworth, Middlesex, England

First published by Roc, an imprint of Dutton Signet,
a division of Penguin Books USA Inc.

First Printing, January, 1996
10   9   8   7   6   5   4   3

ACKNOWLEDGMENTS
"The Dripping" copyright © 1972 by David Morrell. Reprinted by permission
  of the author and his agent, Henry Morrison, Inc.
"The Wringer" copyright © 1996 by F. Paul Wilson
"A Season of Change" copyright © 1996 by Richard T. Chizmar
"Good Vibrations" copyright © 1996 by Richard Laymon
"The Tulsa Experience" copyright © 1994 by Lawrence Block. First published
  in *Some Days You Get the Bear*. Reprinted by permission of the author.
"Trolls" copyright © 1996 by Christopher Fahy
"Small Deaths" copyright © 1993 by Charles de Lint. First appeared in
  Dreams Underfoot, Tor Books. Reprinted by permission of the author.
"White Lightning" copyright © 1996 by Al Sarrantonio
"Hitman" copyright © 1996 by Rick Hautala
". . . And Eight Rabid Pigs" copyright © 1995 by David Gerrold. First ap-
  peared under the title "Satan Claus" in *Alternate Outlaws*. Reprinted by
  permission of the author.
"Vympyre" copyright © 1996 by William Nolan
"Bringing It Along" copyright © 1996 by A.R. Morlan
"Redemption" copyright © 1996 by Dallas Mayr
"The Graveyard Ghoul" copyright © 1996 by Edward D. Hoch
"The Rings of Cocytus" copyright 1996 by Katherine Ramsland
"Late Last Night" copyright © 1996 by John Maclay
"Beasts in Buildings, Turning 'Round" copyright © 1996 by J. N. Williamson
"Dark Side of the Moon" copyright © 1996 by Barbara Collins

(*The following page constitutes an extension of this copyright page.*)

Contents

The Dripping
by David Morrell

That autumn we live in a house in the country, my mother's house, the house I was raised in. I have been to the village, struck more by how nothing in it has changed, yet everything has, because I am older now, seeing it differently. It is as though I am both here now and back then, at once with the mind of a boy and a man. It is so strange a doubling, so intense, so unsettling, that I am moved to work again, to try to paint it.

So I study the hardware store, the grain barrels in front, the twin square pillars holding up the drooping balcony onto which seared wax-faced men and women from the old people's hotel above come to sit and rock and watch. They look the same aging people I saw as a boy, the wood of the pillars and balcony looks as splintered.

Forgetful of time while I work, I do not begin the long walk home until late, at dusk. The day has been warm, but now in my shirt I am cold, and a half mile along I am caught in a sudden shower and forced to leave the gravel road for the shelter of a tree, its leaves already brown and yellow. The rain becomes a storm, streaking at me sideways, drenching me; I cinch the neck of my canvas bag to protect my painting and equipment, and decide to run, socks spongy in my shoes, when at last I reach the lane down to the house and barn.

The house and barn. They and my mother, they alone have changed, as if as one, warping, weathering, joints twisted and strained, their gray so unlike the white I recall as a boy. The place is weakening her. She is in tune with it, matches its decay. That is why we have come here to live. To revive. Once I thought to convince her to move away. But of her 65 years she had spent 40 here, and she insists she will spend the rest, what is left to her.

The rain falls stronger as I hurry past the side of the house, the light on in the kitchen, suppertime and I am late. The house is connected with the barn the way the small base of an L is connected to its stem. The entrance I always use is directly at the joining, and when I enter out of breath, clothes clinging to me cold and wet, the door to the barn to my left, the door to the kitchen straight ahead, I hear the dripping in the basement down the stairs to my right.

"Meg. Sorry I'm late," I call to my wife, setting down the water-beaded canvas sack, opening the kitchen door. There is no one. No settings on the table. Nothing on the stove. Only the yellow light from the sixty-watt bulb in the ceiling. The kind my mother prefers to the white of one hundred. It reminds her of candlelight, she says.

"Meg," I call again, and still no one answers. Asleep, I think. Dusk coming on, the dark clouds of the storm have lulled them, and they have lain down for a nap, expecting to wake before I return.

Still the dripping. Although the house is very old, the barn long disused, roofs crumbling, I have not thought it all so ill-maintained, the storm so strong that water can be seeping past the cellar windows, trickling, pattering on the old stone floor. I switch on the light to the basement, descend the wood stairs to the right, worn and squeaking, reach where the stairs turn to the left the rest of the way down to the floor, and see not water dripping. Milk. Milk everywhere. On the rafters, on the walls, dripping on the film of milk on the stones, gathering speckled with dirt in the channels between them. From side to side and everywhere.

Sarah, my child, has done this, I think. She has been fascinated by the big wood dollhouse that my father made for me when I was quite young, its blue paint chipped and peeling now. She has pulled it from the far corner to the middle of the basement. There are games and toy soldiers and blocks that have been taken from the wicker storage chest and played with on the floor, all covered with milk, the dollhouse, the chest, the scattered toys, milk dripping on them from the rafters, milk trickling on them.

Why has she done this, I think. Where can she have gotten so much milk? What was in her mind to do this thing?

"Sarah," I call. "Meg." Angry now, I mount the stairs into the quiet kitchen. "Sarah," I shout. She will clean the mess and stay indoors the remainder of the week.

I cross the kitchen, turn through the sitting room past the padded flower-patterned chairs and sofa that have faded since I knew them as a boy, past several of my paintings that my mother has hung up on the wall, bright-colored old ones of pastures and woods from when I was in grade school, brown-shaded new ones of the town, tinted as if old photographs. Two stairs at a time up to the bedrooms, wet shoes on the soft worn carpet on the stairs, hand streaking on the smooth polished maple banister.

At the top I swing down the hall. The door to Sarah's room is open, it is dark in there. I switch on the light. She is not on the bed, nor has been; the satin spread is unrumpled, the rain pelting in through the open window, the wind fresh and cool. I have the feeling then and go uneasy into our bedroom; it is dark as well, empty too. My stomach has become hollow. Where are they? All in mother's room?

No. As I stand at the open door to mother's room I see from the yellow light I have turned on in the hall that only she is in there, her small torso stretched across the bed.

"Mother," I say, intending to add, "Where are Meg and Sarah?" But I stop before I do. One of my mother's shoes is off, the other askew on her foot. There is mud on the shoes. There is blood on her cotton dress. It is torn, her brittle hair disrupted, blood on her face, her bruised lips are swollen.

For several moments I am silent with shock. "My God, Mother," I finally manage to say, and as if the words are a spring releasing me to action I touch her to wake her. But I see that her eyes are open, staring ceilingward, unseeing though alive, and each breath is a sudden full gasp, then slow exhalation.

"Mother, what has happened? Who did this to you? Meg? Sarah?"

But she does not look at me, only constant toward the ceiling.

"For God's sake, Mother, answer me! Look at me! What has happened?"

Nothing. Eyes sightless. Between gasps she is like a statue.

What I think is hysterical. Disjointed, contradictory. I must find Meg and Sarah. They must be somewhere, beaten like my mother. Or worse. Find them. Where? But I cannot leave my mother. When she comes to consciousness, she too will be hysterical, frightened, in great pain. How did she end up on the bed?

In her room there is no sign of the struggle she must have put up against her attacker. It must have happened somewhere else. She crawled from there to here. Then I see the blood on the floor, the swath of blood down the hall from the stairs. Who did this? Where is he? Who would beat a gray, wrinkled, arthritic old woman? Why in God's name would he do it? I shudder. The pain of the arthritis as she struggled with him.

Perhaps he is still in the house, waiting for me.

To the hollow sickness in my stomach now comes fear, hot, pulsing, and I am frantic before I realize what I am doing—grabbing the spare cane my mother always keeps by her bed, flicking on the light in her room, throwing open the closet door and striking in with the cane. Viciously, sounds coming from my throat, the cane flailing among the faded dresses.

No one. Under the bed. No one. Behind the door. No one.

I search all the upstairs rooms that way, terrified, constantly checking behind me, clutching the cane and whacking into closets, under beds, behind doors, with a force that would certainly crack a skull. No one.

"Meg! Sarah!"

No answer, not even an echo in this sound-absorbing house.

There is no attic, just an overhead entry to a crawl space under the eaves, and that opening has long been sealed. No sign of tampering. No one has gone up.

I rush down the stairs, seeing the trail of blood my mother has left on the carpet, imagining her pain as she crawled, and search the rooms downstairs with the same desperate thoroughness. In the front closet. Behind the sofa and chairs. Behind the drapes.

No one.

I lock the front door, lest he be outside in the storm waiting to come in behind me. I remember to draw every blind, close every drape, lest he be out there peering at me. The rain pelts insistently against the windowpanes.

I cry out again and again for Meg and Sarah. The police. My mother. A doctor. I grab for the phone on the wall by the front stairs, fearful to listen to it, afraid he has cut the line outside. But it is droning. Droning. I ring for the police, working the handle at the side around and around and around.

They are coming, they say. A doctor with them. Stay where I am, they say. But I cannot. Meg and Sarah, I must find them. I know they are not in the basement where the milk is dripping—all the basement is open to view. Except for my childhood things, we have cleared out all the boxes and barrels and the shelves of jars the Saturday before.

But under the stairs. I have forgotten about under the stairs and now I race down and stand dreading in the milk; but there are only cobwebs there, already reformed from Saturday when we cleared them. I look up at the side door I first came through, and as if I am seeing through a telescope I focus largely on the handle. It seems to fidget. I have a panicked vision of the intruder bursting through, and I charge up to lock the door, and the door to the barn.

And then I think: if Meg and Sarah are not in the house they are likely in the barn. But I cannot bring myself to unlock the barn door and go through. *He* must be there as well. Not in the rain outside but in the shelter of the barn, and there are no lights to turn on there.

And why the milk? Did he do it and where did he get it? And why? Or did Sarah do it before? No, the milk is too freshly dripping. It has been put there too recently. By him. But why? And who is he? A tramp? An escapee from some prison? Or asylum? No, the nearest institution is far away, hundreds of miles. From the town then. Or a nearby farm.

I know my questions are for delay, to keep me from entering the barn. But I must. I take the flashlight from the kitchen drawer and unlock the door to the barn, force myself to go in quickly, cane ready, flashing my light. The stalls are still there, listing; and some of the equipment, churners, separators, dull and rusted, webbed and dirty. The must of decaying wood and crumbled hay, the fresh wet smell of the rain gusting through cracks in the walls. Once this was a dairy, as the other farms around still are.

Flicking my light toward the corners, edging toward the stalls, boards creaking, echoing, I try to control my fright, try to remember as a boy how the cows waited in the stalls for my father to milk them, how the barn was once board-tight and solid, warm to be in, how there was no connecting door from the barn to the house because my father did not want my mother to smell the animals in her kitchen.

I run my light down the walls, sweep it in arcs through the darkness before me as I draw nearer to the stalls, and in spite of myself I recall that other autumn when the snow came early, four feet deep by morning and still storming thickly, how my father went out to the barn to milk and never returned for lunch, nor supper. There was no phone then, no way to get help, and my mother and I waited all night, unable to make our way through the storm, listening to the slowly dying wind; and the next morning was clear and bright and blinding as we shoveled out to find the cows in agony in their stalls from not having been milked and my father dead, frozen rock-solid in the snow in the middle of the next field where he must have wandered when he lost his bearings in the storm.

There was a fox, risen earlier than us, nosing at him under the snow, and my father had to be sealed in his coffin before he could lie in state. Days after, the snow was melted, gone, the barnyard a sea of mud, and it was autumn again and my mother had the connecting door put in. My father should have tied a rope from the house to his waist to guide him back in case he lost his way. Certainly he knew enough. But then he was like that, always in a rush. When I was ten.

Thus I think as I light the shadows near the stalls, terrified of what I may find in any one of them, Meg and Sarah, or him, thinking of how my mother and I searched for my father and how I now search for my wife and child, trying to think of how it was once warm in here and pleasant, chatting with my father, helping him to milk, the sweet smell of new hay and grain, the different sweet smell of fresh droppings, something I always liked and neither my father nor my mother could understand. I know that if I do not think of these good times I will surely go mad in awful anticipation of what I may find. Pray God they have not died!

What can he have done to them? To assault a five-year-old girl? Split her. The hemorrhaging alone can have killed her.

And then, even in the barn, I hear my mother cry out for me. The relief I feel to leave and go to her unnerves me. I do want to find Meg and Sarah, to try to save them. Yet I am relieved to go. I think my mother will tell me what has happened, tell me where to find them. That is how I justify my leaving as I wave the light in circles around me, guarding my back, retreating through the door and locking it.

Upstairs she sits stiffly on her bed. I want to make her answer my questions, to shake her, to force her to help, but I know it will only frighten her more, maybe push her mind down to where I can never reach.

"Mother," I say to her softly, touching her gently.

"What has happened?" My impatience can barely be contained. "Who did this? Where are Meg and Sarah?"

She smiles at me, reassured by the safety of my presence. Still she cannot answer.

"Mother. Please," I say. "I know how bad it must have been. But you must try to help. I must know where they are so I can help them."

She says, "Dolls."

It chills me. "What dolls, Mother? Did a man come here with dolls? What did he want? You mean he looked like a doll? Wearing a mask like one?"

Too many questions. All she can do is blink.

"Please, Mother. You must try your best to tell me. Where are Meg and Sarah?"

"Dolls," she says.

As I first had the foreboding of disaster at the sight of Sarah's unrumpled satin bedspread, now I am beginning to understand, rejecting it, fighting it.

"Yes, Mother, the dolls," I say, refusing to admit what I know. "Please, Mother. Where are Meg and Sarah?"

"You are a grown boy now. You must stop playing as a child. Your father. Without him you will have to be the man in the house. You must be brave."

"No, Mother." I can feel it swelling in my chest.

"There will be a great deal of work now, more than any child should know. But we have no choice. You must accept that God has chosen to take him from us, that you are all the man I have left to help me."

"No, Mother."

"Now you are a man and you must put away the things of a child."

Eyes streaming, I am barely able to straighten, leaning wearily against the doorjamb, tears rippling from my face down to my shirt, wetting it cold where it had just begun to dry. I wipe my eyes and see her reaching for me, smiling, and I recoil down the hall, stumbling down the stairs, down, through the sitting room, the kitchen, down, down to the milk, splashing through it to the dollhouse, and in there, crammed and doubled, Sarah. And in the wicker chest, Meg. The toys not on the floor for Sarah to play with, but taken out so Meg could be put in. And both of them, their stomachs slashed, stuffed with sawdust, their eyes rolled up like dolls' eyes.

The police are knocking at the side door, pounding, calling out who they are, but I am powerless to let them in. They crash through the door, their rubber raincoats dripping as they stare down at me.

"The milk," I say.

They do not understand. Even as I wait, standing in the milk, listening to the rain pelting on the windows while they come over to see what is in the dollhouse and in the wicker chest, while they go upstairs to my mother and then return so I can tell them again, "The milk." But they still do not understand.

"She killed them of course," one man says. "But I don't see why the milk."

Only when they speak to the neighbors down the road and learn how she came to them, needing the cans of milk, insisting she carry them herself to the car, the agony she was in as she carried them, only when they find the empty cans and the knife in a stall in the barn, can I say, "The milk. The blood. There was so much blood, you know. She needed to deny it, so she washed it away with milk, purified it, started the dairy again. You see, there was so much blood."

That autumn we live in a house in the country, my mother's house, the house I was raised in. I have been to the village, struck even more by how nothing in it has changed, yet everything has, because I am older now, seeing it differently. It is as though I am both here now and back then, at once with the mind of a boy and a man . . .

The Wringer
by F. Paul Wilson

Munir stood on the curb, unzipped his fly, and tugged his penis free. He felt it shrivel in his hand at the cold caress of the March wind and shrink from the sight of all these passing strangers.

At least he hoped they were strangers.

Please let no one who knows me pass by. Or, Allah forbid, a policeman.

He stretched his flabby, reluctant member, and urged his bladder to empty. He'd drunk two quarts of Gatorade in the past three hours to ensure that it would be full to bursting, but he couldn't go. His sphincters were clamped shut as tight as his jaw.

Off to his left the light at the corner where Forty-fifth Street met Broadway turned red, and the traffic slowed to a stop. A woman in a cab glanced at him through her window and started when she saw how he was exposing himself to her. Her lips tightened, and she shook her head in disgust as she turned away. He could almost read her mind: A guy in a suit exposing himself on a Sunday afternoon in the theater district—New York's going to hell even faster than they say it is.

But it has *become* hell for me, Munir thought.

He closed his eyes to shut out the bright marquees and the line of cars idling before him, tried to block out the tapping, scuffing footsteps of the pedestrians on the sidewalk behind him as they hurried to the matinees, but a child's voice broke through.

"Look, Mommy. What's that man—?"

"Don't look, honey," said a woman's voice. "It's just someone who's sick."

Tears were a pressure behind Munir's sealed eyelids.

He bit back a sob of humiliation and tried to imagine himself in a private place, in his own bathroom, standing over the toilet. He forced himself to relax, and soon it came. As the warm liquid streamed out of him, the waiting sob burst free, propelled equally by relief and shame.

He did not have to shut off the flow. When he opened his eyes and saw the steaming puddle before him on the asphalt, saw the drivers and passengers and passersby staring, the stream dried up on its own.

I hope that is enough, he thought. Please let that be enough.

Averting his eyes, Munir zipped up and fled down the sidewalk, all but tripping over his own feet as he ran.

The phone was ringing when Munir got to his apartment. He hit the RECORD button on his answering machine as he snatched up the receiver and jammed it against his ear.

"Yes!"

"Pretty disappointin, Mooo-neeer," said the now-familiar electronically distorted voice. *"Are all you Ay-rabs such mosquito dicks?"*

"I did as you asked! Just as you asked!"

"That wasn't much of a pee, Mooo-neeer."

"It was all I could do! Please let them go now."

He glanced down at the call-tracer. A number had formed in the LCD window. A 212 area code, just like all the other calls. But the seven digits following were a new combination, unlike any of the other calls. And when he called it back, he was sure it would be a public phone booth. Just like all the others.

"Let 'em go? Shee-it. You're only part ways through the wringer. You still got a ways to go yet, boy. But you know somethin'? I get the feelin' your heart's not really into this, Mooo-neeer. I'll have to take this up with your family."

"Are they all right? Let me speak to my wife."

Munir didn't know why he said that. He knew the caller couldn't drag Barbara and Robby to a pay phone.

"She can't come to the phone right now. She's, uh . . . all tied up at the moment."

Munir ground his teeth as the horselaugh brayed through the phone.

"Please. I must know if she's all right."

"You'll have to take my word for it, Mooo-neeer."

"She may be dead." *Allah forbid!* "You may have killed her and Robby already."

"Hey. Ain't I been sendin' you pitchers? Don't you like my pretty pitchers?"

"No!" Munir cried, fighting a wave of nausea. Those pictures—those horrible, sickening Polaroids. "They aren't enough. You could have taken all those photographs at once and then killed them."

The voice on the other end lowered to a sinister, nasty, growling tone.

"You callin' me a liar, you lousy, greasy, two-bit Ay-rab? Don't you ever *doubt a word I tell you. Don't even think* about *doubtin' me. Or I'll show you who's alive. I'll prove your bitch and brat are alive by sendin' you a fresh piece of them every so often. A little bit of each, every day, by Express Mail, so it's nice and fresh. You just keep on sayin' doubtin' me, Mooo-neeer, and pretty soon you'll get your wife and kid back, all of them. But you'll have to figure which part goes where. Like the model kits say: Some Assembly Required."*

Munir bit back a scream as the caller brayed again.

"No-no. Please don't hurt them anymore. I'll do anything you want. What do you want me to do?"

"There. That's more like it. I'll let your little faux pas pass this time. A lot more generous than you'd ever be— ain't that right, Mooo-neeer. And sure as shit more generous than your Ay-rab buddies were when they killed my brother over there in the Gulf."

"Yes. Yes, whatever you say. What else do you want me to do? Just tell me."

"I ain't decided yet, Mooo-neeer. I'm gonna have to think on that one. But in the meantime, I'm gonna look kindly on you and bestow your request. Yessir, I'm gonna send you proof positive that your wife and kid are still alive."

Munir's stomach plummeted. "No! Please! I believe you! I believe!"

"I reckon you do, Mooo-neeer. But believin' just ain't enough sometimes, is it? I mean, you believe in Allah, don't you? Don't you?"

"Yes. Yes, of course I believe in Allah."

"And look at what you did on Friday. Just think back and meditate on what you did."

Munir hung his head in shame and said nothing.

"So you can see where I'm comin' from when I say believin' ain't enough," the hated voice continued. *"Cause if you believe, you can also have doubt. And I don't want you havin' no doubts, Mooo-neeer. I don't want you havin' the slightest twinge of doubt about how important it is for you to do exactly what I tell you to do. 'Cause if you start thinkin' that it really doesn't matter to your bitch and little rat-faced kid, that they're probably dead already and you can tell me to shove it, that's not gonna be good for them. So I'm gonna have to prove to you just how alive and well they are."*

"No!" He was going to be sick. "Please don't!"

"Just remember. You asked for it."

Munir's voice edged toward a scream. *"Please!"*

The line clicked and went dead.

Munir dropped the phone and buried his face in his hands. The caller was mad, crazy, brutally insane, and for some reason he hated Munir with a depth and breadth Munir found incomprehensible and profoundly horrifying. Whoever he was, he seemed capable of anything, and he had Munir's wife and child hidden away somewhere in the city.

The helplessness overwhelmed Munir, and he began to sob. He had allowed only a few to escape when he heard a pounding on his door.

"Hey, what's going on in there? Munir, you okay?"

Munir stiffened as he recognized his neighbor's voice. He straightened in his chair, but said nothing. Charlie lived in the apartment next door. A retired city worker who had taken a shine to Barbara and Robby. A harmless busybody, Barbara called him. He couldn't let Charlie know there was anything wrong.

"Hey!" Charlie said, banging on the door again. "I know someone's in there. If you don't open up, I'm going to assume something is wrong and call the emergency squad. Don't make a fool out of me."

The last thing Munir needed was a bunch of EMTs swarming around his apartment. The police would be with them, and who knew what the crazy man who held Barbara and Robby would do if he saw them. He cleared his throat.

"I'm all right, Charlie."

"The hell you are," Charlie said, rattling the doorknob. "You didn't sound all right a moment ago when you screamed, and you don't sound all right now. Just open up so I can—"

The door swung open, revealing Charlie Akers—fat, balding, a cigar butt in his mouth, a newspaper in his hand, dressed in wrinkled blue pants, a T-shirt, and suspenders—looking as shocked as Munir felt.

In his haste to answer the phone, Munir had forgot to latch the door behind him. Quickly, he wiped his eyes and rose to close it.

"Jesus, Munir," Charlie said. "You look like hell. What's the matter?"

"Nothing, Charlie."

"Hey, don't shit me. I heard you. It sounded like someone was stepping on your soul. Anything I can do?"

"I'm okay. Really."

"Yeah, right. You in trouble? You need money? Maybe I can help."

Munir was touched by the offer. He hardly knew Charlie. If only he *could* help. But no one could help him.

"No. Nothing like that."

"Is it Barbara and the kid? I haven't seen them around for a few days. Something happen to—?" Munir realized it must have shown on his face. Charlie stepped inside and closed the door behind him. "Hey, what's going on here? Are they all right?"

"Please, Charlie. I can't talk about it. And you mustn't talk about it, either. Just let it be. I'm handling it."

"Is it a police thing? I got friends down the precinct house—"

"No! *Not* the police! Please don't say anything to the police. I was warned"—in sickeningly graphic terms—"about going to the police."

Charlie leaned back against the door and stared at him.

"Jesus . . . is this as bad as I think it is?"

Munir nodded mutely.

"Wait here." Charlie ducked out the door. He was back in less than two minutes. He had a slip of paper in his hand. "My brother gave me this a couple of years ago. He said if I was ever in a really bad spot and there was no one left to turn to, I should call this guy."

"No one can help me."

"My brother says this guy's good people, but he said make sure it was my last resort because it was gonna cost me. And he said make sure the cops weren't involved because this guy don't like cops."

No police . . . Munir reached for the slip of paper. And money? What did money matter where Barbara and Robby were concerned?

A telephone number was written on the slip, and below it, two words: *Repairman Jack.*

I'm running out of space, Jack thought as he stood in the front room of his apartment and looked for an empty spot to display his latest treasure.

His Sky King Magni-Glow Writing Ring had just arrived from his connection in southeast Missouri. It contained a Mysterious Glo-Signaler ("Gives a strange green light! You can send blinker signals with it!"). The plastic ruby unfolded into three sections, revealing a Secret Compartment that contained a Flying Crown Brand ("For sealing messages!"); the middle section was a Detecto-Scope Magnifying Glass ("For detecting fingerprints or decoding messages!"), and the outermost section was a Secret Stratospheric Pen ("Writes at any altitude, or under water, in red ink!")

Neat. Incredibly neat. The neatest ring in Jack's collection. Far more complex than his Buck Rogers Ring of Saturn, or his Shadow Ring, or even his Kix Atomic Bomb Ring. It deserved auspicious display. But where?

His front room was already jammed with neat stuff. Radio Premiums, cereal giveaways, comic-strip tie-ins— crassly commercial junk from a time before he was born. Mementos from someone else's childhood. Why did they fascinate him? Why did he collect them? After years of accumulating his hoard, Jack still hadn't found the answer. So he kept buying. And buying.

Every flat surface on the mismatched collection of Victorian golden oak furniture that crowded his front room was littered with old goodies and oddities. The walls were papered with certificates proclaiming him an official member of The Shadow Society, the Doc Savage Club, the Nick Carter Club, the Friends of the Phantom, the Green Hornet G-J-M Club, and other august organizations.

Jack glanced at the Shmoo clock on the hutch. He had an appointment with a new customer in twenty minutes or so. No time to find a special spot for the Sky King Magni-Glow Writing Ring, so he placed it next to his Captain Midnight radio decoder. He pulled a red Lands' End jacket over his shirt and jeans, and headed for the door.

Outside in the growing darkness, Jack hurried through the chilly West Seventies, passing empty storefronts that had been trendy boutiques and eateries not too long ago. The stock market had bounced back, but a lot of the yuppies hadn't. They weren't buying and eating like they used to. Some had had to move out. Mostly, they'd been replaced by an affluent yuppie subgroup—dinks. Double income, no kids. It was for them that the surviving dives were charging $7.50 for a side dish of the Upper West Side's newest culinary rage—mashed potatoes.

The drinkers were three deep around the bar in Julio's. Big crowd for a Sunday night. Hundred-dollar shirts and two-hundred dollar sweaters were wedged next to grease monkey overalls. Julio's was far enough uptown to still hang onto some of its old clientele despite the invasion of the Giorgio Armani and Donna Karan set. The yups and dinks had discovered Julio's awhile back. Thought it had "rugged charm," found the food "authentic," and loved its "unpretentious atmosphere."

They drove Julio up the wall.

Julio was behind the bar, under the "FREE BEER TO-MORROW" sign. Jack waved to let him know he was here. As Jack wandered the length of the bar, he overheard a blond dink in a blue Ralph Lauren blazer, holding a mug of draft beer, who maybe had been here once or twice before, pointing out Julio's famous dead succulents and asparagus ferns hanging in the windows to a couple who were apparently newcomers.

"Aren't they just fabulous?"

"Why doesn't he get fresh ones?" one of the women beside him asked. She was sipping white wine from a smudged tumbler.

"I think he's making a statement," the guy said.

"About what?"

"I haven't the faintest. But don't you just love them?"

Jack knew what the statement was: Callousless people go home—this is a workingman's bar. But they didn't see it. Julio was purposely rude to them, and he'd instructed his help to follow his lead, but it didn't work. The dinks thought it was a put-on, part of the ambiance. They ate it up.

Jack stepped over the length of rope that closed off the back half of the seating area and dropped into his usual booth in the darkened rear. As Julio came out from behind the bar, the blond dink flagged him down.

"Can we get a table back there?"

"No," Julio said.

The muscular little man brushed by him and nodded to Jack on his way to assuming the welcoming committee post by the front door.

Jack pulled a Walkman from his jacket pocket and set up a pair of lightweight headsets while he mentally reviewed the two phone calls that had lead to this meet. The first had been on the answering machine he kept in a deserted office on Tenth Avenue. He'd called it from a pay booth this morning and heard someone named Munir Habib explaining in a tight, barely accented voice that he needed help. Needed it bad. He explained how he'd got the number. He didn't know what Jack could do for him, but he was desperate. He gave his phone number and said he'd be waiting. "Please save my family!" he'd said.

Jack then made a couple of calls of his own. Munir's provenance checked out, so Jack had called him back. From the few details he'd allowed Munir to give over the phone, Jack had determined that the man was indeed a potential customer. He'd set up a meet in Julio's.

A short, fortyish man stepped inside the front door and looked around uncertainly. His light camel hair sport coat was badly wrinkled, like he'd slept in it. He had milk-chocolate skin, a square face, and bright eyes as black as the stiff, straight hair on his head. Julio spoke to him, they exchanged a few words, then Julio smiled and shook his hand. He led him back toward Jack, patting him on the back, treating him like a relative. Close up, the guy looked zombielike. Even if he weren't, he would not have a clue that he'd just been expertly frisked. Julio indicated the seat opposite Jack and gave a quick okay behind his back as the newcomer seated himself.

When Julio reached the bar again, the blond guy in the blazer stopped him again.

"How come they get to sit over there and we don't?"

Julio swung on him and got in his face. His was a good head shorter than the blond guy, but he was thickly muscled and had that air of barely restrained violence. It wasn't an act. Julio was feeling mean these days.

"You ask me one more time about those tables, man, and you outta here. You hear me? You *out,* and you never come back!"

As Julio strutted away, the blond guy turned to his companions, grinning.

"I just *love* this place."

Jack turned his attention to his own customer. He extended his hand.

"I'm Jack."

"Munir Habib." His palm was cold, sweaty. "Are you the one who . . . ?"

"That's me."

A few beats of silence, then, "I was expecting . . ."

"You and everybody else." They all arrived expecting

someone bigger, someone darker, someone meaner looking. "But this is the guy you get. You've got the down payment on you?"

Munir glanced around, furtively. "Yes. It is a lot to carry around in cash."

"It's safe here. Keep it for now. I haven't decided yet whether we'll be doing business. What's the story?"

"As I told you on the phone, my wife and son have been kidnapped and are being held hostage."

A kidnap. One of Jack's rules was to avoid kidnappings. They attracted feds, and Jack had less use for feds than he had for local cops. But this Munir guy had sworn he hadn't called the cops. Said he was too scared by the kidnapper's threats. Jack didn't know if he could believe him.

"Why call me instead of the cops?"

Munir reached inside his jacket and pulled out some Polaroids. His hand trembled as he passed them over to Jack.

"This is why."

The first showed an attractive blond woman, thirty or so, dressed in a white blouse and a dark skirt, gagged and bound to a chair in front of a blank, unpainted wall. A red plastic funnel had been inserted through the gag into her mouth. A can of Drano lay propped in her lap. Her eyes held Jack for a moment—pale blue, and utterly terrified. CAUTION: CONTAINS LYE was block printed across the bottom of the photo.

Jack grimaced and looked at the second photo. At first he wasn't sure what he was looking at. A big meat cleaver took up most of the frame, but the rest was—

He repressed a gasp when he recognized the bare lower belly of a little boy, his hairless pubes, his little penis laid out on the chopping block, the cleaver next to it, ominously close. The caption: *Too bad he's already been circumcised.*

Okay. He hadn't called the cops.

Jack handed the photos back.

"How much do they want?"

"I don't believe it is a 'they.' I think it's a 'he.' And he does not seem to want money—at least not yet."

"He's a psycho?"

"I think so. He seems to hate Arabs—all Arabs—and has picked on me." Munir's features suddenly constricted into a tight knot as his voice cracked. "Why me?"

Jack realized how close this guy was to tumbling over the edge. He didn't want him to start blubbering here.

"Easy, guy," he said softly. "Easy."

Munir rubbed his hands over his face, and when he next looked at Jack, his features were blotchy but composed.

"Yes. I must remain calm. I must not lose control. For Barbara. And Robby."

Jack had a nightmarish flash of Gia and Vickie in the hands of some of the psychos he'd had to deal with, and knew at that moment that he was going to be working with Munir. The guy was okay.

"An Arab hater. One of Kahane's old crew, maybe?"

"No, not a Jew. At least not that I can tell. He keeps referring to a brother who was killed in the Gulf War. I've told him that I'm not an Iraqi, that I'm an American citizen just like him. But even if I weren't a citizen, I'm from Saudi Arabia. My people were allies with the United States, they fought at his brother's side against Saddam. But he doesn't seem to hear me. He says an Arab killed his brother over there, and an Arab's an Arab as far as he's concerned."

"Start at the beginning," Jack said. "Any hint that this was coming?"

"Nothing. Everything has been going normally."

"How about someone from the old country?"

"No. I have no 'old country.' I've spent far more of my life in America than in Saudi Arabia. My father was on long-term assignment here with Saud Petroleum. I grew up in New York. I was in college here when he was transferred back. I spent two months in the land of my birth and realized that my homeland was here. I made my hajj, then returned to New York. I finished school and became a citizen."

"Still could be someone from over there behind it. I

mean, your wife doesn't look like she's from that part of the world."

"Barbara was born and raised in Westchester."

"Well, couldn't marrying someone like that drive—"

"No. Absolutely not." Munir's face hardened. There was absolute conviction in his voice. "An Arab would never do what this man has done to me!"

"Don't be so sure."

"He made me . . . made me eat . . ." Munir seemed to be having trouble completing the sentence. ". . . Pork. And made me drink alcohol with it! *Pork!*"

Jack almost laughed. Then he remembered that Munir was probably a Moslem—most assuredly a Moslem. But still, what was the big deal? Jack could think of a lot worse things Munir could have been forced to do.

"What'd you have to do—eat a ham on rye?"

"No. Ribs. He told me to go to a certain restaurant on Forty-seventh Street last Friday at noon, and buy a rack of what he called 'baby-back ribs.' Then he wanted me to stand outside on the sidewalk and eat them, and wash them down with a bottle of beer."

"Did you?"

Munir bowed his head. "Yes."

"So you ate pork and drank a beer to save your wife and child. Nobody's going to call out the death squads for that. Or are they?"

Jack was tempted to ask if he liked the taste, but stuffed the question. Some folks took this stuff very seriously. He'd never been able to fathom how otherwise intelligent people allowed their diets to be controlled by something written in a book hundreds or thousands of years ago by someone who didn't even have indoor plumbing. But then, he didn't understand a lot of things about a lot of people. He freely admitted that. And what they ate or didn't eat, for whatever reasons, was the least of those mysteries.

"He made me choose between Allah and my family," Munir said. "Forgive me, but I chose my family."

"I don't see any reason to apologize for that. If you'd gone the other way, you wouldn't need me right now, would you."

"But don't you see? He made me do it at noon on Friday."

"So?"

"That is when I should have been in my mosque, praying. It is one of the five duties. No follower of Islam would make a believer do that. He is not an Arab, I tell you. You need only listen to the tape to know that."

"Okay. We'll get to the tape in a minute." Munir had told Jack that he'd been using his answering machine to record the nut's calls since Saturday. "So. He's not an Arab. What about enemies? Got any?"

"No. We lead a quiet life. I run the auditing department in Saud Petrol. I have no enemies. Not many friends to speak of. We keep very much to ourselves."

If that was true—and Jack had learned the hard way over the years never to take anything a customer said at face value—then Munir was indeed the victim of a psycho. And Jack hated dealing with psychos. They didn't follow the rules. They tended to have their own queer logic. Anything could happen. Anything.

"All right. Let's start at the beginning. When did you first realize something was wrong?"

"When I came home from work on Thursday night and found our apartment empty. I checked the answering machine and heard a distorted voice telling me that he had my wife and son, and that they'd be fine if I did as I was told and didn't go to the police. And if I had any thought of going to the police in spite of what he'd said, I should look on the dresser in our bedroom. The photographs were there." Munir rubbed a hand across his eyes. "I sat up all night waiting for the phone to ring. He finally called me on Friday morning."

"And told you that you had to eat pork."

Munir nodded. "He would tell me nothing about Barbara and Robby except that they were alive and well, and were hoping I wouldn't 'screw up.' I did as I was told, then hurried home and tried to vomit it up. He called and said I 'done good.' He said he'd call me again to tell me the next trick he was going to make me do. He said he was going to put me 'through the wringer but good.' "

"What was the next trick?"

"I was to steal a woman's pocketbook in broad daylight, knock her down, and run with it. And I was *not* to get caught. He said the photos I had were 'Before.' If I was caught, he would send me 'After.'"

"So you became a purse snatcher for a day—a successful one, I gather."

Munir lowered his head. "I'm so ashamed ... that poor woman." His features hardened. "And then he sent the other photo."

"Another photo? Where? Let me see it."

Munir suddenly seemed flustered. "It's—it's at home." He was lying. Why? "Bull. Let me see it."

"No. I'd rather you didn't—"

"I'll need to know everything if I'm going to help you." Jack said. He thrust out his hand. "Give it."

With obvious reluctance, Munir reached into his coat and passed another Polaroid across. Jack understood his reluctance immediately.

It was the same blond woman from the first photo, only this time she was nude, tied spread-eagle on a mattress, her dark pubic triangle toward the camera, her eyes bright with tears of humiliation; an equally naked dark-haired boy crouched in terror next to her.

And I thought she was a natural blonde was written across the bottom.

Jack's jaw began to ache from clenching it closed. He handed the photo back.

"And what about yesterday?"

"I had to urinate in the street before the Imperial Theatre at a quarter to three in the afternoon."

"Swell," Jack said, shaking his head. "Sunday matinee time for *Phantom of the Opera.*"

"Correct. But I would do it all again if it would free Barbara and Robby."

"You might have to do worse. In fact, I'm sure you're going to have to do worse. I think this guy's looking for your limit. He wants to see how far he can push you, wants to see how far you'll go."

"But where will it end?"

"Maybe with you killing somebody."

"Him? Gladly! I—"

"No. Somebody else. A stranger."

Munir blanched. "No. Surely you can't be ..." His voice trailed off.

"Why not? He's got you by the balls. That sort of power can make a well man sick and a sick man sicker." He watched Munir's face, the dismay tugging at his features as he stared at the tabletop. "What'll you do?"

A pause while Munir returned from somewhere far away. "What?"

"When the time comes. When he says you've got to choose between the life of a stranger and the lives of your wife and son. What'll you do?"

Munir didn't flinch. "Kill the stranger, of course."

"And the next stranger? And the one after that, and the one after that? When do you say enough, no more, *finis?*"

Now Munir flinched. "I ... I don't know."

Tough question. Jack wondered how he'd answer if Gia and Vickie were captives. How many strangers would die before he stopped? What was the magic number? Jack hoped he never had to find out. The Son of Sam might end up looking like a piker.

"Let's hear that tape."

Munir pulled a cassette out of a side pocket in his jacket, and passed it across. Jack slipped it into the Walkman. Maybe listening to this creep would help him get a read on him.

He handed Munir one headset and positioned the other over his ears. He hit PLAY.

The voice on the tape was electronically distorted. Two possible reasons for that. One obviously to prevent voiceprint analysis. But he could also be worried that Munir would recognize his voice. Jack listened to the snarling Southern accent. He couldn't tell through the electronic buzz if it was authentic or not, but there was no question about the sincerity of the raw hate snaking through the phone line. He closed his eyes and concentrated on the voice.

Something there ... something about this guy ... a picture was forming ...

* * *

Munir found it difficult to focus on the tape. After all, he had listened to that hated voice over and over until he knew by heart every filthy word, every nuance of expression. Besides, he was uneasy here. He never frequented places where liquor was served. The drinking and laughter at the bar—they were alien to his way of life. So he studied this stranger across the table from him instead.

This man called Repairman Jack was most unimpressive. True, he was taller than Munir, perhaps five-eleven, but with a slim, wiry physique. Nothing at all special about his appearance. Brown hair with a low hairline, and such mild brown eyes; had he not been seated alone back here, he would have been almost invisible. Munir had expected a heroic figure—if not physically prepossessing, at least sharp, swift, and viper deadly. This man had none of those qualities. How was he going to wrest Barbara and Robby from their tormentor's grasp? It hardly seemed possible.

And yet, as he watched him listening to the tape with his eyes closed, stopping it here and there to rewind and hear again a sentence or phrase, he became aware of the man's quiet confidence, of a hint of furnace-hot intensity roaring beneath his ordinary surface. And Munir began to see that perhaps there was a purpose behind Jack's manner of dress, his whole demeanor being slanted toward unobtrusiveness. He realized that this man could dog your steps all day long and you'd never notice him.

When the tape was done, the stranger took off his headphones, removed the cassette from the player, and stared at it.

"Something screwy here," he said finally.

"What do you mean?"

"He hates you."

"Yes, I know. He hates all Arabs. He's said so, many times."

"No. He hates *you*."

"Of course. I'm an Arab." What was he getting at?

"Wake up, Munir. I'm telling you this guy knows you, and he hates your guts. This whole deal has nothing to

do with the Gulf War or Arabs or any of the bullshit
he's been handing you. This is personal, Munir. Very
personal."

No. It wasn't possible. He had never met anyone, had
never been even remotely acquainted with a person who
would do this to him and his family.

"I do not believe it," he said. His voice sounded
hoarse. "It cannot be."

"Think about it," Jack said, leaning forward, his voice
low. "In the space of three days this guy has made you
offend your God, offend other people, humiliate yourself, and who knows what next. There's real nastiness
here, Munir. Cold, calculated malice. Especially this
business of making you eat pork and drink beer at noon
on Friday when you're supposed to be at the mosque. I
didn't know you had to pray on Fridays at noon, but he
did. That tells me he knows more than a little about
your religion, studying up on it, most likely. He's not
playing this by ear. He's got a plan. He's not putting
you through this 'wringer' of his just for the hell of it."

"What can he possibly gain from tormenting me?"

"Torment, hell. This guy's out to *destroy* you. And as
for gain, I'm guessing on revenge."

"For what?" This was so maddening. "I fear you are
getting off course with this idea that somehow I know
this insane man."

"Maybe. But something he said during your last conversation doesn't sit quite right. He said he was being 'a
lot more generous than you'd ever be.' That's not a remark a stranger would make. And then he said 'faux
pas' a little while after. He's trying to sound like a redneck, but I don't know too many rednecks with *faux pas*
in their vocabulary."

"But that doesn't necessarily mean he knows me
personally."

"You said you run a department in this oil company."

"Yes. Saud Petrol. I'm head of Stateside operations
division."

"Which means you've got to hire and fire, I imagine."

"Of course."

"Look there. That's where you'll find this kook—in

your personnel records. He's the proverbial Disgruntled Employee. Or Former Employee. Or Almost Employee. Someone you fired, someone you didn't hire, or someone you passed over for promotion. I'd go with the first—some people get very personal about being fired."

Munir searched his past for any confrontations with members of his department. He could think of only one, and that was so minor—

Jack was pushing the tape cassette across the table.

"Call the cops," he said.

Fear wrapped thick fingers around Munir's throat and squeezed. "No! He'll find out! He'll—"

"I can't help you, pal. This isn't my thing. You need more than I can give you. You need officialdom. You need a squad of paper shufflers doing background checks on the people past and present in your department. I'm small potatoes. No staff, no access to fingerprint files. You need all of that and more if you're going to get your family through this. The FBI's good at this stuff. They can stay out of sight, work in the background while you deal with this guy up front."

"But—"

He rose and clapped a hand on Munir's shoulder as he passed.

"Good luck."

And then he was walking away ... blending into the crowd around the bar ... gone.

Charlie popped out his door down the hall just as Munir was unlocking his own.

"Thought that was you," he said. He held up a Federal Express envelope. "This came while you were out. I signed for it."

Munir snatched it from him. His heart began to thud when he saw the name *G. I. Gulf* in the sender section of the address label.

"Thanks, Charlie," he gasped, and practically fell into his apartment.

"Hey, wait. Did you—?"

The door slammed on Charlie's question as Munir's fingers fumbled with the tab of the opening strip. Finally, he got a grip on it and ripped it across the top. He looked inside. Empty except for shadows. No. It couldn't be. He'd felt a bulge, a thickness within. He upended it.

A photograph slipped out and fluttered to the floor.

Munir dropped to a squat and snatched it up. He groaned as he saw Barbara—naked, gagged, bound spread-eagle on the bed as before, but alone this time. Something white was draped across her midsection. Munir looked closer.

A newspaper. A tabloid. The *Post*. The headline was the same he'd seen on the newsstands this morning. And Barbara was staring at the camera. No tears this time. Alert. Angry. *Alive.*

Munir wanted to cry. He pressed the photo against his chest and sobbed once, then looked at it again to make sure there was no trickery. No, it was real. How could you doctor a Polaroid?

At the bottom was another one of the madman's hateful inscriptions: *She watched.*

Barbara watched? Watched what? What did that mean?

Just then the phone rang. Munir leaped for it. He pressed the RECORD button on the answer phone as soon as he recognized the distorted voice.

"Finished barfin' yet, Mooo-neeer?"

"I—I don't know what you mean. But I thank you for this photo. I'm terribly relieved to know my wife is still alive. Thank you."

He wanted to scream that he ached for the day when he could meet him face-to-face and flay him alive, but said nothing. Barbara and Robby could only be hurt by angering this madman.

" 'Thank you'?" The voice on the phone sounded baffled. *"Whatta you mean, 'thank you'? Didn't you see the rest?"*

Munir went cold all over. He tried to speak but the words would not come. It felt as if something were stuck in his throat. Finally, he managed a few words.

"Rest? What rest?"

"I think you'd better take another look in that enve-

*lope, Mooo-neeer. Take a real good look before you
think about thankin' me. I'll call you back later."*

"No—!"

The line went dead.

Panic exploded within Munir as he hung up and
rushed back to the foyer. *Didn't you see the rest?* What
rest? Please, Allah, what did he mean? What was he
saying? He snatched up the stiff envelope. Yes, there
was something still in it. A bulge at the bottom, wedged
into the corner. He smacked the open end of the envelope against the floor.

Once. Twice.

Something tumbled out. Something in a small Ziploc
bag.

Short. Cylindrical. A pale, dusky pink. Bloody red at
the ragged end.

Munir jammed the back of his wrist against his mouth.
To hold back the screams. To hold back the vomit.

And the inscription on Barbara's photograph came
back to him.

She watched.

The phone began to ring.

"Take it easy, guy," Jack said to the sobbing man
slumped before him. "It's going to be all right."

Jack didn't believe that, and he doubted Munir did,
either, but he didn't know what else to say. Hard enough
to deal with a sobbing woman. What do you say to a
blubbering man?

He'd been on his way home from Gia's over on Sutton
Square when he stopped off at the St. Moritz to make
one last call to his answering machine. He never used
his apartment phone for that, and he did his best to
randomize the times and locations of his calls. When he
was on Central Park South he rarely passed up a chance
to call in from the lobby of the Plaza or one of its high-
priced neighbors.

He heard Munir's grief-choked voice: *"Please ... I
have no one else to call. He's hurt Robby! He's hurt my
boy! Please help me, I beg you!"*

Jack couldn't say what was behind the impulse. He

didn't want to, but a moment later he found himself calling Munir back, coaxing an address out of the near-hysterical man, and going over there. He pulled on a pair of thin leather gloves before entering the Turtle Bay high-rise where Munir's apartment was located. He was sure this mess was going to end up in the hands of officialdom, and he wished to leave behind nothing that belonged to him, especially his fingerprints.

Munir had been so glad to see him, so grateful to him for coming that Jack had to peel the man off of him.

He helped him to the kitchen and found a heavy meat cleaver lying on the table there. Several deep gouges, fresh ones, marred the tabletop. Jack finally got him calmed down.

"Where is it?"

"There." He pointed to the upper section of the refrigerator. "I thought if maybe I kept it cold . . ."

Munir slumped forward on the table, facedown, his forehead resting on the arms crossed before him. Jack opened the freezer compartment and pulled out the plastic bag.

It was a finger. A kid's. The left pinky. Cleanly chopped off. Probably with the cleaver in the photo of a more delicate portion of the kid's anatomy he'd seen earlier this evening.

The son of a bitch.

And then there was the photograph of the boy's mother. And the inscription.

Jack felt a surge of blackness from the abyss within him. He willed it back. He couldn't get involved in this, couldn't let it get personal. He turned to look back at the kitchen table and found Munir staring at him.

"Do you see?" Munir said, wiping the tears from his cheeks. "Do you see what he has done to my boy?"

Jack quickly stuffed the finger back into the freezer.

"Look, I'm really sorry about this but nothing's changed. You still need more help than one guy can offer. You need the cops."

Munir shook his head violently. "No! You haven't heard his latest demand! The police can *not* help me with this! Only you can! Please, come listen."

Jack followed him down a hall. He passed a room with an inflatable fighter jet hanging from the ceiling; a poster of Jeff Hostetler ready to pass was tacked to the wall. In another room at the end of the wall, he waited while Munir's trembling fingers fumbled with the rewind controls. Finally, he got it playing. Jack barely recognized Munir's voice as he spewed his grief and rage at the caller. Then the other voice laughed.

VOICE: *Well, well. I guess you got my little present.*

MUNIR: You vile, filthy, perverted—

VOICE: *Hey-hey, Mooo-neeer. Let's not get too personal here. This ain't between you'n me. This here's a matter of international diplomacy.*

MUNIR: How ... (a choking sound) how could you?

VOICE: *Easy, Mooo-neeer. I just think about how your people fried my brother, and it becomes real easy. Might be a real good idea for you to keep that in mind from here on in.*

MUNIR: Let them go and take me. I'll be your prisoner. You can ... you can cut me to pieces if you wish. But let them go, I beg you!

VOICE: *(Laughs) Cut you to pieces! Mooo-neeer, you must be psychic or somethin'. That's what I've been thinkin, too! Ain't that amazin'?*

MUNIR: You mean you'll let them go?

VOICE: *Someday—when you're all the way through the wringer. But let's not change the subject here. You in pieces—now that's a thought. Only I'm not goin' to do it. You are.*

MUNIR: What do you mean?

VOICE: *Just what I said, Mooo-neeer. I want piece of you. One of your fingers. I'll leave it to you to decide which one. But I want you to chop it off and have it ready to send to me by tomorrow mornin'.*

MUNIR: Surely, you can't be serious!

VOICE: *Oh, I'm serious, all right.* Deadly *serious. You can count on that.*

MUNIR: But how? I can't!

VOICE: *You'd better find a way, Mooo-neeer. Or the next package you get will be a bit bigger. It'll be a*

> *whole hand. (Laughs) Well, maybe not a* whole
> *hand. One of the fingers will already be missin'*

MUNIR: No! Please! There must be—

VOICE: *I'll call in the mornin' t'tell you how to deliver it.*
> *And don't even think about goin' to the cops. You*
> *do and the next package you get'll be a* lot *bigger.*
> *Like a head. Chop chop, Mooo-neeer.*

Munir switched off the machine and turned to Jack.

"You see how why I need your help?"

"No. I'm telling you the police can do a better job of tracking this guy down."

"But will the police help me cut off my finger?"

"Forget it!" Jack said, swallowing hard. "No way."

"But I can't do it myself. I've tried but I can't make my hand hold still. I want to but I just can't do it myself." Munir looked him in the eyes. "Please. You're my only hope. You must."

"Don't pull that on me." Jack suddenly wanted out of here. Now. "Get this: Just because you need me doesn't mean you own me. Just because I *can* doesn't mean I *must*. And in this case I honestly doubt that I can. So keep all of your fingers and dial 911 to get some help."

"No!" Anger overcame the fear and anguish in Munir's face. "I will not risk their lives!"

He strode back to the kitchen and picked up the cleaver. Jack was suddenly on guard. The guy was nearing the end of his rope. No telling what he'd do.

"I wasn't man enough to do it before," he said, hefting the cleaver. "But I can see I'll be getting no help from you or anyone else. So I'll have to take care of this all by myself!"

Jack stood back and watched as Munir slammed his left palm down on the tabletop, splayed the fingers, and angled the hand around so the thumb was pointing somewhere past his left flank. Jack didn't move to stop him. Munir was doing what he thought he had to do. He raised the cleaver above his head. It poised there a moment, wavering, like a cliff diver with second thoughts, then with a whimper of fear and dismay, Munir drove the clever into his hand.

Or rather into the tabletop where his hand had been.

Weeping, he collapsed into the chair then, and his sobs of anguish and self-loathing were terrible to hear.

"All right, goddamnit," Jack said. He knew this was going to be nothing but trouble, but he'd seen and heard all he could stand. He kicked the nearest wall. "I'll do it."

"Ready?"

Munir's left hand was lashed to the table top. Munir himself was loaded up with every painkiller he'd had in the medicine cabinet—Tylenol, Advil, Bufferin, Anacin 3, Nuprin. Some of them were duplicates. Jack didn't care. He wanted Munir's pain center deadened as much as possible. He wished the guy drank. He'd have much preferred doing this to someone who was dead drunk. Or doped up. Jack could have scored a bunch of Dilaudids for him. But Munir had said no to both. No booze. No dope.

Tight ass.

Jack had never cut off anybody's finger before. He wanted to do this right. The first time. No misses. Half an inch too far to the right and Munir would lose only a piece of his pinky; half an inch too far to the left and he'd be missing the ring finger as well. So Jack had made himself a guide. He'd found a plastic cutting board, a quarter-inch thick, and had notched one of its edges. Now he was holding the board upright with the notch clamped over the base of Munir's pinky; the rest of his hand was safe behind the board. All Jack had to do to sever the finger cleanly from the hand was chop down as hard as he could along the vertical surface of the board.

That was all.

Right.

"I am ready," Munir said.

He was dripping with sweat. His dark eyes looked up at Jack, then he nodded, stuffed a dishrag in his mouth, and turned his head away.

Swell, Jack thought. I'm glad you're ready. But am I? *Now or never.*

He steadied the cutting board, raised the cleaver. He couldn't do this.

Got to.

He took a deep breath, tightened his grip—

—And drove the cleaver into the wall.

Munir jumped, turned, pulled the dishrag from his mouth.

"What? Why—?"

"This isn't going to work." Jack let the plastic cutting board drop and began to pace the kitchen. "There's got to be another way. He's got us on the run. We're playing this whole thing by his rules."

"There aren't any others," Munir said.

"Yeah, there are."

Jack continued pacing. One thing he'd learned over the years was not to let the other guy deal all the cards. Let him *think* he had control of the deck while you dealt from your own.

Munir wriggled his fingers. "Please. I cannot risk angering this madman."

Jack swung to face him. An idea was taking shape.

"You want me in on this?"

"Yes, of course."

"Then, we do it my way. All of it." He began working at the knots that bound Munir's arm to the table. "And the first thing we do is untie you. Then we make some phone calls."

Munir understood none of this. He sat in a daze, sipping milk to ease a stomach that quaked from fear and burned from too many pills. Jack was on the phone, but his words made no sense.

"Yeah, Pete. It's me. Jack ... Right. That Jack. Look, I need a piece of your wares ... Small piece. Easy thing ... Right. I'll get that to you in an hour or two. Thing is, I need it by morning. Can you deliver? ... Great. I'll be by later. By the way—how much? ... Make that two and you got a deal ... All right. See you."

Then he hung up, consulted a small address book, and dialed another number.

"Hey, Teddy. It's me. Jack ... Yeah, I know, but this

can't wait till morning. How about opening up your store for me? I need about ten minutes inside ... That's no help to me, Teddy. I need to get in now. *Now*. . . . Okay. Meet you there in twenty."

Jack hung up and took the glass from Munir's hands. Munir found himself taken by the upper arm and pulled toward the door.

"Can you get us into your office?"

Munir nodded. "I'll need my ID card and keys, but yes, they'll let me in."

"Get them. There a back way out of here?"

Munir took him down the elevator to the parking garage and out the rear door. From there they caught a late-cruising gypsy cab down to a hardware store on Bleecker Street. The lights inside were on but the sign in the window said CLOSED. Jack told the cabbie to wait and knocked on the door. A painfully thin man with no hair whatsoever, not even eyebrows, opened the door.

"You coulda broke in, Jack," he said. "I wouldna minded. I need my rest, y'know."

"I know, Teddy," Jack said. "But I need the lights on for this, and I couldn't risk attracting that kind of attention."

Munir followed Jack to the paint department at the rear of the store. They stopped at the display of color cards. Jack pulled a group from the brown section and turned to him.

"Give me your hand."

Baffled, Munir watched as Jack placed one of the color cards against the back of Munir's hand, then tossed it away. And again. One after another until—

"Bingo. Here it is. Perfect match.'

"We're buying *paint*?"

"No. We're buying flesh—specifically, flesh with Golden Mocha number 169 skin. Let's go."

And then they were moving again, waving good-bye to Teddy, and getting back into the cab.

To the East Side now, up First Avenue to Thirty-first Street. Jack ran inside with the color card, then came out and jumped back into the cab empty-handed.

"Okay. Next stop is your office."

"My office? Why?"

"Because we've got a few hours to kill, and we might as well use them looking up everyone you fired in the past year."

Munir thought this was futile, but he had given himself into Jack's hands. He had to trust him. And as exhausted as he was, sleep was out of the question.

He gave the driver the address of the Saud Petrol offices.

"This guy looks promising," Jack said, handing him a file. "Remember him?"

Until tonight, Munir never had realized how many people he hired and fired—"let go" was the current euphemism—in the course of a year. He was amazed.

He opened the file. Richard Hollander. The name didn't catch until he read the man's performance report.

"Not him. Anyone but him."

"Yeah? Why not?"

"Because he was so . . ." As Munir searched for the right word, he pulled out all he remembered about Hollander, and it wasn't much. The man hadn't been with the company long, and had been pretty much a nonentity during his stay. Then he found the word he was looking for. "Ineffectual."

"Yeah?"

"Yes. He never got anything done. Every assignment, every report was either late or incomplete. He had a wonderful academic record—good grades from an Ivy League school, that sort of thing—but he proved incapable of putting any of his learning into practice. That was why he was let go."

"Any reaction? You know, shouting, yelling, threats?"

"No." Munir remembered giving Hollander his notice. The man had merely nodded and begun emptying his desk. He hadn't even asked for an explanation. "He knew he'd been screwing up. I think he was expecting it. Besides, he had no Southern accent. It's not him."

Munir passed the folder back, but instead of putting it away, Jack opened it and glanced through it again.

"I wouldn't be too sure about that. Accents can be

faked. And if I was going to pick the type who'd go nuts for revenge, this guy would be it. Look: he's unmarried, lives alone—"

"Where does it say he lives alone?"

"It doesn't. But his emergency contact is his mother in Massachusetts. If he had a lover or even a roomie, he'd list them, wouldn't you think? No moderating influences. And look at his favorite sports: swimming and jogging. This guy's a loner from the git-go."

"That does not make him a psychopath. I imagine you are a loner, too, and you ..."

The words dribbled away as Munir's mind followed the thought to its conclusion.

Jack grinned. "Right, Munir. Think about that."

He reached for the phone and punched in a number. After a moment he spoke in a deep, authoritative voice: "Please pick up. This is an emergency. Please pick up." A moment later he hung up and began writing on a notepad. "I'm going to take down this guy's address for future reference. It's almost four a.m. and Mr. Hollander isn't home. His answering machine is on, but even if he's screening his calls, I think he'd have responded to my little emergency message, don't you?"

Munir nodded. "Most certainly. But what if he doesn't live there anymore?"

"Always a possibility." Jack glanced at his watch. "But right now I've got to go pick up a package. You sit tight and stay by the phone here. I'll call you when I've got it."

Before Munir could protest, Jack was gone, leaving him alone in his office, staring at the gallery of family photos arrayed on his desk. He began to sob.

The phone startled Munir out of a light doze. Confusion jerked him upright. What was he doing in his office? He should be home ...

Then he remembered.

It was Jack on the line: "Meet me downstairs."

Out on the street, in the pale, predawn light, two figures awaited him. One was Jack, the other a stranger— a thin man of Munir's height with shoulder-length hair and a goatee. Jack made no introductions. Instead he led them around a corner to a small deli. He stared through the open window at the lights inside.

"This looks bright enough," Jack said.

Inside he ordered two coffees and two cheese Danish and carried them to the rearmost booth in the narrow, deserted store. Jack and the stranger slid into one side of the booth, Munir the other, facing them. Still no introductions.

"Okay, Munir," Jack said. "Put your hand on the table.

Munir complied, placing his left hand palm down, wondering what this was about.

"Now, let's see the merchandise," Jack said to the stranger.

The thin man pulled a small, oblong package from his pocket. It appeared to be wrapped in brown paper hand towels. He unrolled the towels and placed the object next to Munir's hand.

A finger. Not Robby's. Different. Adult size.

Munir pulled his hand back onto his lap and stared.

"Come on, Munir," Jack said. "We've got to do a color check."

Munir slipped his hand back onto the table next to the grisly object, regarding it obliquely. So real looking.

"It's too long and that's only a fair color match," Jack said.

"It's close enough," the stranger said. "Pretty damn good on such short notice, I'd say."

"I suppose you're right." Jack handed him an envelope. "Here you go."

The goateed stranger took the envelope and stuffed it inside his shirt without opening it, then left without saying good-bye.

Munir stared at the finger. The dried blood on the stump end, the detail over the knuckles and around the fingernail—even down to the dirt under the nail—was incredible. It almost looked real.

"This won't work," he said. "I don't care how real this looks, when he finds out it's a fake—"

"Fake?" Jack said, stirring sugar into his coffee. "Who said it's a fake?"

Munir snatched his hand away and pushed himself back. He wanted to sink into the vinyl covering of the booth seat, wanted to pass through to the other side and run from this man and the loathsome object on the table between them. He fixed his eyes on the seat beside him and managed to force a few words past his rising gorge.

"Please ... take ... that ... away."

He heard the soft crinkle and scrape of paper being folded and dragged across the tabletop, then Jack's voice:

"Okay, Cinderella. You can look now. It's gone."

Munir kept his eyes averted. What had he got himself into? In order to save his family from one ruthless madman, he was forced to deal with another. What sort of world was this?

He felt a sob build up in his throat. Until last week, he couldn't remember crying once since his boyhood. For the past few days it seemed he wanted to cry all the time. Or scream. Or both.

He saw Jack's hand pushing a cup of coffee into his field of vision.

"Here. Drink this. Lots of it. You're going to need to stay alert."

An insane hope arose in Munir.

"Do you think ... do you think the man on the phone did the same thing? With Robby's finger? Maybe he went to a morgue and ..."

Jack shook his head slowly, as if the movement pained him. For an instant he saw past the wall around Jack. Saw pity there.

"Don't torture yourself," Jack said.

Yes, Munir thought. The madman on the phone was already doing too good a job of that.

"It's not going to work," Munir said, fighting the blackness of despair. "He's going to realize he's been tricked, and then he's going to take it out on my boy."

"No matter what you do, he's going to find an excuse to do something nasty to your boy. Or your wife. That's the whole idea behind this gig—make you suffer. But his latest wrinkle with the fingers gives us a chance to find out who he is and where he's holed up."

"How?"

"He wants your finger. How's he going to get it? He can't very well give us an address to mail it to. So there's going to have to be a drop—someplace where we leave it, and he picks it up. And that's where we nab him and make him tell us where he's got your family stashed."

"What if he refuses to tell us?"

Jack's voice was soft, his nod almost imperceptible. Munir shuddered at what he saw flashing through Jack's eyes in that instant.

"Oh . . . he'll tell us."

"He thinks I won't do it," Munir said, looking at his fingers—all ten of them. "He thinks I'm a coward because he thinks all Arabs are cowards. He's said so. And he was right. I couldn't do it."

"Hell," Jack said, "I couldn't do it, either, and it wasn't even my hand. But I'm sure you'd have done it eventually if I hadn't come up with an alternative."

Would I have done it? Munir thought. *Could* I have done it?

Maybe he'd have done it just to demonstrate his courage to the madman on the phone. Over the years Munir had seen the Western world's image of the Arab male distorted beyond recognition by terrorism: the Arab warrior bombed school buses and hijacked planes and pistol-whipped helpless passengers; Arab manhood aimed its weapons from behind the skirts of unarmed civilian women and children. That was why Munir had been overjoyed to see the courage and skill of the Saudi pilots and soldiers during the Gulf War displayed on American television for all to see. Now all the world could see how Arab warriors bravely faced an enemy that shot back.

"If something goes wrong because of this, because of my calling on you to help me, I . . . I will never forgive myself."

"Don't think like that," Jack said. "It gets you nothing. And you've got to face it: No matter what you do—cut off one finger, two fingers, your left leg, kill somebody, blow up Manhattan—it's never going to be enough. He's going to keep escalating until you're dead. You've got to stop him now, before it goes any further. Understand?"

Munir nodded. "But I'm so afraid. Poor Robby ... his terrible pain, his fear. And Barbara ..."

"Exactly. And if you don't want that to go on indefinitely, you've got to take the offensive. Now. So let's get back to your place and see how he wants to take delivery of your finger."

Back in the apartment, Jack bandaged Munir's hand in thick layers of gauze to make it look injured. While they waited for the phone to ring, Jack took the finger to the bathroom and washed it.

"We want this to be as convincing as possible," he said. "You don't strike me as the type to have dirty fingernails."

It was well after nine when the call finally came. Munir ground his teeth at the sound of the hated voice.

Jack was beside him, gripping his arm, steadying him as he listened through an earphone he had plugged into the answering machine. He had told him what to say, and had coached him on how to say it, how to sound.

"Well, Mooo-neeer. You got that finger for me?"

"Yes," he said in the choked voice he had rehearsed. "I have it."

There was a pause at the other end, as if the caller was surprised by the response.

"You did it? You really did it?"

"Yes. You gave me no choice."

"Well, I'll be damned. Hey, how come your voice sounds so funny?"

"Codeine. For the pain."

"Yeah. I'll bet that smarts. But that's okay. Pain's good for you. And just think: your kid got through it without codeine."

Jack's grip on his arm tightened as Munir stiffened and began to rise. Jack pulled him back to a sitting position.

"Please don't hurt Robby anymore," Munir said, and

this time he did not have to feign a choking voice. "I did what you asked me. Now let them go."

"Not so fast, Mooo-neeer. How do I know you really cut that finger off? You wouldn't be bullshitting me now, would you?"

"Oh, please. I would not lie about something as important as this."

Yet I *am* lying, he thought. Forgive me, my son, if this goes wrong.

"Well, we'll just have to see about that, won't we? Here's what you do: Put your offerin' in a brown paper lunch bag and head downtown. Go to the mailbox on the corner where Lafayette, Astor, and Eighth come together. Leave the bag on top of the mailbox, then walk half a block down and stand in front of the Astor Place Theatre. Got it?"

"Yes. Yes, I think so."

"Of course you do. Even a bonehead like you should be able to handle those instructions."

"But when should I do this?"

"Ten a.m."

"This morning?" He glanced at his watch. "But it is almost nine-thirty!"

"Aaaay! And he tells time, too! What an intellect! Yeah, that's right, Mooo-neeer. And don't be late or I'll have to think you're lyin' to me. And we know what'll happen then, don't we."

"But what if—?"

"See you soon, Mooo-neeer."

The line went dead. His heart pounding, Munir fumbled the receiver back onto its cradle and turned to Jack.

"We must hurry! We have no time to waste!"

Jack nodded. "This guy's no dummy. He's not giving us a chance to set anything up."

"I'll need the . . . finger," Munir said. Even now, long after the shock of learning it was real, the thought of touching it made him queasy. "Could you please put it in the brown bag for me?"

Jack nodded. Munir led him to the kitchen and gave him a brown lunch bag. Jack dropped the finger inside and handed the sack back to him.

"You've got to arrive alone, so you go first," Jack said. "I'll follow a few minutes from now. If you don't see me around, don't worry. I'll be there. And whatever you do, follow his instructions—nothing else. Understand? *Nothing else*. I'll do the ad-libbing. Now get moving."

Munir fairly ran for the street, praying to Allah that it wouldn't take too long to find a taxi.

Somehow Jack's cab made it down to the East Village before Munir's. He had a bad moment when he couldn't find him. Then a cab screeched to a halt, and Munir jumped out. Jack watched as he hurried to the mailbox and placed the brown paper bag atop it. Jack retreated to a phone booth on the uptown corner and pretended to make a call while Munir strode down to a spot in front of the closed-up Astor Place Theater.

As Jack began an animated conversation with the dial tone, he scanned the area. Monday morning coming down in the East Village. Members of the neighborhood's homeless brigade seemed to be the only people about, either shuffling aimlessly along, as if dazed by the bright morning sun, or huddled on the sidewalks like discarded rag piles. The nut could be among them. Easy to hide within layers of grime and ratty clothes. But not so easy to hide a purpose in life. Jack hunted for someone who looked like he had somewhere to go.

Hollander . . . he wished there'd been a photo in his personnel file. Jack was sure he was the bad guy here. If only he'd been able to get over to his apartment before now. Maybe he'd have found—

And then Jack spotted him. A tall bearded guy traveling westward along Eighth Street, weaving his way through the loitering horde. He was squeezed into a filthy, undersize Army fatigue jacket, the cuffs of at least three of the multiple shirts he wore under the coat protruding from the too-short sleeves; the neck of a pint bottle of Mad Dog stuck up like a periscope from the frayed edge of one of the pockets; the torn knees of his green work pants revealed threadbare jeans beneath.

Piercing blue eyes peered out from under a Navy watch cap.

The sicko? Maybe. Maybe not. One thing was sure: this guy wasn't wandering; he had someplace to go. He was heading directly for the mailbox. When he reached it, he stopped and looked over his shoulder, back along the way he had come on Eighth, then grabbed the brown paper bag Munir had left there. He reached inside, pulled out the paper-towel-wrapped contents, and began to unwrap it.

Suddenly, he let out a strangled cry and tossed the finger into the street. It rolled in an arc and came to rest in the debris matted against the curb. He glanced over his shoulder again and began a stumbling run in the other direction, across Eighth, toward Jack and away from Munir.

"Shit!" Jack said aloud, working the word into his one-way conversation, making it an argument, all the while pretending not to notice the doings at the mailbox.

Something tricky was going down. But what? Had the sicko sent a patsy? Jack had known the guy was sly, but he'd thought the sicko would have wanted to see the finger up close and personal, just to be sure it was real.

Unless of course the sicko was the wino, and he'd done just that a few seconds ago.

He was almost up to Jack's phone booth now. The only option Jack saw was to follow him. Give him a good lead and—

He heard pounding footsteps. Munir was coming this way—*running* this way. Sprinting across the pavement, teeth bared, eyes wild, reaching for the tall guy. Jack repressed an alarmed impulse to get between the two of them. It wouldn't do any good. Munir was out of control and had built up too much momentum. Besides, no use in tipping off his own part in this.

Munir grabbed the taller man by the elbow and spun him around.

"Where are they?" he screeched. His face was flushed; tiny bubbles of saliva collected at the corners of his mouth. "Tell me, you swine!"

Swine? Maybe that was a heavy-duty insult from a Moslem, but it was pablum around here.

The tall guy jerked back, trying to shake Munir off. His open mouth revealed gapped rows of rotting teeth.

"Hey, man—!"

"Tell me or I'll kill you!" Munir shouted, grabbing the man's upper arms and shaking his lanky frame.

"Lemme go, man," the guy said as his head snapped back and forth like a guy in a car that had just been rear-ended. Munir was going to give him whiplash in a few seconds. "I don't know what you're talkin' about!"

"You do! You went right to the package. You've seen the finger—now tell me where they are!"

"Hey, look, man, I don't know nothin' about whatcher sayin'. Dude stopped me down the street and told me to go check out the bag on top of the mailbox. Gave me five to do it. Told me to hold up whatever was inside it."

"Who?" Munir said, releasing the guy and turning to look back down Eighth. "Where is he?"

"Gone now."

Munir grabbed the guy again, this time by the front of his fatigue jacket.

"What did he look like?"

"I dunno. Just a guy. Whatta you want from me any-way, man? I didn't do nothin'. And I don't want nothin' to do with no dead fingers. Now, getcher hands offa me!"

Jack had heard enough.

"Let him go," he told Munir, still pretending to talk into the phone.

Munir gave him a baffled look. "No. He can tell us—"

"He can't tell us anything we need to know. Let him go and get back to your apartment. You've done enough damage already."

Munir blanched and loosened his grip. The guy stumbled back a couple of steps, then turned and ran down Lafayette. Munir looked around and saw that every rheumy eye in the area was on him. He stared down at his hands—the free right and the bandaged left—as if they were traitors.

"You don't think—?"

"Get home. He'll be calling you. And so will I."

Jack watched Munir move away toward the Bowery like a sleepwalker. He hung up the phone and leaned against the booth.

What a mess. The nut had pulled a fast one. Got some wino to make the pick up. But how could a guy that kinked be satisfied with seeing Munir's finger from afar? He seemed the type to want to hold it in his grubby little hand.

But maybe he didn't care. Because maybe it didn't matter.

Jack pulled out the slip of paper on which he'd written Richard Hollander's address. Time to pay Saud Petrol's ex-employee a little visit.

Munir paced his apartment, going from room to room, cursing himself. Such a fool! Such an idiot! But he couldn't help it. He'd lost control. When he'd seen that man walk up to the paper bag and reach inside it, all rationality had fled. The only thing left in his mind had been the sight of Robby's little finger tumbling out of that envelope last night.

After that, everything was a blur.

The phone began to ring.

Oh, no! he thought. It's him. Please, Allah, let him be satisfied. Grant him mercy.

He lifted the receiver and heard the voice.

"Quite a show you put on there, Mooo-neeer."

"Please. I was upset. You've seen my severed finger. Now will you let my family go?"

"Now, just hold on there a minute, Mooo-neeer. I saw a finger go flyin' through the air, but I don't know for sure if it was your finger."

Munir froze with the receiver jammed against his ear.

"Wh-what do you mean?"

"I mean, how do I know that was a real finger? How do I know it wasn't one of those fake rubber things you buy in the five-and-dime?"

"It was real! I swear it! You saw how your man reacted!"

"He was just a wino, Mooo-neeer. Scared of his own shadow. What's he know?"

"Oh, please! You must believe me!"

"Well, I would, Mooo-neeer. Really, I would. Except for the way you grabbed him afterward. Now, it's bad enough you went after him, but I'm willin' to overlook that. I'm far more generous about forgivin' mistakes than you are, Mooo-neeer. But what bothers me is the way you grabbed him. You used both your hands the same."

Munir felt his blood congealing, sludging through his arteries and veins.

"What do you mean?"

"Well, I got trouble seeing a man who just chopped off one of his fingers doing that, Mooo-neeer. I mean, you grabbed him like you had two good hands. And that bothers me, Mooo-neeer. Sorely bothers me."

"Please. I swear—"

"Swearing ain't good enough, I'm afraid. Seein' is believin'. And I believe I saw a man with two good hands out there this mornin'."

"No. Really . . ."

"So I'm gonna have to send you another package, Mooo-neer."

"Oh, no! Don't—"

"Yep. A little memento from your wife."

"Please, no."

He told Munir what that memento would be, then he clicked off.

"No!"

Munir jammed his knuckles into his mouth and screamed into his fist.

"Nooooo!"

Jack stood outside Richard Hollander's door.

No sweat getting into the building. The address in the personnel file had led Jack to a run-down walk-up in the West Eighties. He'd checked the mailboxes in the dingy vestibule and found *R. Hollander* still listed for 3B. A few quick strokes with the notched flexible plastic ruler Jack kept handy, and he was in.

He knocked—not quite pounding, but with enough urgency to bring even the most cautious resident to the peephole.

Three tries, no answer. Jack put his picks to work on the dead bolt. A Quickset. He was rusty. Took him almost a minute, and a minute was a long time when you were standing in an open hallway fiddling with someone's lock. The closest a fully clothed man could come to feeling naked in public.

Finally, the bolt snapped back. He drew the silenced Belgium-made 9mm Browning he'd brought along and entered in a crouch.

Quiet. Didn't take long to search the one-bedroom apartment. Empty. He turned on the lights and did another search.

Neat. The bed was made, the furniture was dusted, clothes folded in the bureau drawers, no dirty dishes in the sink. Hollander either had a maid or he was a neatnik. People who could afford maids didn't live in this building; that made him a neatnik. Not what Jack had expected from a guy who got fired because he couldn't get the job done.

He checked the bookshelves. A few novels and short story collections—literary stuff, mostly—salted in among the business texts. And in the far right corner, three books on Islam with titles like *Understanding Islam* and *An Introduction To Islam.*

Not an indictment by itself. Hollander might have bought them for reference when he'd been hired by Saudi Petrol.

And he might have bought them *after* he was fired.

Jack was willing to bet on the latter. He had a gut feeling about this guy.

On the desk was a picture of a thin, pale, blond man with an older woman. Hollander and his mother maybe? Jack went through the drawers and found a black ledger, a checkbook, and a pile of bills. It looked like he'd been dipping into his savings. His Master Card was almost to the limit, and he'd been paying only the minimum. A lot of late payment notices, and a couple of bad-news letters from employment agencies. Times were tough, and maybe Mr. Richard Hollander was looking for someone to blame.

Folded between the back cover and the last page of the ledger was a receipt from the Brickell Real Estate Agency for a thousand-dollar cash security deposit and first month's rental on Loft #629. Dated last month. Made out to Sean McCabe.

Loft #629. Where the hell was that? And why did Richard Hollander have someone else's cash receipt? Unless it wasn't someone else's. Had he rented loft #629 under a phony name? That would explain using cash. But why would a guy who was almost broke spend a grand on a loft?

Unless he was looking for a place to do something that was too risky to do in his own apartment. Like holding hostages?

He copied down the Brickell agency's phone number. He might need that later. Then he called Munir.

Hysteria on the phone. Sobbing, moaning, the guy was almost incoherent.

"Calm down, damnit! What exactly did he tell you?"

"He's going to cut her ... he's going to cut her ... he's going to cut her ..."

He sounded like a stuck record player. If Munir had been within reach, Jack would have whacked him alongside the head to unstick him.

"Cut her what?"

"Cut her nipple off!"

"Oh, Jeez! Stay right there. I'll call you right back."

Jack retrieved the receipt for the loft and dialed the number of the realtor. As the phone began to ring, he realized he hadn't figured out an angle to pry the address out of the realtor. They wouldn't give it to just anybody. But maybe a cop ...

He hoped he was right as a pleasant female voice answered on the third ring. "Brickell Agency."

Jack put a harsh, Brooklynese edge on his voice.

"Yeah. This is Lieutenant Adams of the Twelfth Precinct. Who's in charge there?"

"I am," she said. Her voice had cooled. "Esther Brickell. This is my agency."

"Good. Here's the story. We've got a suspect in a mutilation murder, but we don't know his whereabouts. However, we did find a cash receipt among his effects. Your name was on it."

"The Brickell Agency?"

"Big as life. A thousand bucks down on loft number six-two-nine. Sound familiar?"

"Not off hand. We're computerized. We access all our rental accounts by number."

"Fine. Then, it'll only take you a coupla seconds to get me the address of this place."

"I'm afraid I can't do that," she said. "I have a strict policy of never giving out information about my clients. Especially, over the phone. All my dealings with them are strictly confidential. I'm sure you can understand."

Swell, Jack thought. She thinks she's a priest or a reporter.

"What I understand," he said, "is that I've got a crazy perp out there, and you think you've got privileged information. Well, listen, sweetie, the First Amendment don't include realtors. I need the address of your six-two-nine loft rented to"——he glanced at the name on the receipt—"Sean McCabe. Not later. Now. *Capsice?*"

"Sorry," she said. "I can't do that. Good day, Lieutenant—if indeed you are a lieutenant."

Shit! But Jack wasn't giving up. He *had* to get this address.

"Oh, I'm a lieutenant, all right. And believe me, sweetie, you don't come across with that address here and now, you've got trouble. You make me waste my time tracking down a judge to swear out a search warrant, make me come out to your dinky little office to get this one crummy address, I'm gonna do it up big. I'm gonna bring uniforms and blue-and-whites units, and we're gonna do a thorough search. And I do mean a *thorough* search. We'll be there all day. And we'll go through *all* your files. And while we're at it, you can explain to any prospective clients who walk in exactly what we're doing and why—and hope they'll believe you. And if we can't find what we want in your computer, we'll confiscate it. And keep it for a while. And maybe you'll get it back next Christmas. Maybe."

"Just a minute," she said.

Jack waited, hoping she hadn't gone to another phone to call her lawyer and check on his empty threats, or call the Twelfth to check on a particularly obnoxious lieutenant named Adams.

"It's on White Street," she said suddenly in cold, clipped tones. "Eighteen-twenty-two. Two-D."

"Thank—"

She hung up on him. Fine. He had what he needed.

White Street. That was in TriBeCa—the triangle below Canal Street. Lots of lofts down there. Straight down Lafayette from where he and Munir had played the mailbox game. He'd been on top of the guy an hour ago.

He punched in Munir's number.

"Eighteen-twenty-two White," he said without preamble. "Get down there now."

No time for explanations. He hung up and ran for the door.

Eighteen-twenty-two White Street looked like a deserted factory. Probably was. Four stories with no windows on the first floor. Maybe an old sweatshop. A "NOW RENTING" sign next to the front door. The place looked empty. Had the Brickell lady stiffed him with the wrong address?

With his trusty plastic ruler ready in his gloved hand, Jack hopped out of the cab and ran for the door. It was steel, a leftover from the building's factory days. An anti-jimmy plate had been welded over the latch area. Jack pocketed the plastic and inspected the lock: a heavy-duty Schlage. A tough pick on a good day. Here on the sidewalk, with the clock ticking, in full view of the cars passing on the street, it would be a *very* tough pick.

He ran along the front of the building and took the alley around to the back. Another door there, this one with a big red alarm warning posted front and center.

Two-D . . . that meant the second floor had been subdivided into at least four mini lofts. If Hollander was here at all, he'd be renting the cheapest one. Usually, the lower letters meant up front with a view of the street; farther down the alphabet you got relegated to the rear with an alley view.

Jack stepped back and looked up. The second-floor windows to his left were bare and empty. The ones on the right were completely draped with what looked like bedsheets.

And running right smack past the middle of those windows was a downspout.

Jack tested the pipe. This wasn't some flimsy aluminum tube that collapsed like a beer can; this was an old-fashioned galvanized pipe. He pulled on the fittings. They wiggled in their sockets.

Not good, but he'd have to risk it.

He began to climb, shimmying up the pipe, vising it with his knees and elbows as he sought toeholds and fingerholds on the fittings. It shuddered, it groaned, and halfway up it settled a couple of inches with a jolt, but it held. Moments later he was perched outside the shrouded second-floor windows.

Now what?

Sometimes the direct approach was the best. He knocked on the nearest pane. It was two foot high, three foot wide, and filthy. After a few seconds, he knocked again. Finally, a corner of one of the sheets lifted hesitantly, and a man stared out at him. Blond hair, wide blue eyes, pale face in need of a shave. The eyes got wider and the face faded a few shades paler when he saw Jack. He didn't look exactly like the guy in the photo in Hollander's apartment, but he could be. Easily.

Jack smiled and gave him a friendly wave. He raised his voice to be heard through the glass.

"Good morning. I'd like to have a word with Mrs. Habib, if you don't mind."

The corner of the sheet dropped, and the guy disappeared. Which confirmed that he'd found Richard Hollander. Anybody else would have asked him what the hell he was doing out there and who the hell was Mrs. Habib?

So now Jack had to move quickly. If he had Hollander

pegged right, he'd be tripping full tilt down the stairs for the street. Which was fine with Jack. But there was a small chance he'd take a second or two to do something gruesome or even fatal to the woman and the boy before he fled. Jack didn't anticipate any physical resistance— a gutless creep who struck at another man through his wife and child was hardly the type for *mano a mano* confrontation.

Bracing his hands on the pipe, Jack planted one foot on the three-inch windowsill and aimed a kick at the bottom pane.

Suddenly, the glass three panes above it exploded outward as a rusty steel L-bar smashed through, narrowly missing Jack's face and showering him with glass.

On the other hand, he thought, even the lowliest rat had been known to fight when cornered.

Jack swung back onto the pipe and around to the windows on the other side. The bar retreated through the holes it had punched in the sheet and the window. As Jack shifted his weight to the opposite sill, he realized that from inside he was silhouetted on the sheet. Too late. The bar came crashing through the pane level with Jack's groin, catching him in the leg. He grunted with pain as the corner of the bar tore through his jeans and gouged the flesh across the front of his thigh. In a sudden burst of rage, he grabbed the bar and pulled.

The sheet came down and draped over Hollander. He fought it off with panicky swipes, letting go of the bar in the process. Jack pulled it the rest of the way through the window and dropped it into the alley below. Then he kicked the remaining glass out of the pane and swung through.

Hollander was dashing for the door, something in his right hand. Jack started after him, his mind registering strobe-flash images as he moved: a big empty space, a card table, two chairs, three mattresses on the floor, the first empty, a boy tied to the second, a naked woman tied to the third, blood on her right breast. Jack picked up speed and caught Hollander as he reached the door. He ducked as Hollander spun and swung a meat cleaver at his head. Jack grabbed Hollander's wrist with his left hand and smashed his right fist into the pale face. The cleaver fell from his fingers as he dropped to his knees.

"I give up," Hollander said, coughing and spitting blood. "It's over."

"No," Jack said, hauling him to his feet. The darkness was welling up in him now, whispering, taking control. "It's not."

The wide blue eyes darted about in confusion. "What? Not what?"

"Over."

Jack drove a left into his gut, then caught him with an uppercut as he doubled over, slamming him back against the door.

Hollander retched and groaned as he sank to the floor again.

"You can't do this," he moaned. "I've surrendered."

"And you think that does it? You've played dirty for days and now that things aren't going your way anymore, that's it? Finsies? Uncle? Tilt? Game over? I don't think so. I *don't* think so."

"No. You've got to read me my rights and take me in."

"Oh, I get it," Jack said. "You think I'm a cop."

Hollander looked up at him in dazed confusion. He pursed his lips, beginning a question that died before it was asked.

"I'm not," Jack said. He grinned. "Mooo-neeer sent me."

Jack waited a few heartbeats as Hollander glanced over to where Munir's naked wife and mutilated child were trussed up, watched the sick horror grow in his eyes. When it filled them, when Jack was sure he had tasted a crumb of what he'd been putting Munir through for days, Jack rammed the heel of his hand against the creep's nose, slamming the back of his head against the door. He wanted to do it again, and again, keep on doing it until the gutless wonder's skull was bone confetti, but he fought the urge, pulled back as Hollander's eyes rolled up in his head and he collapsed the rest of the way to the floor.

He went first to the woman. She looked up at him with terrified eyes.

"Don't worry," he said. "Munir's on his way. It's all over."

She closed her eyes and began to sob through her gag.

As Jack fumbled with the knots on her wrists, he checked out the fresh blood on her left breast. The nipple was still there. An inch-long cut ran along its outer margin. A bloody straight razor lay on the mattress beside her.

If he'd tapped on that window a few minutes later . . .

As soon as her hands were free, she sat up and tore the gag from her mouth. She looked at him with tear-flooded eyes, but seemed unable to speak. Sobbing, she went to work on her ankle bonds. Jack stepped over to where the fallen sheet lay crumpled on the floor and draped it over her.

"That man, that . . . beast," she said. "He told us Munir didn't care about us, that he wouldn't cooperate, wouldn't do anything he was told."

Jack glanced over at Hollander's unconscious form. Was there no limit?

"He lied to you. Munir's been going crazy doing everything the guy told him."

"Did he really cut off his . . . ?"

"No. But he would have if I hadn't stopped him."

"Who are you?"

"Nobody."

He went to the boy. The kid's eyes were bleary. He looked flushed and his skin was hot. Fever. A wad of bloody gauze encased his left hand. Jack pulled the gag from his mouth.

"Where's my dad?" he said hoarsely. Not Who are you? or What's going on? Just worried about his dad. Jack wished for a son like that someday.

"On his way."

Jack began untying the boy's wrists. Soon he had help from Barbara. A moment later, mother and son were crying in each other's arms. He found their clothing and handed it to them.

While they were dressing, Jack dragged Hollander

over to Barbara's mattress and stuffed her gag in his mouth. As he finished tying him down with her ropes, he heard someone pounding on the downstairs door. He ushered the woman and the boy out to the landing, then went down and found Munir frantic on the sidewalk.

"Where—?"

"Upstairs," Jack said.

"Are they—?"

Jack nodded.

He stepped aside to allow Munir past, then he waited outside awhile to give them all a chance to be alone together. Five minutes, then he limped back upstairs. It wasn't over yet. The kid was sick, needed medical attention. But there wasn't an ER in the city that wouldn't be phoning in a child-abuse complaint as soon as they saw Robby's left hand. And that would start officialdom down a road that might lead them to Jack.

But Jack knew a doc who wouldn't call anyone. Couldn't. His license had been on permanent suspension for years.

Jack was sitting and waiting with Barbara and Munir. Doc Hargus had stitched up Barbara's breast first because it was a fresh wound and fairly easy to repair. Robby, he'd said, was going to be another story.

"I still cannot understand it," Munir said for what seemed like the hundredth time but was probably only the twentieth. "Richard Hollander ... how could he do this to me? To anybody? I never hurt him."

"You fired him," Jack said. "He's probably been looney tunes for years, on the verge of a breakdown, walking the line. Losing his job just pushed him over the edge."

"But people lose their jobs every day. They don't kidnap and torture—"

"He was ready to blow. You just happened to be the unlucky one. It was his first job. He had to blame somebody—anybody but himself—and get even with him. He chose you. Don't look for logic. The guy's crazy."

"But the depth of his cruelty ..."

"Maybe you could have been gentler with him when you fired him," Barbara said.

The words sent a chill through Jack, bringing back Munir's plea from his first telephone call last night.

Please save my family!

Jack wondered if that was possible, if anyone could save Munir's family now. It had begun to unravel as soon as Barbara and Robby were kidnapped. It still had been salvageable then, up to the point when the cleaver had cut through Robby's finger. That was probably the death blow. Even if nothing worse had happened from there on in, that missing finger would be a permanent reminder of the nightmare, and somehow it would be Munir's fault. If he'd already gone to the police, it would be because of that; since he hadn't, it would be his fault for *not* going to the police. Munir would always blame himself; deep in her heart Barbara also would blame him. And later on, maybe years from now, Robby would blame him, too.

Because there'd always be one too few fingers on Robby's left hand, always be that scar along the margin of Barbara's nipple, always be the vagrant thought, sneaking through the night, that Munir hadn't done all he could, that if he'd only been a little more cooperative, Robby still would have ten fingers.

Sure, they were together now, and they'd been hugging and crying and kissing, but later on they'd start asking questions: Couldn't you have done more? Why *didn't* you cut your finger off when he told you to?

Even now, Barbara was suggesting that maybe Munir could have been gentler when he'd fired Hollander. The natural progression from that was to: If you had, none of this would have happened.

The individual members might still be alive, but Munir's family was already dead. He just didn't know it yet.

And that saddened Jack. It meant that Hollander had won.

Doc Hargus shuffled out of the back room. He had an aggressively wrinkled face and a Wilfred Brimley mustache.

"He's sleeping," Doc said. "Probably sleep through the night."

"But his hand," Barbara said. "You couldn't—?"

"No way that finger could be reattached, not even at the Mayo Clinic. Not after spending a night in a Federal Express envelope. I sewed up the stump good and tight. You may want to get a more cosmetic repair in a few years, but it'll do for now. He's loaded up with antibiotics and painkillers at the moment. Probably sleep till morning."

"Thank you, Doctor," Munir said.

"And how about you?" he said to Barbara. "How're you feeling?"

She cupped a hand over her breast. "Fine . . . I think."

"Good. Your sutures can come out in five days. We'll leave Robby's in for about ten."

"How can we ever repay you?" Munir said.

"In cash," Doc said. "You'll get my bill."

As he shuffled back to where Robby was sleeping, Barbara pressed her head against her husband's shoulder.

"Oh, Munir. I can't believe it's over."

Jack watched them and knew he hadn't completely earned his fee.

Save my family . . .

Not yet. Hollander hadn't won yet.

"It's not over," Jack said.

They both turned to look at him.

"We've still got Richard Hollander tied up in that loft. What do we do with him?"

"I never want to see him again!" Barbara said.

"So we let him go?"

"No!" Munir spoke through his teeth. "I want him to hang! I want him to fry! He has to pay for what he did to Robby! To Barbara!"

"You really think he'll pay if we turn him in? I mean, how much faith do you have in the courts?"

They looked at him. Their bleak stares told him they felt like everybody else: No faith. No faith at all.

"So your only other option is to go back there and deal with him yourself."

Munir was nodding slowly, his mouth a tight line, his eyes angry slits. "Yes . . . I would like that." He rose to his feet. "I will go back there. He has . . . things to answer for. I must be sure this will never happen again."

Barbara was on her feet, too, a feral glint in her eyes. "I'm coming with you."

"But Robby—"

"I'll stay here," Jack said. "He knows me now. If he wakes up, I'll be here."

They hesitated.

Save my family . . .

If the Habibs were going to make it, they were going to have to face Hollander together and resolve all those as yet unasked questions by settling their scores with him. All their scores.

"Get going," he said. "I never made it past Tenderfoot in the Boy Scouts. Who knows how long my knots will last?"

Jack watched them hurry out, hand in hand. Maybe this would fix their marriage, maybe it wouldn't. All he knew for sure was that he was glad he wasn't Richard Hollander tonight.

He got up and went looking for Doc Hargus. The doc was never without a stock of good beer in his fridge.

A Season of Change
by Richard T. Chizmar

1

If it wasn't for the headlights, I never would've seen it.

The house was a spiderweb of shadows, the porch and front lawn lost in darkness. It was after one in the morning, and I was a little drunk and a lot tired. Four hours of Loughlin's Pub entertainment was all I could handle for one night. Despite a soft spray of moonlight, I never would've seen the broken paper clip if a car hadn't slowed and turned the corner as I reached for the door, its headlights sweeping across the lower half of my home, sparking a tiny glint of silver in the keyhole.

I reacted predictably at the sight of the tampered-with lock. I cussed—not once, but twice—and kicked the door. Made me feel better, too. I knew the key wouldn't make a fit but, seeing that I was pissed off and pickled and the all-too-familiar combination formed a good enough excuse, I tried anyway.

I felt the key push the paper clip further into the hole and immediately wondered why the bastard who'd jammed the lock hadn't stuck around to do the job right. Dog-tired and drunk, and I gotta deal with a goddamned prank. No justice in this world.

I started to turn around and in midturn, my mind flashed: *Or maybe they just didn't have time to finish the job, maybe they're still nearby.*

To my right, under the bay window, one of the shadows moved, and instinctively I moved away from it, knowing that my last thought had been a correct one. A second shadow, to my left this time, elongated and the rosebushes exploded. I heard clothing tear and a

68

grunt of pain. And then I felt my head explode and heard nothing at all.

2

The first thing I saw when I came to was the moon. And the pointy son of a bitch was laughing at me.

I was flat on my back, underneath the den window, a few yards to the right of the porch. Taking deep, slow breaths, I reached down and touched the emptiness in my waistband where my gun had been.

"Son of a bitch," I whispered. Wasn't gonna look good. Over ten years on the street, and a couple of damn thieves kick my ass, take my gun, and roll me under a bush like a dead bird. No sir, wasn't gonna look good at all.

My head roared when I moved to check the time. The familiar glow-in-the dark dials told me that only fifteen minutes had passed. And the fact that I still had the two-year-old Seiko on my wrist told me that the guys who'd nailed me weren't petty crooks.

I felt the back of my skull and my fingers came away wet to the knuckles. "Son of a bitch," I muttered again, shaking my head.

I struggled to my feet, after a couple of sad attempts, and walked very slowly to the porch. My keys were gone, of course, and the door was still closed. Didn't mean the bastards weren't inside, though. With another flash of pain, I bent and checked for the paper clip. It was still in place. This time I didn't bother to try the lock. I'm not *that* stupid.

I crept around the house and found the extra back-door key that I keep hidden underneath the plastic bird-bath. The sliding glass door looked untouched; I unlocked it and stepped inside. In addition to my gun cabinet which I showcase in the den, I keep an extra 9mm in the garage. I swung right in a crouch, slipped through the cluttered breezeway, and retrieved the gun. Then I searched the rest of the house, hitting the down-stairs first. I'd turned on just about every light in the house and checked every room except the bathroom when, as I crossed the hall, I itched my forehead and my fingertips came away smeared in obscene red. Too glossy for blood. I flipped the bathroom overhead on and stepped in front of the mirror.

The harsh light stung my eyes, but I could see my reflection clear enough to start my entire body shaking. My hair was slicked with sweat and blood and a patch near the back was spiked and tangled from where I'd rubbed it. My eyes were wide and nervous, my cheeks flushed with pain and adrenaline. I'd looked worse before—hell, I'd looked worse *without* having my ass kicked—but what scared the very crap out of me was the word that had been written, in smeared lipstick, across the length of my forehead.

The word that read: MAILMAN

3

It took all of six seconds for my brain to register what the word meant and another six for me to reach the phone. I punched the number and waited. Dead air. Nothing.

"Shit." I hung up and hurried down the stairs, falling on my ass the last six or seven steps. I grabbed a backup set of keys from the kitchen, pushed the back door open, and staggered across the side yard. I unlocked the truck door and had the radio transmitter in my hand before my ass hit the seat.

It was worse than I'd feared. Much worse. They didn't even have to run a check for me. They'd been trying to call me, but there'd been problems with my phone. Bastards must've cut the line. I flashed my lights and hit the I-95 exit at a clean eighty.

Ray York, my partner for the past six years, lived one exit south of me, ten minutes closer to Baltimore City. He was a good cop and a good friend. A big bear of a man, he was always happy, always smiling, always seeing the bright side of a situation. Downright unnatural for a cop. We spent plenty of off-duty hours together, but Ray was a big-time homebody, and most of the time we watched videos or ball games in his basement. His family consisted of his beautiful wife Connie—I'd been the best man at the wedding three years ago—and a pampered golden retriever named Cowboy. Cowboy was an only child, but it wasn't likely to stay that way, Ray always joked. He claimed that as soon as Connie got promoted, they were going to start working on a family. He wanted five kids. Just the thought made me cringe.

The call had come in at 12:41. Anonymous, of course. *You'll find him in the back* was all they'd said, along with the street address. The operator ran a check on the address and rushed a call through when she recognized the name.

They'd found him in the backyard. Shot twice in the midsection. Still alive. Barely. Asking only for me. They were waiting for the medivac copter.

4

A pair of patrol cars appeared behind and followed me off the Hanson exit, through an empty intersection, and onto Tupelo, the secluded dead-end street where Ray and his wife lived. An officer recognized me and waved me through the line. He stopped the other two cars and directed them to the curb.

The area was abuzz with activity: officers standing in small groups talking, others shuffling to and from the backyard. I parked at the end of the asphalt driveway and waded through the crowd. A young state trooper sidestepped from my path, looking terrified and sick and embarrassed. Jerry Higney, a fifteen-year vet with a locker near mine, called my name and pointed toward the back. I looked at him, and his eyes told me the same thing the rookie's had.

The ambulance was parked far back in the yard, near the open field that bordered Ray's property. Its overhead lights were flashing, the twin back doors standing open. A ring of on-duties surrounded the scene, shielding all activity. I slowed to a jog, pointing at my badge, when a cop I didn't recognize stepped out to intercept me. He nodded and stepped out of the way, and I saw Ray on his back on a stretcher, surrounded by paramedics.

I stepped closer, moved over him. His eyes flickered open and when he saw me . . . he smiled.

I froze.

His face was perfect, untouched, and smiling. I tried to smile back—I honestly did—but couldn't. Two paramedics knelt at his side, fist deep in his open stomach. I reached for his hand. He took it and squeezed; his grip so very soft, almost nothing. I squeezed hard enough for both of us and leaned closer.

A man with a blood-smeared jumpsuit and a nose the size of Cleveland touched my shoulder. "You'll have to stay back so we can—"

I shook my head and interrupted, "He's my partner."

Someone called him and the paramedic glanced over his shoulder, then looked back at me and said, "Okay, but if I tell you to move, you damn well better do it."

I felt Ray's fingers twitch, and he whispered in a voice that made my heart hurt and my eyes water, "You get a look at his nose? Sucker's almost as big as your's." He smiled again, but this time it hurt him and he gritted his teeth and groaned.

I think I did smile then, despite his pain. His goddamn nose jokes got me every time. I pressed closer. "Take it easy, buddy. Bird's on the way; everything's gonna be all right."

A paramedic knocked me off balance momentarily and when I looked back at Ray, his stare was savage. "Mailman," he hissed.

"I know. I know," I said. "Couple of his boys were waiting for me at the house tonight." I rubbed the back of my head instinctively. "The son of a bitches surprised me."

He shook his head and said, "They were waiting . . . waiting outside. They . . ." He rolled his head to the side and vomited. I cleared his mouth with my fingers.

"Don't talk anymore. Just try to—"

"Listen to me," he whispered, his voice almost gone. "Connie's at her mother's. They were gonna . . . gonna go shopping tomorrow. You tell her, okay? Tell her . . ."

I shook my head, knowing what was coming but not wanting to hear it, not wanting to be there anymore.

"Tell her . . ."

I waited for more, but he just stared at me, eyes pleading for an answer to this mess. "I will," I managed. "Don't worry about that now. I'll take care of it."

And then he closed his eyes and said, "I'm sorry."

I didn't know what the hell he meant, and didn't have much time to think about it before two paramedics pushed me aside, both yelling, "Code Red," and the rest of the crew went bat shit.

It was ugly. The backyard looking like a scene out of one of those high-tech science-fiction flicks. Lights everywhere, big white skylights shining brightly upward. Police red-and-blues flashing through the darkness, a bizarre laser show for the onlookers. Police officers and medics scurrying across the lawn. The paramedics pushing and poking and breathing into Ray, until the one with the big nose is standing up in disgust, snatching the radio, telling the copter to turn around. And then it gets very quiet and the lights blink out like in a stage play, only this act is real, and my partner is dead.

I found Connie's mother's phone number inside the house and called. Connie answered after the fourth ring, sounding sleepy and irritated. A few minutes later, she sounded worse. Her mother took the phone and said they'd be leaving in a few minutes. The courageous bastard that I am, I left before they arrived.

5

I spent the next couple of days inside. Alone. Took the phone off the hook. Didn't dress or shave. Nibbled at something when I got hungry, which wasn't often. Sat staring out the back-porch window. Thinking.

I don't think they meant to kill Ray, just knock him down a lick or two, like they'd done with me. A warning. Ray and I had spent past six weeks heading up a special task force designed to crush the Mailman and were finally, after a month of drawing blanks, making some progress.

Mailman's legal name was Reggie Scales. Black male. Twenty-four. Skinny and ugly. A cold-blooded killer. A self-proclaimed mastermind, he employed others to do his dirty work. Kept his own hands clean. Scales ran Baltimore City's drug trade; heroin, cocaine, crack. Of course, there were still chump-change dealers on the street—always would be—but Scales handled the main traffic. His gang numbered over thirty. And they called him Mailman on the street because he always delivered.

We'd been getting closer and closer—one of his street sellers was starting to get nervous and talk—and he must've figured it was time for a warning. Something nice and subtle, like a little too-close-to-home-for-comfort ass-beating to soften the hard-ons we had for him.

Judging from evidence found in and around Ray's house, I guessed that it'd happened like this: Mailman's men were creeping around the house when Ray opened the back door and let Cowboy out for his final shit break of the night. The dog spotted one of them and attacked. They'd found Cowboy with a bullet in his neck about ten yards from the back door. A guy I know who works K-9 told me that he'd probably died quickly, and I know that would've made Ray feel a little better. Another officer told me that Cowboy had a chunk of human flesh the size of a golf ball in his mouth. Good for him.

Mailman's men must've either panicked after Cowboy attacked or Ray must've fought like a bastard and forced one of them to gun him. Nothing else I can think of. I know that seeing Cowboy gunned down right before his eyes would've made Ray crazy, so I'd bet on the latter. Christ, he loved that mutt.

6

We buried Ray on a Sunday. A seasonally cool morning, the sky stretched a crisp, clean blue. A thin layer of fallen leaves blanketed the cemetery grounds. There was no wind, no rain. Didn't feel like funeral weather.

I wore my dress blues and if I wasn't in such a deep

funk, I would've felt ridiculous. The entire precinct—
and over a hundred other officers from as far away as
Ohio—were in attendance. And, of course, the media
showed up. Reporters, a shit load of camera crews—the
whole damn circus. They tried their best to look sincere,
but just looked hungry. I found out later that the funeral
was the lead news story on all three networks. As usual,
I declined all interviews, and threatened several reporters with bodily harm. Off camera, of course.

I stood behind Connie during the service and felt like
a real bastard. Not only had I left before she arrived at
the scene, but I'd only called her once over the past
three days.

She'd sounded as well as could be expected on the
telephone. Said both her parents were staying with her
and that she'd been taking some pills to help her sleep
and that they were working. She'd asked me a lot of
questions—about Ray and that night, about the Mailman—few of which I had answers for. The conversation
lasted barely fifteen minutes; it was all either of us could
stand. Before I hung up, I told her what Ray's last words
to me had been—*I'm sorry*—and asked if she knew what
he'd meant. She'd answered me with silence; I told her
to forget it and hung up.

After the funeral service, I spoke briefly with Ray's
parents, then wandered around aimlessly for a few minutes, afraid to get in my car and drive away, but more
afraid of staying and saying good-bye to my partner.
Connie spotted me, excused herself from the main
group, and walked over. We hugged without exchanging
words—there was really nothing either of us could say—
and she slipped a piece of paper into my hand before
we parted. I talked to a few other officers, then snuck
away before the media freaks got brave again.

I unfolded the paper and read what was written, once
in the parking lot and again in the car. Then I went
home and got drunk. I read it a third time the next
morning and got drunk again.

7

Baltimore's Inner Harbor is a contradiction of humanity.

If you sit on Federal Hill and look straight ahead out over the harbor, you can see the truth in that statement.

The harbor attracts money—all kinds. Well-dressed tourists, bored locals, hand-holding couples, businessmen and businesswomen doing lunch. Families wait in line at the aquarium, the science center, the shops and food joints. Catch a show on the Bay Lady, ride a miniature motorboat or paddleboat, eat and drink on an outdoor patio, listen to a concert. Summer, winter, hot, cold, it doesn't matter; they flock here like ants on a corpse.

Two blocks away, in the harbor's shadow, it's a different story. Barefooted kids run the streets; uneducated, undernourished, underloved. Doors and windows are open—no air-conditioning. Too many people are on the street; it's a weekday and they should be at work. A whistle sounds from a second-floor window, and the dealers disappear into the cracks. Seconds later, a dented police cruiser turns the corner. The officer inside is hot and bored and anxious to go home to his swimming pool. The squad car passes—the officer never glancing in any direction other than straight ahead—and the dealers reappear with smiles on their faces. Business is good.

Two city blocks . . . two different worlds.

And it's impossible to prevent these two worlds from clashing. Beggars line the store and restaurant fronts. Drug dealers and pimps wait in line next to visiting suburban schoolchildren. Street people sift through trash cans while spoiled teenagers hunt for the latest fashion rage or cuss the slow-walking elders in front of them. Yuppie women complain because no one notices their new outfit or haircut, while real people die a block away and no one notices or even cares.

Coming to the Inner Harbor always depresses me, and when I get depressed—which is more often than I like to admit—I tend to preach. But I preach to an audience of one, so I offer no apologies.

Connie had called late last night to arrange this morning's meeting. Ten in the morning at Federal Hill. I was early, unusual for me. I sat back in the grass and thought about the note while I waited. I supposed I could play dumb, ask her what she meant or just try to change her mind. The problem was I knew exactly what she meant, and wasn't sure that I *wanted* to change her mind.

Kill him.

The words were handwritten in black ink on lined tablet paper, probably the same pad and pen Connie used to record her grocery list every week. But instead of fruit and vegetables, this request was less healthy.

I hadn't been able to accept Ray's death yet—hadn't said good-bye to him at the funeral or returned to work and faced the job alone—but I wasn't sure if taking out the Mailman would allow me to. And I wasn't sure how I felt about Connie. Compassion and pity and ... disappointment?

Revenge was a primitive and intense emotion, one that I experienced fairly often. Hell, I had no *moral* problems with her request. The badge certainly wouldn't stop me. I'd been a terrible human long before I became a cop, and unless you listened to Ray, I'd never stopped being one. But, for some reason, I'd never expected it of Connie. At least, not to this degree. I'm a pompous bastard, I know.

She finally showed at 10:04, walking gracefully down the stone path, looking beautiful in a schoolgirl way, blond ponytail swinging from side to side. I didn't see her swollen eyes until she drew close and kissed me softly on the cheek. She sat beside me in the grass, and we talked for several minutes before silence overtook us. Somewhere in the middle of the quiet she looked at me, green eyes wide and moist, and I nodded. Her body wavered, all her breath leaving her at once, and she smiled. Then she touched my hand and left me alone.

8

Two weeks later and I'm on the street. Past midnight. Light rain falling. Cruising the city, west side, in my beat-up Mustang. I hadn't driven the junker for months—ever since I'd bought my truck—and the clutch was kicking my ass. I was wearing an old army jacket over a sweater and blue jeans. Had a wool cap pulled low over my forehead with some fake hair sticking out the back. I looked pretty damn stupid, but, hell, I valued my life more than my pride.

I had a 9mm in my shoulder holster, a shotgun under the dash, and a plastic baggie of cocaine underneath my jacket on the front seat. Earlier, I'd jumped a dealer on Fayette Street, out by the hospital, and cleaned out his stash. Knocked out two of his teeth in the process. Didn't feel good doing it, but I needed the stuff and wasn't about to pay for it.

After fifteen minutes of driving, I spotted who I was searching for on a dark corner and pulled to the curb. I leaned over and rolled down the passenger window.

"Hey, old man. Hey, Snowman. I'm looking for some information."

The man didn't look up. He was sitting on a crumbled porch, chin resting on his hands, oblivious to the rain. He looked close to sixty, but was actually in his midforties, a well-known veteran of the street. Because of his round belly and choice of drug habit, the street called him Snowman. He was wearing a filthy wool cap and a recycled trench coat down to his knees. I noted the hat and felt a little better about my disguise.

I called him a second time, this time offering to pay for the help, and again he ignored me. A young redneck couple, voices raised, obviously arguing about something, turned the corner, and I leaned back into the driver's seat. I waited for them to pass, then placed the clear bag of cocaine in my lap and poked a hole in the top with two fingers. I scooped a small amount of the powder into my other palm and exited the car, leaving the bag on the seat. Our undercovers had tried unsuccessfully to pry information from the Snowman several times before, using small amounts of money as bait.

The man heard the car door slam and slowly opened his eyes. Dull. Expressionless. Before he could close them again and return to his dream world, I opened my hand in front of his face.

"It's all yours," I said, motioning for him to take the drug.

He eyed me cautiously, then craned his neck up and down the street, eyes scanning.

"This isn't a setup," I said. "All I want is some information. I'm looking for someone and if you can help me find him, there's a bag of this stuff in the car that's yours."

I crouched to a knee and offered my hand again. He lifted a filthy, scarred hand, and I poured the cocaine onto his palm. He touched a finger to the powder, lifted it to his tongue, then, seemingly satisfied that it was the real thing, emptied it onto a scrap of newspaper. He carefully folded the paper and stuffed it under his hat.

"Who?" he asked, not looking at me.

"Mailman."

"Uh uh. Can't help you."

I walked back to the car, checking the street for wandering eyes. I lifted the coke from the seat and held it level to the man's face, feeling guilty as hell. His eyes widened, showing human emotion for the first time. Showing hunger. "All I want to know is where he is," I said. "And all this is yours. No tricks. Otherwise I find someone else to do it."

He stared at the bag, eyes unblinking, tongue snaking out to lick cracked lips. "One hour. Wait here."

I stuffed the bag inside my jacket and smiled. "I'll be waiting."

I watched the old man disappear down the street, then pulled the car around the corner and turned off the engine. I checked the time, then opened a paper bag and pulled out a ham-and-cheese sandwich and a candy bar. Damn if I wasn't prepared.

I had actually packed the same snack, dressed in the same pathetic disguise, and loaded the car twice before, false starting both times. I didn't even leave the curb the first time, and I did a U-turn on I-95 and returned home the second time.

There was no turning back tonight. I knew that.

Premeditated murder. Two words that I'd heard and

said hundreds of times before; they haunted me now. Since the meeting on Federal Hill, I'd found myself thinking of the Mailman less and less, and thinking, instead, of Connie and the note. Ray's death had triggered something inside of her—eaten away something good and pure—and she'd turned to me for help. I didn't know whether to feel honored or ashamed.

Exactly forty-five minutes after he had left, Snowman returned. He walked to the driver's side of the car and waited for me to roll down my window. Without a word, he held out his hands.

"Give it to me first," he said.

"You know where he is?"

He nodded.

I handed him the bag, and it disappeared inside his coat.

"Mama Lucia's," he said, turning to leave.

"Little Italy?"

"Yeah." Then he was gone, humming as he went.

It was easier than it should've been. Easy and quick.

There were only two men guarding him. Both standing outside, hiding from the rain underneath the awning. I popped up behind the first one and forearmed his head a couple of times until he went to sleep, and the second one—a muscle-bound teenager—actually took off running before I could get to him. Guess you can't buy loyalty.

Mama Lucia's was a corner restaurant at the north end of Little Italy. Vine-covered red brick. Two stories. A relatively quiet section of the city. Only three blocks away from the harbor, it attracted plenty of suits and other expensive clientele and served as one of many tourist attractions. And if it was like most of the other ethnic restaurants on the block, there were living quarters on the top floor. Mailman probably had something on the restaurant owner—like an overdue coke bill—and figured it was the last place anyone would look for him.

It was close to three in the morning when I walked in the front door, gloves on, gun in hand. The downstairs dining room was dark and deserted. I headed for the stairs, moving carefully through the cramped maze of tables and chairs. Considering the Mailman's healthy ego, I was surprised that the place wasn't crawling with armed guards. A few seconds later, as I reached the last step and entered a narrow, carpeted hallway, I heard squeals of pleasure, then a deeper-toned groan, and immediately knew why security was minimal. The Mailman was getting laid.

The animals sounds—they sounded like they were mauling each other—were coming from the end of the hall. There was a single door and it was cracked open, a sliver of dim light escaping into the hall. No wonder his men had been waiting outside in the rain.

I had no brilliant plan of action and instead of formulating one now, I simply walked into the room, yanked the flabby woman off the Mailman's lap, and shoved the barrel of my gun under his nose. "Don't move or I swear to God I'll pull it."

"Be cool, man," he said, gold teeth flashing. He was nude, slicked with sweat, sitting up on a tangle of sheets. He held his arms up and I could count the ribs sticking out below his scrawny chest. Christ, he certainly didn't spend his money on food. I'd seen enough pictures of Scales to recognize his face, but still I couldn't believe this was the guy we'd been looking for. He looked like a little kid.

The woman was hysterical behind me. She screamed and cussed me and started clawing my back, so I reached back and pistol-whipped her across the forehead. She hit the carpet and shut up real nice after that.

"Listen, man, I—"

"Just shut up and sit your ass right where you are, and we'll have no problems. I'm just gonna take you out of here and talk to you."

His eyes widened and he nodded his head spastically, looking like a broken puppet. He even smiled, as if to show that he trusted me. It was a sad sight.

I moved quickly, hoping that the downstairs was still clear. I pulled a set of handcuffs from my coat, yanked the Mailman's arms behind his back, and snapped them on his wrists. There was a pair of ugly yellow jockeys on the floor, and I slipped them on him myself. Wasn't my idea of a good time, but I'd seen his naked body long enough.

I guided him down the hall in front of me, shielding myself, in case anyone was waiting. I knew the gorilla downstairs wouldn't be waking up anytime soon, but I wasn't sure if the other one had called for help or grown balls in the meantime and returned.

For once, the horseshoe was up *my* ass, and the downstairs was exactly as I left it. I escorted the Mailman down the block, shoved him in the front seat of the Mustang, got in, and drove away.

"Be careful, man. I told ya I can't swim."

"And I told you to shut your mouth. We're almost there."

We were inside one of the abandoned shipyards outside of Fells Point. Walking single-file down a narrow concrete path above the water. The docks had long been taken out, leaving a sheer drop from the concrete into the black water. The rain was falling harder now, and the walk was dangerously slick. A row of dark, abandoned warehouses stretched several hundred yards in both directions, blocking the view from the street. On the way, I'd told him that someone was waiting in one of the buildings to talk to him. I figured I could waste him down here, and nobody would ever find him. It was almost over.

I studied his silhouette closely as we walked, itching to pull the trigger. He was so damn thin, his body took on an almost elastic appearance. He was a full ten inches taller than me, but I probably outweighed him by twenty pounds. It was too dark to see clearly, but I could hear the squeak of his bare feet on the pavement and the slap of thick gold chains against his chest. Wearing only underwear, he shivered badly in the cold rain.

We passed an ancient loading platform, broken and uneven now, and the pathway widened a bit. I looked back over my shoulder; we were far enough from the street now.

"The building's right up here," I said. He slowed his pace, and I pushed the 9mm's barrel into the center of his back, nudging him forward.

"Damn it, man. Keep me the fuck away from the edge. I can't swim, I tell ya. I can't fuckin' swim."

Suddenly, a flash went off inside my head. My heart hammered.

I can't swim.

I pushed him over the edge to see if he was lying.

He wasn't.

I watched the bubbles until they disappeared.

9

I hate answering machines. The only reason I finally bought one is because I kept missing calls from my bookie. Now I get messages all the time from a Mr. Pony. Clever guy.

I always screen my phone calls, with an emphasis on the always. I pick up maybe one time out of every three or four dozen calls. That's it. But, and it never fails, the single call I answer in the flesh is always the one I wanted most to avoid.

That's how Connie finally tracked me down, a week and four messages later. She didn't ask me why I hadn't returned the calls, so I didn't make up a sorry excuse. I had a feeling she knew, anyway.

"Is it over?" she asked, skipping any casual bullshit.

I'd rehearsed this moment over and over again, but my mouth felt dry and sticky. "Yes," I finally said.

"How are you?"

"Fine," I lied.

Silence. Then she said matter-of-factly, "I'm expecting my sister and her family tonight, but if you'd like to come over and talk—"

"No, no, that's okay," I said. "I've got a lot to catch up on downtown." Another lie.

"Okay, if you're sure." Long pause. "Listen, I've been thinking about what Ray said to you that night."

"Uh huh," I said, knowing precisely what she was talking about.

"Well, you know Ray thought of you as a lot more than just a partner. I mean . . . he really admired you. He loved you."

Her voice was strangled and soft, and I knew she was starting to cry.

"He thought of you as a brother . . . as family. And I think he was saying sorry because he was leaving you alone. He worried about you, you know? He used to talk about it a lot. No wife, no family, not many friends. Just your work. He always told me that if something happened to him, he knew I could go on. I had family members close by, good friends, a job I enjoyed." She sighed. "You were the one he worried about. I think Ray was apologizing for leaving you alone. That was just like him, wasn't it?"

I didn't answer. Couldn't. Just thanked her after a moment and hung up, knowing that what she'd said was the truth.

Later, I made myself a sandwich and ate it outside on the back porch. I watched the leaves dance across the lawn, and the late-afternoon sunshine and the whisper of a breeze felt good on my face. Autumn was in full swing now, and for the first time since I was a teenager, I remembered that it was my favorite time of year. A season of change.

I sat there for a long time nibbling at that sandwich, thinking about Ray. About his unshakable spirit and outlook on life. About the big mouth that had given me so many headaches during so many workdays—his stupid jokes, his boring family talk, his childhood adventure stories. And I thought about the many times when we'd sat, shared a beer or dinner, and just talked. About nothing in particular, about everything that was important to us.

As the afternoon passed, I could feel the heavy weight of guilt slowly ease away. What we'd done wasn't right, but it had cleaned the slate. It had allowed us—Ray's survivors—to survive. And to start over again.

When the sun finally lowered and the chill set in, I took my empty paper plate and went inside. It was the best damn sandwich I ever ate.

10

Later that evening, while reading the newspaper, I found myself staring at the classified advertisements. I turned to the section for household pets and circled a phone number for purebred puppies. I thought about it a bit longer and decided to call in the morning. Someone to keep me company, I thought. One of those shiny gold ones ... like Cowboy.

I know Ray would've liked that.

Good Vibrations
by Richard Laymon

Kim spread her blanket on the sand. She stepped onto the middle of it, set down her beach bag, and pulled off her sneakers and socks. She placed her sneakers at two corners of the blanket in case the wind should pick up.

Then she unbuttoned her blouse.

She wondered who might be watching. The beach was hardly deserted. At least a dozen guys—some playing volleyball, a few tossing Frisbees, others sunbathing alone or with friends or families or lovers—had turned their heads to inspect her as she'd made her way along the beach in search of an empty place to put down her blanket. Some would be staring at her now, eager to watch the clothes come off.

The beach was aswarm with beautiful young women in scanty swimsuits, but most of the guys within range would have their eyes on Kim. Because she was the one still wearing a blouse and shorts. And they wanted to watch her strip.

She'd come to the beach often enough to know how they were.

Right now, any number of men were staring at her back, aware that she'd unbuttoned her blouse, waiting for her to slip it off her shoulders. Most, she suspected, hoped that by some miracle of recklessness or mischance she'd left the top of her swimsuit elsewhere.

Sorry to disappoint you, fellas, she thought.

She removed her blouse, dropped it to the blanket, then quickly pulled down her shorts and stepped out of them. That should pretty much end the suspense for her audience. Now, she was just another gal in a string bikini. She hadn't forgotten to wear a suit, after all. And it wasn't transparent. And it hadn't fallen apart to give them a thrill.

The guys could turn their attention to other matters.

Some, of course, were bound to keep on watching. There were always a few of those.

It's just part of coming to the beach, Kim told herself. You know you'll be stared at and admired. You know you'll be getting some guys turned on. Like it or not, that's the way it is.

Relax and enjoy yourself.

Clasping her hands behind her head, she stretched. She shut her eyes, arched her back, rose onto tiptoe, clenched her buttocks, and moaned with the good feel of her straining muscles. She sniffed the fresh, briny air. She heard the surf roaring in and washing out, the squeals of seagulls and children, laughter and shouts, rock 'n' roll and rap and country music and the manic voices of djs from nearby radios. She felt the heat of the sun. She relished the way the soft, cool breeze stirred her hair and roamed over her bare skin.

This is really the life, she thought. It doesn't get much better than this.

It would be better without the bikini, she thought.

And laughed softly.

The fellas would *really* have something to look at then.

No way.

Kim opened her eyes. Even through the tinted lenses of her sunglasses, the gleam of the sunlit waves was so bright that she was forced to squint. Some kids were playing in the surf. A couple of lovers strolled by, the foam sliding over their feet. A man in skimpy trunks ran past them, muscles leaping, bronze skin flashing.

He didn't look toward Kim. After he'd run by, she watched his back, the way his buttocks flexed under the tight sheath. She was still watching him when she noticed the young man stretched out on the sand a couple of yards off to her left.

He lay on his belly, arms folded under his face. His head was turned toward her. He wore a strange pair of goggles. They didn't look at all like swimming goggles.

They were leather, with small round lenses, the green glass of the lenses so dark that she couldn't see his eyes at all. She felt certain that they were open, though. Open and staring at her.

He'd probably been one of those spying on her from the start.

She frowned at him. "What're *you* looking at?"

He didn't answer. He didn't move. Playing possum.

No point in getting upset, Kim told herself. He has a right to be here. And there's no law against looking at me.

Not even if you are wearing weird goggles.

Something else seemed wrong about him, though.

Something more than the goggles and the sneaky way he was ogling her.

For one thing, she realized, he was sprawled on the actual sand; he had no towel or blanket under him. He didn't have a shirt or shoes. Instead of a real swimsuit, he wore faded cutoff blue jeans.

He didn't look wet at all, so he hadn't simply come wading out of the water and flopped here to let the sun dry him.

His beltless jeans hung so low that the top of his crease showed. A seat pocket was torn loose at one corner, and Kim could see skin through the hole.

The skin there seemed as tanned as the rest of him.

Look who's staring now, Kim thought.

She knew she ought to turn away from him. In those goggles, he just *had* to be a space cadet. She certainly didn't want him to get the impression that she might be interested in him.

All you need is a guy like this deciding to put moves on you.

He's gotta be a nutcase.

But a good-looking one, from what she could see of him. Muscular, slim, with smooth skin tanned a shade darker than the sand and bare all the way down past his hips where his cutoffs hung carelessly low. Or intentionally low. Maybe he wanted her to notice the sleek curve of his back and how it rose to the mounds of his buttocks. Wanted her to think about him being naked under the faded, torn denim.

Kim swung her gaze to his face. It rested on his crossed arms. Those goggles were so damn queer. He might be quite handsome, but who could tell with his eyes out of sight? His hair was cinched in against his head by the leather strap, but neatly trimmed, gleaming like gold, blowing a little in the breeze.

He looked as if he might be a few years younger than Kim. Still a teenager, for sure.

That might explain why he wore the goggles. Teenaged guys often seemed to take a perverse pride in being strange. They enjoyed calling attention to themselves. Not only that, but they were constantly horny. He might be wearing the goggles just so he could spy on the girls in secret.

Maybe he isn't watching me.

Maybe he really is asleep.

His lips suddenly pursed out. Kissed at her twice.

Kim flinched. She turned away fast, knelt on her blanket and stuffed her blouse and shorts into her beach bag.

Her heart was thumping.

He'd been watching her all along, knew she'd been staring at him, the creep.

Those kissing gestures! Only a jerk would do something like that. They'd been like a crude remark—"kiss my ass," or "suck me off."

Or maybe he'd meant nothing of the kind. Maybe he'd only wanted to suggest he wouldn't mind kissing her.

Whatever, it was damned embarrassing.

Kim wondered if she ought to pick up her things and move to a different section of the beach. She didn't want to do that, though. She'd been here first. At least, she *thought* she'd been here first. She certainly hadn't noticed him when she'd picked this spot, or she wouldn't have put her blanket down so close to him.

No, he'd come along afterward. He must've snuck over and flopped nearby to watch the strip show.

Maybe while I was spreading the blanket.

This is where I stay, she decided. I'm not about to let him scare me off.

Scare me off?

I'm not scared. Why should I be? He might be a weirdo, but so what? It's not like he can *do* anything to me, not with so many people around.

All he can do is look. So what?

Let him look to his heart's content.

Jerkoff.

Scared of him. Right. Sure.

Kim dug into her beach bag and pulled out a plastic bottle of suntan oil. She moved the bag out of her way. Then she turned around slowly. Though trembling a bit, she felt quite pleased with herself as she taunted him with a good frontal view of her body shifting and twisting inside the bikini.

Turning you on, goggle eyes?

She resisted a sudden temptation to make kisses at him.

That might start something.

So she kept her face toward the water, stretched out her legs, and uncapped the bottle of suntan oil. She squirted a thin stream of warm fluid down the top of each leg to the ankle. The oil gleamed sunlight, tickled her as it started to dribble. She set the bottle aside. With open hands, she spread the oil over her shins and knees. Then her thighs. She lingered on her thighs, sliding her hands slowly up and down and between them, slicking her skin all the way to the edges of the blue patch that stretched down from its low cord and hugged her like a narrow, glossy membrane.

Catching all this, Goggles?

Eat your heart out.

Done with her legs, she squirted oil into the palm of her right hand and slicked her belly, fingertips drifting along the cord that slanted down from high on both hips. Her hand drifted over the cord, then came up for more oil. This she spread over her sides and across her rib cage below her bikini top.

She oiled her shoulders and arms next. She grinned to herself as she did it.

Make him wait for the grand finale.

She took off her sunglasses. Eyes shut, she carefully dabbed oil on her face.

Bet I'm driving him nuts.

He's probably *already* nuts, or he wouldn't be wearing those idiotic goggles.

Kim put her sunglasses back on, then filled her hand with oil and began to rub it on her chest. She caressed herself, enjoying the hot slippery feel of her skin and savoring the way she must be tormenting the kid. He had to be watching, had to be wishing this was *his* hand sliding between her breasts and stroking their bare sides.

One hand at a time, she eased her fingers beneath the cords that suspended the garment from her neck. She smoothed oil over the top of each breast. She went in under the clinging fabric and brushed her fingertips over nipples already turgid and jutting.

Bet you never expected a show like this, dip shit.

Right hand still inside her top, oily fingers sliding on her nipple, she turned her head for a glance at her spectator.

He was gone.

Nothing there except the shallow imprint his body had pressed into the sand.

Where the hell'd he go?

Kim slipped her hand out from under the bikini and scanned the beach. She looked from side to side. She swept her gaze across the shoreline and the surf. She even twisted her head around to search the area behind her.

She saw plenty of people, even a few guys wearing cutoffs instead of swimsuits. Nobody was near enough, fortunately, to have enjoyed a ringside seat for her show. But the goggled kid who was supposed to be only a few feet away, who was supposed to be agonizing over her, was nowhere to be seen.

The bastard bailed out on me!

Good, she told herself. I didn't come here to get ogled by some freak.

Damn it! How could he just get up and walk away?

Must be gay. No other explanation. A straight guy would've stayed or come over and put moves on me.

Unless he left just to piss me off.

I'm not pissed off.

I'm glad he's gone. good riddance. I didn't come here to get pestered by some freaky teenager.

Kim capped the bottle of oil. Her hands were trembling.

Calm down, she told herself. He's gone. Now you can just forget about him and enjoy yourself.

Twisting around, she propped the bottle against her beach bag. Then she lay down. She closed her eyes. She shifted about on her blanket, snuggling against the sand to shape it with the curves of her body.

She took a deep breath that pushed her breasts more tightly into the bikini's smooth, hugging pouches. She liked the feel of that. She liked the feel of the sun's heat and the way the mild breeze brushed over her skin like gentle fingertips.

It's wonderful, she thought. It's perfect, now that the creep is gone.

Almost perfect. She didn't like the way a lump in the sand pressed against her rump. She squirmed until it settled into the groove between her buttocks.

Probably a beer bottle left behind by some damn litterbug.

She thought about getting rid of it. But that would take so much effort: crawling off the blanket, moving it out of the way, digging into the sand, and then she'd have to *touch* the thing. Somebody else's garbage. Probably filthy. It might not even *be* a bottle. Might be an old bone, or something. Yuck. Forget it.

Besides, it didn't really cause any discomfort now. In fact, it felt rather good. She gave it a squeeze with her buttocks.

I ought to roll over and get the most out of it, she thought.

But she had already oiled her front. And she felt too lazy and contented to move. She yawned. She stretched. She snuggled down against the sand and the bump, and soon she fell asleep.

In her dream, the young man in goggles knelt between her legs and slid his hands up her thighs. "I knew you'd come back," she told him. "I knew you wanted me," he said. She laughed and said, "Don't flatter yourself." He smiled. Then he ducked low and licked her. From the feel of his tongue, she realized her bikini bottom was gone. She looked down at herself. The top was missing, too. Gasping, she flung up her hands and covered her breasts. His mouth went away. "It's all right," he said. "Nobody's watching." She said, "I'll just bet." He opened his button and slid the zipper down. "Would I do this?" he asked, "if we had an audience?" He let the cutoffs fall to his knees. "My God," Kim muttered. "All for you," he said. She let her arms fall to her sides. Bending down, he kissed and licked her breasts. He sucked on them. She moaned and writhed. Then she gasped, "No, wait." He lifted his head. He smiled down at her and licked his glistening lips. "What?" he asked. "I don't even know you." He answered, "That's all right. You want me. That's all that matters." She shook her head. "I don't care about your name," she told him. "But I need to *see* who you are. It's like you're hiding from me behind those stupid goggles." He smiled again. "Help yourself." Easing forward, he lowered himself onto her. As the length of his hot body pressed against her and his tongue slipped between her lips, she reached up and pushed the goggles to his forehead.

He had no eyes.

Empty sockets. Dark, bloody pits.

Kim yelped and pushed him away and flinched awake as she bolted upright. Sweat spilled down her body. She sat there, gasping for breath. A dream. It had just been a dream. A real doozy.

A great dream, there for a while. But those *eyes!*

Yeah. What eyes?

"Man," she murmured. What's wrong with me, imagining something like that?

She leaned back, braced herself up with stiff arms, and rolled her head to get the kinks out of her neck.

And saw him.

He'd returned.

He lay stretched out on the sand a few feet away, but on her right. He'd switched sides. Like before, however, his head rested on his folded arms, turned toward her. Like before, he wore the strange round goggles that hid his eyes behind their dark green lenses.

If he's *got* eyes, Kim thought.

She realized she was grimacing.

"Something wrong?" he asked.

"Yeah. You. What're you doing here?"

"Enjoying the beach."

"It's a big beach. Why don't you go somewhere else?"

"I like it here. A very beautiful view."

"Yeah? I thought maybe you were blind, or something."

He smiled, showing straight white teeth. Then he rolled over and sat up and turned to face her. As he crossed his legs, he brushed sand off his shoulders and chest. "You were asleep a long time," he said.

"And I suppose you were watching me."

"You looked like you were having a nightmare."

"Why do you wear those stupid goggles?"

"They keep the sand out of my eyes."

"They make you look like a dork."

"Sorry." A corner of his mouth turned up. Then he raised his hands to the sides of his goggles.

Kim's heart gave a lurch. Her stomach seemed to fall. She lost her breath.

"No," she gasped. "You don't . . ."

Too late.

He lifted the goggles to his forehead.

And Kim found herself staring at a pair of eyes as blue as the sky, with long silken lashes. They seemed amused, knowing, gentle.

He's gorgeous!

"Is that better?" he asked.

"A lot better," Kim said. Her voice came out husky, barely making its way through the tightness in her throat.

"My name's Sandy," he said. Smiling, he shook his head. Some sand came out of his fine, glossy hair, sprinkling his shoulders, falling past his face.

"You're sandy, all right," Kim said.

"Named after Koufax."

"Ah. I'm Kim."

"Pleased to meet you, Kim. But you're going to burn that lovely skin if you don't turn over pretty soon."

She eased herself down and rolled onto her side. Facing him. Very aware of how her breasts shifted within the flimsy, yielding patches of her bikini.

"If I turn over," she said, "my back will burn. Unless you'd like to help me."

"Help you?"

"With the suntan oil."

"Ah. I suppose I could do that."

"Thanks." She rolled off her side and stretched out. She crossed her arms beneath her face. And watched Sandy gaze at her as she squirmed on the blanket to smooth and shape the sand. She remembered the lump that had been pressing up against her, earlier. She didn't feel it now.

She stopped moving.

Sandy just sat there.

"Well?" she asked. "Coming over?"

He shook his head. Some more sand fell from his hair. "I've got a better idea," he said. "Why don't you come over here?"

Suddenly playing control games?

Maybe he just wants to watch me stand up and walk, wants to enjoy the bod in motion.

"My blanket's here," she said.

"That's what I mean. You don't need it. It's in the way. You should be on the sand."

"I'd get it all over me."

"Shower afterward."

She stared into his wonderful eyes. He's seeing me naked in a shower, she thought. Maybe seeing himself *with* me under the spray. Soaping me.

She pushed herself up. She clutched the slippery bottle of suntan oil and crawled off the blanket. Crawled toward him, head up, watching him, the hot sand sinking under her hands and knees. It was a shame he couldn't see how her breasts swayed, but he must have a nice view of her back, bare except for the two tied cords that held her top on and the third that descended from her hips to the narrow sheath clinging to her buttocks.

She stopped in front of his crossed legs. She pushed herself up. Kneeling, she held out the bottle.

He took it from her.

"Here?" she asked.

"Here's fine."

She turned aside and lay down flat. The sand felt almost hot enough to scorch her. After a few moments, she got used to the heat. She squirmed, enjoying the way the surface molded against her body.

"Doesn't that feel better than the blanket?"

"It's different."

"It's like floating," he said. "Floating on a warm sea that loves you. Feel how it hugs you? Feel how it holds every curve of you, every hollow?"

"I guess so." It's nice, she thought, but it's not *that* nice. This guy may be gorgeous, but he's still a little weird. "Are you going to oil my back for me?"

Smiling, he nodded. As he got to his knees and crawled to her, Kim swept her hair aside to bare the nape of her neck. She untied the cord there. She lowered its ends to the sand, then reached up behind her back and plucked open the bow at her spine.

"I don't want strap marks," she explained.

"More like strings," Sandy said.

"Now there aren't any strings in the way." Kim folded her arms under her face. She stretched and wiggled. It felt very good to be free of the cords, exciting to know that her top was loose, held against her breasts by nothing more than the pressure of the cupping sand. "I'll have to remember to stay down."

"If you forget, I doubt that anyone would mind. I know I wouldn't."

She trembled with delight as Sandy squirted a stream of warm oil across the backs of her shoulders and down her spine. Then his hands were on her, gliding, sliding. They drifted all over her back and sides. They spread the oil. They massaged her. They explored her, even roaming low enough to slick the sides of her breasts. When he did that, she raised herself slightly out of the sand. But he didn't take advantage of it, didn't reach into the space and fill his hand. He simply moved on and Kim, with a sigh, sank down again.

When his hands went away, she lifted her head and looked around. She found Sandy kneeling by her hip. He bent forward and squirted oil down both her legs. His cutoffs hung so low, they looked as if they might fall off.

God, he's fantastic, she thought.

Then she was lost in the feel of him kneading her calves. She lowered her face against her arm and shut her eyes.

When he's done, she thought, maybe he'll let me oil him.

That would be wonderful. But she would need to tie her top again and get up. She didn't want to do that. She liked being just where she was.

I couldn't get up if I wanted to, she thought.

And moaned as his hands worked their way up her thighs. Slid between them. Slicked her bare skin all the way to her groin, then went up and caressed her hips with oil before swirling over her buttocks. He rubbed them, squeezed them. But stayed away from the little that was covered, as if her bikini were a border he didn't dare cross.

Probably doesn't want to stain it with oil.

Or afraid people might be watching.

I've got to take him home with me, Kim thought. I've got to. Take him home to bed. He can oil me all over, and I'll oil him. It'll stain the sheets, but who cares?

Then he was done.

Kim let out a shaky breath. She opened her eyes, and watched Sandy crawl alongside her. He lay down, crossed his arms, and gazed into her eyes.

"That was great," she whispered.

"My pleasure," he said.

"I just wish nobody else was here. And we had the whole beach all to ourselves."

"I know."

"Would you like to come over to my apartment?"

He frowned slightly. "I don't think so."

You can't mean that, Kim thought. Please. "There won't be anyone there. Only us."

"I like it here."

"We don't have to leave right away. We can stay as long as you want." She tried to smile. "I'm not sure I'd be able to move right now, anyway. You've got me so . . . lazy and excited."

"This is where I belong," he said.

"Hey, come on." That sounded a bit whiny. She struggled for control, then tried again. "Don't you get it? I *want* you. I want us to make love."

"So do I."

"Well, then . . . "

Sandy drew the goggles down over his eyes. He straightened his arms overhead, then turned his face downward and pushed it into the sand.

"What're you . . .?"

He began to shake, his whole body shuddering, vibrating.

Kim raised her face. She gaped at him. "Sandy? What're you doing?"

He didn't answer. He kept on quaking.

My God! He's having some kind of fit!

"Are you all right? What's wrong?"

Reaching out, she clutched his shoulder. It juddered in her grip. Then sand was pushing up around her fingertips.

My God! He's sinking!

She jerked her hand away.

The sand shivered around his palsied body, seemed to be melting beneath him, sucking him down. His arms were already gone. His face was buried past the ears.

His shoulders vanished completely. Sand spilled in across his lower back, trembled above his legs.

Gotta help him!

Kim almost thrust herself up, then remembered her loose top. She groped for the strings, found them in the sand beside her breasts, strained her arms up behind her back to tie them. Then let them fall again.

Because all that remained of Sandy was the seat of

his cutoffs and the back of his head—the leather strap matting down his hair.

The goggles.

He's doing this on purpose.

It's what he does.

It's how he disappeared last time.

He's doing it because of me.

Now he was completely gone, leaving behind an imprint of his outstretched body in the sand.

Holy shit!

Kim looked around. Not far away, people were sunbathing. Others were sitting up, reading, talking. One group was having a picnic. A kid walked by with a bottle of soda.

Nobody was gazing, thunderstruck, at the patch of beach where Sandy had pulled his disappearing stunt.

Nobody had noticed.

Nobody knows but me.

Maybe it didn't happen, at all. A person can't just wiggle down like that and vanish. It's impossible.

But I *saw* it happen. And I'm not dreaming now.

Reaching up behind her, Kim stroked the small of her back. Her hand came away slick.

I didn't dream him oiling me. I'm not dreaming any of this. He really buried himself. Somehow.

Her throat felt tight and tickly. She kept her mouth shut to hold in the scream or wild laugh that wanted to burst free. From her nose came a high-pitched humm.

It's crazy! Get the hell out of here!

She slapped her hands against the sand, ready to push herself up, then paused wondering if she should tie her bikini first. No time to lose. Better to risk a little embarrassment than to delay her escape even for a ... the sand beneath her breasts trembled.

Rubbed her.

My God!

All thoughts of fleeing dissolved as the sand shifted against her breasts and fell away. She felt them hanging free inside hollows. Then hands were cupping them, squeezing them gently. Warm, grainy hands on her bare skin. Kim didn't know what he'd done with her bikini top, but she didn't much care.

It's down there somewhere, she thought.

I can worry about it later.

Trembling, she crossed her arms beneath her face.

This is just too weird, she thought.

He's under me. Touching me. And nobody knows. It's our little secret. Our big secret.

How the hell can he breathe?

It's only been a minute or two, she thought. She'd heard of pearl divers who could stay under water forever. Ten minutes? Fifteen?

This is incredible. Fabulous.

She writhed and moaned as the hands plied her breasts, stroked and pulled her nipples.

This is why he didn't want me on the blanket, she realized. So he could get to me.

Something hard nudged her groin.

Something like the mouth of a beer bottle buried in the sand.

Oh, Sandy! You devil!

It tore her breath away as it thrust.

Not here. Is he nuts?

I can't untie my bottoms. Somebody'd notice that, for sure. And I don't want sand in me.

Gasping and moaning as Sandy teased her breasts and pushed at the flimsy shield between her legs, she lifted her head. She began to sweep away the sand beneath her face. All she found was more sand.

"Where are you?" she whispered.

And scooped out more. And more. And uncovered his nose. Then his goggles. Then his lips. They were shut tight, a line of sand resting across the crease between them. Kim blew the sand away. She lowered her face into the depression and kissed them. They parted. His tongue pushed into her mouth. She sucked it, moaning.

The sand beneath her body began to shiver and slide.

His hands went away from her breasts, slid down to her hips, fingered the ties, plucked them open.

Don't. Somebody'll see.

But she didn't want to tell him no. Didn't want to pull

her mouth away from his. Didn't want to stop what was happening. Because now she could feel all of Sandy. Somehow, he'd done away with the thickness of sand keeping them apart. And with his cutoffs.

Who does he think he is, Houdini?

She chuckled softly into his mouth.

He was long and hot against her oiled skin, smooth except for the rough grains that rubbed her as he shook.

He was shaking like crazy.

Vibrating.

It felt wonderful.

He didn't even stop shaking when he plunked the loose fabric, and it slid down between her legs and away.

My ass is bare!

Everyone'll see!

Nobody'll see, she realized. It's all right.

Because sand was rushing in to cover her buttocks. It felt wonderful like warm water flooding down, caressing her bare skin, licking into crevices.

Kissing her shut eyes. Dribbling into her ears.

She realized her face was buried. But she could still breathe. No sand was coming into her nostrils as she sucked air. Couldn't get in between their faces. Not yet. And this shouldn't take long.

As Sandy pushed up at her, she tried to spread her legs wider. The sand held them motionless.

He thrust into her, anyway.

Big and thick and sandy.

Quivering in a frenzy deep inside her while his tongue plunged deeper into her mouth and his lips vibrated against her lips and the tremors of his chest rubbed and shook her breasts and his belly and pelvis and thighs all buffeted her with their mad fluttering.

How does he do this?

Doesn't matter how.

All that mattered was how it felt to be pinned down by the heavy sand, naked against his shuddering body, filled with him, lost in the feel of him.

She gasped into his mouth and quaked.

Sandy jumped in her depths, spurting.

Then he quit the wild shaking. He lay motionless beneath her.

We did it. My God, we actually did it here on the beach right in front of everyone . . . and nobody's the wiser.

His tongue began to slide out of Kim's mouth. She squeezed it between her lips, savoring the thickness of it. When it was gone, she kissed his mouth.

This was the best ever, she thought. I've got to bring him home with me.

She tried to lift her head.

The clutching sand held it firm.

Hey, come on.

"Sandy," she whispered against his lips. "Get us out of here."

His quivering started again.

"Thanks," she whispered.

Ride him up like an elevator.

Uh-oh, she thought. Where's my bikini? I'll be popping up bare-ass.

Then she realized that her beach blanket should be within reach. She could drag it over and cover herself, hide beneath it while she got into her shorts and blouse.

Then she felt sand sliding against her lips. Her next breath sucked dry particles into her nostrils.

Shit!

She blew out air to clear the passages, and held her breath.

Sandy!

Sand, not Sandy, was trembling beneath the length of her body. He was no longer pressed against her. But he was still in her. Hard and vibrating, slowly sliding out.

No!

She willed herself to reach down and grab hold before he was gone entirely. But the sand refused to let her arms move.

She clenched muscles around the retreating shaft. Hugged it, but couldn't stop it.

It went away.

Please! My God!

Don't get crazy, she thought. He'll be back. He's just fooling around, trying to throw a scare into me. Playing some kind of masculine control game. Wants to show me who's boss.

He can't just leave me here!

She tensed her muscles, made them shiver.

Two can play this game. If he can vibrate through the sand, so can I.

But the sand only squeezed her. Didn't slide away at all.

Her lungs began to burn.

She went limp.

He'll be back. He won't let me . . .

The sand began to shimmy beneath her trapped body.

I knew it! Thank God!

A pocket opened beneath her right breast.

A tongue slid against her nipple.

Damn it, Sandy! This is no time to fool around! I'm suffocating here!

She felt his lips, the edges of his teeth, his swirling tongue as he sucked her breast into his mouth.

You bastard! Get me out of here!

When his teeth snapped shut, Kim screamed.

When the scream was done and she gasped for air, sand filled her mouth.

Choking, on fire with agony, she struggled to shove and kick and buck, to get away from his teeth, to get free of the sand.

It clutched her, wouldn't let her move.

Held her for Sandy while he ate.

The Tulsa Experience
by Lawrence Block

They were teasing me Friday at the office. Sharon told me to be sure and send her a postcard, the way she always does, and I said what I always say, that I'd be back before the postcard reached her. And Warren asked which airline I was flying, and when I told him he very solemnly pulled out a quarter and handed it to me, telling me to buy some flight insurance and put him down as beneficiary.

Lee said, "Where's it going to be this time, Dennis? Acapulco? Macao? The south of France?"

"Tulsa," I said.

"Tulsa," he said. "Would that be Tulsa, Spain, on the Costa Brava? Or do you mean Tulsa, Nepal, gateway to the Himalayas?"

"This will come as a shock to you," I said, "but it's Tulsa, Oklahoma."

"Tulsa, Oklahoma," he marveled. "So the Gold Dust Twins are going to glamorous Tulsa, Oklahoma. I suppose Harry is up to it, but are you sure your heart can handle the excitement?"

"I'll try to pace myself," I said.

Harry and I are not twins, Gold Dust or otherwise. He's my brother, two years older than I, and aside from our vacations we actually see very little of each other. Harry, who has never married, still lives in the row house in Woodside where we grew up. After college he helped in the store and took over the business when Dad retired. The house was left to both of us when our parents died, but we worked out a way for him to buy my share.

I was married for several years, but I've been divorced

104

for longer than I was married, and I doubt I'll marry again. I have a nice apartment on East Eighty-third Street. It's small but it suits me, and it's rent-controlled. Work is a short bus ride away, a walk in good weather.

I had taken the bus that morning, although the weather was nice, because I had my suitcase with me. I worked right through lunch hour and then took the rest of the afternoon off and caught a cab to the airport. I got there over an hour before flight time and Harry was already there, his bag checked. "Well," he said, punching me affectionately on the shoulder. "You ready for the Tulsa experience, Denny?"

"I sure am," I said.

I've been at Langford Corporation for almost seventeen years, I had another job for a year and a half when I first got out of college, and then I came to Langford, and I've been with the company ever since. So for the past five years I've been entitled to four weeks of paid vacation a year. I take a week in the spring, a week in the summer, a week in the fall, and a week in the winter, and Harry arranges to close his store during those weeks. When we first started doing this he let his employees take over, but that didn't work out so well, and it's simpler and easier just to lock the doors for a week.

And that's really about the only time we see each other. Each season we pick a city, somewhere right here in the United States, and we take rooms in a nice hotel and make sure we experience the place to the hilt.

Boston was the third city we visited together, or maybe it was the fourth. I could stop and figure it out, but it doesn't matter; the point is that there was one of those multiscreen presentations in a theater near Quincy Market, giving you the history of the city and an armchair tour of the area. *The Boston Experience,* they called it, and ever since we've used that phrase to describe our travels to one another. After Boston we had the Atlanta experience. Now we were going to have the Tulsa experience, and three months ago, give or take a week, we were having the San Diego experience.

I can understand why Lee teases me. I have never been to London or Paris or Rome, and I don't know that I'll ever get out of this country at all. We've talked about it, Harry and I, but whenever it comes time to plan a trip we always wind up choosing an American city. I guess it's not glamorous, and maybe we're missing something, but we always have a great time, so why change?

Founded in 1879, Tulsa has a population of 360,919, and is the second-largest city in Oklahoma. (Oklahoma City, the capital, is larger by about forty thousand; we have not yet had the Oklahoma City experience.) Tulsa is 750 feet above sea level, located in the heart of a major oil- and gas-producing area. More than six hundred energy-oriented firms employ upward of thirty thousand people.

We reviewed this and other facts about Tulsa during our flight. Harry had done the planning, so he had the guidebooks, and we read passages aloud to one another. We both ordered martinis when the stewardess came around with the drinks cart. Harry's not a big drinker, and I hardly drink at all except when we travel. But the drinks are free in first class and it seems silly not to have one.

We always fly first class. The seats are more comfortable and they treat you with special care. It costs more, of course, and it may not really be worth the difference, but it helps make the trip special. And we can afford it. I earn a decent salary, and Harry has always done well with the store, and neither of us is given to high living. Harry has always lived alone, as I believe I mentioned, and my own marriage was childless, and my wife has long since remarried so I don't have any alimony to pay. That makes it easy enough for us to fly first class and stay at a good hotel and eat in the best restaurants. We don't throw money around like drunken sailors, or even like Tulsa oilmen, but we treat ourselves well.

There was an in-fight movie, but we didn't bother watching it. It was more interesting to read the guidebooks and discuss which attractions appealed and which we thought we could safely pass up. The average person would probably think that a week would be more than time enough to experience everything a city like Tulsa has to offer, but he would be very much mistaken.

You've probably heard jokes about Philadelphia, for example. That they had a contest, and first prize was a week in Philadelphia while second prize was two weeks. Well, we've had the Philadelphia experience, and a week was nowhere near enough to experience the city to the fullest. We did well, we went just about everywhere we really wanted to go, but there were still quite a few attractions we had to pass up with some regret.

The flight was enjoyable. Harry had the aisle seat this time, so he got to flirt a little with the stewardess. For my part, I was able to look out the window during our approach to Tulsa. It was still light out, but even on night flights I get a kick out of seeing the lights of the city below, as if they're all lit up just to welcome the two of us.

They delivered our rental car just minutes after our bags came off the luggage carousel. The car was a full-size Olds with a plush velour interior, very quiet and luxurious. Back home I don't even own a car, and all Harry has is the six-year-old panel truck with the name of the store painted on its sides. We could have managed just as well with a subcompact, but if you shop around you can usually get a really nice car for only a few dollars more. We'd had a great deal on a Lincoln Town Car in Denver, with free mileage and no charge for the full insurance coverage, for example.

We stayed downtown at the Westin on Second Street. Harry had booked us adjoining rooms on the luxury level. A double room or even a small suite would have been a lot less expensive, but we both like our privacy, as much as we enjoy being together on our vacations. And, as you probably have gathered by now, we don't stint on these trips. If we have one rule, it's to treat ourselves to what we want.

We made it an early night, unpacking, getting settled, and orienting ourselves in the hotel. First thing after breakfast the next day we took a Gray Line bus tour of Tulsa, which is what we always do when we can. It gives

you a wonderful overview of the city and you don't have
to find your own way around. You get to drive past some
attractions that you might not be interested enough to
see if they required a special trip, but that are certainly
worth viewing through the window of the bus. And you
pick up a familiarity with the place that makes it a lot
easier to get around during the remainder of the stay.
Harry and I are both sold on bus tours, and it's disappointing when a city doesn't have them.

The tour was a good one, and it took most of the
morning. After lunch we went to the Thomas Gilcrease
Institute of American History and Art. They have a
wonderful collection of western art, with works by Rem-
ington, Moran. Charles Russell, and a great many others.
The collection of Indian artifacts was also outstanding,
but we spent so much time looking at the paintings that
we didn't really have time to do the Indian collection
justice.

"We'll get back during the week," Harry said.

We had dinner at a really nice restaurant just a short
walk from our hotel. The menu was northern Italian,
and they made their own pasta. We took a long walk
afterward. When we got back to the hotel Harry wanted
to have a swim in the pool, but I was ready to call it a
night. I've found it's important to not try to do too
much, especially the first couple of days. I took a long
soak in the tub, watched a movie on HBO, and made
an early night of it.

They brought in Tulsa's first oil well in 1901, and
Tulsa invited oilmen to "come and make your homes in
a beautiful little city that is high and dry, peaceful and
orderly, where there are good churches, stores, schools
and banks, and where our ordinances prevent the desola-
tion of our homes and property by oil wells."

Sunday morning we went to services at Boston Avenue United Methodist Church, which had been pointed
out to us on the Gray Line tour. Neither Harry nor I
go to church as an ordinary thing, and we weren't raised
as Methodists to begin with, but that's the whole point
of vacation, to get away from the workaday world and

experience something different. Why, I hardly ever go to museums in New York, where we have some of the best in the world, but when I am in another city I can't get enough of them.

That afternoon, though, we tried a different sort of cultural experience and drove over to Bell's Amusement Park. They had a big old wooden roller coaster, three water slides, a log ride and a sky ride and a pair of miniature golf courses. It was a little cold for the water slides but we did everything else, laughing and shouting and shoving each other like children. Harry threw darts at balloons until he won a stuffed panda, and then he gave it to the first little girl he saw.

"Now in the future," he told her, "don't you take pandas from strange men." And we laughed, and her mother and father laughed, and we went off to play miniature golf one more time.

There was a restaurant called Louisiane that we'd seen a few blocks from the church, and where we were planning to go for dinner. But after we got back to the hotel we arranged to meet in the bar downstairs, and when I got there Harry was knee-deep in conversation with a handsome woman with short dark hair and a full figure. He introduced her as Margaret Cummings, up from Fort Worth for the weekend.

I joined them for a quick drink, and then Harry took me aside and asked if I'd mind if he took Margaret to dinner. "I was talking to her at the pool last night," he said, "and the thing is, she's going back home tomorrow." I told him don't be silly, of course I didn't mind, and wished him luck.

So I ate right there in the hotel myself, and had a fine meal, and then went for a little walk after dinner. At breakfast the next day Harry grinned and said he'd had some fun with Margaret, and she'd given him her address and phone in case he ever got to Fort Worth. We've been to Dallas, and enjoyed that very much, and made a visit or two to Fort Worth at that time, taking in the Amon Carter Museum and some other attractions, so I doubt we'll be ready for the Fort Worth experience for quite a while yet.

"I was sorry to leave you stranded," Harry said, but I told him not to be silly. "You never know," I said. "Maybe we'll both get lucky here in Tulsa."

We started off the morning with an industrial tour of the Prankoma pottery. We both love industrial tours, and take advantage of them every chance we get. One of the highlights of the St. Louis experience was a tour of the Anheuser-Busch brewery, and we followed it up a day later with a half-hour tour of Bardenheier's Wine Cellars, followed by a half hour of wine-tasting. They didn't give you anything to drink at Prankoma, but it was very interesting to see how they made the pottery. Afterward they encouraged you to buy pottery in their shop, and they had some nice things for sale, but we didn't buy anything.

We almost never do. The National Park Service has a motto— "Take only snapshots, leave only footprints." (A side trip to Olympic National Park was one of the highlights of the Seattle experience.) We go them one better by not even taking snapshots. My apartment's too small to clutter it up with souvenirs, and Harry has the same attitude toward souvenirs, even though he has more than enough room for them at the house in Woodside.

As it is, I pick up one souvenir from every trip, a T-shirt with the name of the city we went to. My favorite so far is a fuchsia one from Indianapolis, with crossed black-and-white checkerboard racing flags on it to represent the Indianapolis 500. Most of the Tulsa T-shirts picture an oil well, and Thursday I finally picked out an especially nice one.

But I'm getting ahead of myself, aren't I?

Monday afternoon we went to the Tulsa Garden Center, and spent several hours there and nearby at the Park Department Conservatory. Tuesday we started out at the Historical Society Museum, then went to a synagogue to see the Gerson and Rebecca Fenster Gallery of Jewish Art, the largest collection of Judaica in the Southwest. From there we went to Oral Robert University for a brief campus tour, and picked up tickets for a chamber music concert to be held the following evening.

We went to our rooms for a nap before dinner, arranging to meet in the cocktail lounge. This time I got there before Harry did, and I got into a conversation with a pretty young woman named Lylah. We were hitting it off pretty well, and then Harry joined us, and before you knew it a friend of Lylah's named Mary Eileen came by and made it a foursome. We had two rounds of drinks at a table and Harry said he hoped the two of them would join us for dinner.

Lylah and Mary Eileen exchanged glances, and then Mary Eileen said, "Why should a couple of nice fellows like you waste your money on dinner?"

Well, I won't say I was shocked, because I had the feeling that they were unusually quick to get friendly. Besides, this sort of thing has happened before. The Chicago experience, for example, included a couple of young ladies whose interest in us was purely professional, but we sure had a good time all the same.

The upshot of this was that Lylah came up to my room, and Mary Eileen went with Harry. I had some fun with Lylah, and she seemed happy with the hundred dollars I gave her. On her way out she gave me an engraved business card with just her first name and her phone number on it. Mary Eileen gave Harry one just like it, except with a different name, of course. They both had the same phone number.

"Take only snapshots," Harry said, tearing Mary Eileen's card in two. "Leave only footprints." And I did the same with Lylah's card. It wasn't likely we'd ever be back in Tulsa, and we wouldn't want to see those girls more than once this trip. The Gilcrease Institute might be worth a second visit, but not Lylah and Mary Eileen.

Wednesday we left town right after breakfast and drove fifty-five miles north to Bartlesville, where the founder of a big oil company set up a wildlife preserve with herds of bison, longhorn cattle, and all sorts of wild animals. We stayed right in the Olds and drove around, viewing them from the car. The complex includes a museum, and the western art and Plains Indian artifacts were magnificent, and just wonderfully displayed. They also had what was described as one of the finest collections of Colt weapons in the country, and I could believe it.

We wound up spending the whole day in Bartlesville, because there were other interesting attractions besides Woolaroc. We saw an exact replica of the state's first commercial drilling rig, we saw an exhibit on the development and uses of petroleum, and we saw a tower designed by Frank Lloyd Wright. North of Bartlesville in Dewey we paid a visit to the Tom Mix Museum and saw original costumes and cowboy gear from his movies along with film stills and other interesting items.

We finally got around to having dinner at Louisiane that night and just got to the concert on time at Oral Roberts. Afterward we roamed around the campus a bit, then took a lazy drive around Tulsa, just looking at people. There was a shopping mall Harry wanted to check out, but it was late by the time we got out of the concert so we decided we'd save that for tomorrow.

"We'll do some fieldwork tomorrow afternoon and evening," Harry said, "and I figure Friday night we'll go for it."

I said that was fine with me. He'd been doing all the planning, and the Tulsa experience had been really fine so far.

When I had time to myself I'd read about Tulsa in the guidebook, or in some of the tourist brochures in the hotel room. I liked to pick up whatever information I could.

With the completion of the Arkansas River Navigation System, Tulsa has gained itself a water route to both the Great Lakes and the Gulf of Mexico. The port of Catoosa, three miles from Tulsa itself on Verdigris River, stands at the headwaters of the waterway and is presently America's westernmost inland water port.

Now you might think that a fact like that wouldn't stay with me, but it's funny how much of what we do and see and learn on these vacation trips remains in memory. It's a real education.

*   *   *

Thursday morning we went straight to the Philbrook Art Center after breakfast. It's set on over twenty acres and surrounded by gardens, and the collections ranged from Italian Renaissance paintings to Southeast Asian tradeware. It took the whole morning to do the place justice.

"I like Tulsa," I told Harry. "I really like it."

After lunch for a change of pace we went to the zoo in Mohawk Park. The performing elephants were the highlight, but just walking around and seeing the animals was enjoyable, too. Then toward the later part of the afternoon we went to that shopping mall and wandered around, and that was when I bought my souvenir T-shirt, a nice blue one with an oil well, of course, and the slogan "Progress and Culture." Harry thought it was a dopey slogan, but I liked the shirt. I still like it. The funny thing is nobody ever sees my T-shirts, because I wear a dress shirt and tie to the office every day, and even on weekends I'm afraid I'm not the T-shirt type. I wear them as undershirts beneath my dress shirts, or I'll wear them around the apartment, or to sleep in. I like having them, though, and you could say I'm developing quite a little collection, adding a new one every three months.

The Indianapolis shirt is my favorite so far, but I believe I mentioned that before.

We drove around Thursday night. We checked out the University of Tulsa campus and cruised around Mohawk Park. I was really glad we had the big car instead of an economy compact. I think it makes a difference.

I didn't sleep well Thursday night, and Harry said he was restless himself. We both had the impulse to skip the activity he had planned, but we stuck with it and I'm glad we did. We drove ten miles south of the city to the Allen Ranch, where we were booked for a half-day trail ride on horseback through some really pretty country. Neither of us is much of a rider, but we've been on horseback on other vacations, and the horses they give you are always gentle and well trained. I knew I'd be sore for the next week or so, but it seemed like a small price to pay. We had a really good time, and the weather was perfect for it, too.

I showered as soon as we got back, and then I went downstairs for a whirlpool and sauna. That wouldn't do anything about the saddle sores, but it took some of the ache out of muscles that don't get much use back in New York.

Then I took a long nap and left a call so I'd be up in time for dinner. Dinner was just a light bite at a coffee shop because we were both keyed up and a big meal wouldn't have been a good idea even if we'd been in the mood for it.

We went to the shopping mall and prowled around there for a while, but we didn't find what we were looking for. Then we drove to the hospital and waited in the parking lot for twenty minutes or so without any success. We went back to the University of Tulsa campus and came very close there, but we aborted the mission at the last minute and drove to a supermarket we had researched the day before.

We parked where we could watch people entering and leaving. We were there twenty minutes or so when Harry nudged my arm and pointed to a woman getting out of a Japanese compact. We watched as she walked past us and into the market. I nodded, smiling.

"Bingo," he said.

He parked our car right next to her. She wasn't in there long, maybe another ten minutes, and she came out carrying her groceries in a plastic bag.

Harry had the window rolled down, and he called her over. "Miss," he said, "maybe you can help me. Would you know where this address is?"

She came over for a look. I was by the side of the car and I stepped up behind her and got her in a chokehold and clapped my other hand over her mouth so she couldn't make a sound. I dragged her into the shadows and kept the pressure on her throat and Harry got out of the car and hurried over and hit her three times, once in the solar plexus and twice in the pit of the stomach.

We'd bought supplies yesterday, including a roll of tape. She was pretty much unconscious from the chokehold so it was easy to tape her mouth shut and get her hands behind her back and tape her wrists together.

Harry opened the back door and I got in back with her and he got behind the wheel and drove. I had her groceries in the back of the car with me, and her purse.

Harry headed for Mohawk Park and we drove right out onto the golf course. She came to in the car but she was all trussed up and there wasn't a thing she could do. When he stopped the car we dragged her outside and got her clothes off, and we took turns having fun with her. We both had a really wonderful time with her, we really did.

Finally Harry asked me if I was done and I had to say I was, and he told me in that case to go ahead and finish up. I told him it was his turn, but then he reminded me that he had done the nurse in San Diego. Don't ask me how I'd managed to forget that.

So it was my turn after all, and I got the belt out of my pants and strangled her with it. Then I took her arms and Harry took her legs and we carried her off the fairway and left her deep in the rough. You'd have to hook your tee shot real bad to get anywhere near her.

We threw her purse in a Dumpster outside a restaurant on Lewis Avenue. There was a Goodwill Industries collection box a few blocks away, and that's where we left her clothes. I would have liked to keep something, an intimate garment of some sort, but we never did that. *Take no snapshots, leave no footprints*—that's the National Park Service motto as we've adapted it for our own use.

I'd bought a Dustbuster the day before and I used it to go over the interior of the Olds very thoroughly. They'd vacuum the car after we turned it in, but you don't want to leave anything to chance. The Dustbuster went in another Dumpster, along with the roll of tape. And her bag of groceries, except for a box of Wheat Thins. I was pretty hungry, so I took those back and ate them in the room.

Saturday we pretty much took it easy. I went back for a second visit to the Gilcrease Institute but Harry passed that up and hung around the hotel pool instead. We were planning on another concert that evening but we spent a long time over dinner and wound up taking in a movie instead. Then back to the hotel for a quick brandy in the bar, and then up to bed.

And Sunday morning we flew back to New York.

Monday morning I was at my desk by nine, which was more than some of my fellow workers could claim. Sharon said she hadn't received my postcard, and as always I told her to keep watching the mailbox. Of course I hadn't sent one. Warren breezed in at a quarter to ten and said he guessed he'd wasted another twenty-five cents on flight insurance. I told him he could try again in August. "I'll have to," he said. "I can't quit now, I've got too much money invested."

Lee asked me where I'd be going in August. "Baghdad? Timbuktu? Or someplace really exotic, like Newark?"

I'm not sure. Buffalo, possibly. I'd like to see Niagara Falls. Or maybe Minneapolis—St. Paul. It's the right time of year for either of those cities. It's my turn to plan the trip, so I'll take my time and make the right decision.

In the meantime I go to my office every morning and read guidebooks evenings and weekends. Sometimes when I sit at my desk I'll think about the T-shirt I'm wearing, invisible under my dress shirt. I'll remember which one it is, and I'll take a moment to relive the Denver experience, or the Baltimore experience, or the Tulsa experience. Depending on what shirt I'm wearing.

Lee can tease me all he wants. I don't mind. Tulsa was *wonderful*.

Trolls
by Christopher Fahy

Daddy had said: "You can't be serious, Beth. You actually think you're going to land a job at this late date? Fresh out of college, with no experience other than practice teaching, and you've waited till now to start looking?" He'd shaken his head in despair and left the kitchen.

And now as Beth looked through the tall dorm window, she thought: Well, Daddy, guess what? You're not always right after all.

It had been a close call, though, a very close call. By the third week in August, things had looked really bleak. She was trying to face up to building Big Macs for another year, but then—incredible!—she got the letter, interviewed, and here she was—a teacher!

Okay, so Radbourne wasn't a regular school, certainly not what she'd had in mind when she'd started her job search, but hey—it was better than Egg McMuffins and mopping floors. And it might prove interesting. She'd only had two courses in special ed, it wasn't exactly her cup of tea, but who could tell? She might learn to like it. At any rate, a year at Radbourne would brighten her pallid resume—and it was a *job*. She'd be able to save for a car, pay her student loans, maybe even eat out sometimes.

And the campus was beautiful! With its rolling lawns and towering trees, its yellow brick paths and wooden benches and globe-topped cast-iron lampposts. The buildings themselves, Victorian mansions with wraparound porches smothered in ivy and creepers, were in need of some tender-loving care. Still, the impression was charming—as long as you didn't get too close. Barrington Hall, where she was lodged, was in decent (if gloomy) shape on the ground floor, where library, parlor, and offices were, but its other three stories were sad: the walls hadn't been painted in years and were riddled with cracks, the faucets gave only a trickle of water, the green shades were faded and torn. And as for Beth's personal quarters . . .

A tiny cubicle, a cell, with walls of mint-green beaded pine, a creaky dark varnished floor, one window, a small limp bed, a mismatched bureau, table, and chair. Not the Ritz by a long shot, no, but a place of her own—away from Daddy and Mom!

Kind of spooky, however, especially at night. The window sash behind the green shade would chatter in the slightest breeze. And that door across from her bed, the defunct door to what she'd been told was a storage room—she didn't like that too much. So buried in ancient paint that its hinges were blurs and its plugged-up keyhole was merely a dimple, that door was quite impossible to budge. All the same, it made her uneasy.

Spooky place, you bet—but the view! She was up on the top floor, the window faced west, and the sunsets over the stand of pines behind Branch Hall, the schoolhouse, were spectacular. So far, she'd admired two of them. The other day had been overcast, like today. But even on cloudy days it was pleasant to sit in the wooden chair and look at the manicured lawns, the thick hedge of faded roses that bordered the narrow dirt lane, the students walking dreamily along the yellow paths.

She could hardly believe she had been here for only four days. The world of Daddy and Mom, of McDonald's, seemed so remote—though she was no more than an hour away from her hometown of Clinton by car.

Her first day at Radbourne—endless! She'd wondered more than once if she had what it took to make it here, and she'd fallen in bed exhausted. That scene on the tennis court, when the door to the gym flew open and a rush of students—dozens of odd-looking men and women—came up to her staring, grinning, drooling, shaking her arm like an old water pump as they said hello. Then the dining room: the squealing and moaning, the waving of fingers, the food falling out of slack mouths made her stomach churn. No more. She was already used to it. And now as she watched Jeff T. and Alice M. walk by below, she smiled to think of her fear on the tennis court. It already seemed so comical.

For the truth was that most of the students, no matter how threatening they looked, were quite nice. She had already made some friends, especially among the Down's syndrome people. Freddie P. and Shirley S.—what sweethearts!

Freddie was twenty-five, three years older than Beth. But he looked every bit of thirty-five, and acted no more than ten. Not a *normal* ten, however. He moved so clumsily and slowly, talked in such a halting way. He wasn't like any ten-year-old that *Beth* had ever known. But such good manners. So polite.

Shirley S., who was four years older than Freddie, had milky white skin and silky straight hair, large hands, splayed feet—and a smile that could light up a room. She was good at piano and played for Miss Hemphill, the school's director. Beth hadn't been introduced to Miss Hemphill yet, but had learned that she liked a piano selection or two and a glass of sherry (or two—or three) before dinner, which she ate in her ground floor chambers. Each evening as Beth combed her hair in the chipped wood-framed mirror atop the bureau, soft notes drifted up from Miss Hemphill's suite. Shirley played with a tender touch that made Beth sad: made her wish she were back at her parents' house or at college. But soon the melancholy notes would end, and Beth would descend the steep wide stairs and cross the lawn to the dining room, and once she was there with the rest of the staff and the students, the sick lonely ache would fade.

Tonight, as at every meal so far, her tablemates were Sara, who, like Beth, had been hired just a few days ago, and Pat and Diane, who had been with the school a bit longer, almost a month. They were all in their twenties. The whole staff was young. "Radbourne's a stepping stone," Pat had said during Beth's first breakfast, "a place to get your feet wet." She'd lowered her husky voice and leaned forward. "With what they pay, I mean really, how can they keep anybody?" The others agreed, and Beth told herself that as soon as something better showed up she'd be out of here. But for now this was fine; she was happy to have it.

The teachers had tables to themselves, though Mr. Critch, the principal, encouraged them to mix with the student body. Houseparents didn't have any choice: they *had* to eat with the students. Houseparents, by and large, were males, but Beth had seen nobody promising—yet. Considering the high turnover, though, the prospects looked pretty good.

Radbourne staff members didn't wait tables; the most able students did that, and did it quite well. Nobody had to write down orders or remember who got what, of course (all meals were the same), but aside from that, the dining room work was a lot like work in the outside world, and some of the students had gone on to similar jobs in restaurants and lived in their own apartments. Radbourne was quite a progressive school, Mr. Critch had said with his tight little smile during Beth's interview.

A progressive school without any children, Beth soon learned. For the youngest student, Polly F., was Beth's age, twenty-two. There were quite a few middle-aged people, and several old-timers. One man, Harold G., was eighty-eight. He was the guy with the wicker basket who always smiled at Beth and said, "AT&T, up seven-eighths," or "IBM, down a quarter." He had lived here for sixty years. A weird old guy, but nice, like most of the students.

But not *all* the students. There were some Beth just couldn't relate to.

Like Garth, who was sitting across the way at the table below the window. She looked at him shoveling down his food. His nose was long, his mouth was wide, his eyes were small and sharp. She had him in morning activities class. So far he'd done nothing at all in that class, shown no interest in anything: puzzles, ceramics, drawing.

Adrian was another one. She was in afternoon activities, and could have passed for Garth's sister—same pointed nose, huge mouth. Same sour attitude.

Beth watched her eat and listened to Pat and Diane. They were talking about a store in the Westside Mall that had discount clothes, and wanted to know if she'd like to go shopping some time.

"Oh, sure," Beth said—though she didn't plan to add so much as a pair of socks to her wardrobe this year. She was going to save every penny she made, especially since pennies would be so scarce. And who needed new clothes here in nowhere land, where fashion was not, to say the least, a priority?

"Now who's got a car we can borrow?" Pat wondered aloud. 'Maybe blue eyes?" She winked.

"Who's blue eyes?" Asked Sara.

"Third table over," Diane said. "With curly blond hair?"

"Cute," Sara said. "He has a car?"

"One of the few houseparents who does," Pat said.

"So you're after him for his money," Diane said.

Pat laughed. "If that bomb of his can make it to Westside and back—"

"Dessert?"

It was Edwin M., a tall brown-haired fellow with crooked pale eyes behind glasses with pink plastic frames.

Raising her ample dark eyebrows, Pat said, "What is it tonight, Edwin?"

"Ch-chocolate pudding."

"Yum. I shouldn't, I really shouldn't. But of course I will."

The others decided that they would, too.

"I've been at this place four weeks, and I've gained ten pounds," Diane said ruefully. "I've got to stop."

"Only ten?" Pat said. "I've put on twelve—in three and a half weeks. It must be the starches."

"Starches, protein, fat, who cares? As long as it's food, I'll eat it."

The others laughed, and Beth thought: Got to watch myself. The food, while not gourmet by any means, was better than they'd served at college, and there was a ton of it, all you could eat. And what else was there to do here *but* eat? Pat and Diane were decidedly chubby, and Beth would easily find herself needing an extra size or two if she wasn't careful.

Edwin returned with the four desserts, and set them before the young women. "Oh no, they look *good,*" Pat said.

"I'll just have a bite," Diane said; and then with a nod of her pretty blond head she said, "Right."

They all laughed and dug in.

The following morning, Beth handed out modeling clay.

"Make a thnake," lisped Shirley S. with a lopsided grin.

"Sure, Shirley," Beth said, "that's a fine idea."

"Make a ball—*big* ball," said Freddie P. and Beth gave him the go-ahead. She helped Jimmy Q. and Blenda B., then said, "And how about you, Garth? What are you going to make?"

She flushed at her stupidity, remembering what she had learned last night: Garth couldn't talk. Neither could his lookalike, Adrian M. Some of the students just couldn't talk, and here she had thought they'd been holding out on her.

"A snake?" Beth said. Garth scowled. His eyebrows, black and bushy, formed a solid unbroken line. His eyes were deep-set, tiny, dark.

"A man?" Beth said. "It's easy to make a man, let me show you."

She pulled a chair over, sat in front of him, placed some more clay on his desk. He regarded it sourly, eyebrows furrowed. "Now, watch me, watch what I do," Beth said. She kneaded the clay, then pulled it apart, shaped a torso, rolled arms, legs, head. She assembled the figure, then, taking a pencil, said, "Now we draw some eyes, a nose, a mouth, and—look—we have a man." She placed it beside Garth's lump of clay. "There. Now you try."

Garth scowled at the figure; retracted his upper lip, showing pointed teeth, and tore the appendages off the man; ripped the head off, and squashed it flat. He stared at Beth defiantly.

"No, that's not good," she said. "I want you to *make* something, not destroy it."

He just kept staring at her hard. Deciding not to press the issue, she stood and said, "Well, let's see what Shirley's doing."

She arrived at the dining room late that evening. The only available space was with Mr. Critch, the principal, and two women. Feeling anxious, she sat across from Critch, who introduced the women: secretaries. Sally Z., the waitress, set a large steaming bowl of soup before Beth, who thanked her and then fell silent.

"How are you finding the work so far?" asked Critch as she took her first sip of the soup. He was sixty or so, with silvery hair that was thinning quite badly in back. His charcoal gray suit was expensive-looking, but worn.

Beth swallowed the hot soup quickly and said, "I've already learned so much."

"There is so much to learn," said Critch. "So much that the books don't teach you." With exquisite care he sliced some meat and lifted it to his mouth.

The secretaries daintily ate to the background noise of gnashing teeth, soft moaning, high squeals. Beth had another spoonful of soup, then said, "I was wondering about Garth and Adrian. What kind of syndrome are they?"

"Syndrome?" Critch said. He dabbed at his mouth with his napkin.

Beth blushed. "They look so much alike, I thought—I figured they were a syndrome. And Horace and Roland look like them, too—don't you think?"

"They do?" Critch said. He glanced at the secretary on his left, a thin, lined woman named Marple, then looked back at Beth. "I never noticed any resemblance. However, now that you mention it . . . Hmm. Interesting observation. But no syndrome, so far as I know."

Beth looked at the table that stood near the kitchen doors, where Garth and Adrian sat at opposite ends. They were both quite short, about four feet tall, but extremely stocky and solid-looking; had dark furry eyebrows and long snout-like noses, huge hands, couldn't talk . . . She looked across at Roland and Horace, who couldn't talk, either. All four of them could have been siblings. And there, that other one, what was his name again? Brice?

It certainly seemed like a syndrome to her, and she suddenly thought: Wouldn't that be something? If Daddy's little ne'er-do-well, with her little old bachelor's degree, discovered a brand-new *syndrome?*

"Billie Rae F. is a Treacher-Collins," Critch said as he sliced more meat. "Note the narrow, pinched face. The palate is very high and arched, resulting in nasal speech. Intelligence often isn't affected, but in Billie Rae's case, it was."

"I haven't met Billie Rae yet," Beth said.

"She's at the west wall," Critch said. "The young woman in the yellow dress."

"Oh, yes," Beth said. And there was another one! "Who's that next to Freddie?" she asked.

Critch squinted. "That's Eldreth H."

Another one, absolutely. And Critch had never seen the resemblance? Weird.

As Critch and the women chatted, Beth looked at Freddie. A waiter came by with a tray of desserts. Eldreth gave hers to Freddie, who smacked his lips. Two desserts! He was thirty or forty pounds overweight, and they let him eat two desserts? Didn't anyone supervise diet at Radbourne School?

And now Sally Z. was standing beside her and saying, "Bwownies and ice cweam?"

"Miss Lewis?" Critch said.

"Oh—I shouldn't," Beth said. But then said she would, and so did the others, Miss West, Mrs. Marple (who could certainly stand to gain a few pounds), and Critch himself. Folding his napkin with great precision, Critch said, "We're quite proud of our dining service."

"It's easy to see why," Beth said.

Mrs. Marple smiled. Miss West inspected a fingernail. Beth glanced at the various tables; at Sara and Pat and the new teacher, Marnie, eating dessert; at Shirley, eating, at Freddie—still eating!

And then she saw Garth.

Garth was not eating. He sat there, his arms hanging down at his sides as around him the others swallowed and chewed, his thick single eyebrow frowning. Frowning at her, at Beth. Yes, frowning at *her.*

That night she woke out of a dreadful nightmare and sat straight up in her bed. She listened, cold sweat on her skin.

There. She heard it again. It had been in her dream, but was real—a scream, far off somewhere. It stopped. She lay there, scarcely breathing, as again it rose into the night. She heard the sound of machinery then, a whining, metallic sound, and a pitiful faraway voice pleading, "No! Please! No!"

She got up and went to the window and lifted the shade. The night was totally black, without any moon. The lamps had gone out at ten o'clock, Radbourne's official bedtime, and now she could barely distinguish the pathways snaking across the lawn. No movement, nobody there. And now no sound.

She sat on the bed, her heart beating wildly; took a deep breath, let it out. She looked at the window, the bright high stars far off in the blue-black sky. Somebody coughed down the hall somewhere. Sara? Pat? Beth stared at the door to the hall, which was bolted, then looked at the door to the storage room, its mint-green panels gray in the feeble light. She finally lay down again, pulling the sheet up, and after a while she slept again, but not well.

"She already quit?" Beth said.

She was walking with Pat to her morning class. "Yep, she's gone," Pat said.

"Wow, that didn't last long."

"Hey, let's face it," Pat said, "this job is tough. You have to be right on top of things every second. At the end of a day here, I'm really wrung out. And I'm a high-energy person."

"Yeah," Beth said.

"Diane was not a high-energy person."

"Oh."

Beth was quiet a minute, then frowned at the yellow brick path and said, "Pat?"

"Yeah?"

"Did you hear that screaming last night?"

Pat rolled her cow-like dark brown eyes. "That's another thing. These folks have a nightmare, and bang, they go off the deep end. They think dreams are real, I guess—like those primitive tribes?"

"They were having a rough time, whoever they were."

"I'll say. It's that kind of stuff that gets you. I guess if you're here long enough, you can sleep right through it. To tell you the truth, though, I don't want to be here that long."

They'd reached the schoolhouse, and went inside. "Well, see you at lunch," Pat said.

"Yeah—and save me a seat," Beth said.

The morning did not go well. For some reason, Freddie was not in a very good mood, and swiped a crayon from Yola R., a dour white-haired woman with long ruddy cheeks and gray eyes.

"Give it back," Yola said.

"No."

"Yes! Give it back!"

"No!"

Yola, flushed and furious, sprayed spittle as she said, "You meatball!"

"No!" Freddie said, his eyes suddenly wide. "No meatball! Me ... no meatball!"

Garth, who'd been sullen all morning, grinned at this; then laughed with a series of short loud grunts.

So that's what turns him on, Beth thought. A fight. "Freddie, give it back now," she said.

"Me ... no meatball!" Freddie said, and Beth was surprised to see he was close to tears.

"No, you're no meatball," she said. "Give Yola her crayon now."

"No meatball," Freddie said, shaking his head as he handed the crayon back. "No meatball, no."

Exposing his jagged teeth, Garth laughed again.

"Garth, it's not funny," Beth said sharply.

Garth continued to grin. Beth glared at him, hands on her hips.

A piece of paper floated off Shirley's desk and landed beside Garth's chair. "Ooopth!" Shirley said.

"I'll get it," Beth said, and leaned over; was rising again when she felt a sharp pinch on her arm. "Garth!"

His grin was huge. "That's not funny!" Beth said. "Not at all! We don't pinch people here!"

Garth's grin dissolved. His eyes grew dark.

Pure hatred in those eyes, Beth thought, and she took a step backward, saying, "You do anything like that again, I'll report you to Mr. Critch—or Miss Hemphill, you understand?"

He continued to scowl, and she suddenly wondered: *Did* he understand? After all, he couldn't talk ... The other students looked away—at the floor, at their desks—with sheepish eyes.

Beth gave Shirley her paper. To Blenda she said, "That's a very nice flower. A beautiful flower, good job."

"No meatball," Freddie said with another slow shake of his head. "Me ... no meatball."

"Just forget that now," Beth said, and avoided looking at Garth again, and thought of Diane, who had already quit after only a month at this place. A month could be a long time when you had to face Garth and Adrian every day, she thought. A *real* long time.

The pay phone stood in the first-floor hallway, next to Critch's door.

Beth looked at the massive squat-legged table with its dimly glowing brass globe lamp, at the heavy brown velvet drapes in the archway, the dull Persian runner on the varnished floor, and swallowed against the homesickness lodged in her throat. "Oh yes," she said, quite challenging. I've already learned so much." "Just gorgeous—especially now that the leaves are beginning to turn." "No, not till Thanksgiving, I don't get any time off before then." "I love you, too. Say hi to Daddy. Bye."

As she placed the receiver back in its cradle, the loneliness hit her hard. She looked at the gilt-framed painting above the table: a landscape devoid of human figures, feathery and dark. The hallway suddenly seemed to contain no air. She left it, crossed the vestibule, and entered the library.

They *were* some kind of syndrome, she was sure of it. Garth, Adrian, Horace, Roland, Eldreth, Brice—and Grindle P. They looked alike and acted alike: stubborn, surly, and sometimes downright cruel. She had seen Grindle P. deliberately trip Amos A., sending him sprawling onto the yellow brick path, where he skinned both palms. And Brice had shoved Blenda into the drinking fountain, cutting her lower lip.

Beth wanted to check their files, their medical records, but that was forbidden; administration alone had access to those. What else could you expect from a place that wouldn't even tell you your students' last names? "Confidentiality is paramount at Radbourne," Critch had told her. "Many of our parents are quite . . . sensitive."

Denied the records, she spent three nights in the school's dank library, searching the ponderous volumes on disability, but found no pictures that looked like Garth or the rest. Mucopolysaccharidosis (what a mouthful) came closest, but wasn't quite it. Maybe she *was* onto something new. If so, she wouldn't call it any tongue twister. Beth syndrome? Or maybe Troll syndrome. For that's what they looked like, those mythical, evil elves. Troll syndrome, yes indeed.

"Adrian? Are you kidding?" Sara said, placing her cup in its saucer. "She's done nothing in class for the whole three weeks I've been teaching. Nothing."

"Same here," Beth said, nodding, poking her meat with her fork. "I just can't seem to motivate her. Anything I show her, she refuses to even try."

"She pinched me once," Pat said; and Marnie, who'd been at Radbourne for only a few days, widened her big blue eyes.

"Garth pinched me once," Beth said, "but Adrian hasn't tried it yet."

"Garth," Sara said. "I'm glad I don't have him, he gives me the creeps."

"And Adrian doesn't?" Pat said.

"Well, yeah, she does, but not as bad as Garth."

Pat shrugged. "Horace, Roland, Adrian, Garth—they *all* give me the creeps."

"They're a syndrome," Beth said. "They have to be. I mean look at their faces, the way they behave, their lack of speech. And they all make that grunting noise."

"Isn't it gross?" Sara said. "They sound like a fish I caught in the Delaware Bay."

"What kind of a fish was that?" Pat said.

"A grunt."

"Excuse me for asking."

"No, that's what they're called—really," Sara said, smiling.

Beth swallowed a piece of her meat and said in a soft voice, "I call them the trolls."

Pat giggled.

"I know," Beth said, "it's not professional, it's downright nasty, in fact, but these folks are not nice."

"More coffee?" asked Edwin, their waiter, the pot in his hand.

They declined.

"More meat and eggs?"

"No thank you," Beth said. In spite of her resolution, she'd already gained six pounds—in only two weeks! The others said they were finished too, and Edwin left.

"I'm fat, fat, fat," Pat said. "I think that's really why Diane quit, she was turning into a butterball."

"I can't quit, I need the job," Sara said. "But I can see burnout coming on fast in a place like this. Hard work, long hours, low pay—The Radbourne School has it all. And, as an extra added attraction, it's creepy. I feel like I'm being watched all the time."

Pat frowned. "By Critch?"

"Yeah, by Critch," Sara said, "but not *only* by Critch."

"Yes, I know what you mean," Beth said, "I feel it,

too. I've felt it ever since I first came here. I thought it was probably just me."

"It isn't just you," Pat said.

Marnie said, "No, I've been here for less than a week, and I feel it, too."

They were silent a moment, and then Beth said, "Well, they give us plenty of food, at least."

Pat rolled her eyes. "Another problem to deal with!"

They finished and went outside. As they passed the building that housed the woodworking shop, Pat said, "My God, it smells putrid out here."

Sara wrinkled her nose. "Yeah, what is that, the sewage system?"

"Whatever it is, I wish they'd fix it—fast."

The stench made Beth feel slightly ill, especially after all that food. As the four of them crossed to the schoolhouse, the feeling that Sara had talked about, that feeling of being watched, came over Beth. And then she saw why.

Far off, on the hill behind Kilby Hall, stood Garth, his thick arms at his sides. He was staring right at her.

She tried to deny what she felt, that quick stab of fear. Playing hooky today, Mr. Garth? she said to herself. Not a good idea. Mr. Critch isn't going to like that. In the schoolhouse she told the others she'd see them later, then went to her classroom.

And Garth was sitting there, clutching the edge of his desk, feet dangling above the floor.

So it hadn't been him on the hill after all; it must've been Horace or Roland or Brice. Proof positive they looked alike! "Good morning, everyone," she said, and those with the gift of speech returned the greeting— except for Freddie, whose cheeks were shiny with tears.

She went to him. "What is it, Freddie? Don't you feel well?"

Looking up, Freddie swallowed with effort and said, "Him . . . call me meatball."

"Who?" Beth said. "You mean Yola again?" Freddie got "him" and "her" mixed-up sometimes.

"N—not him," said Freddie. Then, eyes going wide, he pointed his stubby finger at Garth. "H—him!"

Beth frowned. "Garth? But Freddie, Garth doesn't talk."

"Him talk!" Freddie said. "Him ... say meatball!"

"Garth?"

"Him say me meatball, yes!" Freddie said.

Frowning harder, Beth said, "Whoever called Freddie a nasty name, don't you ever do it again. If I catch you, I'll send you to Mr. Critch."

At this, Garth snickered. Freddie, his hooded eyes flashing, sputtered, "You bad! You bad!"

Shirley gasped. Blenda B. bit her knuckles and moaned. Yola, mouth going wide, scraped her fingernails down her flat cheeks.

"All right," Beth said, "enough. We're going to do some drawing now. Jimmy, pass out the crayons, please."

Jimmy, his eyes round and huge in his skinny pale face, got up from his chair and went to the shelf for the crayons. Garth snickered again. Furious now, Beth glared at him.

His eyes locked onto hers and stayed, and a chill went over her spine. Unable to bear his gaze, she turned away.

That evening, on her way back to Barrington Hall after dinner, she looked at the hill where Horace or Roland or Brice had stood staring down, and there, on its crest, she saw Adrian walking with Shirley. But not just walking—prodding her with a stick! Poking at her, herding her along. Shirley would turn every once in a while and utter a protest, lost at this distance, and then would submit again.

Bullies, Beth said to herself. They're bullies, all of them. She started up the hill to intervene; but Adrian flung down the stick and walked away as Shirley went into the dorm.

Beth, tired now at the end of the day, decided not to pursue. But she would tell Critch about this, absolutely, it had to be stopped.

The shouts woke her out of another disturbing dream. She could hear the words plainly this time: "Please! Please! Oh no, my God!"

It sounded like a woman's voice. But maybe it wasn't—for some of the male students' voices were almost falsetto, and some of the women were baritones.

The whining sound she'd heard that other time began, and the screaming stopped. Beth lay on her side, hunched up, and stared at the wall, at the door to the storage room, unable to sleep.

Freddie came forward and sat on the swing, "Okay," Beth said, "can you say it? *My* turn."

"M—my turn," Freddie said.

"Good for you," Beth said. "Whose turn is it, Freddie?"

"M—m—*my* turn."

"All right!" Beth said, and gave him a push. What a lump he was! Jimmy, that twig, had been a breeze, Shirley had been a lot harder, but Blenda and Yola had known how to swing by themselves, giving Beth a break. Freddie's ponderous body swung back and forth as he clung to the ropes, his mouth open, his eyes partly closed. "Is it fun?" Beth asked. Freddie gave no reply, and Beth let him slow down. When the pendulum stopped, she helped him off; he sat cross-legged on the grass.

Her heart gave a sharp little twist as she said, "Okay, Garth, *your* turn."

Garth had stood apart on the sidelines as the others had swung. Now, craning his muscular neck toward Beth, wonder of wonders, he laughed!

"Your turn," Beth said again, puzzled. "Come on, you'll like it."

Garth nodded, his thick grin huge. He went to the swing and sat down.

Beth positioned herself behind him. "Hold tight," she said, and pushed.

His back was as hard and compact as stone, and her fingers recoiled. When again she made contact, he laughed with a bark-like grunt, and she said with a shiver, "Garth likes his turn, don't you, Garth?"

More mirthful grunting sounds. Freddie looked at him indirectly, appearing to cringe.

"Garth likes his turn," Beth said. Garth nodded heartily, laughing and grunting.

Beth backed away, the feel of Garth's loathesome flesh on her fingers, tingling. He slowed and stopped, sat grinning a minute, then stood up and pointed at Beth.

She frowned. "*My* turn?" she said. "You want *me* to swing?"

Garth nodded enthusiastically.

"Well, okay," Beth said, "okay," and she sat on the seat.

Garth went behind her and started to push. The feel of his hands on her back made her shoulder blades crawl. But this was amazing! She was actually breaking through to Garth? She was actually going to have some *rapport* with him?

She went higher—and higher. Garth pushed. And now she was going uncomfortably high, and she said, "Okay, Garth, that's enough." He ignored her, kept pushing. She was high up over the top of the bar now, moving with frightening speed. "Garth! Stop!" she cried, but he pushed again. Her next descent, she scraped her shoes hard on the dirt and the swing spun sideways, crazily, twisting, went up again, crooked, she braked again, and the swing at last stopped.

Garth was laughing without any sound, his mouth a black pit.

"No," Beth said, getting up from the seat, "That wasn't funny. That wasn't funny at *all*."

Garth's expression went sullen. He stood leaning forward, his arms at his sides, his hands in a simian curl.

"All right," Beth said, her heart beating hard, "it's time to go back to class."

Garth continued to stand there. "Let's go," Beth said.

Garth retracted his lip, showing crooked sharp teeth; then grinned again, and slowly began to walk.

There was somebody in the storage room.

Beth rolled over in bed. The clock's red numbers said 2:16. In the feeble light she could make out that door in the wall, and a fear of it suddenly opening seized her.

But no, that couldn't happen; it was painted in place, sealed tight.

She listened. Intermittent murmuring she couldn't understand. What in the world were they doing in there at this hour?

The creak of the storage room's hallway door, then footsteps descending the stairs. They were leaving, whoever they were. A silent space, then Beth heard them again, outside. She left the bed and went to the window and cautiously lifted the shade.

The moon was a pale green slit in the inky sky. She heard more indecipherable words, then saw three shadows huddled together beside the vine-choked porch. The shadows moved off in different directions, and Beth saw how short they were.

Three trolls! She squinted at the dark. Three trolls! And one was Garth! Her heart leapt to her throat—and the shadow she thought was Garth turned and looked at her window.

She pulled away quickly, dropping the shade and pressing her back to the wall. Had he seen her? Her breath was loud in the still, small room. She waited awhile, then risked a quick glance outside again—and they were gone.

Three trolls, she thought. And they were *talking*.

"She's gone?" Beth said. "Just like that, without saying good-bye?"

Sara, fork in her meat, shrugged. "It looks that way."

"I thought we were her friends."

"I thought so, too."

Beth poked at her meat. She pushed it aside and looked at Sara and said, "You aren't going to leave like that, I hope."

"Of course not."

"I'd like us to still be friends—on the outside, I mean."

Sara smiled. "You make Radbourne sound like a prison," she said.

"Well, sometimes I feel like it *is* a prison," Beth said. She frowned. "So Pat is gone."

Sara's smile turned wistful. "And not only Pat," she said. "Do you notice who else is missing?"

Beth looked around quickly. "Who?"

"A certain fellow with blue, blue eyes?"

"Don't tell me he quit, too."

"Yep. Replaced by the guy with the droopy mustache who's pouring Ricky some milk."

"Oh, boy," Beth said.

"My sentiments exactly," Sara said, Frowning at her plate, she said, "This meat is raw."

"And fatty, too," Beth said. She pushed some more of it aside and said, "I'm going to miss Pat."

"You and me both," Sara said. "You know, pretty soon, if this keeps up, we'll be the old-timers here."

They looked at each other thoughtfully—and then started to laugh.

A tremendous crash in the storage room sent her jolting awake with a gasp.

Pressing the sheet against her breasts, she listened, her eyes on the sharp streak of moonlight dividing the wall.

The hoot of an owl in the distance, and that was all. She waited, and then, once her heart had slowed down, put her head on her pillow again. As she stared at the wall, at the sickly light, at that ghostly painted-shut paneled door, her body began to shake. An hour went by before she could sleep, and her sleep was troubled and thin.

"I heard it, too," Sara said as they crossed the lawn. "They told me it was the chairs."

"The chairs?" Beth said.

"Yeah, they hang onto everything here. When a chair falls apart, do they throw it out? No, they put it away in the storage room, till they get around to fixing it. They never do, of course. The room has hundreds of chairs and desks and tables piled up to the ceiling, and last night the chairs fell down."

"It scared me to death," Beth said.

"Me, too," Sara said. As she reached for Branch

Hall's heavy door, she said, "Have you seen Shirley S. this morning?"

"No, she wasn't at breakfast."

"She looks like those chairs fell on *her*," Sara said.

Shirley S. *was* in class—and looked terrible.

Her right eye was swollen and dark, and her forearms were covered with bruises. Beth went with her into the hallway.

"Shirley, who hit you? Who did this to you?"

"N—no," Shirley said with a shake of her head.

"Nobody hit you? What happened, then?"

"Fall down," Shirley said. "Fall down real bad."

"Shirley, look at me," Beth said, taking her chin. "Look at me now and tell the truth. Did Adrian do this to you?"

"No!" Shirley insisted. "Fall down!"

"Okay," Beth said, sighing, taking her hand from Shirley's face. "Okay, well, I'm sorry you hurt yourself."

"Y—yeth," Shirley said.

There were tears in her pale blue eyes.

Vines clotted the tiny window behind Mr. Critch's head. A potted palm spread dusty fronds toward the green-shaded lamp on the mammoth oak desk. Critch leaned back in his leather chair and said, "Specifically?"

"It's about Garth and Adrian," Beth said.

"Oh?" Critch's eyebrows went up.

"They bully the other residents. They physically harm them."

Pursing his lips and frowning, Critch said, "Miss Lewis, that can't be true. The houseparents would have brought it to our attention."

"But it *is* true, I've seen it."

Critch swiveled a quarter turn in his chair. With a tone of impatience, he said, "Garth and Adrian are two of our oldest students, Miss Lewis—and very good Radbourne citizens."

Beth felt her jaw tighten up as she said, "Another thing—they talk."

"They do?" Critch said.

"They certainly do, I've heard them."

Looking slightly incredulous, Critch said, "Now, that *is* news. They've had years of help with their speech, and to no avail—or so we thought. You've heard them talk. And when was that?"

"Two nights ago," Beth said. "They were standing outside my window."

"At night?"

"At night. It was late, very late, after two in the morning. First they were in the storage room, then they went outside."

Critch tilted his head. "Now, what in the world would they want in the storage room? At that late hour?"

"I haven't the slightest idea," Beth said. "All I know is that they were there. And I know that they hurt other students. And Garth—he's even tried to hurt *me* at times. He pinched me once, and once he pushed me so high on the swings—"

"He pushed *you* on the swings?" Critch said.

Beth flushed. "I was teaching the concept of taking turns."

"I see," Critch said. He studied a cuticle for a moment, then said, "I'm sorry you don't like the work, Miss Lewis."

Stunned, Beth said, "Mr. Critch, that's not it. I *do* like the work, it's very rewarding. Most of my students are wonderful; it's just these few who spoil things."

Critch shrugged. "Some students are sometimes difficult—we are a special school, after all—but dealing with that is part of a teacher's job."

"I don't mean difficult," Beth said, "I mean *malicious*."

"Most of our teachers learn to cope," Critch said.

Beth's skin went hot. "Most?" she said. "Is that why your turnover rate's so high?"

Critch paused, his expression perfectly bland, then said, "We want you to be happy, Miss Lewis. We want you to be successful."

"Thanks ever so much," Beth said, and she got up and left the room.

The pay phone was right there beside Critch's door. She wanted to call home, to talk to her mother and father, to hear their voices again. But no, not here, not now, with Critch sitting there in his office. No.

At the sound of piano music, she turned and looked down the hall. Past the squat-legged mahogany table a door was ajar; a strip of pale light creased the dark Persian runner. Miss Hemphill's quarters, Beth thought. That's Shirley playing.

She went toward the music, silently, slowly, and peeked through the crack in the door.

A brown leather chair with an old woman in it, a woman whose feet didn't touch the floor, who smiled and drank from a wineglass, her eyes half closed. A woman who looked—Beth caught her breath—a woman who looked like a troll.

Freddie was not in class the next morning. A note on Beth's desk—from Critch's office—informed her he'd switched to another school.

Sadness welled in her heart as she crumpled the note. Dear Freddie! Without him, it just wouldn't be the same. Radbourne was just too hard, she thought. Too many people you started to get to know, and then—with no warning—were gone. With thoughts of home in her heart, she handed out cardboard and yarn.

"M—mith Freddie," Shirley said, her red eyes moist.

"I miss him, too," Beth said. "We all do, Shirley."

Well, not all. For while Jimmy, Blenda, and Yola looked sad, Garth sat there smiling.

The screams tore her sleep apart and she lay rigid, curled on her side toward the painted-shut door in the wall. "Please! No!" she heard, so thin and distant, pitiful; then that whining, mechanical noise, and she thought: That was Sara screaming! That was Sara's voice! No, no, she told herself, it wasn't, it couldn't have been! But the thought made her cold all through. She clutched the covers, shivering, till the room's tall window filled with morning light.

Sara was not at the breakfast table.

"She quit," said Linda, one of the new houseparents.

Quit? Without saying good-bye? She had promised she wouldn't do that. And she *wouldn't* do that. Beth *knew* that she wouldn't do that.

She fumbled her way through the day. Through all she did, she remembered those screams, those pitiful screams in the night.

There were meatballs for supper. She speared one, looked at it, put it down again; then, slipping the table knife into her purse, she went up to her room.

She sat on her bed and looked at the opposite wall, at that door to the storage room. It hadn't been Sara's voice, she told herself. It had just been a student, a student having a dream. Sara and Pat and Diane had quit, and so had the others, the blue-eyed young man and the others, and Freddie had switched to a different school—

She took the knife out of her purse and went to the storage room door. The keyhole was plugged with a filler as hard as stone. She attacked it, twisting the knife's blunt nose; grains of filler the color of sawdust fell onto the floor.

For over an hour, she worked with the knife as the light in the window died. Hurry! she urged herself. She had to finish before it got dark, while she could see into that room.

You will see only chairs, she told herself as she dug with the knife, her lips pressed tight. It's a room full of furniture, desks and chairs, old tables, that's all it is. She pushed harder, gritting her teeth—and the last of the filler gave way. Holding her breath, she pressed her eye to the opening.

Not chairs.

Not furniture, but bones. A roomful of bones—and skulls.

She put her hand over her mouth and stifled a scream as the table knife fell to the floor.

She would walk through the gate and keep walking. Right now. Pretend she was out for an evening stroll and slip through the gate—

But no: if they saw her she'd have no chance, none at all, the lane was a quarter mile long, and even once she reached the road there wasn't a house for another mile—

A taxi? And where would she call? From the phone outside Critch's office?

No, wait until dark, her chances would be much better—provided the trolls weren't roaming.

She sat in the chair by the window, tense, her heart high and quick in her neck. She heard a radio playing somewhere, heard a laugh. The sky turned inky blue, then black. No moon. Good, good.

When at last it was quiet and very dark, had been quiet for over an hour, she went to her door and opened it slowly; winced at its tiny brief squeak. She stood in the hallway under the naked dim ceiling bulb, then turned and went to the stairs.

And there they were, on the landing, waiting.

Seven cavernous mouths. Seven throats making quick grunting sounds.

Garth moved forward a step. Flexing his knobby fingers slowly, he grinned, displaying his ragged sharp teeth. His eyes went wide. In gutteral but perfectly articulated syllables, he said: "It's your turn, Beth."

Small Deaths
by Charles de Lint

> What unites us universally is our emotions, our
> feelings in the face of experience, and not neces-
> sarily the actual experiences themselves.
> > —Anais Nin

"I feel like I should know you."

Zoe Brill looked up. The line was familiar, but it usually came only after she'd spoken—that was the down
side of being an all-night DJ in a city with too many
people awake and having nothing to do between midnight and dawn. Everybody felt they knew you; everybody was your friend. Most of the time that suited her
fine, since she genuinely liked people, but as her mother
used to tell her, every family has its black sheep. Sometimes it seemed that every one of them tended to gravi-
tate to her at one point or another in their lives.

The man who'd paused by the café railing to speak to
Zoe this evening reminded her of a fox. He had lean,
pointy features, dark eyes, the corners of his lips constantly lifted in a sly smile, hair as red as her own, if not
as long. Unlike her, he had a dark complexion, as though
swimming somewhere back in the gene pool of his fore-
bears was an Italian, an Arab, or a Native American.
His self-assurance radiated a touch too shrill for Zoe's
taste, but he seemed basically harmless. Just your average single male yuppie on the prowl, heading out for an
evening in club land—she could almost hear the Full
Force-produced dance number kick up as a sound track
to the moment. Move your body all night long.

He was well dressed, as all Lotharios should be, casual, but with flair; she doubted there was a single item in his wardrobe worth under two hundred dollars. Maybe the socks.

"I think I'd remember if we'd met before," she said.

He ignored the wryness in her voice and took what she'd said as a compliment.

"Most people do," he agreed.

"Lucky them."

It was one of those rare, supernaturally perfect November evenings, warm with a light breeze, wedged in between a week of subzero temperatures with similar weather to follow. All up and down Lee Street, from one end of the Market to the other, the restaurants and cafés had opened their patios for one last outdoor fling.

"No, no," the man said, finally picking up on her disinterest. "It's not like what you're thinking."

Zoe tapped a long finger lightly against the page of the opened book that lay on her table beside a glass of red wine.

"I'm kind of busy," she said. "Maybe some other time."

He leaned closer to read the running head at the top of the book's left-hand page: *Disappearing Through the Skylight.*

"That's by O. B. Hardison, isn't it?" he asked. "Didn't he also write *Entering the Maze?*"

Zoe gave a reluctant nod and upgraded her opinion of him. Fine. So he was a well-read single male yuppie on the prowl, but she still wasn't interested.

"Technology," he said, "is a perfect example of evolution, don't you think? Take the camera. If you compare present models to the best they had just thirty years ago, you can see—"

"Look," Zoe said. "This is all very interesting, and I don't mean to sound rude, but why don't you go hit on someone else? If I'd wanted company, I would've gone out with a friend."

He shook his head. "No, no. I told you, I'm not trying to pick you up." He put out his hand. "My name's Gordon Wolfe."

He gave her his name with the simple assurance inherent in his voice that it was impossible that she wouldn't recognize it.

Zoe ignored the hand. As an attractive woman living on her own in a city the size of Newford, she'd long ago acquired a highly developed sense of radar, a kind of mental dah-*dum,* dah-*dum* straight out of *Jaws,* that kicked in whenever that sixth sense hiding somewhere in her subconscious decided that the situation carried too much of a possibility of turning weird, or a little too intense.

Gordon Wolfe had done nothing yet, but the warning bell was sounding faintly in her mind.

"Then, what do you want?" she asked.

He lifted his hand and ran it through his hair, the movement so casual it was as though he'd never been rebuffed. "I'm just trying to figure out why I feel like I should know you."

So they were back to that again.

"The world's full of mysteries," Zoe told him. "I guess that's just going to be another one."

She turned back to her book, but he didn't leave the railing. Looking up, she tried to catch the eye of the waiter, to let him know that she was being bothered, but naturally neither he nor the two waitresses were anywhere in sight. The patio held only the usual bohemian mix of Lower Crowsea's inhabitants and hangers-on—a well-stirred stew of actors, poets, artists, musicians, and those who aspired, through their clothing or attitude, to be counted in that number. Sometimes it was all just a little too trendy.

She turned back to her unwelcome visitor, who still stood on the other side of the café's railing.

"It's nothing personal," she began. "I just don't—"

"You shouldn't mock me," he said, cutting in. "I'm the bringer of small deaths." His dark eyes flashed. "Remember me the next time you die a little."

Then he turned and walked away, losing himself in among the crowd of pedestrians that filled the sidewalk on either side of Lee Street.

Zoe sighed. Why were they always drawn to her? The weird and the wacky. Why not the wonderful for a change? When was the last time a nice normal guy had tried to chat her up?

It wasn't as though she looked particularly exotic: skin a little too pale, perhaps, due to the same genes that had given her her shoulder-length red hair and green eyes, but certainly not the extreme vampiric pallor affected by so many fans of the various British Gothic bands that jostled for position on the album charts of college radio and independent record stores; clothing less thrift shop than most of those with whom she shared the patio this evening: ankle-high black lace-up boots, dark stockings, a black dress that was somewhat tight and a little short, a faded jean jacket that was a couple of sizes too big.

Just your basic semi-hip working girl, relaxing over a glass of wine and a book before she had to head over to the studio. So where were all the nice semi-hip guys for her to meet?

She took a sip of her wine and went back to her book, but found herself unable to concentrate on what she was reading. Gordon Wolfe's parting shot kept intruding on the words that filled the page before her.

Remember me the next time you die a little.

She couldn't suppress the small shiver that slithered up her spine.

Congratulations, she thought to her now-absent irritant. You've succeeded in screwing up my evening anyway.

Paying her bill, she decided to go home and walk Rupert, then head in to work early. An electronic score with lots of deep, low bass notes echoed in her head as she went home, "Tangerine Dream" crossed with B-movie horror themes. She kept thinking Wolfe was lurking about, following her home, although whenever she turned, there was no one there. She hated this mild anxiety he'd bestowed upon her like some spiteful parting gift.

Her relief at finally getting home to where Rupert waited for her far outweighed the dog's slobbery enthusiasm at the thought of going out for their evening ramble earlier than usual. Zoe took a long roundabout way to the station, letting Rupert's ingenuous affection work its magic. With the big galoot at her side, it was easy to put the bad taste of her encounter with Wolfe to rest.

An old Lovin' Spoonful song provided backdrop to the walk, bouncing and cheerful. It wasn't summer any longer, but it was warmer than usual, and Newford had always been a hot town.

The phone call came in during the fourth hour of her show, "Nightnoise." As usual, the music was an eclectic mix. An Italian aria by Kiri Te Kanawa was segueing into a cut by the New Age Celtic group from which the show had gotten its name, with Steve Earle's "The Hard Way" queued up next, when the yellow light on the studio's phone began to blink with an incoming call.

"Nightnoise," she said into the receiver. "Zoe B. here."

"Are we on the air?"

It was a man's voice—an unfamiliar voice, warm and friendly with just the vaguest undercurrent of tension.

"I'm sorry," she said. "We don't take call-ins after three."

From one to three a.m. she took on-air calls for requests, commentaries, sometimes just to chat; during that time period she also conducted interviews, if she had any slated. Experience had proven that the real fruitcakes didn't come out of the woodwork until the show was into its fourth hour, creeping up on dawn.

"That's all right," her caller said. "It's you I wanted to talk to."

Zoe cradled the receiver between her shoulder and ear and checked the studio clock. As the instrumental she was playing ended, she brought up the beginning of the Steve Earle cut and began to queue up her next choice, Concrete Blonde's cover of a Leonard Cohen song from the *Pump Up the Volume* sound track.

"So talk," she said, shifting the receiver back to her hand.

She could almost feel the caller's hesitation. It happened a lot. They got up the nerve to make the call, but once they were connected, their mouths went dry and all their words turned to sand.

"What's your name?" she added, trying to make it easier on him.

"Bob."

"Not the one from *Twin Peaks* I hope."

"I'm sorry?"

Obviously not a David Lynch fan, Zoe thought.

"Nothing," she said. "What can I do for you tonight, Bob?" Maybe she'd make an exception, she thought, and added: "Did you have a special song you wanted me to play for you?"

"No, I . . . It's about Gordon."

Zoe went blank for a moment. The first Gordon that came to mind was Gordon Waller from the old UK band, Peter & Gordon, rapidly followed by rockabilly great Robert Gordon and then Jim Gordon, the drummer who'd played with everybody from Baez to Clapton, including a short stint with Bread.

"Gordon Wolfe," Bob said, filling in the blank for her. "You were talking to him earlier tonight on the patio of The Rusty Lion."

Zoe shivered. From his blanket beside the studio door, Rupert lifted his head and gave an anxious whine, sensing her distress.

"You . . ." she began. "How could you know? What were you doing, following me?"

"No. I was following him."

"Oh."

Recovering her equilibrium, Zoe glanced at the studio clock and queued up the first cut from her next set in the CD player, her fingers going though the procedure on automatic.

"Why?" she asked.

"Because he's dangerous."

He'd given her the creeps, Zoe remembered, but she hadn't really thought of him as dangerous—at least not until his parting shot.

Remember me the next time you die a little.

"Who is he?" she asked. "Better yet, who are you? Why are you following this Wolfe guy around?"

"That's not his real name," Bob said.

"Then what is?"

"I can't tell you."

"Why the hell not?"

"Not won't," Bob said quickly. "*Can't.* I don't know it myself. All I know is he's dangerous, and you shouldn't have gotten him mad at you."

"Jesus," Zoe said. "I really need this." Her gaze flicked back to the studio clock; the Steve Earle cut was heading into its fade-out. "Hang on a sec, Bob. I've got to run some commercials."

She put him on hold and brought up the volume on her mike.

"That was Steve Earle," she said, "with the title cut from his latest album, and you're listening to 'Nightnoise' on WKPN. Zoe B. here, spinning the tunes for all you night birds and birdettes. Coming up we've got a hot and heavy metal set, starting off with the classic 'Ace of Spades' by Motorhead. These are *not* new kids on the block, my friends. But first, oh yes, even at this time of night, a word from some sponsors."

She punched up the cassette with its minute of ads for this half hour and brought the volume down off her mike again. But when she turned back to the phone, the on-line light was dead. She tried it anyway, but Bob had hung up.

"Shit," she said. "Why are you doing this to me?"

Rupert looked up again, then got up from his blanket and padded across the floor to press his wet nose up against her hand. He was a cross between a golden lab and a German shepherd, seventy pounds of bighearted mush.

"No, not you," she told him, taking his head in both of her hands and rubbing her nose against the tip of his muzzle. "You're Zoe's big baby, aren't you?"

The ads cassette ran its course, and she brought up Motorhead. As she queued up the rest of the pieces for this set, she kept looking at the phone, but the on-line light stayed dead.

"Weird," Hilary Carlisle agreed. She brushed a stray lock of hair away from her face and gave Zoe a quick smile. "But par for the course, don't you think?"

"Thanks a lot."

"I didn't say you egged them on, but it seems to be the story of your life: put you in a roomful of strangers and you can almost guarantee that the most oddball guy there will be standing beside you within ten minutes. It's"— she grinned —"just a gift you have."

"Well, this guy's really given me a case of the creeps."

"Which one—Gordon or Bob?"

"Both of them, if you want the truth."

Hilary's smile faded. "This is really getting to you, isn't it?"

"I could've just forgotten my delightful encounter at The Rusty Lion if it hadn't been for the follow-up call."

"You think it's connected?"

"Well, of course it's connected."

"No, not like that," Hilary said. "I mean, do you think the two of them have worked this thing up together?"

That was just what Zoe had been thinking. She didn't really believe in coincidence. To her mind, there was always connections; they just weren't always that easy to work out.

"But what would be the point?" she asked.

"You've got me," Hilary said. "You can stay here with me for a few days if you like," she added.

They were sitting in the front room of Hilary's downstairs apartment, which was in the front half of one of the old Tudor buildings on the south side of Stanton Street facing the estates. Hilary in this room always reminded Zoe of Mendelssohn's "Concerto in E Minor," a perfect dialogue between soloist and orchestra. Paintings, curtains, carpet, and furniture all reflected Hilary's slightly askew worldview so that Impressionists hung side-by-side with paintings that seemed more the work of a camera; an antique sideboard housed a state-of-the-art stereo, glass shelves held old books; the curtains were dark antique flower prints, with sheers trimmed in lace, the carpet a riot of symmetrical designs and primary colors. The recamier on which Hilary was lounging had a glory of leaf and scrollwork in its wood; Zoe's club chair looked as though a bear had been hibernating in it.

Hilary herself was as tall as Zoe's five-ten, but where

Zoe was more angular and big-boned, Hilary was all graceful lines with tanned skin that accentuated her blue eyes and the waterfall of her long straight blond hair. She was dressed in white this morning, wearing a simple cotton shirt and trousers with the casual elegance of a model, and appeared, as she always did, as the perfect centerpiece to the room.

"I think I'll be okay," Zoe said. "Besides, I've always got Rupert to protect me."

At the sound of his name, Rupert lifted his head from the floor by Zoe's feet and gave her a quick, searching glance.

Hilary laughed. "Right. Like he isn't scared of his own shadow."

"He can't help being nervous. He's just—"

"I know. High-strung."

"Did I ever tell you how he jumped right—"

"Into the canal and saved Tommy's dog from drowning when it fell in? Only about a hundred times since it happened."

Zoe lips shaped a moue.

"Oh, God," Hilary said, starting to laugh. "Don't pout. You know what it does to me when you pout."

Hilary was a talent scout for WEA Records. They'd met three years ago at a record launch party when Hilary had made a pass at her. Once they got past the fact that Zoe preferred men and wasn't planning on changing that preference, they discovered that they had far too much in common not to be good friends. But that didn't stop Hilary from occasionally teasing her, especially when Zoe was complaining about man troubles.

Such troubles were usually far simpler than the one currently in hand.

"What do you think he meant by small deaths?" Zoe asked. "The more I think of it, the more it gives me the creeps."

Hilary nodded. "Isn't sleep sometimes referred to as the little death?"

Zoe could hear Wolfe's voice in her head. *I'm the bringer of small deaths.*

"I don't think that's what he was talking about," she said.

"Maybe it's just his way of saying you're going to have bad dreams. You know, he freaks you out a little, makes you nervous, then bingo—he's a success."

"But why?"

"Creeps don't need reasons for what they do; that's why they're creeps."

Remember me the next time you die a little.

Zoe was back to shivering again.

"Maybe I will stay here," she said, "if you're sure I won't be in your way."

"Be in my way?" Hilary glanced at her watch. "I'm supposed to be at work right now—I've got a meeting in an hour—so you'll have the place to yourself."

"I just hope I can get to sleep."

"Do you want something to help you relax?"

"What, like a sleeping pill?"

Hilary shook her head. "I was thinking more along the lines of some hot milk."

"That'd be lovely."

Zoe didn't sleep well. It wasn't her own bed, and the daytime street noises were different from the ones outside her own apartment, but it was mostly the constant replay of last night's two conversations that kept her turning restlessly from one side of the bed to the other. Finally, she just gave up and decided to face the day on less sleep than she normally needed.

She knew she'd been having bad dreams during the few times when she had managed to sleep, but couldn't remember one of them. Padding through the apartment in an oversize T-shirt, she found herself drawn to the front window. She peeked out through the curtains, gaze traveling up and down the length of Stanton Street. When she realized what she was doing—looking for a shock of red hair, dark eyes watching the house—she felt more irritable than ever.

She was not going to let it get to her, she decided. At least not anymore.

A shower woke her up, while breakfast and a long

afternoon ramble with Rupert through the grounds of
Butler University made her feel a little better, but by
the time she got to work at a quarter to twelve that
night and started to go through the station's library to
collect the music she needed for the show, she was back
to being tense and irritable. Halfway through the first
hour of the show, she interrupted a Bobby Brown/Ice
T./Living Colour set and brought up her voice mike.

"Here's a song for Gordon Wolfe," she said as she
queued by an album cut by the local band No Nuns
Here. "Memories are made of this, Wolfe."

The long wall of an electric guitar went out over the
airwaves, a primal screech as the high E string was fingered down around the fourteenth fret and pushed up
past the G string, then the bass and drums caught and
settled into a driving back beat. The wailing guitar broke
into bar chunky chords as Lorio Munn's voice cut across
the music like the punch of a fist.

> *I don't want your love, baby*
> > *So don't come on so sweet*
> *I don't need a man, baby*
> > *Treats me like I'm meat*

> *I'm coming to your house, baby*
> > *Coming to your door*
> *Gonna knock you down, right where you stand*
> > *And stomp you on the floor*

Zoe eyed the studio phone. She picked up the handset
as soon as the on-line light began to flash. Which one
was it going to be? she thought as she spoke into the
phone.

"Nightnoise. Zoe B. here."

She kept the call off the air, just in case.

"What the hell do you think you're doing?"

Bingo. It was Bob.

"Tell me about small deaths," she said.

"I *told* you he was dangerous, but you just—"

"You'll get your chance to natter on," Zoe interrupted, "but first I want to know about these small deaths."

Silence on the line was the only reply.

"I don't hear a dial tone," she said, "so I know you're still there. Talk to me."

"I . . . Jesus," Bob said finally.

"Small deaths," Zoe repeated.

After another long hesitation, she heard Bob sigh. "They're those pivotal moments in a person's life that change it forever: a love affair gone wrong, not getting into the right post-graduate program, stealing a car on a dare and getting caught, that kind of thing. They're the moments that some people brood on forever; right now they could have the most successful marriage or career, but they can't stop thinking about the past, about what might have happened if things had gone differently.

"It sours their success, makes them bitter. And usually it leads to more small deaths: depression, stress, heavy drinking, or drug use, abusing their spouse or children."

"What are you saying?" Zoe asked. "That a small death's like disappointment?"

"More like a pain, a sorrow, an anger. It doesn't have to be something you do to yourself. Maybe one of your parents died when you were just a kid, or you were abused as a child; that kind of a trauma changes a person forever. You can't go through such an experience and grow up to be the same person you would have been without it."

"It sounds like you're just talking about life," Zoe said. "It's got its ups and its downs; to stay sane, you've got to take what it hands you. Ride the punches and maybe try to leave the place in a little better shape than it was before you got there."

What was *with* this conversation? Zoe thought as she was speaking.

As the No Nuns Here cut came to an end, she queued in a version of Carly Simon's "You're So Vain" by Faster Pussycat.

"Jesus," Bob said as the song went out over the air. "You really have a death wish, don't you?"

"Tell me about Gordon Wolfe."

The man's voice echoed in her mind as she spoke his name.

I'm the bringer of small deaths.

"What's he got to do with all of this?" she added.

Remember me the next time you die a little.

"He's a catalyst for bad luck," Bob said. "It's like, being in his company—just being in proximity to him—can bring on a small death. It's like . . . do you remember that character in the *L'il Abner* comic strip—the one who always had a cloud hanging over his head. What was his name?"

"I can't remember."

"Everywhere he went he brought bad luck."

"What about him?" Zoe asked.

"Gordon Wolfe's like that, except you don't see the cloud. You don't get any warning at all. I guess the worst thing is that his effects are completely random—unless he happens to take a dislike to you. Then it's personal."

"A serial killer of peoples' hopes," Zoe said, half jokingly.

"Exactly."

"Oh, give me a break."

"I'm trying to."

"Yeah, right," Zoe said. "You feed me a crock of shit and then expect me to—"

"I don't think he's human," Bob said then.

Zoe wasn't sure what she'd been expecting from this conversation—a confession, perhaps, or even just an apology, but it wasn't this.

"And I don't think you are, either," he added.

"Oh, please."

"Why else do you think he was so attracted to you? He recognized something in you. I'm sure of it."

Wolfe's voice was back in her head.

I feel like I should know you.

"I think we've taken this about as far as it can go," Zoe said.

This time she was the one to cut the connection.

The phone's on-line light immediately lit up once more. She hesitated for a long moment, then brought the handset up to her ear.

"I am not bullshitting you," Bob said.

"Look, why don't you take it to the tabloids—they'd eat it up."

"You don't think I've tried? I'd do anything to see him stopped."

"Why?"

"Because the world's tough enough without having something like him wandering through it, randomly shooting down people's hopes. He's the father of fear. You know what fear stands for? Fuck Everything And Run. You want a whole world to be like that? People screw up their lives enough on their own; they don't need a . . . a *thing* like Wolfe to add to their grief."

The scariest thing, Zoe realized, was that he really sounded sincere.

"So what am I, then?" she asked. "The mother of hope?"

"I don't know. But I think you scare *him*."

Zoe had to laugh. Wolfe had her so creeped out, she hadn't even been able to go to her own apartment last night, and Bob thought she was the scary one?

"Look, could we meet somewhere?" Bob said.

"I don't think so."

"Somewhere public. Bring along a friend—bring a dozen friends. Face-to-face, I know I can make you understand."

Zoe thought about it.

"It's important," Bob said. "Look at it this way: if I'm a nut, you've got nothing to lose except some time. But if I'm right, then you'd really be—how did you put it?— leaving the world in a little better shape than it was before you got there. A lot better shape."

"Okay," Zoe said. "Tomorrow noon. I'll be at the main entrance of the Williamson Street Mall."

"Great." Zoe started to hang up, pausing when he added: "And Zoe, cool it with the on-air digs at Wolfe, would you? You don't want to see him pissed."

Zoe hung up.

"Your problem," Hilary said as the two of them sat on the edge of the indoor fountain just inside the main entrance of the Williamson Street Mall, "is that you keep expecting to find a man who's going to solve all of your problems for you."

"Of course. Why didn't I realize that was the problem?"

"You know," Hilary went on, ignoring Zoe's sarcasm. "Like who you are, where you're going, who you want to be."

Rupert sat on his haunches by Zoe's knee, head leaning in toward her as she absently played with the hair on the top of his head.

"So what're you saying?" she asked. "That I should be looking for a woman instead?"

Hilary shook her head. "You've got to find yourself first. Everything else'll follow."

"I'm not looking for a man."

"Right."

"Well, not actively. And besides, what's that got to do with anything?"

"Everything. You wouldn't be in this situation, you wouldn't have all these weird guys coming on to you, if you didn't exude a kind of confusion about your identity. People pick up on that kind of thing, even if the signals are just subliminal. Look at yourself: You're a nice normal-looking woman with terrific skin and hair and great posture. The loony squad shouldn't be hitting on you. Who's that actor you like so much?"

"Mel Gibson."

"Guys like him should be hitting on you. Or at least, guys like your idolized version of him. Who knows what Gibson's really like?"

Over an early breakfast, Zoe had laid out the whole story for her friend. Hilary had been skeptical about meeting with Bob, but when she realized that Zoe was going to keep the rendezvous, with or without her, she'd allowed herself to be talked into coming along. She'd left work early enough to return to her apartment to wake Zoe and then the two of them had taken the subway over to the mall.

"You think this is all a waste of time, don't you?" Zoe said.

"Don't you?"

Zoe shrugged. A young security guard walked by and eyed the three of them, his gaze lingering longest on Rupert, but he didn't ask them to leave. Maybe he thought Rupert was a seeing-eye dog, Zoe thought. Maybe he just liked the look of Hilary. Most guys did.

Hilary glanced at her watch. "He's five minutes late. Want to bet he's a no-show?"

But Zoe wasn't listening to her. Her gaze was locked on the red-haired man who had just come in off the street.

"What's the matter?" Hilary asked.

"That's him—the red-haired guy."

"I thought you'd never met this Bob."

"I haven't," Zoe said. "That's Gordon Wolfe."

Or was it? Wolfe was still decked out like a high roller on the make, but there was something subtly different about him this afternoon. His carriage, his whole body language had changed.

Zoe had a moment of frisson. A long shiver went up her spine. It started out as a low thrum and climbed into a high-pitched, almost piercing note, like Mariah Carey running through all seven of her octaves.

"Hello, Zoe," Wolfe said as he joined them.

Zoe looked up at him, trying to find a physical difference. It was Wolfe, but it wasn't. The voice was the same as the one on the phone, but people could change their voices; a good actor could look like an entirely different person just through the use of his body language.

Wolfe glanced at Hilary, raising his eyebrows questioningly.

"You . . . you're Bob?" Zoe asked.

He nodded. "I know what you're thinking."

"You're twins?"

"It's a little more complicated than that." His gaze flicked to Hilary again. "How much does your friend know?"

"My name's Hilary, and Zoe's pretty well filled me in on the whole sorry business."

"That's good."

Hilary shook her head. "No, it isn't. The whole thing

sucks. Why don't you just pack up your silly game and take it someplace else?"

Rupert stirred by Zoe's feet. The sharpness in Hilary's voice and Zoe's tension brought the rumbling start of a growl to his chest.

"I didn't start anything," Bob said. "Keep your anger for someone who deserves it."

"Like Wolfe," Zoe said.

Bob nodded.

"Your twin."

"It's more like he's my other half," Bob said. "We share the same body, except he doesn't know it. Only I'm aware of the relationship."

"Jesus, would you give us a break," Hilary said. "This is about as lame as that episode of—"

Zoe laid a hand on her friend's knee. "Wait a minute," she said. "You're saying Wolfe's a schizophrene?"

"I'm not sure if that's technically correct," Bob replied.

He sat down on the marble floor in front of them. It made for an incongruous image: an obviously well-heeled executive type sitting cross-legged on the floor like some panhandler.

"I just know that there's two of us in here," he added, touched a hand to his chest.

"You said you went to the tabloids with this story, didn't you?" Zoe asked.

"I tried."

"I can't believe that they were't interested. When you think of the stuff that they do print. . . ."

"Something . . . happened to every reporter I approached. I gave up after the third one."

"What kind of something?" Hilary asked.

Bob sighed. He lifted a hand and began to count on his fingers. "The first one's wife died in a freak traffic accident; the second had a miscarriage; the third lost his job in disgrace."

"That kind of thing just happens," Zoe said. "It's awful, but there's no way you or Wolfe could be to blame for any of it."

"I'd like to believe you, but I know better."

"Wait a sec," Hilary said. "This happened after you talked to these reporters? What's to stop something from happening to us?"

Zoe glanced at her. "I thought you didn't believe any of this."

"I don't. Do you?"

Zoe just didn't know anymore. The whole thing sounded preposterous, but she couldn't shake the nagging possibility that he wasn't lying to her. It was the complete sincerity with which he—Bob—Wolfe—whatever his name was—spoke that had her mistrusting her logic. Somehow she just couldn't see that sincerity as being faked. She felt that she was too good a judge of character to be taken in so easily by an act, no matter how good; ludicrous as the situation was, she realized that she'd actually feel better if it was true. At least her judgment wouldn't be in question, then.

Of course, if Bob was telling the truth, then that changed all the rules. The world could never be the same again.

"I don't know," she said finally.

"Yeah, well better safe than sorry," Hilary said. She turned her attention back to Bob. "Well?" she asked. "*Are* we in danger?"

"Not at the moment. Zoe negates Wolfe's abilities."

"Whoa," Hilary said. "I can already see where this is going. You want her to be your shadow so that the big bad Wolfe won't hurt anybody else—right? Jesus, I've heard some lame pick-up lines in my time, but this beats them all, hands down."

"That's not it at all," Bob said. "He can't hurt Zoe, that's true. And he's already tried. He's exerted tremendous amounts of time and energy since last night in making her life miserable and hasn't seen any success."

"I don't know about that," Zoe said. "I haven't exactly been having a fun time since I ran into him last night."

"What I'm worried about," Bob said, going on as though Zoe hadn't spoken, "is that he's now going to turn his attention on her friends."

"Okay," Zoe said. "This has gone far enough. I'm going to the cops."

"I'm not threatening you," Bob said as she started to stand up. "I'm just warning you."

"It sounds like a threat to me, pal."

"I've spent years looking for some way to stop Wolfe," Bob said. The desperation in his eyes held Zoe captive. "You're the first ray of hope I've found in all that time. He's scared of you."

"Why? I'm nobody special."

"I could give you a lecture on how we're all unique individuals, each important in his or her own way," Bob said, "but that's not what we're talking about here. What you are goes beyond that. In some ways, you and Wolfe are much the same, except where he brings pain into people's lives, you heal."

Zoe shook her head. "Oh, please."

"I don't think the world is the way we like to think it is," Bob went on. "I don't think its one solid world, but many, thousands upon thousands of them—as many as there are people—because each person perceives the world in his or her own way; each lives in his or her own world. Sometimes they connect, for a moment, or more rarely, for a lifetime, but mostly we are alone, each living in our own world, suffering our small deaths."

"This is stupid," Zoe said.

But she was still held captive by his sincerity. She heard a kind of mystical backdrop to what he was saying, a breathy sound that reminded her of an LP they had in the station's library of R. Carlos Nakai playing a traditional Native American flute.

"I believe you're an easy person to meet," Bob said. "The kind of person that people are drawn to talk to— especially by those who are confused, or hurt, or lost. You give them hope. You help them heal."

Zoe continued to shake her head. "I'm not any of that."

"I'm not so sure he's wrong," Hilary said.

Zoe gave her friend a sour look.

"Well, think about it," Hilary said. "The weird and the wacky are always drawn to you. And that show of yours. There's no way that Nightnoise should work—it's just too bizarre a mix. I can't see head bangers sitting through the opera you play, classical buffs putting up with rap, but they do. It's the most popular show in its time slot."

"Yeah, right. Like it's got so much competition at that hour of the night."

"That's just it," Hilary said. "It does have competition, but people still tune in to you."

"Not fifteen minutes ago, you were telling me that the reason I get all these weird people coming on to me is because I'm putting out confused vibes."

Hilary nodded. "I think I was wrong."

"Oh, for God's sake."

"You do help people," Hilary said. "I've seen some of your fan mail, and then there's all of those people who are constantly calling in. You help them, Zoe. You really do."

This was just too much for Zoe.

"Why are you saying all of this?" she asked Hilary. "Can't you hear what it sounds like?"

"I know. It sounds ridiculous. But at the same time, I think it makes its own kind of sense. All those people are turning to you for help. I don't think they expect you to solve all of their problems; they just want that touch of hope that you give them."

"I think Wolfe's asking for your help, too," Bob said.

"Oh, really?" Zoe said. "And how am I supposed to do that? Find you and him a good shrink?"

"In the old days," Hilary said, "there were people who could drive out demons just by a laying on of the hands."

Zoe looked from Hilary to Bob and realized that they were both serious. A smart-ass remark was on the tip of her tongue, but this time she just let it die unspoken.

A surreal quality had taken hold of the afternoon, as though the Academy of St. Martin-in-the-Fields was playing Hendrix, or Captain Beefheart was doing a duet with Tiffany. The light in the mall seemed incandescent. The air was hot on her skin, but she could feel a chill all the way down to the marrow of her bones.

I don't want this to be real, she realized.

But she knelt down in front of Bob and reached out her hands, laying a palm on either temple.

What now? she thought. Am I supposed to reel off some gibberish to make it sound like a genuine exorcism?

She felt so dumb, she—

The change caught her completely by surprise, stunning her thoughts and the ever-playing sound track that ran through her mind into silence. A tingle like static electricity built up in her fingers.

She was looking directly at Bob, but suddenly it seemed as though she was looking through him, directly into him, into the essence of him. It was flesh and blood that lay under her hands, but rainbowing swirls of light were all she could see. A small sound of wonder sighed from between her lips at the sight.

We're all made of light, she thought. Sounds and light, cells vibrating. . . .

But when she looked more closely, she could see that under her hands the play of lights was threaded with discordances. As soon as she noticed them, the webwork of dark threads coalesced into a pebble-size oval of shadow that fell through the swirl of lights, down, down, until it was gone. The rainbowing pattern of the lights was unblemished now, the lights faded, became flesh and bone and skin and then she was just holding Bob's head in her hands once more.

The tingle left her fingers, and she dropped her hands. Bob smiled at her.

"Thank you," he said.

That sense of sincerity remained, but it wasn't Bob's voice anymore. It was Wolfe's.

"Be careful," he added.

"What do you mean?" she asked.

"I was like you once."

"Like me how?"

"Just be careful," he said.

She tilted her head back as he rose to his feet, gaze tracking him as he walked away, across the marble floor and through the doors of the mall. He didn't open the doors, he just stepped through the glass and steel out into the street and continued off across the pavement. A half dozen yards from the entrance, he simply faded away like a video effect and was gone.

Zoe shook her head.

"No," she said softly. "I don't want to believe this."

"Believe what?" Hilary asked.

Zoe turned to look at her. "You didn't see what happened?"

"Happened where?"

"Bob."

"He's finally here?" Hilary looked around at the passersby. "I was so sure he was going to pull a no-show."

"No, he's not here," Zoe said. "He . . ."

Her voice trailed off as the realization hit home. She was on her own with this. What had happened? If she took it all at face value, she realized that meeting Wolfe *had* brought her a small death after all—the death of the world the way it had been to the way she now knew it to be. It was changed forever. *She* was changed forever. She carried a responsibility now of which she'd never been aware before.

Why didn't Hilary remember the encounter? Probably because it would have been the same small death for her as it had been for Zoe herself; her world would have been changed forever.

But I've negated that for her, Zoe thought. Just like I did for Wolfe, or Bob, or whoever he really was.

Her gaze dropped to the floor where he'd been sitting and saw a small black pebble lying on the marble. She hesitated for a moment, then reached over and picked it up. Her fingers tingled again, and she watched in wonder as the pebble went from black, through gray, until it was a milky white.

"What've you got there?" Hilary asked.

Zoe shook her head. She closed her fingers around the small smooth stone, savoring its odd warmth.

"Nothing," she said. "Just a pebble."

She got up and sat beside Hilary again.

"Excuse me, miss?"

The security guard had returned, and this time he wasn't ignoring Rupert.

"I'm sorry," he said, "but I'm afraid you'll have to take your dog outside. It's the mall management's rules."

"Yes," Zoe said. "Of course."

She gave him a quick smile, which the guard returned with more warmth than Zoe thought was warranted. It was as though she'd propositioned him or something.

Jesus, she thought. Was she going to go through the rest of her life, second-guessing every encounter she ever had? Does he know, does she? Life was tough enough without having to feel self-conscious every time she met somebody. Maybe this was what Wolfe had meant when he said that he had been just like her once. Maybe the pressure just got to be too much for him, and it turned him from healing to hurting.

Just be careful.

It seemed possible. It seemed more than possible when she remembered the gratitude she'd seen in his eyes when he'd thanked her.

Beside her, Hilary looked at her watch. 'We might as well go," she said. "This whole thing's a washout. It's almost twelve-thirty. If he was going to come, he'd've been here by now."

Zoe nodded her head.

"See the thing is," Hilary said as they started for the door, Rupert walking in between them, "a guy like that can't face an actual confrontation. If you ask me, you're never going to hear from him again."

"I think you're right," Zoe said.

But there might be others, changing, already changed. She might become one of them herself if she wasn't—

Just be

Her fingers tightened around the white pebble she'd picked up. She stuck it in the front pocket of her jeans as a token to remind her of what had happened to Wolfe, of how it could just as easily happen to her if she wasn't

—careful.

White Lightning
by Al Sarrantonio

We'd been talking about drinking the white lightning the whole week, but when it finally got to this morning, and we stood in the woods near Pisser Johnson's busted still with a jar of it in our hands, Billy didn't want to do it.

"Could be bad stuff," he said. "Could make us blind, or go crazy. I heard from Jodie McAfrey that Pisser's whiskey drove a man crazy in Dobbinsville a couple years ago. That's why Sheriff Mapes had to finally let the feds get at 'im. I heard the man got himself a gun and shot up the town, killed most of his family, then himself. I heard—"

"You a pussy?" I finally said, sick of his whining.

"I ain't no pussy," he said, getting red in the face. That's about as far as he ever went in anger, getting red in the face. Soon he would look at the ground, then give in to me, just like always.

"Well, only pussys won't drink," I said. "You're tired of stealing your old man's bottle beer, ain't you? Here we got a whole box of jars, just to ourself. Remember the special beating my old man gave me 'time he found me watering his gin after we drank half of it?" I was yelling pretty loud, and Billy was looking at the ground.

"I ain't no pussy," he repeated.

I held the jar out. "Then drink. Chances are, it'll only make us feel real good."

"Or kill us," he said, still looking at the ground.

"You *are* a pussy," I said.

So I drank from the jar first, closing my eyes, holding my breath, and felt the hot stuff go down my throat, then shoot up into my head.

I opened my eyes, and for a second I saw only stars,

and thought I was blind. But then I saw Billy and the woods around him real bright, like they were lit up all around, and knew everything was just fine.

"Holy shit," I said, and Billy looked at me kind of scared, but then I gave a whoop and took another long drink. The world flashed brighter, and I felt warm all through, like the Sun was inside me.

"Even pussys've got to try this!" I laughed, and handed him the jar, and he laughed and took a big swallow.

So we drank the rest of the jar, and took another with us, and hid the rest away in Pisser's storm cellar where we'd found them, where the stupid feds had missed them, and set off back to town to get Billy's old man's gun.

It was two o'clock by the time we got back, which meant Billy's old man was drunk, so we had to sneak around back. We heard Billy's old man raving around in front, yelling at the television, kicking the furniture.

"Let's get it," I said, whispering.

The gun was in the back of the closet shelf in Billy's old man's room. We had to move some stuff aside; we'd had it down to play with a couple of times and knew exactly where everything was and where it had to go back. Billy's old man was a drunk, and drunks know where things should be and are always looking out for people doing them wrong.

The shoe box was there, along with the cardboard box full of clips. We brought them down, took everything out. I hefted the gun, pushed a 9mm clip into it.

"Feels good," I said, smiling.

"Ought to," Billy said. His head looked bigger, brighter, than it was supposed to. Everything he said came out large, like it was written in balloons above his head. "My old man took it from the cop's body they found down by the Housack River last year."

I kept smiling. "Time we put it to some good use. Let's kill your old man."

Billy started to protest, so I said, "Why not?"

"He's my old man."

"So what," I said. "He beat you this week?"

"He beats me every week."

"So I'll kill him."

I stared at him while he got red in the face, stared hard at the ground, then finally said, "Go ahead."

"Take the rest of the clips," I said, and Billy emptied them into his jeans pockets.

We walked down the hall, me in front, smiling, to the living room. Billy's old man was up at the TV, fiddling with the knobs on the back, cursing at the wavy-lined picture on the screen. "Fuckin' shit," he said, and then he said it again. I held the gun up in front of me, two hands, the way they do it on TV. I know I was smiling. I kept walking, the gun in front of me, until he put his head up to get his beer can on top of the TV and saw me.

"What the shit—" he said, but then I pointed the gun up at his head and pulled the trigger, and it kicked me back but it made a hole in his forehead just like I wanted it to. It was a neat round hole, and then blood started to come out of it like a red waterfall, and Billy's old man fell back down behind the television, his hand out trying to catch the bullet already in his head; and it was funny because when he went down he hit the TV, the picture went clear.

"Fuckin' shit," I said, and then I put a slug into the TV to watch the screen bust, and we walked outside.

It was a low, aluminum-colored cloud day. Warm and cold at the same time. The block was empty.

Then it wasn't. The mailman was coming down the street. Billy looked at me and I smiled, and I said, "You do him," and handed him the gun.

"But—"

I opened the jar and handed it to him. "Drink."

He tilted it up, took a swallow.

"More," I said.

He took another swallow, closed his eyes.

"That's enough," I said.

He opened his eyes, handed the jar back to me.

"Do it," I said.

The mailman was heading for us, rolling his funny cart

to an angle stop in front of Mrs. Welsh's gate and flipping through his handful of letters, peeling a couple off and then pushing through the gate to the front of the house.

The dog came at him then, but the mailman was already in position for it, snugged to the right of the walk, and the dog's chain went taut and he couldn't get at the mailman.

I was staring at Billy, seeing him all shiny-bright, watching him looking at the ground, and then finally he said, "Okay."

"Good." I put the jar into the front pocket of my pants, and by then the mailman, whose name was Mr. Masters, and had a big Adam's apple in his long neck that was always bobbing up and down, was coming back down Mrs. Welsh's walk, and Billy walked up to meet him.

"H-Howdy," Billy stammered, holding the gun up.

Masters just looked at the gun, kind of frozen in place, and then the gun began to shake in Billy's hand. Finally Masters smiled a little and said, "Howdy, yourself. Got a new toy for your eleventh birthday, Billy?"

"Sure did," I said, stepping up beside Billy, taking the gun from his hand, aiming it and pulling the trigger.

I hit ole Mr. Masters right in the Adam's apple. Sounded like a bone crack but there was plenty of blood, and Mr. Masters said "Oh, my God," and threw his hands up at his neck, and I popped him one right in the eye.

Billy looked at me, but by then I was pushing through the gate of Mrs. Welsh's house.

The dog was on me, but I didn't care. I kept to the middle of the walk and timed it perfect so that when the dog jumped, just reaching me at the end of its chain, I let the dog's teeth close around the gun barrel and then pulled off two quick shots.

The dog's head sort of went cloudy red and split into two parts. The top part with the eyes still wide fell off and landed on the sidewalk.

I waved for Billy to follow.

I saw Mrs. Welsh staring out at me through the curtains, frozen like a statue, a black phone to her ear. I heard her start screaming, saw her drop the phone and amble away as I mounted the creaky porch steps. "Need fixin'," I said, and then I laughed because Mrs. Welsh was there at the front door, behind the faded door-window curtains, fumbling with the lock.

I took a quick step and planted my foot on the door, knee-jerking it in.

Mrs. Welsh fell back and started to squawk like a chicken before Sunday dinner. "Get in," I said to Billy, and as he stepped in I shut the door.

Mrs. Welsh was laying on the ground, shaking, saying, "No no!" in a high voice, covering her face with her hands, which was good because I started shooting in a line through the floor at her shaking feet and all the way up her body till I split a good shot between her hands and blood pumped out.

I turned to leave as her hands fell away from her face, but then there came a sound from the back of the house.

"You hear that?" I said. "Sounded like a splash. Come on."

We searched until we heard a sound coming from the kitchen, which we'd just looked in. We turned back, and there on the counter under a window was a fish tank, with a goldfish the size of a small carp in it. The water was rocking, and the fish took a jump and popped through the surface, then fell back in again. Next to the tank was a big cardboard canister of fish food.

"Watch," I said, and when the fish made its next leap I shot it through its middle. I shot the fish-food canister for good measure, then turned and walked out of the kitchen.

Way off in the distance, I heard the whine of a police siren.

"Time to go," I said.

As we passed the living room, there was a faint sound coming from the telephone receiver Mrs. Welsh had dropped. I stopped to pick it up and said into it, laughing, "See you soon!"

We went out through the back of Mrs. Welsh's house. There was a fence, easy to climb, which brought us out onto the next block.

My old man's garage was two blocks down and one over, and we got near it by cutting through backyards. Which was just as well, because by now the police sirens were real close, and one of the cars screamed down the street just behind us as we cut into the hedges bordering a big house.

"Ain't this Jodie McAfrey's place?" I said, and stopped to ring the side bell.

Jodie didn't answer, but his mother did, opening the door a crack. I aimed and missed her face. She turned and ran, so I elbowed my way in.

I aimed careful this time, and gave her two quick ones in the spine. After she went down, I put my foot on her back and planted a final one in her head.

"Ain't you gonna ask me why I shot her in the back?" I said to Billy as we headed for the fence between the McAfreys' yard and my old man's garage. I laughed loud and said, "Because her front was too far away!"

We climbed the fence, passed a line of worked-on cars, and then got to the mouth of the garage. I popped the clip on the gun, tossed it away, and put the gun in Billy's hand. "Put a new clip in, and do it," I said.

Billy got red in the face, looked at the ground real hard, but then he did what I said and went in. I stayed outside, sipping from the jar, but after a minute there was no sound so I ducked inside, moving around the open hood of a Chevy and saw Billy at the door to my old man's dirty office.

"You still a pussy?" I asked.

"He ain't here," Billy said.

I stared at him hard, until he looked at the ground, and then I smiled, taking a key ring off the pegboard next to my old man's desk.

"Give me the gun," I said. I held out my hand, and he put the gun in it.

Everything had gone bright and sharp again. I tilted the jar back up to my mouth and felt the white lightning burn down the back of my throat and jump straight into my head.

"I'll drive," I said, walking outside, tucking the jar

back into the front pocket of my pants. The key fit the door of a late model 4×4.

"Hey," I said, "it's got a CD player!"

Billy climbed in. I started the truck up, rolled out, and bent to see if there were any CDs in the case under my seat when a police car roared past and then stopped dead.

"Hold on," I said, and hit the floor, pulling left as the police car squealed around.

I headed for the narrow side lot between the last two houses on the block. We had drunk beer here some nights, and there was no way a police cruiser could climb the curb and make it over the mess of broken bottles and rusting old appliances. Sure enough, the cop braked behind us, took a long look, and roared ahead, hoping to cut us off on the next block.

I drove into the woods beside the back of the lot, instead of bouncing out on Barger Street behind it, where the stupid cop was no doubt waiting for us now.

The path in the woods widened just enough for the 4×4 to get through. I leaned over, looking for CDs. I reached under my seat, found a case with a stack of them, and put the first one I found into the machine.

Christian music came out, telling us about how Jesus was all around us and was going to save us.

"Sounds good to me," I said, laughing, so I put my foot on the brake, stopped the 4×4, put the muzzle of the gun to Billy's ear, and pulled off three shots into his head.

His body was still twitching when I pulled it out of the 4×4 and dumped it on the side of the dirt road. I put two more shots into his head, both nostrils, just to make sure.

The white lightning jar was uncomfortable in the front pocket of my pants, so I took it out and emptied it into my throat. I had to close my eyes, but it felt like I still had them wide open. They felt like they were on fire. All of me felt like I was on fire. I threw the empty jar out the window, and it rolled to Billy's head and stopped there.

The 4×4 was bulky at the end of the narrow woods

road, but I got it through. I knew they'd be roadblocking on the two-lane ahead, and wanted to avoid it, but when I tried to climb the piney bank across the road, the truck nearly flipped over and I couldn't find a way through.

I put the gun on the seat next to me, and turned toward where the roadblock would be.

As I came around the corner toward it, I thought of the one way out. The cops were so fucking stupid. There was another narrow access road just to the left of the crossroads they'd set up on, and I barreled down on them and then clutched and cut back to second gear and turned sharp left. They were all ready with their shotguns and they let go at me, but they were fifty yards away and I got behind the trees fast.

It was bumpier in here, but I knew where I was going and pretty sure I'd get there. Behind me, I heard one of the police cruisers try to follow and then hit something.

Just for the hell of it, I rolled down the window, picked up the gun, and shot at a bluejay I saw up in the trees.

Ahead, a doe leaped across the path, and I braked hard, leaped out, and chased it, pulling off shots. I hit it in the flank and it slowed, and I ran up on it and jumped on its back and fired shots into its head all around, even after it was down on the ground. For good measure I hit the skull with the butt of the gun and kicked it in until there wasn't much left that said deer. I noticed a bulge in the belly and saw that it was pregnant, nearly to term. Something was kicking around inside, so I reared back with my foot a couple of times and planted it in until the movement stopped. One last time I kicked, hard, and my boot went into the belly, making a nice hole, and something bloody with a tiny deer's head fell out.

I went back to the 4×4, checked the clip in the gun, saw that there was only five shells left. I reached into my pocket, found it empty, thought of all the clips in Billy's pockets.

"Shit."

I thought of going back, heard cops, maybe on foot,

getting close behind. I floored the 4×4, kicking leaves, and drove on.

Pisser Johnson's still was only a half mile off the road, and I was at it in another couple of minutes. The shack holding it hadn't been knocked down by the feds, so I slammed the 4×4 into it.

The jars were in the brush-covered storm cellar ten feet away from the still. I paced out ten long steps due west, hit the sill plate with the toe of my boot, and bent down to brush away the pine needles and dry leaves that covered the door. We'd already busted the lock, so all I had to do was flip off the latch and pull the doors back.

It was rotten-smelling down there, and the steps were slippery. There was enough light to see about halfway down, then things got dark. I felt around with my boot, trying to find the last step, but I calculated wrong, and slipped, and went down forward. I felt the gun pop out of my belt and slide away from me in the dark.

It was then that I heard the first voice outside. I knew it was Sheriff Mapes right away; the old bastard was loud and heavy as a hog, and I heard him crunching away in the leaves and twigs. He halted, and there were other crunchings and what sounded like a motorcycle that roared to a stop.

"Jimmy Connel, you in there?" Mapes roared in his bellowed voice. He didn't sound too happy. "You listen to me, boy!"

I scratched around on the floor in front of me, coming up with a handful of wet.

"You come out of there now, you hear me?"

I heard him, and wanted to let him know. I crawled forward, scuttling around now like a crab, and my hand fell on one of the jar cases. I reached up and in, finding the empty spot where me and Billy'd taken our two jars, and there was another one next to it. I lifted it out, unscrewed it quick, and drank some down. I waited while the fire roared around my eye sockets, and when it subsided, I could suddenly see a little in the damp dark and saw the gun laying about a foot to my right.

"I hear you, fat boy!" I shouted, jumping at the gun

and scrambling halfway up the steps, holding the gun out and firing off a couple of shots.

I heard someone shout, "Oh, *shit!*" and heard Sheriff Mapes say, "Is he hit? Get him the hell out of here."

"Come and get me, Sheriff!" I yelled, and then scrambled down to get the jar and drink off some more.

"I want you to listen to me, Jimmy Connel," Mapes said. "We know what you and your friend did. We found Billy lying back there, all shot up. What I want you to do is toss the gun out of the hole and walk right up to me. I'll get you a lawyer and everything. I don't want nobody else hurt. You hear me?"

Again I scrambled up the steps. I stuck my head up real quick, before they could get a good shot at me. I saw a couple of faces, one of them a deputy, the thin tall one with the hair lip who'd only been with Mapes a year, real close by, almost to the door of the hole, on his belly like a commando. I startled him, aimed, and put a hole right through the top of his skull.

He screamed once and then went quiet.

They shot at me, but I was already back down the hole. I went for the jar again. When the white lightning went down, it felt like it was burning me all the way from the inside out to my skin. I threw the jar aside, fumbled back to the box, and got another out.

I heard them arguing outside, and then there was some more crunching in the leaves. I checked the clip in the gun, angling it toward the light, and sure enough there were only two more shells. I snapped the clip back in and waited while they argued.

A lot of them wanted to come in, storm the hole, but Mapes didn't want that. There was more discussion about tear gas. They all decided on that except Mapes, who wanted to try something else first. The rest of them said the hell with it, but Mapes was loud and he got them to shut up.

"Now, Jimmy," Mapes yelled out to me, "I'm going to try one more thing with you. I'm going to try it, and then you're going to throw the gun out of the hole and come out of it with your hands in the clouds."

He didn't wait for me to say anything or shoot, but

then I heard Mapes say, "Go ahead" and I heard my old man's voice.

"Jimmy boy, you hear me?"

I said nothing, but unscrewed the jar lid quick and took a long swallow down.

"Jimmy, I know you hear me, so listen to me now. You've done a lot of bad things here today. I want you to stop it now. I think you know what kind of trouble you're in. What if your Momma—"

I couldn't help myself. I started to cry. I clutched the jar hard, and took a hard swallow. "Don't you do that!" I shouted out.

"Now, Jimmy," my old man said, reasonable, "these folks out here want to help you. No one's gonna hurt—"

"Tell them about my Momma!" I shouted out. I took another swallow of white lightning. "Tell 'em how you beat her when I was four till she left! How you beat her again when she came back to get me, so bad she had to crawl away on her hands and knees! Tell them what you told her, that you'd cut my balls off if she came near the house again! Tell 'em what you been doing to me every night for the past eight years, how you been buggering me and making me use my mouth on you, and what you told me you'd do if I ever told anybody!" I was crying big tears and screaming. "Tell 'em!"

There was no sound out there, just silence. I heard myself weeping. Then I stood up tall, right out of the hole, and took a shot at my old man. But he was hiding behind Mapes, and I winged the fat sheriff instead in the shoulder, and heard him curse and saw him go down to one knee.

They fired more shots at me then, and I ducked back down and swallowed the rest of the jar, and waited until the commotion calmed down.

"You listen to me, Jimmy," Mapes said, a little of the bellow out of his voice, 'cause he was breathing hard. I heard him tell someone, "Leave me alone!" before he talked to me again. "Jimmy, you listen to me. You know what we're going to have to do."

I was still crying a little bit, but I made myself stop and yelled good and loud. "That's all right, Sheriff! I'm just going to sit here and drink the rest of this white lightning!" I took the empty jar in my hand and tossed it out of the hole as far as I could in the sheriff's direction, then opened another jar.

No one said anything, and then Mapes said, "Now, Jimmy, you got to realize that Pisser Johnson never did anything with those jars. We checked them with the fed man last week. There's nothing in 'em but good, clean Housack river water."

But I guess I already knew that, so I put the barrel of the gun in my mouth as far up as it would go and pulled off the last shot.

Hitman
by Rick Hautala

1

3:52 P.M.

Fifteen minutes after Angelo Martelli shot his boss, Tony Vincenza, Angelo's rented car broke down. It didn't cough or sputter or stall even once; it just seized up and died. Angelo gripped the steering wheel tightly as he jerked it hard to the right, and the car coasted to a dead stop on the gravel shoulder of the road. Clenching his fists in controlled frustration, he pressed his hands against his forehead, sucked in a deep breath, and glared out at the snow-covered road ahead.

"You *lou*-sy *mot*-her-*fuck*-er!" he said.

Each syllable came out a tiny puff of steam. Then, with a tight, high grunt, he brought one fist down hard against the dashboard. That was all; his only demonstration of anger. Now that this new situation had presented itself, he had to clear his mind so he could think things through.

Closing his eyes for a moment, he leaned back against the car seat and mentally ran through everything he had done so far to cover his tracks. He was a hitman, and in his line of work it didn't pay to be sloppy or leave *any* loose ends. Angelo was one of the best in the business. He made up operating procedures Tony had always teased him were overly cautious. In fact, Tony and a few of his close associates had nicknamed Angelo *Overkill,* but that pleased rather than bothered Angelo. Besides, he didn't have to concern himself with Tony anymore. But Angelo prided himself on his caution. He wasn't the kind of man who left *anything* to chance. He never traveled with a weapon, always making arrangements through a third party to have what he needed at his destination. He had enough phony IDs to fill ten wallets, and he could come up with iron-clad alibis that would convince the Supreme Court ... but *this*! He couldn't have counted on *this*. A goddamned breakdown!

Right now, fifteen minutes after a hit, a broken-down car was a loose end Angelo couldn't afford or tolerate. He reassured himself that, of course, he hadn't rented the car under his own name. That was standard procedure, but he had taken the extra precaution of wearing thick horn-rim glasses and a blond wig when he picked up the car; so even if someone had photographed him, no one was going to connect him with anything. The major consideration right now was, should he stay with the car or abandon it?

The smart thing might just be to find some other way to get the hell out of this boondock state. He knew the police had equipment that could identify a tire print almost as accurately as a fingerprint. If they matched the tires of this car with evidence they'll eventually find at Tony's isolated cottage on Echo Lake—whenever they discover his body—then maybe it'd be wisest to leave the car, get the hell out of Maine as fast as he could.

Then again, if there wasn't anything seriously wrong with the car and he could get it repaired quickly, it might be smart to return it to the rental agency as if nothing had happened. With what Phil Belario had fronted him for this most recent job, he could easily pay for repairs and return the car rather than cause any kind of fuss that would draw undue attention to him. Hell, he could buy six or seven of these babies with what would be in his bank account as of nine o'clock tomorrow morning. Right now, the important thing was just to get his ass back to Philly.

"Lousy mother*fucker*," he said again, glancing up and down the lonely stretch of country back road. The sky was the color of soot, and snow-draped pines leaned heavily over the road. With evening no more than an hour away, everything looked lonely and cold. Angelo had no idea how far it was to the nearest phone. He thought he remembered passing a gas station a few miles back, but for all he knew there might be something closer up ahead. Maybe doing the hit out here in the boondocks hadn't been such a great idea. If only he had been on the Maine Turnpike, maybe across the New Hampshire border before the rental car shit the bed.

"Okay, okay," Angelo reassured himself. "No need to panic. Nothing to worry about. Everything's covered."

Pulling his leather gloves tightly up to his wrists, he snapped open the car door and stepped out into the cold, January afternoon. His first breath nearly froze his lungs and made him cough so hard he almost choked. He was doubled over by the driver's door, coughing, when a battered pickup truck loaded high with bales of hay roared past him. Hay chaff and black exhaust swirled in its wake like a tornado as Angelo straightened up and—too late—waved his arms to signal the driver to stop.

"Fuckin' hick!" He shook his gloved fist high in the air. "I hope to fuck I see *you* broken down on the side of the road next!"

He was watching the receding truck, so he didn't notice the mud-splattered Subaru that had glided to a stop behind his stalled rental until the driver's door opened and slammed shut.

2

4:07 P.M.

"So, Frank, what did you say you do for work?"

Momentarily distracted as he stared at the road ahead, Angelo shook his head and, glancing at the driver, offered a standard line.

"Oh, I sell insurance—life insurance out of an office in Boston."

The driver, a young man in his late twenties or early thirties, had introduced himself as Mark St. Pierre, a history teacher at a local high school. He seemed like a nice enough fellow, but right now Angelo had enough on his mind; he was in no mood for making friends on the road.

"So, were you up this way for business or pleasure?"

Angelo chuckled. "I can't for the life of me imagine why *anyone* would come up to Maine in January for *pleasure*."

"Not unless they were going skiing. But then again— No offense, Frank, but you don't exactly strike me as the skiing type."

"No, no—I'm not," Angelo replied. "I was seeing a client in Augusta." His gaze shifted to the road ahead. His hands clenched in his lap when he saw the overloaded hay truck up ahead. It was moving slower now, spouting thick, black exhaust as it struggled to make the steep grade of the hill. Angelo smiled and, shaking his head, said, "That's the lousy son-of-a-bitch who almost clipped me when I got out of my car."

"Yeah, I saw that," Mark replied. "I thought it looked like he came pretty close. Well, don't worry. I think there's a long stretch of open road after the top of this hill. We'll leave him in the dust."

He pressed down on the accelerator. The car leaped forward, rapidly closing the distance between them. Angelo stared with cold-eyed hostility at the swaying stack of hay bales on the truck bed, earnestly praying that the precariously balanced load would spill out onto the road as soon as they had passed. As he came up close behind the truck, Mark eased out toward the center line and clicked on the turn signal, indicating his intention to pass.

Suddenly he shouted, "Jesus Christ!" His foot came up off the accelerator, and the car slowed down, dropping back rapidly.

"You gonna pass the motherfucker or what?" Angelo asked. He narrowed his gaze as he turned to look at the driver.

"Jesus *Christ*," Mark repeated, holding the steering wheel tightly with one hand as he stared, gape-mouthed, and pointed at the truck just as it crested the hill. "What the—? Did you *see* that?"

"Yeah, so what? The asshole's got his truck overloaded," Angelo said. "Looks to me like he's gonna spill the whole fuckin' load all over the road. I'd either hurry up and pass him, or hang way the hell back if I was you."

The truck rapidly pulled away from them as Mark slowed down. He was gnawing on his lower lip as he looked back and forth between his passenger and the road ahead.

"No! No! It wasn't that at all!" he said. His voice was twisted up high and tight, and his eyes were round and bulging with surprise. "No, it was—I thought I—"

Rather than say more, Mark stepped down hard on the accelerator again and sped up to catch up with the truck, which was now gaining speed on the down slope. When they were less than fifty feet behind it, Mark pointed and said softly, "Look! There! Between those hay bales on the left side."

Angelo squinted as he leaned forward; then he almost shouted aloud when he saw a hand—a naked, pale, motionless human hand sticking out from between two of the hay bales.

"Jesus Christ. Well what d'yah know?" Angelo said. His voice was faint and flat; he hoped it registered at least a bit of surprise.

"For Christ's sake! What the hell are we gonna *do*?" Mark asked. He kept flicking his eyes over at Angelo, worry and concern written all over his face.

"What do you mean, what are we gonna do?" Angelo said flatly. This was far from the first time he had seen a dead person—or a dead person's hand. "We ain't gonna do a goddamned thing about it."

"But there's—"

"Could be just one of the hayseed's gloves stuck between the bales."

"That sure as hell looks like a real hand to me," Mark replied, not taking his eyes off the swaying back of the truck.

"Well, I'll tell you this," Angelo said in a pleasant but forceful drawl. "We're gonna head to the nearest gas station so I can get a wrecker back out to my car. I have—" He cleared his throat noisily. "I have an important meeting back at the home office tomorrow morning, and I ain't about to piss my time away on bullshit like this."

"But that person— What if that's a dead person in the back of that truck? What if they—I don't know. What if they had a passenger back there, and they don't even know something's happened?"

"Who the fuck would be stupid enough to ride in the back of a truck in weather like this?"

"Then, what if—what if those guys have *killed* someone. What if they're taking the body someplace to get rid of it? We can't just—just *ignore* it! What if—"

"What if *nothing!*" Angelo said, squeezing his gloved hands into tight fists. For once in his life, he wished he carried a gun so he could threaten this man to do what he wanted him to do. But that would have been foolish. He had to get—and maintain—control of this situation. "I don't have the time or the inclination to get involved in anything like this. I think it looks like a glove, but even if there *is* some dead guy in the back of that truck, so what? Big fucking deal! It don't concern either me *or* you!"

"But what if—"

"For all you know, these might be guys you don't want to be messin' with," Angelo said, adding just a touch of menace to his voice.

Mark glanced over at his passenger, obviously trying to gauge just how dangerous he might be. Then, when he saw the truck up ahead slowing down for a left-hand turn, he pulled to a stop on the side of the road. Gritting his teeth, he took a deep, controlled breath, then let it out slowly and said, "Look, Frank, I have to follow that truck—at least to see where they're going. I think there's a gas station a mile or two up the road from here. You can walk or hitchhike to it if you want."

The sun was low on the horizon; it was going to be dark soon. Angelo considered how ball-busting cold it was outside; then he grunted. "Too fucking bad you don't have a car phone," he said. He settled back in the car seat, thinking—*Okay, let this do-gooder find out what's going on; then I'll be rid of him.*

"I swear to God," Mark said, gripping the steering

wheel with both hands, tracking the overloaded truck as it moved down the long stretch of country road. "This isn't a main road or anything, so they can't be going far. Just let me follow them to see where they're going. Then—I swear to God—I'll drive you to the gas station. You can get a wrecker to pick up your car, and I can call the cops from there. I can't ignore something like this. I have to find out where they're going."

Angelo smiled grimly and said, "Okay, then. Better step on it, though. You don't want to lose them, do you?"

With a loud squealing of tires, Mark cut across the main road and sped after the pickup truck. Fighting back a surge of anger, Angelo settled back in the car seat, wishing to hell someone else—*anyone* else—had stopped to help him, but what could he expect out in the boondocks like this?

3

4:29 P.M.

"End of the line, Markie-boy," Angelo said when he saw the pickup truck slow for a turn into a driveway. "Turn around and let's get the fuck out of here." Both he and Mark stared down the one lane dirt drive lined with snow-covered pines and high, dirt-streaked snowplow ridges.

Mark braced his hands on the steering wheel as he pulled a quick U-turn across the road and then stopped the car opposite the driveway entrance. His face was pinched tight with concentration as he looked down the darkening, tree-lined alley.

"You don't think we should check it out first?" he asked.

Angelo shook his head tightly and said, "No way. I think you should get your ass out of here." He looked thoughtfully down the driveway and added, "You have no idea what you might be getting yourself into."

Mark gnawed on his lower lip while he considered. Then, after glancing up and down the road, he sucked in a deep breath and turned off the ignition. Pocketing the keys, he snapped open the car door and put one foot out onto the road.

"You can sit here and wait while I check it out," he said, staring a moment at the screen of trees that blocked his view of whatever was down that road; then he glanced at his wristwatch. "I won't be more than fifteen minutes or so."

"The fuck you will!" Angelo stopped himself from lunging across the seat and grabbing Mark to force him back behind the steering wheel. With the heater turned off and the door open, cold air invaded the car, probing under Angelo's coat collar and down his back like icy fingers. He couldn't repress the shiver that wracked his body.

"Look, man," Mark said in a trembling voice. "I don't know where the fuck you're coming from, but something . . . something really weird is going on here, and I have to check it out." Again, he glanced down the driveway. "You can either sit here and freeze your ass off, or you can come with me."

Angelo tempered his response and, smiling thinly, said, "Or you could leave the car running so I can have some heat."

Mark smiled and shook his head. "Look, Frank, I'm not exactly saying I don't trust you, but what's to stop you from driving off once I'm gone?"

Angelo's thin smile widened. "Nothing at all—except my word."

"Why don't you just come with me," Mark said. "Look, we don't have to go down the driveway. We can cut off across that field there and stay in the woods the whole time. No one's gonna see us if we keep to the woods."

"You got a description of the truck and where it is. Why not just give that to the cops."

"'Cause I have to see what the hell they're up to," Mark answered.

"You're full of shit, you know that?" Angelo said, shivering wildly inside his coat. He wondered which would be colder, sitting here in an unheated car or traipsing through the woods with this asshole do-gooder. After a moment, he decided that, at least if he was walking he might work up enough of a sweat to stay warm. Looking warily up at the darkening sky, he nodded slowly.

"Okay," he said as he clicked open his door. "I'll take a little pleasure walk with you." He got out and slammed the car door shut. Glaring at Mark across the car roof, he jabbed a gloved forefinger at him and said, "But we're talking fifteen minutes at most. I ain't about to get myself lost in the fucking woods, not with night coming on."

Mark nodded agreement, and the two of them dashed across the road. They followed the driveway for no more than fifty feet, then darted into the snow-filled woods. As soon as they were out of sight in the woods, Angelo wished for the dozenth time this afternoon that he was packing a gun so he could waste this jerk. He could take the asshole's car, get back in Philly, and ditch the car long before anyone would miss the sorry bastard.

But he didn't have a gun; so instead, he trudged through ankle-deep snow, all the while silently cursing himself for being a fool. If he was going to be walking in the cold, he should be heading to the nearest gas station. At least there wasn't much snow under the trees; it was sheltered and did feel a bit warmer than it probably would have been in the car.

"I think I see a building over there," Mark said, crouching behind a tree and pointing off to his right. Angelo looked in the direction he was pointing and shrugged when he saw the dark bulk of a barn and an unoccupied farmhouse. A single bare light bulb glowed inside the barn. The overloaded pickup truck was backed up and parked in front of the barn door.

"Great," Angelo said. "You've seen where they were going, now let's get the fuck out of here."

"Just a minute. I want to see what they're doing in there."

"You know," Angelo said, "did it even occur to you that it might not have been what you thought it was?"

Mark turned and regarded him with one raised eyebrow.

"I mean, now that I think about it, I ain't so sure *I* saw any *hand*. For Christ's sake! For all I know, it could have been a piece of rope or a feed bag or something."

"All the more reason to check it out then, don't you think?" Mark said. "I'd feel kind of foolish, getting the police involved if that *wasn't* a hand." He straightened up and began moving carefully between the trees, angling his way over toward the barn. "You coming or not?"

Angelo glanced back the way they had come, then followed a pace or two behind Mark as they moved in a direction that would take them out behind the barn. When they were halfway there, they heard the sound of grinding gears and the sputter of the truck's engine. Mark pointed to the overloaded truck as it started backing up into the wide-open barn doors.

"I'll bet there's a window or an opening out back where we can see inside," Mark said.

Angelo scowled and considered leaving the jerk behind and heading back to the car to wait; but he sucked in a deep breath and followed, mentally cursing both himself and Mark for fools.

They crouched in the fringe of pine trees that backed the barn and spent several seconds studying the battered, ship-gray structure. It was old and weathered. In fact, it looked as though the next strong gust of wind would knock it over. In the gathering gloom, it had a hulking, dark presence that bothered Angelo. For some unaccountable reason, he imagined that indeed the barn was barely supported, and it could come crashing down on top of both him and Mark at any moment.

"So, Frank—" Mark whispered, "—what do you think?"

From inside the barn, they could hear the chugging of the pickup truck, muffled voices of men talking, and heavy thumping sounds as the men tossed the hay bales to the ground. The surrounding woods were perfectly silent except for the faint hiss of wind in the pines high overhead. Angelo shivered, thinking how he could have been comfortably eating a seafood dinner at *The North Pier* in Boston by now if that goddamned rental car hadn't died.

"You want to take a peak through that window there?" Mark asked, indicating a small, dark rectangle on the backside of the barn. Most of the panes had been painted out, but on the lower left side was a hole about the size of a golf ball, through which filtered the mellow yellow glow of light.

"I could just about give two shits what they're doing in there," Angelo said, barely above a whisper. "And if you had half an ounce of brains, you'd—"

"Keep it down, will you?" Mark said. "I just gotta take a look, I mean, what if they're, like, burying the body in there or something?"

"It ain't none of *my* concern," Angelo said with a derisive snort. He stood back in the snowy darkness of the trees, slapping his arms to stay warm now that they had stopped moving.

After casting a cautious glance along either side of the barn, Mark skittered out across the open ground and flattened himself against the side of the barn to one side of the window. He edged around and, crouching low, peered in through the opening. Angelo tried to deny his own slight stirrings of curiosity as he watched the light-trimmed edge of Mark's face. His curiosity rose sharply when, his eyes rounded in shock and his mouth a wide *O,* Mark jerked away from the window.

"Jesus Christ!" he said, staggering backward and grabbing Angelo's arm for support. His voice was a raw, ragged gasp. "They've got a—Oh, my God! There's a dead—a dead *man* in there! For real!"

Angelo smirked, only half-believing Mark as the young man gripped his wrist and tugged him in the direction of the barn.

"You've gotta see it!" he whispered. "I want you to verify what it is, so when we go to the police, they'll believe me."

"We ain't going to no police," Angelo said firmly, but he allowed himself to be led over to the window.

"Go on. Look," Mark whispered. His voice assumed a deep tone of command. "See for yourself!"

Squinting one eye as though looking through a telescope, Angelo bent down and peered through the opening. The strong, musty smell of rotten hay assailed his nostrils and almost made him sneeze, but he checked himself. His heart did a cold, hard flip in his chest when he saw the dead man lying on the barn floor. It was his boss, Tony Vincenza—the man he had killed less than an hour ago.

"Mother of *Christ*!" Angelo muttered. His legs went all rubbery. He turned and collapsed back against the side of the barn, gasping for breath.

"Yeah, I know," Mark said softly. "I haven't seen many dead people, either." He shook his head. "I can't imagine that I'd ever get used to seeing a stiff."

Angelo opened his mouth to say something, but nothing would come out. All he could think was, how in the hell had this happened? Tony had hired him to kill Phil Belario because Phil was muscling in on some of his business concerns, but Angelo had cut a better deal with Phil and taken out Tony instead. So what the hell was Tony's body doing out here? How had these men found it so fast, and what the fuck were they doing with it?

"I can't—No!—I don't"—but that was all Angelo managed to say before dropping to his knees in the snow and throwing up. He leaned forward, his face almost buried in the puke-stained snow as wave after violent wave squeezed his body.

Mark knelt down beside him and gently placed a hand on Angelo's shoulder.

"Hey, man, take it easy there," he said. "I know seeing something like that's gotta be pretty upsetting, but you have to keep quiet." He hooked his thumb toward the barn and looked around cautiously. "I mean, what if those guys in there hear us?"

Angelo's vision was blurred. Vomit dribbled down his chin as he looked up at Mark and stammered, "We've got to—to get the hell—out—out of here." He ran his forearm across his mouth, smearing the vomit across his cheek as he struggled to stand. "These guys—I don't know how they—I'm not sure what the hell's going on here, but we gotta get moving!"

"Come on, then," Mark said calmly as he eased his arm around Angelo's shoulder and directed him toward the woods. "Lets' get back to my car. We have to find someplace to call the cops—"

"No!" Angelo snarled. He trembled as he walked into the dark shadows under the pines. "No cops! Not while I'm around!"

"Why?" What's the problem?"

"Nothing. I just don't want to—"

He cut himself short when a wash of yellow headlights swept down the driveway. Both men flattened themselves to the ground as a tow truck pulled into the door yard. Angelo's stomach went cold and watery when he saw his broken-down rental car attached to the tow.

"Oh, sweet Jesus! Oh, shit!" he whispered, squinting as he watched the truck pull to a stop in front of the barn door. Two men got out. They were nothing more than black shadows in the gloom as they walked around to the back of the truck and lowered Angelo's car to the ground.

"Say," Mark said close to Angelo's ear. "Isn't that your car?" His breath washed over Angelo's face like warm water, but Angelo could barely nod agreement as he looked in amazement from his car to the dark farmhouse.

"Wait just a fucking second," he said, easing himself up into a crouch and brushing snow from his coat. "Just what the fuck is going on here?"

"Nothing much, Angelo," a cold voice from behind them said suddenly.

Angelo let out a startled shout as both he and Mark spun around to see who had spoken. Silent figures resolved out of the darkness as they came around the back of the barn. Angelo couldn't tell for sure, but it looked like four or five men. As soon as he realized that one of them was Phil Belario, he knew there must be at least half a dozen more staying behind cover with guns trained on him and Mark. Snow crunched underfoot as the group of men moved slowly toward them.

"Sorry 'bout this, kid," Angelo said to Mark, "but I tried to warn you. I think you got yourself into something you ain't gonna like."

"What?" Mark asked, his voice high, constricted. "How do you know these men? And why'd he call you Angelo?"

"Just shut the fuck up and let me do the talking. Maybe I can convince them to let you go." Taking a bold step forward with his arms upraised, he called out, "Hey! Jesus Christ, Phil!" He laughed a high, dry laugh and shook his head as though dazed. "Goddamn, I got to hand it to you. You really had me going there." He looked around casually. "So what the fuck is all this about, anyway?"

"Why Angelo, I'm surprised at you," Phil said in a soft, grating tone of voice. "One of the best in the business, and you haven't figured it out?"

"Wha—? What are you talking about?"

"This is a hit, Angelo," Phil said. "I'm taking you out."

"What the *fuck*?" Angelo took a few steps backward, but he knew damned well there were several armed men behind him to stop him if he turned and ran. "What the fuck you talking about?"

"You're a loose end, Angelo," Phil said. "You worked for Tony—how many years? Ten? Twelve?"

"Yeah—'bout twelve, I guess," Angelo said, fighting the trembling in his voice.

"And when he put a contract out on me, how long did it take you to cut a deal with me, huh? Not even one full day! You betrayed your boss like *that*!" He snapped his fingers with a sound like a gunshot.

"Well, now, wait—wait just a second there, Phil," Angelo stammered. "You and me—we've known each other a long time." His chattering teeth diced every word as he spoke. "I've known you almost as long as I've known Tony, and—to tell you the truth—I couldn't see what he was getting all bent out of shape about. I told him I didn't want the contract, but he insisted on using me, so I figured—you know—that I'd tip you off."

"And it didn't take you very long to decide to double-cross your boss, now, did it?"

Finally at a loss for words, Angelo merely shrugged.

"So you have to see why I can't trust you, Angelo," Phil continued. "I'm taking over *all* of Tony's interests, and I have to have people around me that I *know* are gonna be there for me, one hundred percent."

"But *I* was there for you, Phil! I didn't clip you even though there was a hundred grand in it for me."

"But I have to be sure no one's gonna double-cross me at the first opportunity," Phil said mildly. "You can appreciate my problem, can't you?"

Angelo was silent a moment; then he frowned deeply and said, "So what the fuck—? How'd you set this up."

Phil snickered and smiled broadly. "A little dash of sugar in your gas tank took care of the engine," he said. Before Angelo could say more, Phil reached into his coat and withdrew a pistol equipped with a silencer.

"Recognize this?" he said, holding the weapon up so Angelo could see it against the darkening sky.

"Yeah—I think so," Angelo replied.

"This is the gun you used to clip Tony," Phil said with mock earnestness as he sadly shook his head. "And I'm afraid I'm going to have to use it to silence you. You must have heard of Larry Fiero."

Angelo nodded and took one more step backward. "Yeah, sure. Operates out of Chicago."

"That he does, but just this afternoon you've been out for a little joyride with him. Here yah go, Larry." Phil held the gun out, and Mark stepped forward to take it. "Angelo—I'd like to introduce you to Larry Fiero: Larry—this here's Angelo Martelli."

"End of the line, *Frankie-boy*," Mark said as a wide, mean-looking grin spread across his face. "Or should I say *Overkill*?"

"Fiero! What the—?" Angelo was stopped cold when Mark raised the pistol and aimed it squarely at his forehead.

"That's right," Phil said with a snorting laugh. "And you must know that, like you, Larry's one of the best in the business. Hell!" He sniffed with laughter. "After tonight, he'll be the *best*."

"You lousy motherfucker!" Angelo said, glaring at Mark, who was bracing his right arm with his left hand and taking careful aim.

"And that's the *last* time I'll have to hear you use *that* expression," Mark said.

"Wait just a fucking minute!" Angelo said. "This is goddamned ridiculous. How'd you—why'd you go to all this trouble to get me out here like this?"

Unable to believe that any of this was really happening, he stared earnestly back and forth between Mark and Phil. Mark coolly squinted at him over the circled opening of the gun.

"Christ!" Angelo said, helplessly raising his hands. "You could have whacked me anytime after I left the state. Why'd you set me up like this?"

"Yeah, you lousy motherfucker, I could have," Mark said with a cold steeliness in his voice as he started to apply pressure to the trigger. "But don't you think it's been a lot more fun doing it *my* way?"

Vympyre
by William F. Nolan

Blood. My own. Sweet Christ, my own! Seeping along my chest, soaking my white pullover, a spreading patch of dark red. So this is how it finally ends? With the stake being driven in another inch, each blow of the hammer like a thunderclap ... closing my eyes in Paris with blood everywhere on the tumultuous streets, tasting it on my cool lips, with the guillotine hissing down, severed heads thumping wicker baskets ... King Richard there (was it the Third Crusade?), his battle ax cleaving through the enemy's shoulder, sundering down through muscle, bone, and gristle, and watching the stricken rider topple from the tall back of the sweating gray horse ... in Germany's Black Forest, barefoot, my flesh lacerated by thorn and stone, pursued by the shouting villagers, the flames of their torches wavering, flickering through the trees, a strange, surreal glow ... gulls above the sun swept English Channel as I lower my head toward the child's white, delicately tender throat, with the warm sweet wine of her blood on my tongue. (So many myths about us. They call us creatures of the night, but many of us do not fear the bright sun. In truth, it cannot harm us, although we often hunt at night ... so many myths) ... on the high seat of the carriage, pitching and plunging through moonlit Edinburgh, wheels in thunderous clatter over the narrow, cobbled streets, hatless, my cape blown wild behind me as I lash at the straining team ... the impossibly pink sands of the beach, with a stout sea wind rattling the palm fronds, the waves blood-colored, sunset staining the edge of horizon sky and the young woman's drugged, open, waiting flesh, and my lips drawn back, the needled penetration, and the lost cry of release

... the limo driver's rasping voice above the surging current of Fifth Avenue traffic, recounting the intensity of the police hunt, and my quiet smile there with my back against the cool leather, invincible, the girl's corpse where no one can ever find it, with the puncture marks raw and stark on her skin ... the stifling, musky darkness of the cave, the rough-grained face of the club against my cupped fingers, the fetid tangle of beard cloaking my face, my lips thick and swollen, the hot roar of the saber-tooth still echo-sharp in my mind, and thinking not of the dead, drained female beside me but of the brute eyes of the beast ... the stench of war, of cannon-split corpses, the blue-clad regiment sprawled along the slope, the crackling musket fire in the cool air of Virginia, the stone wall ahead of me in the rushing smoke ... the plush gilt of the Vienna opera house, the music rising in a brassy tide and the tall woman beside me in bloodred velvet as I watch the faint heartbeat in the hollow of her arching throat, flushed ivory from the glow of stage lamps ... the bitter-smoked train pulling into the crowded Istanbul station, the towers of ancient Byzantium rising around me, the heavy leather suitcase bumping my leg, the thick wool suit pressing against my skin, the assignation ahead with the dark-haired little fool who trusts me ... the bone-shuddering shock along my right arm as my sword sparks against the upthrust shield, the gaunt Christian falling back under the fury of my attack, the orgasmic scream of the Roman crowd awaiting another death ... the long, baked sweep of sun-blazed prairie, suddenly quiet now after the vast drumming of herded buffalo, the young, pinto-mounted Indian girl riding easily beside me, with the flushed red darkness of her skin inviting me, challenging me ... standing with Rameses II among the fallen Hittites, with the battle-thirst raging through me like a fever, the sharp odor of spilled blood everywhere, soaking deep into parched Egyptian sands ... the reeking London alehouse along the Thames, the almond-eyed whore in my lap, giggling, her breath foul with drink, her blood-rich neck gleaming in the smoky light ... the slave girl in Athens, kneeling in the dirt at my booted feet, begging me to spare her wretched life as the pointed tip of my sword elicits a single drop of crimson from her fear-taut throat ... at the castle feast, soups spiced with sage and sweet basil, the steaming venison on platters of chased silver, the hearty wines of Auvergne aglow in jeweled flagons, with the Queen facing me across the great table, my eyes on the pale blue tracery of veins above the ruffled lace at her neck ... and, at last, here—with all the long centuries behind me, their kaleidoscopic images flickering across my mind—hunted and found, trapped like an animal under a fog-shrouded sun along the soft Pacific shore, in this fateful year of one thousand nine-hundred ninety-six, as the ultimate anvil-ringing stroke of the hammer sends the stake deep into my rioting heart ... to a sudden, unending darkness.

The final blood is mine.

... And Eight Rabid Pigs
by David Gerrold

When I first became aware of Steven Dhor, he was talking about Christmas. Again.

He hated Christmas—in particular, the enforcement of bliss. "Don't be a scrooge, don't be a grinch, don't be a Satan Claus taking away other people's happiness." That's what his mother used to say to him, and twenty years later, he was still angry.

There were a bunch of them sitting around the bar, writers mostly, but a few hangers-on and fringies, sucking up space and savoring the wittiness of the conversation. Bread Bryan loomed all tall and spindly like a frontier town undertaker. Railroad Martin perched like a disgruntled Buddha—he wore the official Railroad Martin uniform, T-shirt, jeans, and potbelly. George Finger was between wives and illnesses, he was enjoying just being alive. Goodman Hallmouth pushed by, snapping at bystanders and demanding to know where Harold Parnell had gone; he was going to punch him in the kneecap.

"Have a nice day, Goodman," someone called.

"Don't tell me to have a nice day," he snarled back. "I'll have any damn kind of a day I want."

"See—" said Dhor, nodding at Hallmouth as he savaged his way out again. "That's honest, at least. Goodman might not fit our pictures of the polite way to behave, but at least he doesn't bury us in another layer of dishonest treacle."

"Yep, Goodman only sells honest treacle," said Railroad Martin.

"Where do you get lie-detector tests for treacle?" Bread Bryan asked, absolutely deadpan.

"There's gotta be a story in that—" mused George Finger.

"—But I just can't put my *finger* on it," said one of the nameless fringies. This was followed by a nanosecond of annoyed silence. Somebody else would have to explain to the fringie that a) that joke was older than God, b) it hadn't been that funny the first time it had been told, and c) he didn't have the right to tell it. Without looking up, Bread Bryan simply said, "That's one."

Steven Dhor said, "You want to know about treacle? Christmas is treacle. It starts the day after Halloween. You get two months of it. It's an avalanche of sugar and bullshit. I suppose they figure that if they put enough sugar into the recipe, you won't notice the taste of the bullshit."

"Don't mince words, Stevie. Tell us what you really think."

"Okay, I will." Dhor had abruptly caught fire. His eyes were blazing. "Christmas—at least the way we celebrate it—is a perversion. It's not a holiday; it's a brainwashing." That's when I started paying *real* attention.

"Every time you see a picture of Santa Claus," Dhor said, "you're being indoctrinated into the Christian ethic. If you're good, you get a reward, a present; if you're bad, you get a lump of coal. One day, you figure it out; you say, hey—Santa Claus is really Mommy and Daddy. And when you tell them you figured it out, what do they do? They tell you about God. If you're good, you get to go to heaven; if you're bad, you go to hell. Dying isn't anything to be afraid of, it's just another form of Christmas. And Santa Claus is God—the only difference is that at least, Santa gives you something tangible. But if there ain't no Santa, then why should we believe in God either?"

Bread Bryan considered Dhor's words dispassionately. Bread Bryan considered everything dispassionately. Despite his nickname, even yeast couldn't make him rise. Railroad Martin swirled his beer around in his glass; he didn't like being upstaged by someone else's anger— even when it was anger as good as this. George Finger, on the other hand, was delighted with the effrontery of the idea.

"But wait—this is the nasty part. We've taken God out of Christmas. You can't put up angels anymore, nor a cross, nor even a crèche. No religious symbols of any kind, because even though everything closes down on Christmas day, we still have to pretend it's a non-secular celebration. So, the only decorations you can put up are Santa Claus, reindeer, snowmen, and elves. We've replaced the actual holiday with a third-generation derivation, including its own pantheon of saints and demons: Rudolph, Frosty, George Bailey, Scrooge, and the Grinch—Santa Claus is not only most people's first experience of God," Dhor continued, "it's now their *only* experience of God."

Dhor was warming to his subject. Clearly this was not a casual thought for him. He'd been stewing this over for some time. He began describing how the country had become economically addicted to Christmas. "We've turned it into a capitalist feeding frenzy—so much so that some retailers depend on Christmas for fifty percent of their annual business. I think we should all 'Just Say No to Christmas.' Or at least—for God's sake—remember whose birthday it is and celebrate it appropriately, by doing things to feed the poor and heal the sick."

A couple of the fringies began applauding then, but Dhor just looked across at them with a sour expression on his face. "Don't applaud," he said. "Just do it."

"Do you?" someone challenged him. "How do you celebrate Christmas?"

"I don't give presents," Dhor finally admitted. "I take the money I would normally spend on presents and give it to the Necessities of Life Program of the AIDS Project of Los Angeles. It's more in keeping with the spirit." That brought another uncomfortable silence. It's one thing to do the performance of saint—most writers are pretty good at it—but when you catch one actually *doing* something unselfish and noteworthy, well . . . it's pretty damned embarrassing for everyone involved.

Fortunately, Dhor was too much in command of the situation to let the awkward moment lie there unmolested. He trampled it quickly. "The thing is, I don't see any way to stop the avalanche of bullshit. The best we can do is ride it."

"How?" George Finger asked.

"Simple. By adding a new piece to the mythology—a new saint in the pantheon. *Satan Claus*." There was that name again. Dhor lowered his voice. "See, if Santa Claus is really another expression of God, then there has to be an equally powerful expression of the Devil too. There has to be a balance."

"Satan Claus. . . ." Bread Bryan considered the thought. "Mm. He must be the fellow who visited my house last year. He didn't give me anything I wanted. And I could have used the coal too. It gets *cold* in Wyoming."

"No. Satan Claus doesn't work that way," said Dhor. "He doesn't give things. He takes them away. The suicide rate goes up around Christmastime. That's no accident. That's Satan Claus. He comes and takes your soul straight to hell."

Then Railroad Martin added a wry thought—"He drives a black sleigh, and he lands in your basement." — and then they were all doing it.

"The sleigh is drawn by eight rabid pigs—big ugly razorbacks," said Dhor. "They have iridescent red eyes, which burn like smoldering embers—they *are* embers, carved right out of the floor of hell. Late at night, as you're lying all alone in your cold, cold bed, you can hear them snuffling and snorting in the ground beneath your house. Their hooves are polished black ebony, and they carve up the ground like knives."

Dhor was creating a legend while his audience sat and listened enraptured. He held up his hands as if outlining the screen on which he was about to paint the rest of his picture. The group fell silent. I had to admire him, in spite of myself. He lowered his voice to a melodramatic stage whisper, "Satan Claus travels underground through dark rumbling passages filled with rats and ghouls. He carries a long black whip, and he stands in the front of the sleigh, whipping the pigs until the blood streams from their backs. Their screams are the despairing sounds of the eternally tormented."

"And he's dressed all in black," suggested Bread Bryan. "Black leather. With silver buckles and studs and rivets."

"Oh, hell," said George Finger. "*Everybody* dresses like that in my neighborhood."

"Yes, black leather," agreed Martin, ignoring the aside. "But it's made from the skins of reindeer."

"Whales," said Bryan. "Baby whales."

Dhor shook his head. "The leather is made from the skins of those whose souls he's taken. He strips it off their bodies before he lets them die. The skins are dyed black with the sins of the owners, and trimmed with red-dyed rat fur. Satan Claus has long gray hair, all shaggy and dirty and matted; and he has a long gray beard, equally dirty. There are crawly things living in his hair and beard. And his skin is leprous and covered with pustules and running sores. His features are deformed and misshapen. His nose is a bulbous monstrosity, swollen and purple. His lips are blue, and his breath smells like the grave. His fingernails are black with filth, but they're as sharp as diamonds. He can claw up through the floor to yank you down into his demonic realm."

"Wow," said Bread Bryan. "I'm moving up to the second floor."

The cluster of listeners shuddered at Dhor's vivid description. It was suddenly a little too heavy for the spirit of the conversation. A couple of them tried to make jokes, but they fell embarrassingly flat.

Finally, George Finger laughed gently and said, "I think you've made him out to be too threatening, Steve. For most of us, Satan Claus just takes our presents away and leaves changeling presents instead."

"Ahh," said Railroad. "That explains why I never get anything I want."

"How can you say that? You get T-shirts every year," said Bread.

"Yes, but I always want a tuxedo."

After the laughter died down, George said, "The

changeling presents are made by the satanic elves, of course."

"Right," said Dhor. He picked up on it immediately. "All year long, the satanic elves work in their secret laboratories underneath the South Pole, creating the most horrendous ungifts they can think of. Satan Claus whips them unmercifully with a cat-o'-nine-tails; he screams at them and beats them and torments them endlessly. The ones who don't work hard enough, he tosses into the pit of eternal fire. The rest of them work like little demons—of course they do; that's what they are— to manufacture all manner of curses and spells and hexes. All the bad luck that you get every year—it comes straight from hell, a gift from Satan Claus himself." Dhor cackled wickedly, an impish burst of glee, and everybody laughed with him.

But he was on a roll. He'd caught fire with this idea and was beginning to build on it now. "The terrible black sleigh isn't a sleigh as much as it's a hearse. And it's filled with bulging sacks filled with bad luck of all kinds. Illnesses, miscarriages, strokes, cancers, viruses, flu germs, birth defects, curses of all kinds. Little things like broken bones and upset stomachs. Big things like impotence, frigidity, sterility. Parkinson's disease, cerebral palsy, multiple sclerosis, encephalitis, everything that stops you from enjoying life."

"I think you're onto something," said Railroad. "I catch the flu right after Christmas, every year. I haven't been to a New Year's party in four years. At least now I have someone to blame."

Dhor nodded and explained, "Satan Claus knows if you've been bad or good—if you've been bad in any way, he comes and takes a little more joy out of your life, makes it harder for you to want to be good. Just as Santa is your first contact with God, Satan Claus is your first experience of evil. Satan Claus is the devil's revenge on Christmas. He's the turd in the punch bowl. He's the tantrum at the party. He's the birthday spoiler. I think we're telling our children only half the story. It's not enough to tell them that Santa will be good to them.

We have to let them know who's planning to be bad to them."

For a while, there was silence, as we all sat around and let the disturbing quality of Dhor's vision sink into our souls. Every so often someone would shudder as he thought of some new twist, some piece of embroidery.

But it was George Finger's speculation that ended the conversation. He said, "Actually, this might be a dangerous line of thought, Steve. Remember the theory that the more believers a god has, the more powerful he becomes? I mean, it's a joke right now, but aren't you summoning a new god into existence this way?"

"Yes, George," Dhor replied, grinning impishly, "There *is* a Satan Clause in the holy contract. But I don't think you need to worry. Our belief in him is insufficient. And unnecessary. We can't create Satan Claus—because he already exists. He came into being when Santa Claus was created. A thing automatically creates its opposite, just by its very existence. You know that. The stronger Santa Claus gets, the stronger Satan Claus must become in opposition."

Steven had been raised in a very religious household. His grandmother had taught him that for every act of good, there has to be a corresponding evil. Therefore, if you have heaven, you have to have hell. If you have a God, you have to have a devil. If there are angels, then there have to be demons. Cherubs and imps. Saints and damned. Nine circles of hell—nine circles of heaven. "Better be careful, George! Satan Claus is watching." And then he laughed fiendishly. I guess he thought he was being funny.

I forgot about Steven Dhor for a few weeks. I was involved in another one of those abortive television projects—it's like doing drugs; you think you can walk away from them, but you can't. Someone offers you a needle and you run to stick it in your arm. And then they jerk you around for another six weeks or six months, and then cut it off anyway—and one morning you wake up and find you're unemployed again. The money's spent, and you've wasted another big chunk of your time and your energy and your enthusiasm on something that will never be broadcast or ever see print. And your credential has gotten that much poorer because you have nothing to show for your effort except another dead baby. You get too many of those dead babies on your resume, and the phone stops ringing altogether. But I love the excitement, that's why I stay so close to Hollywood—

Then one Saturday afternoon, Steven Dhor read a new story at Kicking The Hobbit—the all science-fiction bookstore that used to be in Santa Monica. I'm sure he saw me come in, but he was so engrossed in the story he was reading to the crowd that he didn't recognize me. *". . . The children believed that they could hear the hooves of the huge black pigs scraping through the darkness. They could hear the snuffling and snorting of their hot breaths. The pigs were foaming at the mouth, grunting and bumping up against each other as they pulled the heavy sled through the black tunnels under the earth. The steel runners of the huge carriage sliced across the stones, striking sparks and ringing with a knife-edged note that shrieked like a metal banshee.*

"And the driver—his breath steaming in the terrible cold—shouted their names as he whipped them, 'On, damn you, on! You children of war! On Pustule and Canker and Sickness and Gore! On Monster and Seizure and Bastard and Whore. Drive on through the darkness! Break through and roar!" Dhor's voice rose softly as he read these harrowing passages to his enraptured audience.

I hung back away from the group, listening in appreciation and wonder. Dhor had truly caught the spirit of the Christmas obscenity. By the very act of saying the name aloud in public, Dhor was not only giving his power to Satan Claus, he was daring the beast to visit him on Christmas Eve.

". . . And in the morning," Dhor concluded, *"—there were many deep, knifelike scars in the soft dark earth beneath their bedroom windows. The ground was churned and broken, and there were black sooty smudges on the glass. . . . But of their father, there was not a sign. And by this, the children knew that Satan Claus was in-*

deed real. And they never ever laughed again, as long as they lived."

The small crowd applauded enthusiastically, and then they crowded in close for autographs. Dhor's grin spread across his cherubic face like a pink glow. He basked in all the attention and the approval of the fans; it warmed him like a deep red bath. He'd found something that touched a nerve in the audience—now he responded to them. Something had taken root in his soul.

I saw Dhor several more times that year. And everywhere, he was reading that festering story aloud again: *"Christmas lay across the land like a blight, and once again, the children huddled in their beds and feared the tread of heavy boot steps in the dark. . . ."* He'd look up from the pages, look across the room at his audience with that terrible impish twinkle and then turn back to his reading with renewed vigor. *". . . Millie and little Bob shivered in their nightshirts as Daddy pulled them onto his lap. He smelled of smoke and coal and too much whiskey. His face was blue and scratchy with the stubble of his beard, and his heavy flannel shirt scratched their cheeks uncomfortably. 'Why are you trembling?' he asked. 'There's nothing to be afraid of. I'm just going to tell you about the Christmas spirit. His name is Satan Claus, and he drives a big black sled shaped like a hearse. It's pulled by eight big black pigs with smoldering red eyes. Satan Claus stands in the front of the carriage and rides like the whirlwind, lashing at the boars with a stinging whip. He beats them until the blood pours from their backs and they scream like the souls of the damned—'"*

In the weeks that followed, he read it at the fundraiser/taping for Mike Hodel's literacy project. He read it at the Pasadena Library's Horror/Fantasy Festival. He read it at the Thanksgiving weekend Lost-Con. He read it on Hour 25, and he had tapes made for sale to anyone who wanted one. Steven was riding the tiger. Exploiting it. Whipping it with his need for notoriety.

" 'Satan Claus comes in the middle of the night—he scratches at your window, and leaves sooty marks on the glass. Wherever there's fear, wherever there's madness— there you'll find Satan Claus as well. He comes through

*the wall like smoke and stands at the foot of your bed
with eyes like hot coals. He stands there and watches you.
His hair is long and gray and scraggly. His beard has
terrible little creepy things living in it. You can see them
crawling around. Sometimes, he catches one of the bugs
that lives in his beard, and he eats it alive. If you wake
up on Christmas Eve, he'll be standing there waiting for
you. If you scream, he'll grab you and put you in his
hearse. He'll carry you straight away to hell. If you get
taken to hell before you die, you'll never get out. You'll
never be redeemed by baby Jesus. . . .'"*

And then the Christmas issue of *Ominous* magazine
came out, and *everybody* was reading it.

*"Little Bob began to weep, and Millie reached out to
him, trying to comfort his tears; but Daddy gripped her
arm firmly and held her at arm's length. 'Now, Millie—
don't you help him. Bobby has to learn how to be a man.
Big boys don't cry. If you cry, then for sure Satan Claus
will come and get you. He won't even put you in his
hearse. He'll just eat you alive. He'll pluck you out of
your bed and crunch your bones in his teeth. He has teeth
as sharp as razors and jaws as powerful as an ax. First
he'll bite your arms off, and then he'll bite off your legs—
and then he'll even bite off your little pink peepee. And
you better believe that'll hurt. And then, finally, when he's
bitten off every other part of you, finally he'll bite your head
off! So you mustn't cry. Do you understand me!' Daddy
shook Bobby as hard as he could, so hard that Bobby's
head bounced back and forth on his shoulders and Bobby
couldn't help himself; he bawled as loud as he could."*

People were calling each other on the phone and asking if they'd seen the story and wasn't it the most frightening story they'd ever heard? It was as if they were
enrolling converts into a new religion. They were all having
much too much fun playing with the legend of Satan Claus,
adding to it, building it—giving their power of belief to
Father Darkness, the Christmas evil . . . as if by naming
the horror, they might somehow remain immune to it.

*" 'Listen! Maybe you can hear him even now? Feel
the ground rumble? No, that's not a train. That's Father
Darkness—Satan Claus. Yes, he's always there. Do you*

*hear his horn? Do you hear the ugly snuffling of the
eight rabid pigs? He's coming closer. Maybe this year he's
coming for you. This year, you'd better stay asleep all
night long. Maybe this year, I won't be able to stop him
from getting you!' "*

Then some right-wing religious zealot down in Orange
County saw the story; his teenage son had borrowed a
copy of the magazine from a friend; so of course the
censorship issue came bubbling right up to the surface
like a three-day corpse in a swamp.

Dhor took full advantage of the situation. He ended
up doing a public reading on the front steps of the Los
Angeles Central Library. The *LA Times* printed his picture, and a long article about this controversial new
young fantasy writer who was challenging the outmoded
literary conventions of our times. Goodman Hallmouth
showed up of course—he'd get up off his deathbed for
a media event—and made his usual impassioned statement on how Dhor was exposing the hypocrisy of Christmas in America.

*"The children trembled in their cold, cold beds, afraid
to close their eyes, afraid to fall asleep. They knew that
Father Darkness would soon be there, standing at the foot
of their beds and watching them fiercely to see if they
were truly sleeping or just pretending."*

Of course, it all came to a head at Art and Lydia's
Christmas Eve party. They always invited the whole
community, whoever was in town. You not only got to
see all your friends, but all your enemies as well. You
had to be there, to find out what people were saying
about you behind your back.

Lydia must have spent a week cooking. She had huge
platters piled with steaming turkey, ham, roast beef, lasa-
gna, mashed potatoes, sweet potatoes, tomatoes in basil
and dill, corn on the cob, pickled cabbage, four kinds of
salad, vegetable casseroles, quiche, and deviled eggs. She
had plates of cookies and chocolates everywhere; the bath-
tub was filled with ice and bottles of imported beer and
cans of Coca-Cola. Art brought in champagne and wine
and imported mineral water for Goodman Hallmouth.

And then they invited the seven-year locusts.

All the writers, both serious and not-so, showed up; some of them wearing buttons that said, "Turn down a free meal, get thrown out of the Guild." Artists too, but they generally had better table manners. One year, two of them got trampled in the rush to the buffet. After that, Lydia started weeding out the guest list.

This year, the unofficial theme of the party was "Satan Claus is coming to town." The tree was draped in black crepe and instead of an angel on top, there was a large black bat. Steven Dhor even promised to participate in a "summoning."

"Little Bob still whimpered softly. He wiped his nose on his sleeve. Finally, Millie got out of her bed and crept softly across the floor and slipped into bed next to little Bob. She put her arms around him and held him close and began whispering as quietly as she could. 'He can't hurt us if we're good. So we'll just be as good as we can. Okay. We'll pray to baby Jesus and ask him to watch out for us, okay?' Little Bob nodded and sniffed, and Millie began to pray for the both of them. . . ."

I got there late, I had other errands to run, it's always that way on the holidays.

Steven Dhor was holding court in the living room, sitting on the floor in the middle of a rapt group of wanna-bes and never-wases; he was embellishing the legend of Satan Claus. He'd already announced that he was planning to do a collection of Satan Claus stories, or perhaps even a novel telling the whole story of Satan Claus from beginning to end. Just as St. Nicholas had been born out of good deeds, so had Satan Claus been forged from the evil that stalked the earth on the night before Jesus' birth.

According to legend—legend according to Dhor—the devil was powerless to stop the birth of baby Jesus, but that didn't stop him from raising hell in his own way. On the eve of the very first Christmas, the devil turned loose all his imps upon the world and told them to steal out among the towns and villages of humankind and spread chaos and dismay among all the world's children. Leave no innocent being unharmed. It was out of this beginning that Satan Claus came forth. At first he was small, but he grew. Every year, the belief of the children gave him more and more power.

"The children slept fitfully. They tossed and turned and made terrible little sounds of fear. Their dreams were filled with darkness and threats. They held onto each other all night long. They were awakened by a rumbling deep within the earth, the whole house rolled uneasily—"

Dhor had placed himself so he could see each new arrival come in the front door. He grinned up at each one in a conspiratorial grin of recognition and shared evil, as if to say, "See? It works. Everybody loves it." I had to laugh. He didn't understand. He probably never would. He was so in love with himself and his story and the power of his words, he missed the greater vision. I turned away and went prowling through the party in search of food and drink.

"They came awake together, Millie and little Bob. They came awake with a gasp—they were too frightened to move.

"Something was tapping softly on the bedroom window. It scraped slowly at the glass. But they were both too afraid to look."

Lydia was dressed in a black witch's costume, she even wore a tall pointed hat. She was in the kitchen stirring a huge cauldron of hot mulled wine and cackling like the opening scene in *Macbeth,* "Double, double toil and trouble, fire burn and cauldron bubble—" and having a wonderful time of it. For once, she was enjoying one of her own parties. She waved her wooden spoon around her head like a mallet, laughing in maniacal glee.

Christmas was a lot more fun without all those sappy little elves and angels, all those damned silver bells and the mandatory choral joy of the endless hallelujahs. Steven Dhor had give voice to the rebellious spirit, had found a way to battle the ennui of a month steeped in Christmas cheer. These people were going to enjoy every nasty moment of it.

"A huge dark shape loomed like a wall at the foot of their bed. It stood there, blocking the dim light of the hallway. They could hear its uneven heavy breath sounding like the inhalations of a terrible beast. They could

smell the reek of death and decay. Millie put her hand across little Bob's mouth to keep him from crying.

" 'Oh, please don't hurt us,' she cried. She couldn't help herself. 'Please—' "

I circulated once through the party, taking roll—seeing who was being naughty, who was being nice. Goodman Hallmouth was muttering darkly about the necessity for revenge. Writers, he said, are the Research and Development Division for the whole human race; the only *specialists* in revenge in the whole world. Bread Bryan was standing around looking mournful. George Finger wasn't here, he was back in the hospital again. Railroad Martin was showing off a new T-shirt; it said, "Help, I'm trapped inside a T-shirt."

And, of course, there was the usual coterie of fans and unknowns—I knew them by their fannish identites: the Elephant, the Undertaker, the Blob, the Duck.

"And then—a horrible thing happened. A second shape appeared behind the first, bigger and darker. Its crimson eyes blazed with unholy rage. A cold wind swept through the room. A low groaning noise, somewhere between a moan and an earthquake resounded through the house like a scream. Black against a darker black, the first shape turned and saw what stood behind it. It began to shrivel and shrink. The greater darkness enveloped the lesser, pulled it close, and—did something horrible. In the gloom, the children could not clearly see; but they heard every terrible crunch and gurgle. They heard the choking gasps and felt the floor shudder with the weight.

"Millie screamed then, so did little Bob. They closed their eyes and screamed as hard as they could. They screamed for their very lives. They screamed and screamed and kept on screaming—"

Steven Dhor got very drunk that night—first on his success, then on Art and Lydia's wine. About two in the morning, he became abusive and started telling people what he really thought of them. At first, people thought he was kidding, but then he called Hallmouth a poseur and a phony, and Lydia had to play referee. Finally, Bread Bryan and Railroad Martin drove him home and poured him into bed. He passed out in the car, only rousing himself occasionally to vomit out the window.

The next morning, Steven Dhor was gone.

Art stopped by his place on Christmas morning to see if he was all right; but Dhor didn't answer his knock. Art walked around the back and banged on the back door too. Still no answer. He peeked in the bedroom window, and the bed was disheveled and empty, so Art assumed that Steven had gotten up early and left, perhaps to spend Christmas with a friend. But he didn't know him well enough to guess who he might have gone to see. Nobody did.

Later, the word began to spread that he was missing. His landlady assumed he'd skipped town to avoid paying his rent. Goodman Hallmouth said he thought Steven had gone home to visit his family in Florida, and would probably return shortly. Bread Bryan said that Steve had mentioned taking a sabbatical, a cross-country hitchhiking trip. Railroad Martin filed a missing person report, but after a few routine inquiries, the police gave up the investigation. George Finger suggested that Satan Claus had probably taken him, but under the circumstances, it was considered a rather tasteless joke and wasn't widely repeated.

But . . . George was right.

Steven Dhor had come awake at the darkest moment of the night, stumbling out of a fitful and uncomfortable sleep. He rubbed his eyes and sat up in bed—and then he saw me standing there, watching him. Waiting.

I'd been watching him and waiting for him since the day he'd first spoken my name aloud, since the moment he'd first given me shape and form and the power of his belief. I'd been hungry for him ever since.

He was delicious. I crunched his bones like breadsticks. I drank his blood like wine. The young ones are always tasty. I savored the flavor of his soul for a long long time.

And, of course, before I left, I made sure to leave the evidence of my visit. Art saw it, but he never told anyone: sooty smudges on the bedroom window, and the ground beneath it all torn up and churned, as if by the milling of many heavy-footed creatures.

Bringing It Along
by A. R. Morlan

Oily sweat pooled in the shallow cup of skin below Carey's larynx; indifferently she ran her right forefinger through the sweat, tracing invisible paths along the swell of each breast and up under her chin. Eyes shut tight against the writhing shadows smeared on the skin of the tent, Carey told herself that this time, she wouldn't give in to Gary, wouldn't *freak* again.

I'm in another part of the world, another place, another time, she tried to remind herself, while listening to the skabble and screech of the birds beyond the tent, the arrhthmic breathing of the tropical forest around her (odd-leaved trees and scrubby bushes rubbing against each other, snicking in the warm, moist trade winds) . . . but the maddening sense of sameness, of never leaving home at all persisted anyhow.

Wisconsin was thousands of miles, and Carey didn't know how many time zones away, yet as she lay in the thin-skinned tent Gary had set up that morning, eyes crumpled in a wet-lashed line across her face, Carey couldn't help but think that the differences of time and location had been overcome, bridged with her fear.

Stiff and warm in her hiking clothes—save for the ankle-killing heavy boots Gary had bought for her—Carey tried holding her breath, ears straining for the sound of Gary's soft breathing, but the chitter of birds *(bats? The booklet in the travel bureau said they have* bats *here)* and the chitinous snapping of foliage in the distance masked any smaller noises around her.

Letting out breath in a shaky rush, Carey ever so slowly ran her left hand along the bumpy air mattress, a half inch at a time, feeling for Gary. The brightly colored booklet in the London Square Mall travel-bureau stand down in Eau Claire had warned—in a breezy, reassuringly offhand manner—that centipedes and other crawlies flourished in the more primitive areas of the islands, but they could be avoided with proper care. Carey didn't know if they could squirm into the tent; slither up through paper-thin cracks, to scuttle along the velour surface of the air mattress, toward warm flesh ... but turning on the flashlight near her right side would only make it worse. Better to quickly brush a hand against some recoiling, swiftly gone thing, rather than illuminate the tent and see dozens of slithering, slimy *things* adhering to the tent skin, ready to drop down on her when shaken loose by the vibrations of her screams.

Carey inched her arm out to its full extended length—no Gary. Placing her left arm over her stomach, she rubbed her tense, cramping abdomen, and told herself, *The tent* is *big, plenty big ... leave it to Gary to go for the biggest damn tent in Honolulu. Just like that time in the Blue Hills last summer. Stupid tent was as big as a Wausau Home* ... As she swallowed, Carey's throat made a little clicking noise, while she extended her blistered stocking feet forward, toes pointing sharply toward the far wall of the tent, until her right foot came in contact with something warm, rounded, and hairy.

Gotcha, she thought, gently feeling the smooth roundness with her sore-soled foot, almost saying aloud, "Gary?" before she heard the steady drone, a new yet comfortable sound within the tent.

Tweetie Pie. At first she'd balked at the thought of bringing along their cat on the long ride from the Eau Claire airport to their connecting flight, and beyond; the baggage handlers might lose his white plastic-and-metal cage, or let him freeze or die of thirst. But Tweetie was a hardy little stinker; he'd done fine up in the Blue Hills, hadn't he? Not so much as one picked-up flea, or a single hopping flea. At the airport he'd curled up into a gray-striped and white-pawed ball, broad, curved back exposed to the noise and confusion beyond his cage, nose tucked in close to his tail.

Just as he was curled up now, an incredibly hard little

ball of cat; only his purr revealed that he was a living animal. Relaxing slightly, Carey gently caressed his back; his body was so sleekly fat that even the tiny knobs of his spine were coated, hidden. But her foot was so blistered and tender that Carey was surprised she'd been able to feel Tweetie Pie in the first place. The pressure of Tweetie's flesh against her own was soon unbearable, so she shifted her foot so that the ridge of skin along the side of her foot (near the little toe) barely rested against the sleeping cat. Just enough contact to assure her that she wasn't all alone, helpless, under an alien sky, while resting on strange, hostile soil.

Dipping her fingertip in the cup of sweat over her neck, she drew tight circles along her collarbones, not unlike those she drew upon her flesh *last* August, in that cow-barn of a tent in the Blue Hills as she listened with gritted teeth to the song of the displaced killdeer near their tent. . . .

"Caw-wee, Caw-*wee*," the infernal thing called, mournful and shivery-thin in the darkness. Beside her, Gary had mocked, " 'Caw-wee, Car-*ree*' . . . they're calling for you, Car-ree—"

She had rolled over, shielding Tweetie with her flopping breasts, holding the cat tight against the chill inside her. Gary knew she hated the cry of the killdeer; hated that aching cry which hung like morning mist over the ponds and lakes of Ewerton, their hometown. For those birds seemed to be calling *her,* chanting her name in that eerie whistle-caw that sent shivers up and down her like someone tracing thin lines along her spine with long, sharply pointed fingernails—Freddy Kruger gone avian.

The cry of those thin-legged, skittering birds was better suited to shrill keening winds and sopping-wet cold marshland—not the towering pine-scented hills around them, not the gentle rustle of needles rubbing needles high above them.

To Carey, the killdeer was a thing of the water, of spongy ground and instability . . . and she hated it when they taunted her by name.

She had pressed Tweetie ever closer, bending her

head down close to his purring warmth, trying to drown out that mournful cry—and in so doing, she missed hearing Gary slither out of the tent, to pad around outside and come around to her side. . . .

The travel brochure promised mild temperatures in Hawaii—by Midwest dog-days standard—a mean temperature of only 74.9 blissful degrees, with an August high of a measly 78.3 tempered by northeast trade winds . . . but when they deplaned in Honolulu, it was a dizzying 99 degrees and the announcer for the early evening news show they caught in their motel room was at a loss to explain the heat wave.

Gary, toweling off after a quick shower—he'd left on his lei, a floppy purple thing that bounced on his bony chest—said matter-of-factly, "Talk about bringing it *along,*" before padding back into the bathroom, leaving deeper-tan wet footprints on the light sand-colored carpeting. Carey stopped unpacking long enough to shout back, "What?" then continued to place newly bought J.C. Penney Hawaiian print shirts into the dresser drawers. The idiocy of the shirts hit her then; thousands of dollars spent to come to Paradise, plus whatever Gary'd spent to bribe the airport, taxi, and motel people into letting Tweetie bypass quarantine (oh, Gary claimed, there wasn't any quarantine for house pets, but Carey knew better—yet remained silent), and they'd brought along mainland Hawaiian shirts.

From the echoing bathroom, Gary shouted back, "Your fault, y'know," before turning on his blow-dryer. From the bathroom doorway, she watched Gary wave the dryer at his close-clipped coarse hair, until he noticed her and said, "The truth, y'know. No use running from the heat, it was bound to find us somewhere."

"You talk like an ass," she said flatly, bending down to pick up Tweetie and cuddle him close. A shield between herself and Gary. He'd never hit her while she held the cat in her arms.

Gary aimed the dryer at her for a second, a blast of hot dry air which dried the frown onto her face. "Just like you couldn't hide from them killdeers ... re-*mem*-ber, Car-wee?"

She refused to satisfy him with tears or shudders of memory. Turning off the dryer, setting it on the edge of the sink, Gary leaned in toward the mirror, his lei swinging from his neck over the bowl of the sink. She wished the lei would have pulled the hair dryer into the sink ... if it had still been filled with water.

As Gary checked over his hairdo, patting stray hairs into place (he used hair spray, even on his mustache, something Carey didn't like to think about too much), he continued. "Yeah, that killdeer musta been gunnin' for you ... was a long way from where he was 'sposed to be, huh? Maybe he was sweet on Car-wee—"

Holding Tweetie like a baby, his head tucked under her chin, Carey had left the room, unwilling to hear Gary rehash the Blue Hills debacle yet another time ... but within the week, Gary found a way to get even with her.

First, he grew tired of Honolulu; the *luau* at the motel was a bore, *poi* reminded him of instant oatmeal, leis were for jerks, and he couldn't find anything worth buying to send home to their friends in Ewerton. Likewise, Wahiawa, Waipahu, and Kaneoke were "nothing joints;" only fit for *Hawaii Five-O* cultists, in Gary's expert, world-traveler opinion. Gary, who had yet to set foot in Canada; Gary, who considered a jaunt down to the London Square Mall true adventure. So they'd crossed the Kaiwi Channel by private plane (Carey prayed their credit card would cover Gary's bored spell), but Molokai was likewise "*Magnum P.I.* country," and they finally found themselves back in their original motel, looking out the big window at the countless white-sided buildings below. By that time, their leis were long wilted, tossed away in neat motel garbage-basket liners.

Gradually Carey began to pack away the printed JC Penney shirts, decreasing the number of them resting in Gary's side of the dresser. Then came the morning, yesterday morning, when Gary came back to their room, arms loaded with bags from some sporting goods store a taxi driver had recommended. From the size of the stash Gary brought back with him, the taxi driver had to be getting commissions for steering customers to the store. Carey had been half glad to see Gary charged up over something, until he pulled out a pair of hiking boots for her. . . .

Raindrops *plashed* against the tent; in her mind's eye Carey pictured the droplets darkening the nylon skin, sending tiny writhing shadows slithering down to the ground. Rubbing her aching foot against Tweetie's solid back, Carey decided that Gary had to be somewhere at the far end of the tent—Tweetie liked to sleep near their feet (in his good moods, Gary called the cat Tweetus-Feetus), and since *she* hadn't felt the cat until just a few minutes ago . . .

Knowing—or at least being *almost* sure—where Gary was comforted Carey, made her relax muscle by sore muscle. The heat might have been the same; the fierce, uncharacteristic humidity might have come with them, but *this* time, in *this* patch of wild flora, things were going to be different. Not at all like that time in the Blue Hills, when Gary goaded her into going to pieces, "pussy out," as he'd laughingly told all their friends later on that summer.

I have you beat this time, her mind shouted at him. *You can't pull the same stunt twice, buster.* For a moment, Carey felt galled by Gary's nerve; he'd gone through a lot of trouble (climbing around in brutal heat, plowing through strange plants, risking contact with dozens of scuttling bugs) just to bring her to a place in Hawaii that would remind her of that weekend in the Blue Hills. All because she hadn't *appreciated* his joke the first time around. . . .

Lying under the trees in the Hills, wishing that they'd never come to Rusk County, let along the infernal Blue Hills, Carey had pillowed her head on Tweetie's flank, until the cat's soothing purr lulled her into an uneasy sleep . . . while Gary was circling the tent, seeking the best spot, waiting until he was certain she was deep in sleep—

" '*Car-wee!*' " The noise was monstrous. The mama killdeer of all killdeers crying just scant *inches* from her unprotected head. Tweetie jumped up in a scrabble of claws and bushy fur; her head and arms were clawed before she was fully awake. And she'd done some clawing of her own ... By the time she was aware of what had really happened, she'd somehow ripped the tough shell of the domed tent, her nails broken and jagged— while all around her the Hills echoed with Gary's laughter. Face flushed red up to his hairline, he was barely able to wheeze, " '*C-cu-car-weeeeee!*' " before she came after him, talons out and ready to scratch that convulsing face to an oozing pulp.

Afterward, it was weeks before she talked to him, let alone let him touch her again. . . .

The rain's drone softened, faded to a steady drip drip off the broad stiff leaves nearby. Through her eyelids, Carey could see the first red-black haze of predawn light. True, Gary had gone through a lot of trouble (down to making sure Tweetie was nearby, to shred her face again) to make the terror keen enough to disarm her, but Carey smiled a sweat-oiled grin in the darkness, telling herself that the fact that they were on some little bird-dropping of an island off the coast of Kahoolawe wasn't going to make a bit of difference. *Fool me once, shame on you, fool me twice, shame on me.* She'd heard that line on an old *Star Trek* rerun; it would've been more fitting coming from Jack Lord's lips, or maybe Magnum's pal Higgins, but no matter who said it first, the expression was apt.

And Gary had hired a helicopter to fly the three of them out to this godforsaken area of rock and scruffy vegetation, just to make sure that there would be no hopping in the car and driving back to Dean county, and home, and supportive friends coming when he pulled his little killdeer joke again. And they'd toted in enough food to last three days, until the chopper pilot came back to pick them up. Time enough to rub it in, laugh until his jaws ached over her "pussy" reaction. . . .

As her eyelids let in more and more reddish light,

Carey tensed again; foot rubbing slightly against Twee-tie's unmoving flank or back or whatever for luck, wait-ing for Gary's expertly mimicked, " ' *Car-wee!* ' "

Oh, she'd noticed that devil glint in his eyes as they'd tramped through bushes and low-branched trees to reach this clearing. And the way he'd swung poor Tweetie's cage, as if it were a railroad lantern back at his Soo Line job. *Jaunty prick, aren't we?* she'd thought, as she helped set up camp. And the way he'd stayed awake, so she couldn't hear his slight snore as he slept—very clever. But no joke could ever be as . . . *funny* the second time around. A thing which Gary couldn't realize—but she'd let him have the fun of setting up his little ha-ha, just to see his face fall when it didn't work. . . .

More light, definitely. She felt a pang at missing what had to be a beautiful sunrise, and hated Gary for spoiling the moment for her. Sweat plastered her clothes to her body, a gummy shroud. Gently, she rubbed Tweetie's body, thinking, *Be calm, he'll probably* shout *it next to your ear, a blast of* " 'Car-weeeeee!' " *before the roar. At least Tweetie Pie won't claw me up this—*

Reflexively, she jerked about in a thrash of arms and stiff legs when the cat pounced on her chest, white paws flexing, sending dagger nails into her breast, her neck. At the last second she stifled her scream. Opening her eyes, she saw huge green ones an inch from her nose. Tweetie purred furiously, intent on kneading her upper body. Grateful that she hadn't made *too* much noise, Carey pressed her cat close to her chest. Relaxing, she extended her feet and—

—Her right foot touched Tweetie Pie's back again.

Eyes wide open, breath coming in ragged puffs through her quivering lips, she sat up, trying to make out the semidark interior of the tent, trying to see just what her foot was touching—

What she saw sent her scrambling on hands and knees out of the tent, damn the centipedes and whatnot, she just had to get *out* of that tent, away from Gary's lifeless head jutting through the bottom of the tent. Tweetie wound around her legs as she finally stood at a distance, staring at Gray. He had left the tent all right, most likely with the coming of darkness. Then, just as he had done before, he scuttered around the tent, ready to stop on her side, to wait for the moment when she was completely asleep ... only *this* time, he hadn't seen or expected the vine extending out of the bushes. The vine thick and strong enough for him to get a clumsily booted foot tangled in it. And when he fell down, his neck was impaled on one of the tent spikes....

And somehow his head popped through the bottom hem of the tent, just the crown of short, coarse hair, so much like Tweetie Pie's rough coat—

They got the saying wrong, she told herself, even as she kept backing away from the rain-and-blood-splattered tableaux by the tent, *Fool me twice,* death *on you ... oh Gary, you look so* funny, *what a joke, what a crazy* joke *... and you didn't even get to say—*

From somewhere in the dense dripping foliage, dark foliage she didn't recognize and would never stop fearing, Carey heard that mournful, utterly displaced cry:

"*Caw*-wee? *Caw*-wee? *Car-reeeeee?*"

Redemption
by Jack Ketchum

Dora followed them down into the Forty-second Street station, standing well back in the line as he paid for both their tokens.

Big spender.

She watched him take her hand as they went through the turnstiles side by side, then fished a token out of her change purse and followed them down the stairs to the uptown local waiting on the tracks. Her luck was holding—she slipped into the car ahead of theirs just as the doors slid closed in the face of the old black bag lady behind her. The woman howled and swatted at the door like she was chasing flies.

So many of these women. So many flies.

She could see them through the door windows, standing, straphanging, swaying together as the train pulled away. The back of Howard's suit looked wilted with heat and humidity. The woman was smiling.

Dora gave him this much, he'd always had taste.

The woman wore a black silk jumpsuit, possibly Versace—*black,* for God's sake, on a day like this—looking fresh and clean despite the ninety-degree weather. Her skin was pale, drawn tight across the delicate facial bones, her hair long and black, lips stained bright red and teeth very white.

Her body was not unlike Dora's, but built on a different scale. The woman had easily three inches on her and maybe four—five seven or five eight—so that the slim thighs looked even slimmer, the breasts and buttocks fuller by contrast.

Early thirties.

Irish, probably.

And money. The jumpsuit was expensive. So were the heavy silver bracelet and the ruby-studded earrings.

She was the best one yet as far as Dora was concerned.

Good for you, Howard, she thought.

Bastard.

They got off at Sixty-sixth, walked out of the station and up to Sixty-eighth and then eastward toward the park. A homeless woman in front of the Food Emporium was hawking the *Daily News*. To Dora she looked like one of those dust bowl photos by Walker Evans, all gaunt angles and sad hard lines. The teeth in her mouth would be rotten. Her flesh would smell of mildew and old leaves.

She felt a flash of pity for the woman that was not entirely free of pity for herself.

It was rush hour. Yet this far uptown the sidewalk traffic was light, and she had no trouble following them. At Columbus they turned north past Fellini's, and he took her hand again as they stopped for a moment in front of a boutique, gazing in at the lingerie in the window, while Dora ducked inside a store and picked up the latest copy of *Elle*. The *Elle* fit nicely with the light tailored Burberry suit and Mark Cross briefcase.

Just another pretty young career woman on the rise.

The magazine was an accessory.

With the first one it had been glasses. For some reason no one ever worried about a woman wearing glasses, and the girl, some goddamn secretary no less, had opened the door immediately. All Dora'd said was that she was looking for Howard, she was an old friend from school and he'd given her this address in case he wasn't at his own apartment—and since he wasn't here, either, would the girl mind if she left him a note? Sure, said the girl and turned her back on Dora to show her in. She took the six-inch stainless-steel carving knife out of her handbag, reached up into the girl's frizzy red hair, pulled her head back, and slit her throat.

The rest of it was harder. She had to get the body into the bedroom, up on the bed, and strip it naked, making

*it look like a sex crime and not what it was, an execution,
and the girl was heavier than she looked, heavier in fact
than Howard usually liked them, so that she had to wonder what it was the girl had—she wasn't all that pretty,
really—not like this one—and she supposed it was the
sex, it had to be; Howard always did think with his prick.
And considering that took some of the unpleasantness out
of inserting the handle of the electric broom and then,
rolling her over, the bottle.*

On Seventy-first street they moved east again. Halfway between Columbus and Central Park West they
turned up the stairs of a renovated brownstone. Number
thirty-nine. The woman opened the door. Dora crossed
the street, staring up at the windows, slowly walking by.
It was dusk by then, and the apartment would be dark
inside. She watched. Once again her luck was good. The
woman had a front apartment. She saw the light go on
the third floor, had a brief impression of high white ceil-
ings and plants hanging in the window. She looked away
and continued walking.

At Central Park West she turned back the way she
came. She glanced at the apartment and saw that the
curtains were drawn now, their color indistinguishable.
Dark, heavy material. At Pizza Joint Two she asked the
waiter for a table by the window and seated herself facing east so she could watch the entrance to number
thirty-nine across the street.

She ordered shrimp parmigiana, antipasto, and a glass
of wine.

She looked at her watch. Six-thirty-five.

If her luck still held, he wouldn't stay the night.

*And then this would be the easiest yet. Easier even—
and far less dangerous—than pushing MaryBeth Chap-
man, budding blond account exec for Shearson, in front
of the Seventh Avenue express at Thirty-fourth Street. If
anyone had noticed her hands on MaryBeth's back, they
hadn't said anything. Maybe there was too much shock
at the sound of it for anyone to have reacted even if they
had noticed—the liquid crack like a huge balloon full of
water bursting and a tree-limb snapping, both at once.
The enormous red spray.*

Easier than both the others because he'd brought the others to his apartment first, and she'd had to wait and follow them once they were alone, planning it, getting to know their habits somewhat—where they lived, who they saw, and where they went.

Here she only had to wait till he left. Then she could go in asking for him the same way she had with the secretary holding the copy of Elle *in front of her because it looked right there, a prop. Subliminal. She was neat and fashionable and wasn't any threat to anybody, and the brand-new* eight-inch *knife was handy in the briefcase. She would cut her a little differently. Rob her this time. Nothing sexual. No connection from a police point of view. Clean and tragic.*

The talking heads on television all loved the word "tragic."

An abandoned baby in a dumpster was tragic. A kid caught in a cross fire between crack dealers was tragic. A rising young businesswoman falling in front of a subway train—oh yes. That was tragic, too.

Nonsense.

To be tragic you had to have *stature.* Your suffering— and you—had to be somehow bigger than life. The Electras, the Medeas, the Lears, and the Hamlets. You had to fall from great heights, endure great pain. You had to have all the world to lose—and then you had to lose it.

Take Howard, now. Nothing tragic there.

Though on the surface there were arguments to be made.

A successful corporate lawyer. Yes. *Very* successful. A modicum of stature was implicit in any success.

Then his mother had died two months ago. Sad.

And then the inexplicable, seemingly random loss of two of his lovers. *Each* of his lovers following Dora, *whom he'd dumped after five long years of practically tying his damn shoelaces for him.* Pitiable.

And now a third to follow.

All this. But still—nothing tragic.

Because Howard was a worm, essentially. Small. Small enough to tell her that the sex was her fault—though *he* was the one who couldn't get an erection—and small

enough to blame her when the bank had laid her off—
along with thirty other people, thank you very much—to
say she wasn't aggressive enough. Wasn't sharp enough.

Small enough to try to make her feel that much
smaller just because his ego needed boosting. And then
to dump her entirely.

No. No tragic figure there.

Just a weak little man with a lot of bad luck when it
came to romantic involvements.

And his luck would not improve. Not ever. Not if
Dora could help it.

Not one of them would live. Not one.

Until finally, one day, sometime in the future, he saw
himself for the evil jinx virus he was and stopped trying altogether.

She knew what sex meant to him. For years, until he
developed his ... problem, it meant plenty.

It would absolutely kill him.

Redemption, she thought. It meant to recover something pawned or mortgaged. What she'd mortgaged to
Howard.

To set something free.

Her sense of self. Her own *true* self.

She thought, *I need some damn redemption.*

At eight o'clock he left the building.

She was dawdling over a second cup of coffee, and
she almost missed him—he walked right by her seated
in the window. Dora thought he looked sort of sad
somehow, thoughtful.

Perhaps upstairs things were not going all that
smoothly.

It didn't matter.

She finished the coffee slowly and paid the bill in cash.
No records. A cabbie was picking up a fare—a dapper
old man in an expensive suit, wearing a bow tie and
carrying a cane—directly across the street from number
thirty-nine. She thought of the Walker Evans woman in
front of the market. It was still a man's world. Even an
old man's. She waited until they pulled away and then
crossed the street, walked up the stairs, opened the door,

and scanned the mailboxes in the hall. Three F was B. Querida. The name surprised her. She'd been sure the woman was Irish.

She buzzed her.

"Yes?"

"Hello. yes. It's Janet."

"Janet?"

"Yes. Is Howard there?"

There was a pause.

"Hold on. I'll buzz you up."

The buzzer sounded. She opened the door and went to the elevator and pushed 3.

There were only two apartments on the floor, which said something about their size. And the location was a block from Central Park West. B. Querida was doing rather well for herself, she thought. Probably as well as Howard.

The woman stood in the open doorway, still wearing the black silk jumpsuit—or was that *wearing it again?*— looking poised and smiling and faintly curious.

"Sorry. You just missed him," she said.

Dora stopped just outside the doorway.

"Damn!" she said. She looked momentarily confused and flustered. "I work with him. I've got some papers for him to sign. Oh, God."

"He gave you this address?"

"He said he'd be here till about eight, eight-thirty. And I just now got away. Did he say where ... ?"

"No. Afraid he didn't."

"Listen. Would you mind ... ? Do you think I could use your phone and try to call someone on this?"

"Sure. Of course. Come on in."

The woman stood aside.

The room in front of Dora was cluttered, almost Victorian, though spotlessly clean. And not nearly as large as she would have guessed. Overstuffed chairs in front of what looked like a working fireplace. Heavy maroon curtains. Bric-a-brac and vases filled with long-stem roses.

The room was dark. Deep reds. Mahogany furniture. Even the paintings were dark. Landscapes in storm.

Undecipherable forms. One of them, she thought, might be an Albert Ryder.

It was not what she'd expected.

"The phone's in the bedroom. This way."

The woman was walking in front of her now, through a paneled corridor, black-and-white prints and old sepia photos on the walls, their subjects mostly a blur to her. A closed oak door lay directly ahead of them. The corridor was narrow.

Dora opened the briefcase. Her fingers found the hardwood handle.

It was awkward here, the space too tight.

Better to wait until the bedroom, she thought. Even fake the phone call if she had to.

There would be plenty of opportunity. B. Querida had turned her back on her. She wasn't afraid. If she'd do it once, she'd do it twice.

The woman's fingers closed over the cut crystal doorknob, turned it, and gently pushed open the door. And now she was standing in profile, half her face visible to Dora and smiling in the dim hall light, the other half lost in the bedroom's dark.

"I'll get the light," she said. She stepped inside.

Dora stepped in silently behind her, into darkness. And at once felt oddly out of place here, as though she were not in the city at all anymore but in some room in Vermont or New Hampshire, out in the country somewhere on some night when there was no moon and no stars, when the darkness seemed to swallow every shred of light. New York was never *black*. Never. It glowed.

Not now. Her eyes could make out nothing of the woman inside. She could only hear her cross the room with the practiced ease of someone long blind in a wholly familiar darkness.

And stop. And wait.

And she almost turned away then because there was something wrong with that, somehow it wasn't right, there was a trick here somewhere, and she didn't much care to know where or how but this blackness was *all wrong* and something was telling her to get the hell out of there when she heard a *click* and suddenly the dark exploded, flooded her with light.

So that *she* was the blind one for the moment, unaware of the woman moving back across the room until she was already leaning toward her through the beam like some sudden evil angel bathed in light, aware only of heat and scalding brightness until the woman grabbed her arm and her briefcase and shoved her forward into the room, tore the briefcase from her hands and sent her sprawling across the floor.

The door slammed shut.

Dora thought of her father.

The door slammed shut behind him. The lock turned. Whiskey on his clothes and on his breath as he leaned over.

Whose little girl are you?

The woman walked directly toward her out of the klieg light trained on the door.

"Some of my clients want to feel like movie stars," she said. "Or maybe political prisoners." She laughed. "Sometimes a little of both."

The room was strung with track lighting. Out of the beam of the klieg, Dora could see normally. She sat up and looked around, and the woman saw her looking.

She extracted the knife from the briefcase.

As though she knew it was there all along.

"I lied about the bedroom," she said. "That's over on the other side of the apartment. And nobody goes there but me. Sorry."

Dora looked up and felt the hysterical urge to laugh and then the urge to run.

The room was long and narrow, and except for a wooden chair and small oak linen cabinet, empty of conventional furniture. There were no windows. She could see where there had been one, the sill and frame were there, but the window itself had been bricked over and painted black. The rest of the room was like the padded cell of an asylum—except that the padding, too, was black. Thick steel rods webbed the ceiling. Chains, harnesses, and manacles dangled from them irregularly, some connected by ropes to pulleys on the wall. There was a wall of instruments made of steel and wood—instruments to clamp and probe, to cut and to pierce and tear.

Another wall displaying masks, belts, whips, some of them tipped with metal balls.

In the center of the room stood two huge eight-foot black beams intersecting to form the letter X.

The wall in front of it was a mirror.

She saw what looked like an outdoor grille made of old rusted iron.

A wooden barrel lying on its side, studded with nails.

She saw a scarred butcher-block table arrayed with weights and clamps and knives.

To this the woman added Dora's carving knife, setting it down gently, almost lovingly.

"He comes here, you know? He feels guilty."

"Guilty?"

"Of course he does. Look at what he did to you."

"Me? How do you know . . . ?"

"Oh, I know you all right. I knew you right away. See, Howard always pays cash. You'd think a guy like him, with the kind of job he's got, you'd think he'd go with a credit card just to get the float. Not Howard. Always cash. Did you know he still carries a picture of you in his wallet?"

"I . . . he does?"

"I told you. He feels guilty. I bet you didn't think he had it in him, did you?"

The woman was serious. *Her picture was in his wallet.* Amazing.

"Of course it's not just you. There's the broker and the secretary. He feels guilty about them, too. Though I never could figure out why. Hell, I think he even feels guilty about his *mother* dying. Howard's got a lot of guilt. A lot to answer for. At least *he* thinks so." She laughed again. "Don't look so shocked. In this business you hear a lot of stories. People confess. I make them confess."

She stepped closer.

"Stand up, Dora."

She did as she was told.

"Take off your jacket. Let me look at you."

She hesitated.

"I'm a whole lot stronger than you. Without your little toy there. You know that, don't you?"

Dora looked up into her wide green eyes and nodded. She slipped the jacket off her shoulders. And suddenly felt naked there.

The woman reached out and lightly touched her hair. Her touch was electric.

"So what about you?" she said. "What have *you* got to answer for?"

You've got to get out of here, she thought. *Now.*

The woman turned away, walked to the klieg light and switched it off.

"Let's see if I've got this correct," she said. "Once you had him, you didn't want to fuck him anymore, am I right?" She shrugged. "It happens. For some people, the capture's everything. Once you've proven you can *do* it, once he's yours, it's not so much, is it? Kind of turns to ashes. Especially if you don't really like yourself much. And you don't, do you?"

Dora felt her eyes on her again, probing.

"Of course it took *him* awhile to catch on to that—to catch *up* with you, to become the incredible shrinking dick you really preferred him to be in the first place. And then once he did, he sort of retaliated, he started to belittle you, tried to make you feel like somebody small and stupid and powerless. Which part of you *really thinks you are.* He knew exactly which buttons to push, didn't he."

She walked to the table and picked up Dora's knife again, fingering the edge she'd honed this morning.

"I do, too," she said.,

And Dora believed her.

"Did it occur to you that he was only whittling you down to size in a way? So he could finally leave you, get free of you without feeling like something was wrong with *him,* prove to himself that it was really you all along? And it *was* you, wasn't it. Part of you really *is* small. You didn't want to fuck him. You'd already got what you wanted. Simple as that."

The woman walked back to where Dora stood in front of the huge black *X* and pointed the knife at her, at the top button of her blouse. Dora stood frozen. The woman turned her wrist and the button was gone.

"So," she said. "I'll say it again. What've *you* got to answer for?"

She felt the coolness of the knife as it parted her blouse, its flat edge moving down. Another flick.

Another button falling to the bare hardwood floor.

"I . . . I didn't . . ."

"Mean to? Of course you did, Dora!"

She trembled. The knife moved down over her cream silk bra, over her sternum. To the next button.

Flick.

The woman shook her head and smiled ruefully.

"And he still keeps your picture in his wallet. You're standing on the rocks by the shore. You're wearing a halter and jeans and the waves are crashing white foam and you're smiling."

The flat of the blade moved down across her belly. The blade felt warmer now. She could feel the woman's breath on her cheek. It smelled of rain and fresh open air. The woman was beautiful.

They had all, in their ways, been beautiful.

"Dora. Don't you feel *guilty*?"

She couldn't help it. She began to cry.

"Oh. No need for that," said the woman. "Just step back."

She felt the point of the knife in her belly now, pressing her gently toward the wooden structure behind her. But the woman was wrong—there was plenty of need to cry. Whether the tears came out of guilt or fear seemed almost irrelevant now, they were practically one and the same.

The woman knelt and fitted her ankles into the soft black leather manacles at the base of the structure and strapped them tight. When she parted Dora's legs to set the second strap she felt all volition leave her, expelled in one long breath.

"Raise your arms."

She felt the manacles tighten over her wrists, smelled leather and rich scented oil. The woman stepped back.

"And the others, Dora. Have you thought about the others?"

She hadn't.

She had.

Of course she had.

She gazed at herself in the mirrored wall, and then at the woman's long sleek back. I'll see everything, she thought. Everything.

Both of us. All the while.

It was terrifying. Also thrilling. As though she and the woman were part of a single entity and both were Dora—*essentially Dora*—the punisher and the punished.

"You killed them. You were going to kill me."

Her heart pounded. In the mirror she saw the rise and fall of her breasts, nipples hard and aching beneath the thin filmy surface of the bra.

The woman sighed. "You've been a very bad girl," she said. "They didn't deserve it. Certainly not because of you and Howard. I think you've got a lot to answer for. Don't you?"

In the mirror she watched herself respond. She nodded.

And thought, *I was only looking for some redemption.*

She watched as the knife slit through her skirt from waist to hem, the sweat of the day cooling suddenly on her as the skirt fell away, then moved up to the final two buttons of her blouse and trailed up along her arms to slit the sleeves, so that blouse and skirt formed a pool on the floor in front of her like a snake shedding its skin.

The woman paused and stepped away and allowed her a moment to see herself in the mirror.

That was good. She found that she needed to see.

She walked to the linen cabinet, took out two black sheets, and spread them around Dora's feet both front and back. She unbuttoned the jumpsuit and shrugged it off her shoulders. Beneath it she was naked. She placed the jumpsuit neatly on the back of the chair, then took a long pearl-handled straight-edge razor from the table and opened it. The razor gleamed in the track lighting. She thought that it was very much like her father's.

"This is going to take awhile," she said. "And it's going to get somewhat messy. But we'll get to the bottom of you, you and I. I promise you that. Your own true inner self."

When the razor plucked through the straps and center of her bra and the sides of her panties, she felt a sudden rush of freedom bound tight to a sudden sense of dread. It was perfectly right that this should be so.

"We'll set you free," said the woman.

For the first but not the last time, the razor descended.

The Graveyard Ghoul
by Edward D. Hoch

"My friend," Simon Ark told me as we sat waiting for our host's arrival, "it has been said that everyone has three lives—the public one, the private one, and the secret one. Certainly the secret life is the most interesting, especially in a person of some renown."

"You're thinking of government leaders, statesmen, generals?"

"Or mere poets and essayists like Ralph Waldo Emerson."

The idea made me chuckle. "I'm sure a preacher and philosopher like Emerson had no secret life. He was a very open man."

"Open indeed! Are you aware that his first wife, Ellen, died of tuberculosis at the age of nineteen? He took to walking to her tomb every morning, and one day after she'd been dead for thirteen months, he opened her coffin."

"My God! What did he find?"

Simon Ark shook his head sadly. "We can be thankful he didn't tell us. His journal for March of 1832 records only that, 'I visited Ellen's tomb & opened the coffin.' After thirteen months in her coffin, even the most beautiful of young women would have been terrifying to behold, especially by the young man who had loved her so deeply."

"Why would he have done that? Why would he replace the living memory of her with—"

My question went unfinished, for at that moment our host walked through the wide double doors of the club library. He was a slender gray-haired man named George Mitchner, and after shaking hands with them he led the way to the dining room. "I though my club would be the best place to dine, gentlemen. We won't be disturbed here."

I knew Mitchner slightly because our firm, Neptune Books, had published a slender volume of his on old cemeteries. It hadn't been a big seller, and another editor had handled it, but I'd met him once when he was in the office. It was this fact, and my well-known friendship with Simon Ark, that led to the present dinner invitation at one of Manhattan's more exclusive clubs.

After the drinks had been ordered he turned to Simon, openly examining his black suit and aged face. "I understand you're something of a psychic detective."

Simon Ark smiled slightly. "Only to those who must categorize everything. I am merely a mortal in search of evil—in search of the devil, if you will. Sometimes I find traces of him in the most unexpected places."

"Be that as it may, I need your advice about some unexplained events on my estate."

"Grave robbers," I said, getting right to the point. I'd already told Simon that much, which had brought to mind his story about Emerson.

"Let us wait until after dinner," George Mitchner said with a gesture of his muscular hands. "It is not a topic to discuss before eating."

Over dinner Mitchner went at his food with determination, his angular brow dipped toward the thick steak on his plate. When he spoke at all, it was of other meals he'd eaten in distant places. "The best food in Cairo, you know, wasn't at Shepheard's Hotel but at a little café off Ramses Street."

Simon perked up at mention of Cairo. "You lived there?"

"During the war—World War II. I was very young then. I helped the British build a wall of bricks and sandbags under the chin of the Sphinx. It offered some protection against air-raid damage, though the city had no serious bombing even when the German tanks were only a hundred miles away."

After dinner, when the plates had been cleared and we were almost alone in the large dining room with our cups of coffee, George Mitchner announced, "And now to business. I live on the family estate up in Duchess County, with my wife and son. The Mitchners have owned land there since Revolutionary times, and we have a family cemetery on the property."

Simon Ark interrupted with a question. "How many are buried there?"

"Counting babies who died at birth, I suppose there are about fifty. My parents are both there. Lately, there's been a rash of grave robbing, coffins dug up and opened, the main crypt invaded. The local police put it down to vandalism by teenagers, but I think it's something more. Certain Satanic symbols have been found nearby."

"This interests me," Simon admitted, "though even Satanic symbols can be painted by teenagers."

George Mitchner shook his head. "No, this is a clear case of grave robbery, or at least desecration."

"There are two motives for grave robbery," Simon told him, taking a sip of coffee. "One is to steal valuable objects that were buried with the deceased, as in ancient Egyptian tombs. The other is to steal the body itself, as Burke and Hare did in nineteenth-century Scotland, for sale to medical schools."

"The bodies were not taken. Nothing was taken. It's as if the vandal simply wanted to view the remains."

My mind went back to Emerson again, opening the coffin of his dead wife after thirteen months. "What sort of a sick person would do that?" I asked.

A flicker of pain crossed George Mitchner's face. "That is why I appeal to you, Mr. Ark, to come see for yourself. I have every reason to believe that the graves are being opened by my son Andrew."

When we finally met him, in the big old house at the end of a tree-shaded lane in Duchess County, Andrew Mitchner hardly seemed like the classic representation of a grave-robbing ghoul. He was a personable, mild-mannered young man with a ready smile and a firm handshake. Some of his father's features were apparent, especially in the shape of his brow and the curve of his shoulders.

"I'm pleased to meet you both," he said. "Father tells me you're here to suggest some security measures for the family graveyard. We've been troubled by vandals lately."

"Have you seen anyone in the area?" Simon Ark asked.

"Not at night. The graveyard and crypt are over the hill. They can't be seen from the house."

If we had wondered at the source of the Mitchner family income, it became obvious the moment we walked into what must have been the drawing room. The walls were lined with black-and-white photographs of giant cargo ships, and a scale model of one occupied a place of honor on a side table. "We're a maritime family," George Mitchner explained. "Always have been. Andrew's learning the business."

I guessed the son's age in the late twenties, a bit old for youthful pranks. I was still studying him when his father announced, "And this is my wife Abby."

If Simon and I expected to be greeted by a woman of Mitchner's age, we were startled by our first glimpse of her. She was a second wife, of course, a woman closer to Andrew's age than his father's. Her red hair may not have been natural, but her smile was warm and sincere as she greeted them. "It's a pleasure to have visitors here," she said, striding up to shake our hands. "We're too far from Manhattan for most people."

"It's wonderful country up here," I said. "Those Italian cypresses are like something on a picture postcard."

"All credit for the landscaping belongs to my father," George Mitchner said. "He remodeled the house and greatly improved the grounds. But we should get moving if you wish to see the cemetery while it's still daylight."

I thought for a moment that all of us would be going, but Andrew and Abby Mitchner stayed behind. Simon Ark had been unusually quiet during our time in the house, but once outside and striding through the crisp April air, he seemed to return to his usual self. He often claimed to be two thousand years old, and at that age I suppose anyone can grow a bit quiet at times. Still, I suspected there was more to it than that. The Mitchner family hadn't been what either of us expected.

"There's one of the Satanic symbols I told you about," Mitchner said.

We'd approached the old family cemetery, bounded by an iron fence. There were stone posts where a gate might once have been, and it was on one of these that a crude pentagram had been spray-painted in red. Simon made a sound of derision. "Anyone can draw a pentagram. The dictionary tells you it's an occult symbol. True Satanists would be much more imaginative."

"Are there any teenagers in the area?" I asked Mitchner.

"Sure, there are a few on neighboring estates."

"How about the one next door?"

"A boy named Ronnie, around sixteen. He likes to ride horses. Ronnie King. Sometimes I have to chase him off my property."

"Maybe he's—"

But now we could see the first of the open graves, only partly filled in. Digging down to reach the coffin would have been hard work, a lot harder than spray-painting pentagrams. "This is the grave of my great-grandfather. It was the first one to be opened, two weeks ago. A few nights later, the crypt was broken into." He indicated what was really a stone mausoleum, built into the side of a hill. I could see from this distance that the padlock on the door had been recently replaced, shining like new.

"Exactly what does this graveyard ghoul do?" Simon Ark questioned. "I can see that the coffin has been opened—"

"He does nothing! Perhaps he looks at the bodies, but nothing more. In all cases the remains seemed intact. Nothing obvious was removed."

"Why do you suspect your son?"

"Four nights ago I was standing by the bedroom window just before retiring. There was a full moon, and suddenly I saw Andrew coming out of the garage, heading in this direction. He was carrying a shovel. The following morning I came down here to look and discovered that my wife's grave had been desecrated. His own mother's grave!"

"Have you reported this vandalism to the police?"

"Of course! I've called them all three times. All they told me was that they'd increase the road patrols in this area. That was when I decided I needed private help. If it is Andrew, I don't want him arrested."

Simon and I stood at the edge of the newest grave, staring down at the coffin. "Was there evidence that it had been opened?"

"Oh, yes! The lid was still ajar. When I think of Margaret suffering an indignity like this, after all she went through— And from her own son!"

"When did she die?" I asked.

"Four, almost five, years ago. She had a great many things wrong with her. She'd been in and out of hospital, and finally it got to be too much for her poor body. She was only fifty-five."

Simon Ark pushed a bit of the dirt into the grave with his foot. "What was Andrew's reaction to all this? I gather you haven't confronted him with your accusation."

"Not yet. I wanted your opinion first, Mr. Ark. He seemed as shocked as I was at this outrage, so I made no reference to seeing him with the shovel."

Simon nodded. "It may be good for us to depart and then return after dark. If four nights have passed since the last outrage, it may be time for this ghoul to return."

Mitchner's face revealed a depth of pain we hadn't previously observed. "Why is he doing it, Mr. Ark? Has some devil taken control of him?"

"That's what I intend to find out."

We returned to the house, but now young Andrew Mitchner was nowhere to be seen. Abby was in the garden, tending to the season's first tulips. "The magnolias are ready to blossom," she told her husband. "One more warm day should bring them out."

"She's a wonder with flowers," Mitchner said as we went inside.

"Does she know of your suspicions?" Simon asked.

He shook his head. "I've told no one but you two."

"Still, I should speak with her. She may have observed something that would be helpful."

Abby got up from her knees as we approached, shielding her eyes from the afternoon sun. She still held a trowel in one hand. "What do you think? Can we install a security system down there?"

"A really effective one would be quite expensive," I told her. "Of course, a simple alarm siren would scare them off. That might be all you need."

She rubbed a dirt-stained hand against the side of her jeans, then turned toward Simon as he asked, "Do you have any ideas about this vandalism, Mrs. Mitchner? It always helps to know if we're dealing with wild teenagers on a lark or adults with some darker purpose in mind."

She thought for a moment before responding, then said, "The spray-painted symbols seem more the work of young people, but I can't imagine anyone opening a coffin years after burial. That would have to be an awfully sick individual."

"Perhaps. If the symbols are to be believed, this could be the work of Satanists."

"Why would they open the graves? George tells me nothing was removed. It's not as if they wanted a skull or something for their obscene rites."

At that moment Mitchner called her from the house. "Abby, could you come in now? Dinner is almost ready."

"We have to be going anyway," I told him. "I'll phone you in the morning with a quote on the job."

"Do that."

We drove down the highway a couple of miles as darkness began to settle over the land. "We have some hours yet," Simon Ark said. "Remember, Mitchner spotted his son with the shovel at bedtime."

"You think it'll be tonight?"

"That depends."

We had a light supper at a restaurant overlooking the Hudson River and drove back to the Mitchner estate shortly after eight o'clock. "We'll take up a position near the graveyard and watch until midnight," Simon suggested. "If nothing happens by then, we'll try again tomorrow."

Happily, the night was not too chilly. I found a good spot on the hill above the crypt, giving us a good view of the cemetery's entrance. "No one would climb the fence when there's an open gateway," Simon reasoned.

We were silent for a time, but after a while I became convinced no one would come. I started making conversation in a low voice. "I suppose Abby Mitchner is right. It would take a really sick individual to go about opening coffins."

"But what about Emerson? Was he sick or unbalanced? He opened his wife's coffin, remember."

"I don't know, but there is a possible explanation for that."

"Which is?"

"In those days people were occasionally buried alive, by accident. You have only to read Poe on the subject."

"And you think Emerson opened the coffin to be certain she was dead? After thirteen months?"

"Well—"

"He must have been certain of her death or he would never have allowed her burial. And he must have known that after all those months nothing would be left to stir memories of their days together."

"Then why? Was it something so obscene that we could never imagine it?"

"Hardly, my friend. Remember when we talked of the public life, the private life, and the secret life? Emerson was a minister at the time, a man of God. I doubt if he had a secret life, and if he did he would hardly have written about it in his journal."

"Then what explanation has been offered for his behavior?"

"Students of Emerson say it never happened—that it was a dream or a metaphor. Are we really to believe this, when the remainder of the journals are quite rational and true? Whatever else may have happened, Emerson really did open that coffin."

I was about to continue the conversation when I spotted a light moving among the trees on the other side of the cemetery. "Simon!" I whispered. "Look there!"

"Get down," he cautioned.

"Is it—?"

The light was one of those battery-powered camping lanterns. The figure, dressed in dark clothing, set it on the ground and produced a can of spray paint. This time he began spraying the ground itself, running a long red line over earth and grass and stones, all along one side of the graveyard fence.

"We must catch him and get to the bottom of this," Simon decided. "Go around behind him, and I'll head him in your direction."

I was getting a bit old for playing games in the middle of the night, especially with an opponent who might be both dangerous and deranged, but I followed Simon's instructions and made a wide sweep of the paint sprayer in his circle of light. When I had him between me and the little hill where Simon was hiding, I gave a short, owlish hoot. The figure paused in his spraying to glance in my direction, and that was Simon's signal to rise up and bellow in his deepest voice, "Stop this blasphemy in the name of the Lord!"

The figure dropped his spray can and turned to run, knocking over the lantern as he sprinted directly toward me. I had only to move a few paces to grab him with ease. Hanging onto him was something else again.

"Slow down, mister! We want to talk to you."

"Get your hands off me!"

He lunged for freedom, and we both went down together, hitting the ground with a bone-jarring thud. He rolled over on top of me with ease, and I quickly realized that my fighting days were long past—if they'd ever existed in the first place. Luckily for me, Simon was behind him by this time and took the fight out of him with a blow to the back of his neck.

"Get the lantern," he told me.

If I'd expected it to be young Andrew Mitchner with the spray paint, I was disappointed. It was a spike-haired teenager in black leather who looked as if he'd escaped from some third-rate biker movie. Beneath his pants I could see brown leather riding boots.

"Who are you?" I asked.

"None of your business!" Despite the defiant attitude,

somehow he didn't look like a street punk. Maybe it was the setting. Up there we were a long way from Manhattan.

We helped him to his feet, and Simon asked, "Why would you want to desecrate these graves?"

"I didn't desecrate anything," he muttered, rubbing his neck where Simon's blow had fallen. "I was just having some fun with my spray paint."

"You dug up those coffins."

"Like hell I did! The old guy probably did it himself. He's a nut about cemeteries. Did you ever read his book?"

That was my first clue, though Simon had tumbled to it much sooner. Leather-clad biker punks with spray cans don't read obscure books by obscure authors. They probably don't read any books at all. This kid was a neighbor.

"Do you want us to take you home to your family?" Simon asked. "Your father might not approve of what you've been doing."

"You don't know my family."

"I imagine you're Ronnie King from the neighboring estate. Mitchner's been chasing you off his property when you come riding, hasn't he?"

"Yeah. So what?"

"So you decided on this form of revenge," Simon told him. "Does it give you special pleasure to dress like this when you go out vandalizing property? The ultimate revolt against your parents' values?"

Simon Ark's words had somehow subdued him, as if he'd been a circus lion facing the trainer's whip. "You don't need to take me home," he mumbled. "I know the way."

"Who's been digging up the graves?"

"I don't know! Honest, I don't!"

"You must have seen someone around."

"Nobody, I swear! I saw the gardener partly filling the first grave the morning after it was opened, that's all."

"Yet he left this last grave open."

"The police were here looking at it. I watched them from our place. Old man Mitchner was with them."

"Didn't you know you'd be blamed if you kept returning here with your spray can?"

The kid looked away. "I don't care."

Simon nodded. "You wanted to be caught, didn't you?"

Ronnie King didn't answer.

"Go on, go home," Simon said finally. "Don't come back here again."

He picked up his lantern and trudged off, head down. After a moment we could see only the glow of it, receding into the woods.

"How'd you know it was Ronnie King?" I asked Simon.

"He was wearing brown riding boots under his black leather pants. I remembered Mitchner saying he'd chased Ronnie and his horse off the property. That camping lantern seemed a bit fancy for a town kid, too. I guessed it might be the neighbor."

"You know, Simon, until he mentioned it I'd forgotten George Mitchner's little book on cemeteries. I should find a copy at the office and read through it."

"You can do that tomorrow, my friend. I think we can head home now. The graveyard ghoul won't be appearing tonight."

"How do you know it wasn't Ronnie King?"

"He didn't bring a shovel."

We kept a complete file of all Neptune Books titles in the executive editor's spacious office. It took me only a moment to locate the slim volume with its lavender jacket. At first glance it looked like a book of poetry, which might have been one reason why its sales were disappointing at the time it was published. Actually, it was a 135-page essay on cemeteries, beginning with the burial customs of the ancient Egyptians and their habit of burying treasures and even favorite pets along with the deceased. Everything he would need for the afterlife was provided.

There was even some discussion of the nineteenth-century fear of being buried alive, and of the short-lived fad for coffins with a small bell attached, so help could be summoned if a person found himself in that predicament. The book closed with a mention of modern pet cemeteries, with speculation that someday soon city land might be too valuable to devote to burial grounds. I decided the thing would have made a better magazine piece than a book, but then again I hadn't handled it.

I sought out the editor I wanted—genial, pipe-smoking Chris Billican, who had an office down the hall from me. "Remember George Mitchner?"

"Cemeteries. How could I forget? We sold nineteen hundred copies and remaindered the rest."

I sat down in his visitors' chair. "Wrong jacket. It looked like a book of poems. You should have appealed to the ghoulish crowd. Anyway, what do you remember about the author?"

"Country squire type. A real gentleman. Owned a lot of ships, as I remember it."

"What made him write a book about cemeteries?"

"There's one on the family property up in Duchess County. He told me they fascinated him since he was a kid."

"Nothing else?"

"Not that I can remember. It's a book I try to forget."

"Thanks, Chris."

I wondered if George Mitchner's fascination with cemeteries might extend to digging up coffins in the dead of night. When I suggested this to Simon Ark later that day, he tended to downplay it. "Unless he has a split personality, Mitchner would hardly call me in to investigate if he were the villain."

I had to agree with that. "What do we do next?"

"Mitchner and his son are in the city today. I have telephoned Abby Mitchner to ask if we could visit her."

"Now?"

"As soon as we can drive up there."

It meant another call to my wife Shelly to explain why I wouldn't be home for dinner. She'd put up with Simon Ark's antics for most of our married life, but I knew she grew tired of them at times. I phoned her, and it went about as I'd expected. Then Simon and I were off to the Mitchner estate once more.

Abby Mitchner was waiting at the door for us when we pulled up to the house. "I don't know what I can tell you that George hasn't already gone over," she told Simon.

"He's often away, while you are on the scene. I want to know about servants, neighbors, anyone else who could be desecrating those graves."

"There's no one. We have only two regular servants—a woman who cooks and cleans, and a gardener. Neither of them live in, so they wouldn't have been here overnight." She spoke the words like an actress still uncomfortable in her role as lady of the manor. "As for the neighbors, the only nearby ones are the Kings. Their boy, Ronnie, likes to ride his horse on our property, but otherwise he seems to be a good kid."

"Could I see your stepson's room?" Simon asked suddenly, as if the thought had just occurred to him.

"Whatever for?"

"I want to get some idea of his interests."

She weighed the idea and then decided, "I'll allow you to glance into his room. Naturally, I couldn't allow a search of his drawers or closet."

"Just a glance would be helpful."

She led the way to the second floor and stopped before a closed door. "He's been known to lock it," she informed us, but it was unlocked this day. The bed had been made, and the room was quite neat. Simon's attention was immediately drawn to a shelf of books near the bed, and I focused on them myself. There were a few classics—Shakespeare, Cervantes, Dante—and some textbooks that might have been left over from his college days—*A Brief History of the United States, A Handbook of Toxicology, Advanced Calculus.* At the end of the shelf was a thick volume entitled *A History of Witchcraft,* by Montigue Summers.

"He has a wide variety of interests," Simon murmured.

"I never see him reading. He dislikes modern novels."

There was a television set in the room, with its own VCR and a few tapes of recent popular films. Nothing else of interest seemed visible. Simon strode to the window and gazed out on a view that took in the driveway up to the house. "Your room is around back?"

She nodded. "George and I have the master bedroom. Would you like to see that, too?"

"It won't be necessary."

We went back downstairs, and Simon asked her a few other questions. "Do you visit the graveyard much yourself, Mrs. Mitchner?"

"No. I went over with George to inspect the damage, but before that I hadn't been there in a year. They're not my family."

"How long have you known young Andrew?"

She smiled at the question. "He's not much younger than me. I met him, I believe, on the day of Margaret Mitchner's funeral."

"You knew your husband's first wife?"

"No, but I had a business relationship with George at the time. I was doing some freelance public relations work for his shipping company, and felt I should attend the funeral."

"How would you describe your relationship with Andrew?"

She shrugged. "He hasn't moved out yet. I assume if he didn't like me, he'd find a place of his own."

We finished up then, and Abby Mitchner walked us to the door. "I'll have to tell them you were here," she said.

"Oh, it's no secret," Simon assured her. "Tell them, by all means."

I knew before Simon told me that we'd be spending another night in the graveyard. "He'll be coming tonight," Simon assured me.

"The ghoul?"

"If that's what you wish to call him."

"Andrew Mitchner. But why tonight?"

"Because she'll tell him we looked in his room. He'll know his time is running out."

"The witchcraft book!"

"We shall see, my friend."

We didn't have long to wait that night. We'd taken up the same vantage point on the hill above the mausoleum, and shortly after dark we heard someone approaching through the woods. The figure carried no lantern, and seemed to rely upon instinct or familiarity to find its way among the grave markers. Simon spotted the figure first, when the moon came out from behind a cloud, and touched my arm lightly.

"He's coming right toward us!" I whispered.

"Toward the mausoleum," he corrected.

By moonlight I saw the shovel raised and heard the clang of metal as it hit the padlock. He gave it two more blows and then paused, reaching into his pocket. He'd wanted to avoid using the key, but now he had to. This padlock must have been stronger than the first one.

"He's inside," I whispered.

Simon drew a flashlight from his pocket. "Come on!"

We made our way silently down the hill and to the open mausoleum door. I heard the squeak as another coffin lid was raised. Simon pointed the flashlight and turned it on. The graveyard ghoul had been busy at his tasks and hadn't heard our approach. Now he turned, startled, and the full horror of it met my eyes. It was young Andrew Mitchner, as Simon had known it would be. By the light of a single candle stub, he had opened another coffin and was using a scissors to cut a few strands of long white hair from the decomposing corpse inside.

"There is no need for that, Andrew," Simon told him calmly. "You took what you needed the last time."

"How did you—?"

"Close down that lid and we will talk."

I didn't know quite what there was to talk about when we'd caught him in the act, and I was beginning to wish that one of us had brought a weapon. We waited outside while he screwed down the lid and then joined us. By the light from Simon's flash, I could see his face clearly, and if I'd expected the twisted, hairy features of some werewolf-like creature, I was disappointed. Even his eyes showed none of the madness one might have expected, only a look of concern.

"Will you tell my father?"

"He'll learn your true purpose quickly enough," Simon remarked.

"Then, you know—?"

"Yes, I know. Things are not always what they seem. You had no ghoulish motives in opening these coffins as you did. You were only trying to prove that your mother Margaret was murdered by your father five years ago."

Later, when we were alone, I told Simon, "I thought it was the book on witchcraft that gave you the clue."

"No, no, my friend. Montigue Summers's volume is merely a popular history, with no mention of ghouls or graveyards. Your eye was drawn to that instead of to Shakespeare."

"What docs Shakespeare have to do with it?"

"Just as Hamlet avenges the murder of his father, Andrew set out to avenge the murder of his mother, another victim of poison."

"The book on toxicology!"

"Of course. Such a book on the effects and detection of poisons would hardly have figured in the ordinary college course. He didn't become a doctor, after all."

"What could the toxicology text possibly tell him that would make him dig up his mother's body five years after her death?"

"That traces of arsenic can be found in the victim's hair even after hundreds of years. A recent examination of Napoleon's hair suggests that he was poisoned."

"My God! But why did he dig up the other grave, and open two coffins in the mausoleum?"

"As with a killer who murders four people to hide the identity of his true victim, Andrew wanted to keep his father from learning the purpose of his desecration, at least until he'd gotten a lab report on the hair. Tonight's final coffin opening, as he told us, was to further cloud the motive while also obtaining another sample of hair to be tested against his mother's hair. Virtually everyone's hair has a tiny amount of arsenic in it. The quantity is the important thing."

"What will you tell his father?"

"Nothing. He'll learn the truth quickly enough without our help."

I thought about the young second wife, about how she'd been working with George Mitchner already at the time of Margaret's death. Motive enough, I supposed, especially if a messy divorce would have meant a huge settlement and endless alimony.

The story made the papers a few weeks later: *Police Question Shipping Tycoon About Wife's Death; Exhumed Body Shows Traces of Arsenic.*

"You saw the papers?" I asked Simon Ark when we met for lunch the following week.

"I saw them. Young Andrew tells me an indictment is expected."

"As you say, Simon, things are not always what they seem. Do you think you could clear Ralph Waldo Emerson's name as easily?"

"I already have."

"How could you?"

He leaned back and sipped his drink, smiling at my reaction. "I can never prove it, of course, not at this late date. But I can supply an explanation that has nothing to do with ghouls or madness or burial alive."

"What's that?"

"Emerson opened his wife's coffin after thirteen months simply to retrieve something he'd buried with her."

"Like what?" I asked dubiously.

"Remember that Emerson was a poet, my friend. What could be more natural than for him to have composed a poem on his beloved wife's death and have slipped it into the coffin with her. More than a year later, he wanted that poem back. His journal says only that he visited Ellen's tomb and opened the coffin, not that he looked upon her body. I think he retrieved that poem and published it. Possibly it was *To Ellen* or one of several others he wrote about her death."

Perhaps Simon was right, as he has been about so many things. I like to think so.

The Rings of Cocytus
By Katherine Ramsland

What's scary about serial killers is how their violence can be tripped by almost *anything* and you can't predict what will trigger it. A random gesture, the color of someone's hair, even the style of a house, and they're out of control. So when the guy came to my door, I wasn't ready.

I answered the insistent knock pondering other things: the dust on my chairs, my uncombed hair, my paint-spattered sweatpants. It was odd having a visitor in the middle of the morning. My friends always called first, and everyone I knew was working. I should have been thinking more clearly, but I wasn't. Not that it would have mattered much, I guess.

I pulled my sweater together and opened the door to a man standing on my porch. His dark hair was cropped close to his skull and his wide black eyes, set into a round face, lacked sincerity. He wore only a faded denim shirt and jeans, although it was cold out, with snow on the ground. A yellow belt held up his pants. I noticed he hadn't shaved that morning, and he stank of chicken soup. It was the way my father had always smelled, and I suddenly disliked the guy. I glanced across the street, spotted a beat-up blue Chevy, and knew I should never have answered the door.

The man held out a tattered atlas, opened to Pennsylvania, with a berry jam smudge on my hometown—as if he'd targeted me with a glob of blood. He claimed he needed help.

That's when my knees started to shake.

I had few close neighbors, and what there were kept to their own business. I had no protection, not even a chain on the door. How stupid could I have been? But if I showed him I was scared, that might seal my doom. I steadied my hands and gripped the doorjamb, sharply aware of my parakeet chirping in the background.

"There's a road that goes over the hill," the man said. "But I can't find it on this map. I want the shortcut to Highway 612."

I tried to think what I should do. He pushed the map toward me, inviting closer inspection. I tightened my hold, poised to run. I knew the scenario. Stick your head out, he puts on a choke-hold, forces you inside, and has his way.

"Do you know what road I'm talking about?" he asked.

I wondered what he'd do. Would he pull a gun, a knife, or hit me over the head?

"Look," I said, straining to keep from my voice the shiver that weakened my knees. "There's a gas station down the road. Go ask them."

What had attracted him to me? Had he seen me somewhere, then followed me? How long had he been watching? Did I act like a victim? Did I seem vulnerable?

"Can't you just show me?" he implored.

What if he made a sudden move? Should I slam the door? Run for it? I mentally inventoried the room—the lamp, a heavy book, the telephone—wondering how they'd serve as cudgels.

"Just keep going north on this road," I told him, avoiding his eyes. "You'll see it."

But he kept looking at me. He didn't seem to understand my directions, and he gestured again toward the map in his muscular hand.

"I don't know the area," he said. "Can't you show me?"

Was that a glimmer in his eye? Was he getting ready? He must realize I'm afraid, I thought. He's making a decision. Perspiration gathered at my armpits. He could probably smell it from where he stood. *This was happening, it was really happening!* He'd locked onto me, scoped out my house, and devised the best approach for maximum vulnerability. He was asking for help, as if he knew how my father had always lectured me to be hospitable lest I inadvertently entertain an angel out to test my Christian goodwill. I couldn't get away from Daddy's ideals even now when my life depended on it. All I could see as I looked at this stranger on my porch was that perennial, cold, hopeless *disappointment* in Daddy's eyes, the way his shoulders sagged when I failed to live up to his expectations. If this guy *wasn't* a serial killer, I'd be a paranoid jerk for not helping him, and the guilt from that was almost worse. The ambiguity paralyzed me, and I couldn't bring myself to close the door. I cursed myself for it. No doubt it was idiotic ambivalence that had drawn him to me in the first place.

"Ma'am?" he asked.

I shook my head, withdrawing. I wasn't getting any closer to his map.

"Please." He stepped closer and broke the spell.

I took a breath, steeled myself, and just did it. I closed the door and knew at once I'd made a mistake. I locked it and put my ear to the crack. Now that he realized I was on to him, he couldn't just let me go. He'd find another way in. I strained closer, holding my breath, to hear what he was doing.

I'd been reading about serial killers for the past year, spurred on by my friend, Terri, who collected them. I don't mean she collected actual killers, but she had a huge file of clippings, trial transcripts, and photographs that she'd been compiling for years. She knew all about John Wayne Gacy, who'd buried boys in his crawl space; Ted Bundy, who'd lured girls by acting helpless; Henry Lee Lucas, who'd claimed to have stashed hundreds of victims in shallow graves. Lots of them just went door to door like this. As I listened to the footsteps retreat from my porch, I reviewed our conversations for some clue about what to do. Terri could recite the killer profile by heart.

"Gerald Stano killed thirty-nine people in Florida," she'd told me proudly. "Vaugn Greenwood slashed his victims' throats and filled a cup with their blood."

"But what gets them going?" I'd asked.

"Someone in their life pushes them around. They

withdraw into a turmoil of fear and anger. I mean, they become time bombs, just waiting for a person who reminds them of their pain to flick on the switch, and that person becomes their victim. Something happens in their head, like a chemical reaction."

Who did I remind him of? A mother who beat him when he was a kid? I glanced out the window but didn't see the dark-haired man. The hedge was in the way—the one I'd been meaning to cut. He could be on his way to his car ... *or heading around toward the back where my door was unlocked!* I crept to another window and strained to see. Terri's words filled my brain with gruesome images.

"The killer gets into this aura phase, like being on drugs. His perception changes, and he loses control. Kind of like PMS, I guess, only worse. He starts seeing reality differently; he might even see a person who's not there. Then it starts."

"What?"

"The trolling. Cruising. Looking for his prey. He hooks into some past trauma and targets an innocent person. The victim gives him power. Like John Wayne Gacy—you know, he got his start screwing corpses at a funeral home—he'd have sex with boys, then kill them to preserve the manhood his father ridiculed."

Was that guy outside whacked out, I wondered. Was he hallucinating? I moved around to another window but still couldn't see anything. What happens next? What had she told me?

"They go into these ritualistic patterns and do whatever it takes to get satisfied. They sort of have an orgasm by causing death."

Shit! She'd got me sweating with her spooky stories. What did this guy want? What would he do?

"That's the pinnacle, and some of them claim to find truth at that moment. Others say they'd just disintegrate if they didn't kill. But the satisfaction doesn't last. That's why some of them take a trophy—cut off an ear or, like Eddy Gein did, the genitals, so they can relive the experience."

My God, I breathed. What did this guy have in mind?

Had he *done* others? Taken "trophies?" Would he cut something off me or have sex with my corpse? My legs closed together in reflex. I glanced out again and thought I saw movement—something blue between the branches. I briefly pondered opening the door and inviting him back. I could catch him off guard before he got me. Or maybe he'd just disintegrate. I giggled a little at the image of him liquified on my floor. Then it gave me an idea.

I could play him a bit, get him wound up tight. Let him circle the house, thinking of me as some terrified victim within. Then frustrate him, repulse his advances. Suddenly I was intrigued about what would happen. The adrenaline was pumping, clearing my head. I mentally rooted through what I knew about these guys.

Terri had told me the FBI estimated there are some five hundred unidentified serial killers at large in this country. *Five Hundred!* I couldn't stand the thought. It made the probability of becoming a victim almost staggering. I'd sometimes hated going to Terri's house, as if I'd be contaminated by touching her files and make myself more vulnerable. She'd always get me to take home a book, and I'd send it right back as soon as I got sick to my stomach. Guys sawing up women or gutting them. It was as if opening those books invited maniacs into my house, and the images of what they'd done log-jammed my dreams—even my daydreams. After reading how Ed Gein dug up corpses and flensed women he'd killed so he could wear their skin, I'd had enough.

"Why do you like this stuff?" I'd asked Terri once. "It's sick!"

"I just do," she'd said. "There's something compelling about the psyche of a totally deranged person who seems for all the world like the rest of us on the outside."

"Yeah, right!"

"It's really about society, you know. Serial killers show us the architecture of what lurks beyond law."

I'd snorted. She was always talking about how we project crap from ourselves onto others, making for a screwy society, which then gave birth to even screwier people. Now I wished I'd listened. I'd be able to figure this guy out, come up with a plan.

I looked out the window again. Where the hell *was* he? My heart was pumping, and I feared I'd black out. I had to think. How could I lure him, then overpower him? If he got away, then I was *really* in trouble. I heard blood rushing in my ears, pounding out my panic. Even my bird stopped singing.

Then the guy came around the hedge into view. He crossed to his car and turned, catching my eye. For a moment we were bonded. Then his face blurred. My hands shook as I clung to the curtains. He was leaving. My plan wouldn't work. He'd go now and then come back when I was more vulnerable, I just *knew* it. I *belonged* to him. I started breathing harder. *Damn* him!

But he didn't move. He just stood there looking at me, like he had some right to make me so scared. Sweat beaded up around my hairline. Then it happened. You just can't predict what will trigger it. His shoulders sagged, and he climbed into his car.

My head snapped back, and I almost growled in my rage. *No more!* He wasn't going to hurt me again with his impossible expectations! I caught his license number as he drove away, but I didn't need it. I knew who he was. I grabbed my coat and went to my car.

Look out, Daddy, here I come!

Late Last Night
by John Maclay

He was set down in the Philly bus station, on his way from Baltimore to Easton, in the middle of the night. He'd been dozing, lulled toward sleep by the security of not driving himself, the warm interior and gentle roll of the larger vehicle, and the cocoon-like environment formed by the high seat backs and the dark inside and outside the windows. For a while he'd watched the passing lights of lonely, anonymous towns, but then his eyes had unfocused, he'd turned inward. He'd been only dimly aware of the orange glow of the approaching city, then the bus's plunging into a narrow tunnel to the underground station whose atmosphere again matched his consciousness.

Brushing his long, black hair back from his forehead, stretching his lanky, twenty-year-old body and rising from the seat, shrugging into his leather jacket and grabbing his duffel bag and guitar case, he stumbled down the narrow aisle and steps onto the oily concrete. Followed the other sleepy passengers through a door in a plate-glass wall—windows between a dark interior and a lighted interior—and into the waiting room. His eyes still downcast, he noticed a dirty, tiled floor, punctuated by cigarette butts, then watched his booted feet climb a flight of stairs. A stop in the filthy men's room, then some more steps, past a menacing guard, to the main lobby, where he mumblingly bought a ticket for the next local bus—hand plunged into jeans pocket to pull out crumpled bills—from a sleepy agent. Then a burger from the near deserted fast-food place, a time spent sitting in a molded plastic chair, red, then down again to another, blue, in the waiting room.

He sat staring out into the false underground night.
He knew bus stations well, from this past year of traveling: college dropout, sometime guitar player, wanderer
from job to odd job. Ironically, this was one of the best
of them; there'd been cold gas stations, street corners
with nothing but a sign, tiny lobbies with nothing but
stale vending-machine food. The places were all tired,
like the people who rode, long and tired, in the vehicles
they harbored. In 1995, they were the lowest in the hier-
archy of plane, train, bus. Even in the daytime, they
called forth perpetual night.

Now, for the first time, he looked around at the other
travelers in this fuzzy purgatory. The black woman, pos-
sessions in four fat shopping bags, two thin children kicking a soda can on the tiled floor in front of her. The old
guy, hanging onto respectability by wearing a stained
suit jacket, but surely on his way from nowhere to nowhere, now and for a long time. All the lost people of
the bus world, waiting in the underground station's glare
that somehow gave no light.

But then, as they sometimes did in such places, his
eyes found the young woman, the girl.

She was sitting several seats over from him, and as
usual, was close to a perfect match. Same long, tousled
hair, same leather jacket, same jeans, same boots. Same
look of the wanderer, the dropout, in her tired and too
soon knowing eyes. Hair blond instead of black like his,
those eyes blue instead of brown, knit top instead of
wrinkled shirt, but the same. And her body, though a
complement to his—swell of breast, slope of hip, swell
of thigh—still more like than unlike, the same.

And in their shared, soporific state, as usual, they
came together.

He knew how it went. A few words in the station, not
really looking at each other, though they might have
found faces and minds attractive, then a narrow seat
on the next bus. The warmth of the vehicle's heater,
and that of their touching bodies, now doing more
than words, being all that was needed against the
world outside. Then some kissing of tired mouths,
some furtive groping of breast and groin, and the un-

spoken agreement to get off at the next stop. A walk across cold concrete, a moment in the glaring office of a cheap motel, a room that looked like any other. Finally, at the time of nakedness and beyond, an unaccustomed waking, a brief thrill, even the thought that it could be different after all. Nothing suddenly becoming everything at the moment of peak and release, and the sleep in each other's arms afterward almost a home.

But then, when the dawn light penetrated the faded curtains, nothing again. And the bus waiting in the mist outside the door.

Now, in the Philly station, he simply followed the ritual. Moved down next to her, repeated the words.

"Hi. Where you headed?"

"Hi. Up to Easton."

"Me too. Go to school?"

"No. Used to."

"Me too. Ride with me?"

"Yeah." And that was all there was.

Now the bus pulled in, a former Greyhound with the shadow of the dog—running where?—under the new, local paint. Twin duffel bags were picked up, half dragged across the tiles, out the glass door to the oily cement; tickets, small and simple like the mode of transportation, handed to the burly driver. Then up the narrow metal steps again, down the aisle past sleeping and cloth-smelling huddled forms under weak amber lights, to a double seat, and the closeness.

No talk, just the contact of leather on leather, denim on denim, only the hint, like half-remembered dream, of flesh of a different gender underneath. The driver climbed behind the wheel—a sign, "Safe, Reliable, Courteous"—the amber lights went off, removing whatever wakefulness there'd been, and the bus backed out of its stall like a heavy cow, then moved, powerful and ponderous, up the ramp and out into Philadelphia again. City of deserted sidewalks, naked orange lights, cold blocky buildings, none of it basically different from the mood inside and below.

Winter-dark Eastern city, he thought, and the eyes of his female companion, lit alternately by passing street lamps, seemed to reflect it. Drives you deep into your soul.

Accelerating, the bus swung ship-like around the few landmarks: gray bulk of City Hall, with its phallic tower; castellated Temple, home of the rooms of some order traveling east unknown to him. The few lighted windows of the tall buildings—stacked cages by day—seemed menacing, hinting at the inanimate bulk of that which couldn't be seen; he moved a bit closer to the warmth of the girl. Then they bore north, toward even bleaker landscapes, toward the university and the bombed-out rows.

The academic buildings, close without campus on this city street, seemed mocking, though he tried not to let them. He'd known he was right to seek the road again, the wide-open vistas of Montana, the revelatory moments with real people, even the soporific state of the bus. Guthrie-like, Seeger-like, he'd gone forth, living and believing in something that was so true, even if only a few saw it, even if everyday life seemed to go on without it, maybe had to forget it in order to go on. The Indians had it, the Orientals had it, Whitman was its American Christ. Why spend four years learning, over and over, only the dry facts that surrounded it, proving for the millionth time things that needed no proof, or were even irrelevant or counter? In vain were the arguments that dues had to be paid, rituals had to be performed, before even this truth would be credited. His guitar spoke louder to his mind than his mind did. Still, there were the unpleasant memories of buildings like these. And the memories of the friends he'd left behind, who'd made the really tiny accomodations he couldn't, who'd in turn received the larger world while he was alone with the real one.

But now the university was behind him again, and the bus floated on, through timed lights on a wide, trafficless street, past the rows of derelict houses. If he'd been an entrepreneur, he'd have salvaged houses so close to a college, as had been done in Baltimore; made of them yuppie and preppy havens and along with that, a fortune. As it was, three-storied places identical to one in which he'd once lived were gutted, burned-out, their copper bays and pillars stripped for scrap. Menacing, again, to see, like a nightmare of one's home after a future war.

Yet the bus, safe and reliable, went on, and the girl was beside him. His mind subtly switching gears to sleep as positive, removal as positive, he began to think again of the warm bed, the moment, however transitory, of peace and release.

"Place to stay in Easton?"

"Uh-uh. Find one."

"Stay with me?"

"Guess so."

"Sleep with me?"

"OK." A tired smile, and a hand on his jacketed arm. Sleep ... A rumbling underneath the floor. An uncanny noise. A sudden cessation of power, a soundless coasting. Smoke. The bus ground to a halt.

Five minutes later, and he and the girl were standing on cold concrete again, but not on the way to a warm bed, or to Easton, or to anywhere. The late cocoon of the bus sat smoking, then outrageously beginning to burn, no longer even a temporary shelter while help came. Soon it would be a blackened hulk, like the rows of dark houses its former occupants could feel at their backs, empty and menacing. The two dozen people, driver, suddenly stripped of his power, included, stood huddled together, collars turned up, hands in pockets, stamping their feet like a lost herd of cattle. They'd been birthed from a dark womb into an equally dark, surreal night.

The others would stand there, probably, shaking with cold and city-slum fear, until a police car or fire truck happened by and some sort of accommodation was made. But he and the girl, unspokenly, being part of a life that was already flow, fugue, and imperative motion, shrugged, shouldered their gear, and started walking back toward the hazy orange of downtown.

... Booted feet crunching broken glass of wine bottles, even an occasional syringe. Bare trees, dead and broken trees, of what had once been a neighborhood. The three-story housefronts, beyond short, paper-strewn yards, staring open-doored, no doored, windowless, obscene. No lights inside, not even a late night drunk in the street to disturb what was no longer peace, no longer anything. A neighborhood that, in no longer being one, had reserved itself into a dark mirror image, a cold, dark hell. And everywhere the smell of charred wood, infinitely worse than a burning.

Guitar case on back, duffels in hands, hand in hand. Long hair ruffled by vagrant air, chill breath in lungs.

"Scared."

"Sort of."

"Me too."

"Been through worse. Got raped once."

"Damn. Nothing like that. Once went in a house like these, sleep the night, old man, red eyes, breath like acid, stuck his face in mine, kitchen knife in ribs, ripped off my money. He was like metal, I was only skin and bones."

"Yeah. Know what you mean."

Walk another dead black block, another. The chill, the fear, now digging deep, moving over the line to the physical; heavy gut, fast heart, weak legs. But atmosphere still worse than actuality, maybe . . .

At the end of the next block, silhouetted by what light there was, legs spread, arms braced: the four figures, black or white.

Don't turn. Don't run. Just walk up to them, by them, nod. Though it's three A.M. in the city of death, don't show you're afraid.

Boots sound too loud, hearts the same. But almost there . . . Almost past . . . The four guys hard, inhuman, dirty denims, on drugs but no less sinewy, catlike. The other strain of American rebel, bred of violence, reacting with it. Past . . . Oh God, some distance now . . .

"Hey, guitar man!"

"Hey, little mama!"

Footsteps quick behind, flash of knives seen over shoulder.

Run!

Surreal. The life, the road, the bus, the dreams and nightmares, hundred seats, hundred gravelly highway shoulders, motel rooms, strangers, rare kindred spirits, even the long-ago not-so-long-ago time of childhood, innocence, security, all come to this. Real enough.

They dash down the dark cold sidewalk, baggage dropped, only guitar case thumping on his back, stripped like prey for flight. Boots pound, hearts pound, lungs start to ache, legs move faster than willed, automatic. He runs a bit ahead, propelling, hand locked on hers, feeling cold sweat. What's passed, what's seen of it, looks like the day after Dresden, day after some future holocaust, feels like worse. A dream he once had flashes, of a burning row of houses, flames rising to orange night sky, and a boy and girl fleeing to the cold country, he maybe to become a prophet, she a saint before they die. But what's behind . . .

Suddenly, a pitch-dark corner. He turns sharply, nearly slips, drags, they dart down a side street. Without looking, up the cracked steps of the first dead house, across the broken porch—ankles turning— inside. Up the filthy stairway—glass crunching underfoot, paper slipping—through the first solid door, closed behind, inside. A bedroom, bare, couple of chairs, cracked paint, peeling wallpaper, dust, raw gust in through glassless windows, wan streetlight beyond.

But no steps following, for now.

"Gee."

"Yeah."

"Looked back once, they were half a block behind."

"Won't give up. Not them."

"Right. No witnesses. Kill us if they find us."

"Yeah. Their turf. Jungle."

"Can't run anymore. Ankle."

"God . . ."

Then slowly, with no more words, the merging of the same but different happens, not in a hot motel room in the not-to-be north, but here, here. He isn't protector, she isn't consoler, they're just two becoming one. Arms reach, hug, long hair's smoothed back with caring hands, still panting lips meet, denim presses denim, through hard leather jackets, breasts meet breast. He sinks back into a shaky chair, unbuckles like an out-of-date warrior, she smiles, reaches to her belt, jeans below ankles, flash of white thigh, shuffles forward like a lost goddess . . .

Only the dark, and the soft sound. On his lap, facing, he holding, the local warmth, sharp thrill of entry, slight motion, but then all of it getting lost again in space and time, especially since it could be the last. Go this way, maybe, right beyond the peak into nothingness. Could be worse, the life we've led, free at least, the dream, true at least, this, real at least.

Only the dark, and the soft sound, the beautiful lost music from her throat.

Afterward, they buckle up, sit cross-legged, facing, on the dusty floor. She reaches in pocket, pulls out a candy bar, breaks it in half. He digs in jeans, comes up with a crumpled pack, one last smoke, passes it. Leaves the lighter open, sets it between them, not enough for outsiders to see, but enough for them till it dies. Cold and death kept at bay one more time. Enough.

Then he opens the battered case, takes out guitar . . . and tries to echo, not loud enough for them, what he's just heard from her.

It was never any good, really. Thinking you could say something that would change it. Stop the machine, the death in life. The people who held the towns and the daylight, who put you off onto the roads and into the night while they slept even deeper. Into the drift, the state of the bus world that was nevertheless more valid than they'd ever know. And now to this, to an end maybe fittingly at the raw hands of those even farther lost or found in the darkness. But at least you could try.

A song, now, rising on the night. A gentle voice, words, guitar strings, all of it peace. Enough, after all, despite the other voices, the things they wanted, the cold hard facts. Something somehow, still, running under or above it all, from the real Jesus, through Walt, through Woody, a song, America, Russia, all of it that was ever any good was a song, a forgotten song. As this one would be, since only he knew it, and now she.

And a noise, of the four sets of feet instinctively, finally on the stairs outside, then kicking at the wooden door. Making a sounding box of the death room, like the smaller box of the instrument. Bursting in ... they're gonna come get you sometime ...

In the end, before the blood, there was only the sound of a guitar, and a song.

Beasts in Buildings,
Turning 'Round
by J. N. Williamson

If she'd had a premonition that morning that she was going to die that day, it probably wouldn't have occurred to her that her life would end in the bomb shelter.

Certainly not with her throat cut.

Three people with her in the old, reopened shelter saw the start of the woman's death if not, in all cases, the cause of it. They were among those who weren't praying for the missiles to pass by the hotel again that afternoon, though they certainly wished for another miracle. One of them merely happened to turn his head in her direction at the moment it appeared that the taut skin at the front of her neck and just above the collarbone was splitting, opening up of its own accord. Fascinated, he had the impression as well that the gap immediately began to widen—as though something inside her was pushing out, trying to escape. But that was only the blood.

A second person saw the death start, too, but looked away. He was too frightened by the noise above the hotel to allow anything to register in his mind except his personal terror.

The third person who observed the arrival of death and had not been praying was the murderer. By the time the dead woman was pitching forward with no sound escaping her lips—moving for an instant as if she might be on the verge of standing—that person was already sitting alone in a concave hollow of the shelter even more steeped in shadow than the rest of the bare and colorless, utterly functional room.

He didn't point, cry out, or rise until the first witness was already emitting piteous cries, which drew the complete attention of the other fifteen living people present, and by then, an unsuppressed smile didn't matter much.

Under the circumstances, it was safe to consider himself successful.

Safe, successful, and self-satisfied for the third time running.

Three women murdered inside a stale and poorly illumined bomb shelter built to fend off the weapons of other, half-forgotten wars and taking up less than half the cellar of the modest old hotel. Just one exit, too! Three, during a total of nine raids spread over four days—let the foreign army devil see a pattern in that! Three down, fourteen to go, some men, some women— it was delicious to picture them trying to decide whether the males were to be spared, and only the females stalked and slaughtered! Fourteen human beings of varying faiths and several nations, the imbeciles huddled together because they already feared for their worthless lives—incapable of going anywhere else from terror of the bombs!—and they had no way to discover who was cutting their throats!

His solitary risk lay in the likelihood that they'd no longer think, after this, that two or more nationals were killing each other; they'd *know* there was just one murderer. But that added another element of challenge, of delight! The trick was to take them when they least expected it, and to destroy as many of them as possible prior to the eventual evacuation.

So, since they wouldn't anticipate consecutive attacks, the next victim must die during the next sortie of planes and missiles. Perhaps—if they were rattled badly enough—his total might climb to five or six, even more.

And they would never discover the motive behind the killings in ten thousand risings of the sun—in one hundred thousand!

Because there was none.

The three men from the embassy had taken the best table in the restaurant of the besieged hotel with as little to-do as if magnetized by it, and the headwaiter had passed out menus without giving a thought to their right to the table. There was that kind of dignity to the graying ambassador, whether anyone else in the place knew his profession or not. His aide was trying hard—fine-haired mustache meant to age him, twitching whenever he wiggled his upper lip—to do a good impression of the old man.

As to the uniformed man with the short-cropped, wiry hair, he had his own sort of dignity, but would have felt badly about his small group commandeering the big table if the ranks of people staying at the hotel hadn't been thinned. In addition to the trio of women killed in the basement shelter, a number of frightened individuals had run off into the war-torn city to vanish, and some patrons, obviously, had stayed in their rooms tonight.

Not that he blamed them. He'd been stunned when the latest victim's throat was slashed. *Dead bodies work up very little appetite*, he thought, and began to survey the other tables, counting those who were present until it was time to place his order. *"That,"* he said, blindly jabbing an index finger at the menu. He wouldn't be in the dining room at all except the ambassador desired the views of his attaché.

Three of them, seven other customers scattered around the sizable, candlelit room. The hotel was trying to conserve the generator. Since only three employees remained—the maids had taken off so there was the dark-skinned cook, an aged runt of a bellhop, and the hotel manager obliged to double as headwaiter—that meant two folks were alone now in their rooms. The captain remembered. An exotic-looking woman who reminded him of some fifties actress, and an Alexandrian business type; they were not present and accounted for.

It dawned on him with distaste that he was beginning to look at the others as if one was the worst kind of murderer he'd ever imagined and, with a shock akin to a minor electrical jolt, that one of them undoubtedly was.

"My money's on a terrorist," said the ambassador. His voice and chin were low; he seemed to be addressing his silverware. "Who else could manage such a thing in the midst of other people?"

The young aide bobbed his head. "That's a given." He didn't admit he was contradicting his own first impression that there were conflicting groups of nationals.

"Well, how hard is it to imagine a psycho at work," the captain said slowly, "considering the shelter is half-dark and folks are already terrified by bombs? No nation or race is free of madness." He let his gaze wander. Counting the actress-type in her room, there were only four women left. With surprise, he saw that one of them was seeking his gaze. "This fellow's a planner who takes his time."

"Terrorists can calculate matters down to the fine details," the aide argued, appealing to his employer with a glance. "There may be some clever *pattern* that—"

"Planners of terrorism plan," the captain told him. "They send emotional types to get the job done. Expendable fanatics full of passion, high as kites."

The distinguished ambassador remarked, "I find that most interesting."

"Thank you, sir." He broke eye contact with the young woman. It was a night of surprises. This old man in the gray, perfectly tailored suit rarely offered a compliment. "I have my ideas, but their only value is that they are mine."

A crinkled smile. The ambassador peered up with a disturbingly challenging expression. "They're about to acquire added weight, Captain. No one else in this place can get to the bottom of things but you. Not so far as I know."

The captain frowned, sat back. He had just walked straight into one of the old diplomat's famous traps. "I have no authority here if you mean I should conduct an investigation." He really meant that none of them did. Suddenly, he felt quite tired. The embassy had been closed with little prior notice. Everyone had piled into vehicles headed for the airport, and their own car hadn't made it. Only decent luck had gotten them to this hotel in one piece. Their driver hadn't been that fortunate.

The old man's blue eyes had a way of frosting out to

colorlessness when he'd gotten into something; they were like that now. "I doubt anyone will raise an objection if you stop the son of a bitch. Look. The phone lines are down, even if we could persuade a policeman to jeopardize his life in coming here. I know your record, Captain. A hitch in Intelligence. You are the best man for the job."

Sensing an approach, he leaned forward to reply, just above a whisper. "All right. Because he probably *will* do it again if no one volunteers. What else is there to it, sir?"

"Shrewd question." The old man's voice was scarcely audible. "Before losing the phones, we were informed that command will provide a little lift for us in the morning, whenever it looks clear. The hotel will be evacuated."

"Keep it quiet," the aide added. "There'd be panic if the bird couldn't land for any reason."

Yet if an Apache *did* make it in tomorrow morning, thought the captain, everybody there would be airlifted out, ultimately dispersed to God knew how many nations—

And the damned killer would get by with the vilest crimes he had ever heard of. He would be free to go on slicing up innocents whenever and wherever he—

"Please," said the standing woman, "pardon me. But if you're the best man to find the murderer, we should get acquainted."

He stared up, startled that she was speaking flawless English. "How did you hear what we were saying?"

"I didn't." She gave him a fleeting smile. "I read lips. As to what was discussed, don't worry. I'll keep it quiet about the helicopter."

She was in her late twenties, her auburn hair tousled as if she'd brushed at instead of brushing it, and very, very short. The captain had the impression that her mammoth purse with the strap was far too large for her ... of demureness, and mental gears furiously shifting ... of western dress hastily assembled over a figure that was probably cute (a type he'd never much appreciated) ... and of an icy challenge with the same flinty self-confidence he associated—loved and hated—with the ambassador.

"If we can have a moment," she went on, "at my table"—she tilted her head—"I'll have my say before your meals arrive."

Irritation flared, but the ambassador answered her before he could. "We'll excuse you, Captain," he said, rising to nod at their petite intruder. He smiled down, benignly. "Perhaps the young lady believes she knows the identity of the murderer." Everything in his face but the smile asked the captain to take over, and be discreet.

Fuming, he followed her to her table, saw her seated, went around to face her. "Under the circumstances, I don't see how I can shout to make myself understood."

"You needn't." She watched him lower himself to a chair. "My hearing is excellent. I learned to lip-read to deal better with patients suffering psychosomatic deafness."

"You're a doctor, then?"

"No." Her way of staring directly at him and seldom blinking was unnerving, and it made him glance down at her hands. Folded on the edge of the table, they might have been those of a small, tiny, child. "I'm a clinical psychologist with a background in experimental, comparative, and social psychology as well as criminology."

"How impressive, *Ms.*—?"

"Sister," she said. "Sister Bethany will do." His lips parted, she saw and giggled like a five-year-old. "A nun, that's correct."

The captain sat up straight. "Forgive me for asking, but what are you doing in this part of the world?"

"And, 'Why in heaven's name would *I* want to talk with the best man to find a killer?'" She closed and opened her eyes. "A clinical psychologist not only diagnoses and tries to treat mental disorders, but does research into the subject of mental illnesses."

"And these days there's no better place for you to come," he said, smiling.

"Captain," she said—"I'm the best *woman* for the job. The murders."

"Why?" He put the question before thinking.

"Perhaps it's crossed your mind that a possible motivation of the person killing these women is religious."
A shrug. "I'm a psychologist *and* a nun."

"And a woman."

"How perceptive," she said. "But I won't take the killer's work personally."

"As a nun?"

"No," Sister Bethany said, "as a psychologist." Something turned her eyes to green flame for an instant. "As a nun, I'm afraid I take it quite personally."

"Criminology, too," he noted. He lifted the tips of his fingers to suggest the others in the restaurant. "What do you deduce, looking around you, Sister?"

She shook her head, and a faint line appeared between her eyes, above her small nose. "Such remarks will lead us nowhere, Captain. Sherlock Holmes might study the faces, hands, clothing of the others present to determine where they came from, their vocations, why they came here—and that's quite pointless to us now."

He asked bluntly, "Why?"

"Because, sir, you and I could simply stand, and go *ask* them!" her cheeks reddened. "The murderer in this case lives life as an ordinary person who won't even lie if there's no need for it. You'll find no fangs sank into the women's throats."

Annoyed, the captain motioned to the waiter for coffee, turned up a cup the nun had not used, pointed. "Some of us at my table believe the murderer is a terrorist. After all, the victims were very neatly, efficiently executed. As if the man had practice."

She waited until the swarthy hotel manager doubling as maître d' filled both their cups. His thick mustache a work of patience and the passage of years, he paused, lips moving nervously, but Sister Bethany waved him away. "Isn't it possible that what you cite as practiced efficiency is necessary speed? Even in a shelter that size, there's no time for admiring his handiwork."

Her forthrightness was off-putting. "I suppose. But—"

"But you neither believe he's a terrorist or care for that reasoning," she interposed, "and neither do I." She smiled charmingly, stunningly. "As James Thurber said,

'The conclusion you jump to may be your own.' The individual we intend to stop, Captain, isn't a terrorist, not in the usual sense. He or she is either a psychopath or a sociopath."

"If I have to choose, as a working theory," he said, "I think of the psycho as a man compelled to—well, destroy his victim. Maul, disfigure, annihilate." He realized his curiosity about this little woman's ability was growing in pace with his annoyance. His meal and the meals of the ambassador and his aide were being put on a tray by the headwaiter, and he might be wasting time on the nun. But he wasn't Catholic, was military, and his training prompted him to be properly courteous. "Am I mistaken in that?"

"Not if one assumes he's acting at the crest of his rage. At that moment, he definitely would be out of control." Her smile was gone. She seemed to peer at him above the rim of her cup with new respect. "And it's difficult to imagine the psychopathic personality regaining his control the next second after he's killed. In time to move away from the victim's body before she even slumps to the floor."

She was telling him he was right, and that flustered him. "I must rejoin the others in a moment," he said. "Tell me, Sister. What is it you intend to do to help me stop this lunatic?"

Sister Bethany replaced her cup in its saucer demurely. For the first time it occurred to him to wonder how natural diffidence and humility were to her. And how much justification there was for the self-assurance he was beginning to pick up from her attitude and comments.

"Gradually, I'm developing a profile of the troubled and terrible person who is stalking us even as we finally start to stalk him. With no undue modesty, I'm quite good at this kind of thing." Her face was heart-shaped, he realized; it occurred to him she was the prettiest unpretty woman he had met. "If we had the time, I might be able to pick the killer out of such a limited number of suspects and talk with him, *reach* the person on one level or another, forestall an early attack."

"We don't have the time." He said it under his breath while he stood. A "troubled" person!

"Then, all I can promise," Sister Bethany said quietly, "is that even if the murderer kills one of us during the next raid, I'll determine his identity—and there'll be no further killings after the helicopter has evacuated us."

A promise! Feeling enormous and clumsy looking down at her, he bent slightly. "Most people here heard that the first two victims were Jews, and that this afternoon's victim had a British passport and name. Before you rule a terrorist out completely, Sister, you'd better know that her maiden name was Epstein."

She sighed sadly. "Alas, Captain, that only stresses a factor for which we simply do not have the time."

He opened his mouth, astonished. "But a fact is a fact."

"Those." She spoke with disdain. "Modern people, in trying to be better than nature, or not a part of it, have used facts to make the devastating weapons that military men then bend over backward to refrain from using! We handpick the facts that serve us, ignore the rest. Well, that's what *I'll* do. It's just that I belong to realms of nature and authority which fail to conform with the realms you prefer."

He saw the mustached manager with the food at his table. "I think you're talking about the supernatural," he corrected her gently, "not the natural."

"Oh? Your logic would force us to see that the killer has a means of identifying the victims. You might find he knew them all before coming to the hotel or that they were all familiar with each other. You might—*if* we all remained in this place indefinitely. Where's your logic, your appreciation of facts, in that?"

"Such information may be instrumental in learning the monster's identity."

Her expression pitied him. "I've learned that it's under conditions of great difficulty that people may bypass the bothersome facts and fears, and realize we're conscious creatures primarily for the purpose of discovering how to direct our own lives. We're never free until then. Cows *think* they have the liberty to go where they please."

"Sister Bethany—"

"If we didn't have a good chance to improve ourselves by learning ways to deal with crises, God would give us neither the wit to achieve nor the problems!" She, too, stood. "There would be no utter failures like mass killers, then. But we'd be nothing more than erect beasts in buildings, and God alone could truly shelter us. Captain, we can't have it both ways—the opportunity to cope with our problems, and the godlike indulgence of comprehending every conceivable *aspect* of them."

Well, he hadn't gotten a dressing-down in a long time. "You equate opportunity with crisis, intelligence with ordinary decency? Studying all the facts thoroughly with self-indulgence?"

Sister Bethany took her check. And his, for the coffee. "Thurber also wrote, 'The noblest study of mankind is Man, says Man.' When I said we'll learn who the killer is even if he attacks again, I told you that as a clinical psychologist. I also said the murders will stop then." She patted his wrist just before the sirens began anew. "That was a pledge of faith—because an element of what I'm saying to you is definitely supernatural!"

He hadn't cut the throat of a celebrity before, and the foreign slut actress was the most interesting of his remaining possibilities, but she was a luxury for a later time. The devil in the uniform would be expecting Four to be another woman. Additionally, the captain might think her an Israeli and expect her to be next.

His selection was neither Jewish nor female.

With no doubt, he was making the right choice. Everyone in the shelter was frightened that the missiles would crush or burn them to death, and most—particularly the females and Jews left—were equally terrified, at least, of him.

But a few obviously thought they were invulnerable, unassailable—immune to any attack within the bomb shelter, certainly. And those foreign fools were actually

doing their best to *watch out for* the four remaining
women! It was clear to see!

Fleetingly—so briefly only the blood racing in the
veins took note—there was enough of a break in the
cacophony of war raging in the air above the hotel for
the majority of people uncomfortably huddled in the
badly lit room to catch a sigh of relief. He moved then,
in the silence—in his perfectly controlled composure—
to cross a space of no more than ten meters to his favored victim. Not while the sound was all but deafening
and they waited in tense expectancy. He crossed it at a
normal, suitable speed with neither nonchalance nor
stealth. He went to the elderly man appearing concerned
but bravely reassuring, he went to him with an air that
said he was one of them, he belonged—and he was!
Then, clear as lake water about what was customary and
what wasn't, displaying no sign of disjoined stress or passion, he paused ...

Until, automatically, the distinguished gentlemen sat
erect and looked up expectantly from where he sat on
the wooden bench.

Just as the blue eyes focused upon him and immediately before the ambassador could say "Yes?" he drove
the knife into the soft folds of flesh under the prominent
jaw. The blade's tip stopped short of the bone that might
have pinioned it in marrow and came out cleanly on a
line like a red kite tail.

Neither the young aide nor the body of the diplomat
moved until he was three paces away, raising his bare
hands to the unseen skies as if beseeching the gods to
halt the new torrents of sound, the screams of death-
dealing missiles.

Then when the youth cried out about his murdered
leader, *he* was sitting next to a woman on the other side
of the shelter, pretending to comfort her. Later and luxury were now.

The actress from another world rested her head grate-
fully, momentarily, against his arm.

"Are you from Israel?" He appeared to be trying to
soothe and distract her. He had to repeat the question

in two other languages before she understood, but that could have been terror.

"I am not." She stared at him blankly without turning her head, eyes midnight smudges of confusion and fear. They were breathtakingly beautiful.

"It doesn't matter," he said, bringing his hand up from where it had dangled between his knees. The hand was not empty now.

In the darkness he wasn't able to judge just where the blade entered, but he was able to drag the knife around, in a sawing motion, and to withdraw it before either his hand or cuff were soaked.

Now, perhaps, she understood what was happening. If not, the matter was of no interest to him. He kissed Five on the side of the cheek because he could, and then jumped up to join the others in a general uproar of shouts at the foreign devil in the captain's uniform to "do something."

There were twelve to go. Excluding, of course, himself.

The actress's body fell rather noisily to the shelter floor, and it was another instant of triumph when he saw from their faces that no one at all imagined she had fainted.

If only for this wonderful interval, he had become more terrible than war.

Because they'd turned to him in the shelter, the captain had fulfilled half the ambassador's order. He had taken command of the investigation.

The main part, stopping the son of a bitch, was already a washout.

He had thought of confining the last dozen people to their rooms until morning, then dismissed the plan for various reasons. As a group, they'd still be in greater danger from missiles than from the murderer; they'd be sitting ducks, since there were no men to post as guards in front of their rooms; it would garner him no more information via interrogation than it would in the restaurant, which was nearer to the bomb shelter; and they probably wouldn't stay put anyway. Civilians didn't understand the necessity of orders or obey them faithfully regardless of nationality, and that went for the nun, too.

He turned his head to check on Sister Bethany where she sat at the same table she'd had before the last two deaths, rubbed his burr head with the palm of one hand, sighed. In the end, he'd rounded all the survivors up where they could at least get something to eat or drink, make believe the world wasn't changing. Candles provided sparse light to save the almost-drained generator, and the restaurant looked both romantic and eerie as the anteroom to hell. He'd come to have feeling for the ambassador, and that rather surprised him. He supposed he should be pleased about that, even if the feeling wasn't pure, or purely affectionate. A long while back— when he decided to stay in, make a career of it—there'd been feeling for every goddamn thing that moved. Even when that altered, he'd felt for anything on his side. Anybody. This was the first time in decades there was enough to be bothered by, and he wished detesting the politician in the old man was not a big part of the feeling.

The first person he'd questioned had been the businessman from Alexandria. He didn't know why. Probably because he and the actress had been the only ones to remain in their rooms during the dinner hour. Maybe they'd used only one room, it was a sexual thing, maybe her death had been unconnected with the other murders (since this was the only time two were killed); maybe the Egyptian had remembered a wife.

But the man (in textiles, he said) offered nothing to work with, and neither did the rest who followed him. As the manager/maître d' walked off muttering to himself, the captain realized there probably weren't a dozen suspects, not bonafide. He himself had killed nobody, the boyish aide was in a state of useless shock, and the surrender of the allied coalition to Saddam Hussein would not have surprised the captain more than discovering the tiny nun was sprinting around in the cellar with a razor-sharp knife.

Leaving nine viable suspects. Nine who could become

victims of the pervert before the bird showed up eight or nine hours from then. One who was the murderer.

Two women (other than Sister Bethany), both fifty if a day and only one conceivably attractive to a sighted man; a journalist from New Zealand, a Tel Aviv native who turned out to be a rabbi, two Turkish brothers who claimed to be importers; and the three men still working in the hotel: the bellhop, smaller than the nun and as old as some sins she fretted about. Another, the dark-skinned cook who was so heavyset and stank so much it was hard to believe anybody in a shelter could fail to see his movements. And the manager, lips always working under his mustache, hands shaking so badly he couldn't pour water.

Which left *her* to interrogate. That word, this context, was absurd. He wondered if her promises were, too—if the deaths would stop, the madman's identity be known before the morning evac. Also absurd was thinking she could be right. But like the stalker, Sister Bethany wouldn't be around to crow over him when they were airlifted out; she'd go her own way, too.

He was wondering why he disliked the thought of that when, before he could rise and walk to her table, she was heading toward his. Fast, like the answer to a short and reasonable prayer.

"You're ready for me."

"Sit down." It wasn't a question, and he was glad since he couldn't have answered it. Other women sat down in segments, as if hiding things or emphasizing things. Sister Bethany just sat. "The actress wasn't a Jew. Neither was the ambassador."

"Black Elk remarked that Native Americans did everything in circles and was asked why. 'That is because the Power of the World always works in circles, and everything tries to be round.' "

"And that means?"

"If one begins with Jews and isn't stopped, he'll proceed to the rest, but come back to Jews. He's trying to be the Power; to be round. Wherever one starts, he circles, returns." She drew herself to her seated height, little hands in her lap, clasped. "I agreed that the murderer wasn't a terrorist or a psychopath. That left you with a sociopath to stop."

"What goes around comes around, I follow that. Go on."

"Unlike the psycho, this person cannot be broken emotionally by questioning him. He has no impossible dreams, he suffers no guilt, he can't be ruffled by authority or by his own emotions—for the very sound reason that he may have none."

"No feelings sounds as crazy to me as having fantasies or delusions."

"It can be, but you don't follow me." She placed her fingertips on the table edge, tablecloth and candlelight painting the nails red. "In his delusions, the psycho can't distinguish between reality and unreality. Everyone fantasizes except, perhaps, the sociopath. He makes painstaking plans, enacts them with full knowledge. You and I can't imagine what it would be like to have absolute control of our acts regardless of *what* we were doing. Automatically, we consider what others think and, unlike him, how they may feel."

His mind was wandering and he blamed the hour, the lighting. What this woman said sounded like meaningless philosophizing, and he had to remind himself that, in fact, he had nowhere else to look for help. "The socio does none of that?"

"He *tries* to do so, at times," Sister Bethany said, "in my opinion. But because he has only the intellectual capacity to estimate how we'll react, it's just when we pin a label to him that he can start forming a clear picture of us, or of himself. Captain, he *cannot care.*"

He leaned back. "Please don't tell me he feels unloved."

"But he does—and unhated, too!" The hollows of her face were darkened by light from their candle. "He sees no reason why we should detest him until he has individually attacked us. However, because he's usually very bright and knows *about* feelings, he believes he would be fine and content if he was given enough *attention.* It's my theory that since he is incapable himself of loving, he comes to see our observance and scrutiny—our *notice*—as the range of emotions we call love!"

He was so startled, he threw out his hand and nearly knocked the candle off the table. "You're talking about notoriety, being in the *spotlight!*"

"And having enough of it," she nodded. "We see it in many leaders who are sociopathic, yet never take a life. They *have* enough time in the limelight. When they do kill, it's because someone whom they imagine loved *them* died, so that person is symbolically both punished and avenged in some way and replaced by another admirer. Captain, you looked askance when I called this man—a sociopath is almost always male—troubled; but how else can I see someone who must content himself with apparent regard, the look of being cherished or admired?" She shuddered. "To never feel or know *love* . . ."

He sat forward. "Forgive me for wanting even more to stop him."

"I would," Sister Bethany said, "except you really mean—to kill him. I will stop both of you."

For one heartbeat he didn't grasp what she had said so matter-of-factly. "In the morning, Sister," he said tightly, "he'll be gone."

"So shall we all, one morning." Abruptly, her girlish giggle escaped. "James Thurber pointed out, 'Where most of us end up there is no knowing, but the hell-bent get where they are going.' I just can't let you do what you plan to yourself. The sociopath, to put it in the vernacular, doesn't give a damn. I mean that literally, Captain—but you don't get the gravity of what I'm saying. Which is why he and his kind are usually undetected in an open society. And why he seized the chance to do what he pleased in this artificially closed one."

"I suppose maybe I *don't* get it," he retorted. He made sure he was wearing his sidearm. "I suppose *I* don't care what makes him the way he is. Sister—why should I?"

"He looks no different, utters no word to indicate the presence of an abnormal mind," she went on as if he hadn't spoken, "he thinks logically—and he is incredibly dangerous to your soul, because he will do *anything* at all."

"My soul?"

"Yours, mine." The candlelight flickered. "With no treasured memories, no beloved family, no law or moral principle dear to him—no childhood crony, no pet, not even the psychopath's release when he's killed—the man we seek may possess the kind of secret knowledge that often summons . . ." She broke off.

"Supernatural powers?"

Sister Bethany beamed so happily it was as if he'd strolled into one of the old ambassador's little traps. "I'm so glad you chose those words."

"I?" he repeated with a scowl.

"I won't let you harm your soul to punish a person who has none."

"What was that?" he demanded. "*No* soul?"

"Perhaps not. But *especially*," she finished her original remark, "when he'd think you were showing you cared for him. That's an obscenity." Impulsively, she put out her hand, tried to take his. Grudgingly, he gave her the tips of his fingers. "About the mistake he makes in taking recognition for emotions we can experience, imagine this: the man who has no feeling for society will end by accepting society's opinion of him."

"You're remarkable, Sister." He extricated his fingers gently. "Yet nothing you said suggests to me you can keep the promises you made."

"True. But don't be concerned." She drew a mirror from her purse, brushed a straying auburn wave back into place. "If the bombs fall again, that will mark the end of the murders." That second her eyes provided no more light than the candle. "I know the identity of this sociopath, and I'll point him out to you."

All hell burst out in the skies. And though he did not much like the expression, it would burst out again, now, in the cellar shelter.

Missiles were soaring into the city at such a rate that, combined with return fire, it sounded like a machine-gun war. He had heard every kind of explosive except the atomic bomb, but one could not remember the music those weapons made. Not with one's ears. Possibly in the part of the mind that lingered, hovered.

He had selected his target before this raid began. Killing two again had seemed a child's dream. However, this sortie was so powerful that most of the dozen people with him were wrapping their arms around their heads or staring blankly straight ahead, teeth chattering. Only a coward would utterly rule out an unexpected opportunity.

It occurred to him as he shifted his hips in apparent nervous discomfort, but in readiness to rise and begin, that a direct hit could cave in the ceiling of the shelter in such a way that seven or eight mightn't die, could merely be badly wounded. If so, *he*—

The building tremored as if the earth itself had quaked in fear, but the danger was not from beneath them. When he saw the hotel would stand, he willed himself erect, willed his heart to be calm, his brain to operate efficiently, willed his feet to carry him—a terror-stricken appearing man, arm upraised, lips mutely moving—toward Six.

His victim's sex, race, age, religion were no more and no less evident to him than they would have been to any normal person; they did not hypnotize or revulse him. The victims, the numbers, meant nothing except as the details physically delineating themselves individually helped fix them in memory. Not that he'd have a sexual climax, a nostalgic chill, even a sense of satisfying revenge when he recalled them and their deaths someday.

He would know just that he had fully outsmarted—bested—some of the many people who'd ordered him about and stared through him as if intuiting his essential substancelessness. And had acquired an image of *his* face—his drab, unexciting, normal face—in their memories forever.

Since no one told how long that was, a fraction of one second was enough.

"*El qounboulas*," he complained, whining. *The bombs.* Twisting his head right to left, he seemed to be speaking to nobody in particular; like them, he was only scared, weary, seeking human contact at an instant when death confronted them all. And so he was, but *he functioned*.

Six, scarcely raising his head, scarcely saw him.

Beside the intended target, however, the young woman was lifting her head to stare into his eyes ... and bringing her palms together in a quickening beat he could not for another second understand.

She kept the rhythm up—smiling, at him, green eyes seeming to flash her approval, admiration—as he realized with amazement that *she was applauding him!*

She recognized and was *cheering* him. "Bravo!" she cried, breaking off long enough to touch the top of his hand where it clutched a knife inside his unbuttoned suit coat. Her fingers—warm, *warm*. "Bravo!"

Next to her, after a moment, the foreign devil in uniform joined her—clapped for him, too! Across the shelter, the youth who'd sat next to Number Four also acknowledged and greeted him with applause.

But the captain stopped clapping long enough to touch his hand as the woman had—and the masculine, businesslike fingers spread as if to ensnare his wrist.

Flushed, filled with confusion, he spun on his heel and raced toward the door in a bewildered daze.

—And was through it, mentally searching for a place to hide in the building he knew better than any other, when he realized tears were streaming down his cheeks into his mustache.

"You tried to trick him, to capture him!" Sister Bethany and the captain had rushed after the murderer, but he'd slammed the shelter door in their faces. By the time they were emerging from the basement stairwell and were stepping into a deserted lobby, the hotel manager was nowhere to be seen. "You have no *trust*. Another moment and everyone present would have been applauding!"

"And then what?" Side arm drawn, the captain proceeded carefully across the lobby to the doors. One stood wide. "Would he have had to cut the throats of the Third Armored Division for an encore?"

Realizing they hadn't needed to shout to be heard,

staring through the open door at a smoke-filled but otherwise clear sky, they turned to each other. "You won't find him out there."

"There'll only be looters in those streets," he said, "except him."

She saw the sudden, horizon-eating flash of missiles miles in the distance.

"Stay here," he commanded, paused. "How did you spot him?"

Shrugging, she began to walk slowly back across the lobby. "He kept referring to *mawt*, Arabic for death, even while he was serving us. When you questioned him and let him go, he muttered *gharib*—foreign—and *qatzir*—dirty. Then a term I would rather not repeat. He promised you 'mawt,' Captain."

He stared dumbfounded from the door. "He didn't say a damn word like that," he called. "I was listening."

"You forget. I read lips. And they definitely were *damning* words."

She was at an alcove leading off the lobby. He had to raise his voice, and the tremor he heard in it made him aware of some problems his conscious mind hadn't confided clearly. "Where are you going, Sister?"

"I didn't question your ability to find him in the city, Captain. I only meant that a man who regards himself as infinitely superior wouldn't have gone out among looters to hide." She was small as a speck across the long lobby. "Neither you nor he would've had to open those doors, Captain. The glass was already shattered by the blasts."

He glanced down at the floor and saw that he was crunching shards under his feet. Looking up, he saw that the speck had vanished.

She remembered reading the sign indicating the *lukanda* manager's office when she checked in, and she wasn't surprised when the door yielded to her slight weight and opened. The only reason she hesitated in the entrance was to let her vision adjust to the darkness.

"Hiding can be rather demeaning, I think." The office door went back all the way to the wall with a light push.

"I really do believe your timing and planning have been brilliant." No reply. "Between the two of us, your hotel is being evacuated in a few hours. You can see for yourself, it *is* over."

Yellow as urine, his face materialized in a flare of dim light. When he put the lantern down, his eyes still had a uremic cast to them, and the mustache that managed to conceal and distort the lower part of his face looked as if he had pulled his head out of a toilet. No startlement, no apprehension in the eyes. They didn't even swing to a position beyond her to search for the uniformed man.

He stood in a corner of his office—not crouching but bracing himself on the wall with one hand, idly. The knife in the other hand was gripped as if he'd just completed a business call and hadn't put the phone back in its cradle. Sirens screeched above the hotel, and a low hum began building with such incremental steadiness that it suggested to Sister Bethany an abnormally swift growth of tissue around the building. He glanced up, casually curious, as though trying to gauge distances with astronomical precision. "Gounod's *Ave Maria* is lovely."

"I think so." She went in, closed the door quietly behind her. There were other marked offices along the corridor, and the captain couldn't read Arabic. "I didn't write it, of course. Neither the music nor the words." A flag hung from one wall, framed photographs of other mustache-wearing men from another. "You're aware of my vocation, then." The humming grew much closer now; the cocoon around the *lukanda* was hardening.

"I saw that you were intelligent. You were to be one of the last." He didn't quite imply it, but she inferred his belief that she could still be. His gaze dropped from the heavens, came at her like tracer fire. "It may be of *faida*—interest—to know I hoped to keep you awhile, with me. Now," his eyelids went back to show tears standing in them, "I must decide swiftly the degree of your sincerity, your touch. Were you really appreciative or, filled with your churchly arrogance, just pretending, and hungry to watch me at work?"

She raised her arms slightly and walked nearer. *By-*

pass the bothersome facts and fears, she thought. "I think it wouldn't be quite reasonable to question my sincerity. Other qualities, perhaps." She thought she heard the captain cautiously trying other doors outside the office but couldn't be sure with the *qounboulas* falling again. "You see that I noticed you, singled you out."

"*Naam,*" he agreed, appearing curious.

"I am prepared now to tell you what I think about you—if it matters."

He didn't move. He considered that. "How can I know if it matters until I have heard what it is?" he said. "Come; tell me. And I"—he left the wall, outstretched both his arms, the knife no more unconventional to him than a wristwatch or a belt—"I shall tell you what is in my heart."

God alone can comprehend all aspects at times of crisis, Sister Bethany told herself. It wouldn't be possible to forget how he looked then, or the feeling that she might have grown vain in her knowledge. *Direct your life, Sister!*

One framed photo shot across the room. Simultaneously, the wall behind him collapsed, a missile hitting the corner of the hotel directly. The noise for an instant was too varied, too consuming, to be bearable. It was all there was.

. . . She was kneeling with no notion how she had gotten there—

And the sociopath seemed to have been obliterated.

Something, partly slithering; the sound of cloth and bone worming free. A clenched fist, the blade of a knife naked against suddenly visible bursts of explosive in the midnight sky. He, he was wrenching himself out of the rubble into a sitting position. His mustache was a smoky remnant, yet the smile was beneath it.

Sister Bethany realized he either had no legs or they were crushed under him.

"A hug." He said it plainly, neither plea nor command. It was what he wanted. Gouts of blood were on his teeth, others snapped out when he spoke. "Hug me, and I shall speak my heart."

She got to her feet. Pain somewhere. She walked toward the man with no legs.

The sharp sound like something cracking made her turn her head, and the captain stood in the doorway, partly crouching, aiming. He did not seem to see her.

She whirled and tried to run the rest of the distance to the partly buried man. "I think God—"

"*Muzlim,*'" he bit off the word. Eyes roved from her to the captain, back. And when she stood in the captain's line of sight and was inches away from her goal, she saw nothing in the eyes for her to recognize. "You—I—we're all *muzlim*, all is."

He dragged the edge of the knife across his throat, deeply.

It stayed in his hand, was covered with blood immediately, and his eyes weren't appreciably dimmer than they had been in life.

"Darkness." Sister Bethany touched his cheek, then herself. The captain was attempting to draw her away. "He said everyone is—darkness."

Because the war went on, she allowed herself to be guided into the undamaged portion of the hotel, wishing the man who had managed it had allowed her to say what she'd meant to tell him.

That she thought God loved him.

"We must remember that one is able to see only to the limits permitted by one's structure, for the instrument of seeing is oneself."

——James Wyckoff, 1975.

Dark Side of the Moon
by Barbara Collins

Harriett Gipple clutched the silk black crotchless panties tightly to her chest, her eyes squeezed shut, an expression of pain etched on her pasty, lumpy face.

She sat that way, in a frumpy brown dress, on the edge of a pink satin bed—in a room that seemed designed more for sex than sleep—for nearly a full minute. Then she sighed, letting the panties fall down, onto her protruding stomach.

To Jack Lawson, who stood by quietly, the sixty-plus-year-old woman with her slight balding spot and facial hair, appeared about as out of place—and uncomfortable—as a nun in a cathouse.

It just wasn't like her.

He went to the woman, squatted down next to the bed, and put one hand tentatively on her knee. "Maybe something in the closet . . . ?" he asked anxiously.

"No," she said firmly, shaking her head, looking at him with her only redeeming feature: a pair of shockingly beautiful green eyes. God mercifully must have given them to her, Lawson supposed, to keep people from running screaming into the night at the sight of the *rest* of her.

Lawson stood up, and now he sighed. He was baffled by Harriett's lack of response, which—as long as he'd known her—had never before happened. And even more disturbing was his own reaction: beads of sweat were forming on his brow.

Had he come to need this woman so much, that, without her, he couldn't function? As he stood looking down at her, he suddenly wished she'd never come in to his life at all.

It was two years ago—April to be exact—when Roy Kautz, C.E.O. of a multibillion dollar chemical plant, became a victim of corporate kidnapping. He was snatched—appropriately enough—while visiting his mistress. The unfortunate woman was killed. A ransom note sent to the company demanded a mere five million.

Jack Lawson, then new to the force, was at the station, working into the night, when the woman named Harriett Gipple came in. She started babbling about having an autographed copy of the industrialist's best-selling book, *How to Get Ahead and Climb on Top*. And, when she heard Kautz was missing, she had gotten out the book. That's when she "saw" him buried in a coffin, equipped with some water and a hose for air.

She thought he was alive. She thought she could find him.

Lawson thought she was nuts.

Back in Chicago he'd dealt with psychics before: a bunch of self-professed, self-serving, egotistical misfits that would—dollars to donuts—send him scurrying off in the wrong direction every time. Like when the DA turned up missing, her car abandoned in an empty lot, court papers and briefs thrown to the wind. Yes, they were called in, to give their pronouncements of "lake" and "train trestle" and—in the case of something that needed interpretation—"frisbee." And all the while the DA was at the bottom of a dumpster just fifty feet away.

The skepticism must have showed on Lawson's face because Harriett Gipple had reached out across the desk, taken his coffee cup, closed her eyes, then opened them and said, "Prostrate problems in a man of your youth are unusual."

With the help of Harriett Gipple, Lawson found Kautz, buried in a cornfield in a wooden box. Though the executive was alive, physically, the traumatic experience rendered him dead, mentally.

As Roy Kautz's brilliant career went nova, Lawson's lackluster one began to shine.

"We're all done out here, Lieutenant," said a sergeant who stood in the bedroom doorway.

Lawson looked at Harriett, who was rising up from the bed and avoiding his stare.

"I guess we are too," he said, picking up the black panties that had fallen onto the floor. He went over to a dresser, its top covered with perfume bottles and makeup, and put them away, in the drawer where he'd found them.

"Probable homicide, Lieutenant?" asked the sergeant.

"Missing person," said Lawson. "Until we find a body."

Lawson followed Harriett out, into the living room, which was as blandly decorated as a Montgomery Ward floor display. The beige carpet looked new, spotless—except for the thin trail of blood leading off to the bathroom.

Lawson and Harriett left out the back, down a short flight of steps, and into the alley behind the house. The night was lit by a ghostly white moon; shapeless black clouds floated across it, spirits from another world.

The late fall wind sent dry leaves and debris dancing and swirling around their legs as they walked quickly along. At the mouth of the alley, a cat digging in garbage saw them, arched its back and hissed.

Around the corner, Harriett's car was parked at the curb. They stopped on the sidewalk a few feet from it.

"What happened?" asked Lawson quietly as he faced the woman. "Why didn't you see her?"

Harriett was silent for a moment before she said, "I didn't say I didn't."

"Then, what? Is it so horrible ... ?"

Harriet shook her head.

"Tell me!" said Lawson, putting his hands on her shoulders. "Where *is* she?"

Harriett looked up, toward the source of the light. "She's there."

"Where?"

"There. On the moon."

The women stood motionless, all in a row, their clothes splotched red, their hands bound in front, slashes of gray duct tape covering their mouths.

Despite the thick ropes that looped around their hands, many held sticks. And at the end of those sticks were signs that read: STOP VIOLENCE AGAINST WOMEN!

Jane Yeoman squinted her eyes against the brilliant autumn-day sun as she watched Jack Lawson enter the police station, just across the street. She put down her sign, shook off the ropes, untaped her mouth, and said to the woman standing next to her, "I'll be back."

Then she picked up her bag from the sidewalk, and started across the street, weaving in and out of the traffic that had slowed to a crawl as drivers and passengers gawked at the demonstrators.

Once in the building, she hunted him, her ketchup-stained corduroy skirt swishing, brown loafers slapping the tiles as she walked. On the third floor she found him, bent over a water fountain.

"Mr. Lawson," she said, approaching the sandy-haired man of average build who she guessed was in his early thirties.

He stopped drinking and straightened up. Water dripped from his unshaven chin, and he wiped it away with the back of one hand. His white long-sleeved shirt and black trousers looked slept in.

"Ms. Yeoman," he said with a smile she didn't believe for a moment.

"Why haven't you found Rita Cato?" Yeoman demanded.

Lawson's smile turned patronizing. "We're working around the clock," he said. "Now, if you don't mind, I'm very busy."

He turned away from her, walking on.

"I see," said Yeoman, standing her ground by the water fountain. "Of course, you found Roy Kautz in twenty-four hours. But then, he was an important citizen . . . not an insignificant housewife. He was a man . . . not a woman."

Lawson stopped in his tracks, looked back at her with what she thought was amused disgust. He started to say something, but must have thought better of it. Then he continued down the hall, disappearing into a room.

"And I'd like to know," asked Yeoman, now standing

in the doorway of his office, "why that husband of hers isn't in jail!"

Lawson, seated behind his desk, shuffling papers, didn't bother to look at her. "I'm not at liberty to discuss the case with you," he said flatly.

Yeoman moved in front of his desk. "You know she's been murdered ... from the rope and the tape and the blood in the bathroom! *And he did it!*"

Now Lawson looked at her. "Ms. Yeoman, we're pursuing every available avenue to solve this thing. But there'll be no arrest until we have proper evidence."

Yeoman rummaged around in her bag, pulled out a videotape, and placed it on the desk. "Then perhaps," she said, "*this* might help."

Lawson looked at the black cassette, then back at her.

"It 'stars' Rita Cato," Yeoman explained. "She came to see me last month at the Women's Resource Center."

Lawson leaned back in his chair. "Do you always videotape your clients?" he asked.

"No," she said. "But if they've been battered—like Rita—I do. In case they change their mind and want to file charges." She paused. "They're aware I do it," she added.

Lawson reached out, picked up the tape, turning it over, like he'd never seen one before.

"Well?" Yeoman said after a moment. "Shouldn't we look at it?"

" 'We'?" He used the word disdainfully. "*I'll* look at it when I get around to it. Now, why don't you be a good girl and run along, back to your little group."

"Disturbing you, are we?" Yeoman sneered.

"Can I give you some advice?"

"What? Not 'friendly' advice?" she smirked.

"If I were you, I'd be careful about picking a team mascot until I found out the score."

"If you were me, you wouldn't be a condescending sexist jerk."

His smile was typically smug. "Wouldn't I?" he asked.

She grunted, threw her bag onto her shoulder, and stormed out.

On the front steps of the police station, Yeoman spotted a TV crew, across the street, filming the bound and gagged women, and her frown disappeared.

"Jane!" called out the perky, petite newscaster Yeoman recognized as Heather Hart, coanchor of the local Channel Eight News.

"Could you answer a question for our six o'clock edition?" she asked the approaching Yeoman, then laughed, "No one else here seems to be able to talk!"

"Certainly," said Yeoman, businesslike.

Heather gave her long blond hair a toss and licked her pink lips as the cameraman with Minicam stood nearby, ready to roll.

Then she pointedly asked Yeoman, into the microphone, "Just how *long* do you plan on keeping up this vigil?"

Yeoman looked into the camera. "The Women's Resource Center, along with friends and concerned citizens of Rita Cato, will keep up our vigil—here in front of the police station—until *they* find her, and the *man* responsible for this horrible atrocity is brought to justice."

Yeoman went on. "Nearly every ten seconds a woman becomes the victim of a brutal crime and . . ."

"Thank you, Jane Yeoman. Founder of the Woman's Resource Center. This is Heather Hart, Channel Eight Eyewitness News."

"Sorry, Jane," said Heather after a moment when the cameraman stopped filming. "Sound bites. We need sound bites."

As the woman walked away, Yeoman pursed her lips and glared. "Airhead," she said under her breath.

She was the worst, thought Yeoman, watching Heather leave in the news van. The real lack of support for women's rights didn't come from men—who could be made to feel guilty—it came from the white-collar women who saw their suffering sisters as just less competition.

"I'm going home," Yeoman said, disgruntled, to the woman she'd talked to earlier when she'd spotted Lawson. "Can you handle the second shift?"

The silent, muzzled woman nodded.

"I'll see you in the morning."

Yeoman walked to her car, which was parked on the
street a block away. She got in and started the engine.

"Hey! There's Jane Yeoman, the women's libber!"
she heard a bystander say as she drove off.

How Yeoman hated that label. But there were worse
ones, like troublemaker, lesbian, and PMSer. Men who
fought injustice received distinguished titles like "advo-
cate," and "protector of consumer affairs." Hell, even
comic-book superheroes got more respect—there was no
"Justice League of America" for those who fought the
feminist battle.

But Yeoman hadn't planned on becoming a feminist.

As a little girl, growing up in a small town in Iowa in
the 1960s—the heyday of the women's movement—Jane
didn't even know what a feminist was. The third child
born to Elizabeth and John Yeoman, she remembered
being told more than once that her arrival "wasn't
planned."

Her mother, a cold and calculating social climber, and
father, a never-at-home auto parts salesman, paid little
attention to the girl. Jane spent her childhood starved
for affection. Though she had older twin brothers, they
teased her relentlessly, nicknaming her "Clarabell the
Clown" because of her thick red hair. When the boys
went off to college, her father saw his responsibility as
done and moved out.

But there were a few bright spots in Jane Yeoman's
life. In high school, with the help of a kind drama
teacher, she excelled in theater. A shy, quiet introvert,
she blossomed when performing on the stage. Then an
unexpected scholarship let her escape to the University
of Colorado.

It was there, on a ski slope in Boulder during Christmas break, that she ran into Bob. Literally. She tripped
him, coming down a run, and they landed in a twisted
pile, him hurting his shoulder and her an ankle. They
hobbled back to the lodge, where, as an apology, she
bought him a drink. As they sat in front of a crackling
fire, she couldn't believe how funny and attentive he
was. Tall and muscular, dark and handsome, he was a
Prince Charming if ever she saw one. And they found

an immediate common ground: both hadn't gone home for the holidays because they hated their families.

After a short, whirlwind, passionate courtship, they drove off to Las Vegas and got married. And she happily sacrificed her scholarship to go to work in a bank in Boulder so he could continue his studies. But then, just a few months into the marriage, Jane began to discover that her Prince Charming was really a toad.

It began in the form of what he called "constructive criticism," but really it was vindictive browbeating, designed to undermine her assertiveness and chop away at her self-esteem. At first she complied with his wishes and tried not to "be so selfish," thinking, because of her upbringing, she just didn't know what it took to make a good marriage.

But then nothing she seemed to do was right, and he would fly off the handle, throwing and breaking things; if she threatened to walk out, he would cry and promise her the moon. So they would make up, and he would be nice—for a while. But pretty soon it would start all over again.

It was such a shame, Jane had thought, because he was so good in bed!

When he broke her nose, though, she moved out, taking the cat, to an apartment of her own. That's when he started in with the threats and harassment that sent her into a tailspin of fear. He began following her, and phoning her at all hours and hanging up. Once when she went out to her car, it was covered with raw eggs; another time her tires were slashed. But the final blow came when she arrived home from work and could tell someone had been in her apartment. The place wasn't ransacked, but drawers had been gone through, and a bottle of what used to be their favorite wine had been left, empty, by the sink as a calling card.

And the cat was missing.

When she called Bob on the phone and confronted him, he denied ever being there, acting all sweet and innocent, saying he was concerned that she might be losing her mind.

It was pretty damn frightening.

The next day, putting groceries away, she found the cat. In the freezer. She sat hysterically crying, holding her dead pet, until the poor thing thawed out. Then a calmness settled over her.

Something had to be done.

That night, she waited in the darkness, behind the wheel of her Cherokee Jeep, in the parking lot of a bar outside Boulder on Shadow mountain. When Bob came out with a slut on his arm, Jane slumped down in her seat and watched as they got drunkenly into his Pinto. They made out for a few minutes before Bob started the car and eased it out, heading down the winding hill.

Jane followed; lights out.

On a particularly treacherous stretch of road, she floored her accelerator and rammed into him, hard. To her amazement, the rear of the Pinto burst into flames and the tremendous jolt caused the car to crash through a guardrail, where it sailed over the edge.

Jane, unhurt, pulled her scorched Cherokee over, jumped out and looked down at the burning car, which was flipping ass over teakettle down the mountainside.

She hadn't meant for him to die. Exactly. But as she stood staring at the crimson flames, it reminded her of the beginning of their fire-side romance; and she was as happy as she was back then.

With a large check from an insurance policy Bob had taken out on himself shortly after they were married, Jane returned to college, but back in her home state, at the University of Iowa. On campus she was active in school politics, off campus she worked for the passage of the Equal Rights Amendment, and was instrumental in bringing to the public's attention the dangerous rear-end collision problem of the Pinto. Eventually she changed her major to political science.

After graduation, with the help of state and local funds, along with the last of the insurance money, she started the Women's Resource Center in Iowa City. She wanted to help other women who had been abused like herself.

But as of late, the Women's Resource Center had fallen on hard times; the recession had put a stranglehold on community donations, and government dropped its funding. If something didn't happen soon, the facility would go under.

The high profile the center was now attracting, however, by rallying around Rita Cato, was beginning to help.

Yeoman pulled her car in the driveway of her rustic, A-frame condominium on the outskirts of the city, and got out. She walked up the wooden flight of steps and around the tree-lined deck where yellow and orange mums, along with other potted plants, sat like patio guests, whispering in the cool breeze. Wind chimes dangled from the overhang, twisting, singing their monotonous tunes.

She unlocked the back door and let herself in.

Gloria, her calico cat, greeted her, weaving in and out of her master's legs. Yeoman bent over and petted it. Then she threw her bag on a chair and went to the kitchen to pour herself a drink. She took the glass of wine to the couch, where she flopped down, kicking off her shoes.

She sat there, sipping her drink, staring into space, recharging herself, until at last she focused on a videotape on top of the TV. The tape was a dub of the one she'd given Lawson. She got up, turned on the TV, and put the cassette in the VCR.

She'd never actually viewed the tape of her meeting with Rita—after all, she'd *been* there—and had only partially screened it, to make sure the tape wasn't defective before dubbing it.

Yeoman returned to the couch to watch.

The woman filled the screen, from the waist up. She was lovely—beautiful really—despite her bruised face and distraught expression. She had long, raven-black hair, a delicately turned-up nose, and full, rounded lips. She spoke softly, hesitantly, like a little lost girl. She said her husband abused her.

Yeoman leaned forward, eyes glued to the set. Even though her senses were dulled from the wine, something suddenly seemed wrong. She was reminded of a performance she had given in a high school play. She thought she had been wonderful, but later, watching a videotape a friend had made, she looked bad, stilted, over-rehearsed.

Like Rita.

Now the woman was emptying her purse into her lap looking for a Kleenex, and Yeoman saw something that made her drop down, off the couch, onto her knees, and crawl like a baby toward the screen to see better.

Then Yeoman got up, grabbed her bag and coat, and went to her car.

Rita Cato floated, dreamily, inside the tiny crater, its hot, bubbling liquid soothing her naked, voluptuous body. She looked upward. The earth, brown with swirling blue and white masses, seemed so very far away. Lazily, she turned her head, smiling at the sight of the silver space capsule, which rose phallically off the floor just a few yards away.

She drifted, self-absorbed, until a rap-rap-rapping in the distance brought her back to reality.

"Who's there?" she called out.

"Room service!"

Rita got out of the whirlpool, reached for a white towel resting among man-made moon rocks, wrapped herself up, and answered the door.

"Hello, Jaimie," she smiled to the young dark man standing with a covered tray in his hands. "Come on in . . . there's a beautiful earth out tonight."

She blocked the doorway, provocatively, forcing him to squeeze by her. About her height, he was real Chippendale material, in spite of his crater-like acne.

She closed the door.

"Where . . . where you want it?" he stammered, then seemed to get flustered by his own phrasing.

She smiled, amused, undulating past him, letting the towel fall open to reveal the perfect full moon of her ass. "Why, over here," she purred, pointing to the round white bed in the bottom of the capsule, "where you . . . put it . . . yesterday."

He took the tray to the capsule and bent over, leaning

in the hatch door. Rita reached out and ran her hand along his cute butt, and down between his legs.

He jumped, surprised, hitting his head on the metal frame, spilling the food from the tray.

She laughed.

"No," he said, pulling her hand away. "I don't want to lose job!"

"But you'll come back later?" she asked with an exaggerated pout. "To turn down the bed?"

Getting no reaction, she pressed forward, looking into his eyes. "You can be Luke Skywalker, and I'll be Princess Leia," she said playfully.

He looked confused by her words, and sidestepped her, to make his escape.

She waited until he reached the door before calling out, "Hey! I forgot to give you a tip!"

He stopped and looked back.

"Bring some inner-galactic condoms!" she said, then howled with laughter.

When he had gone, she discarded the towel and climbed inside the capsule, onto the bed. She poured herself another scotch on the rocks from a small bar hidden behind a fake control panel, and chugged the booze down.

"He'll be back," she smirked, running a long red-nailed finger around the rim of the glass.

She leaned against the pillows. What a great place, she thought. And what a great idea! A hotel designed to fulfill your every fantasy.

She saw the Minneapolis playground advertised in the *Iowa City* paper. Wouldn't it be fun to go there, she had thought—of course, not with her husband.

And that had given her a wicked little idea.

What if she just disappeared? That would fix him. She would teach that bastard never to bat her around. So what if she started the fight by clobbering him with the clock radio. He still shouldn't have hit her. She was a *woman,* wasn't she?

Vindictively, she'd gone to the Women's Resource Center, to get him into trouble. But when the woman there wanted her to go to the police, she thought she'd better back off.

Then a few days later, while shaving her legs, she sliced her ankle; she hadn't realized she'd done it until she saw all the blood on the carpet.

Suddenly that little idea that had been revving its engine in the back of her mind, raced to the front! Here was her chance ...

So she'd planted the tape and rope in the bathroom, got her secret nest egg of cash, and caught a bus, leaving behind her purse and ID.

When she arrived in Minneapolis after a six-hour ride, the hotel was nearly booked. She had wanted to be Cleopatra, in the ruins of Rome, but the only beds left were the space capsule, or a '57 Chevy.

She took the capsule. She'd done enough fucking in a car.

And was she ever thrilled with her choice! When the antigravity force was simulated, screwing in the capsule was a cosmic blast! It gave the big bang theory new credence.

There was a knock at the door.

Rita put on a robe and answered it, eagerly, expecting Jaimie.

But instead, it was that woman, Jane Yeoman, from the Resource Center!

"Hello, Rita," she smiled.

Rita was so startled she didn't know what to say—caught with her pants down ... if she'd been wearing any.

"May I come in?" the woman asked.

Rita hesitated, then stepped aside, letting her by.

Jane Yeoman, in a black coat, her red hair pulled back from a tired face, stood for a moment, taking in the lunar decor.

"Tasteful," she finally said.

"How did you *find* me?" Rita asked, pulling the robe more securely around herself.

Jane Yeoman walked farther into the room, then stopped and bent over to pick up a stray rock in her path. "I saw you at the ice machine, a little while ago."

"But how the hell did you know I was *here*?" Rita demanded.

"From the videotape," the woman said, stopping at the whirlpool, where she stood, turning the rock in her hands, looking down at the now still water. "The advertisement fell out of your purse."

Rita thought for a second, then grunted, realizing her mistake. She went to the woman, faced her, and said, "So what! Since when is it a crime to take a vacation?"

"Rita," she answered, looking at her, "I don't think you realize the magnitude of the trouble you've caused."

"Like what?" Rita asked, hands on hips.

"Everyone thought you were dead. The police have worked hundreds of hours trying to locate you. Concerned citizens raised thousands of dollars in your behalf. We held daily vigils for you. I put my reputation— and the future of the Women's Resource Center—on the line for you. I trusted you, and you used me. And you used our cause to get back at that misogynist husband of yours."

Now the bitch was starting to irritate Rita. "Look," she snapped, "he really did slap me around! And I just wanted to get the bastard in a little hot water—not that it's any of *your* goddamn business!"

"I think you can do better where your 'better half' is concerned," she said, with a thin, nasty smile.

"What do you mean?"

"Why don't you *leave* him in the hot water—to boil?"

Rita narrowed her eyes. "How? I don't understand."

"It's easy," she said. "But first, you need to do me a little favor."

"Such as?"

"Really die."

And Jane Yeoman swung the rock in a savage arc.

Yeoman checked the hallway, to see if it was clear.

She looked back at Rita, submerged lifelessly in the pool, the bottom half of her robe floating peacefully on the water's crimson surface.

She tucked the bloody rock wrapped in a towel under her coat, and slipped out. The rock would disappear out her car window somewhere between here and home. She followed the red-carpeted corridor to the nearest exit.

Outside, a fierce northern wind slapped her around, waking her up from the numbness she felt.

Disposing of Rita was not a task Yeoman enjoyed; but it was a responsibility she had had to face. In a war, soldiers died; this time a deserter would be seen as a valiant martyr. But sometimes the truth, like Rita Cato, had to be sacrificed. It meant the survival of the Resource Center and the future well-being of other sisters.

Yeoman vowed to make it up to Rita. She would give her a unique gift: life after death.

With yearly vigils and charity events commemorating her violent disappearance, there could be a new facility—the Rita Cato Women's Resource Foundation.

And, with a little luck, Rita's misogynist husband might get tried for her disappearance. Yeoman would work toward that end. That wife-battering son of a bitch had it coming.

As for the unidentified dead woman found in the pool—that would, if there were any justice, be written off as the work of some unknown male assailant. If Rita had been spending her vacation in and out of bed, with the likes of that busboy Yeoman spotted coming out of the room, then some innocent man might find himself in hot water. But so be it. After all, in this male-dominated society, what man was truly "innocent," anyway?

Yeoman smiled, feeling better.

At her car, she looked in her purse for her keys, using the light of the silvery moon.

She had the keys in her hand.

"Leaving so soon?" a voice asked.

Yeoman spun around, keys flying. She saw someone standing between two parked cars. A man . . .

He moved toward her, out of the shadows, and Yeoman was horrified.

He was Jack Lawson.

Thrown, she took the defensive. "You scared me to death! What the *hell* are you doing here?"

"I was just going to ask you that," he said, coming closer.

Now Yeoman noticed that Lawson wasn't alone. A figure—a witchy old woman—emerged from the shadows behind him; she bent down and picked up Yeoman's keys on the ground.

Yeoman was freaking. Lawson must have also seen the newspaper ad on the tape! She commanded herself to be calm.

"I thought Rita might be here," she said matter-of-factly. "But I checked at the desk, and there's no one registered under that name."

"Ah," said the old woman, "but she *is*." She turned to Lawson. "Rita Cato is as I first saw her. But dead. Killed by this woman." She pointed a knobby, accusing finger.

Yeoman's mouth fell open, and before she had a chance to speak or move, Lawson was in front of her, patting her down.

Finding the moon rock.

And inside Yeoman's mind, the Resource Center came crumbling down.

She had to admit—as he almost gently held her by the arm, helping her walk back to the hotel—that no matter how much she hated him, he was conducting himself professionally. He didn't smirk, or gloat, or look condescendingly at her.

And she was thankful for that.

Then his professional mask slipped as he guided her up the winding stone stairway to the hotel.

"Watch your step," he said. "You might stumble—it's just one small step for a man, you know . . . but a large step, for womankind."

His irony was not lost on her, but it held no sting. She was too busy crossing over onto the dark side of the moon.

Honor Bound
by J. M. Morgan

Gershom Hillel woke from his vivid dream and sat up on the side of the bed. The white sheets were twisted cords beneath him; he had struggled again. The dream always left him like this. It was coming more often now.

His T-shirt was damp with sweat and sticking to his skin. It smelled like onions. He pulled it over his head and threw it into the corner of the room, where a wicker clothes hamper overflowed with JCPenny underwear, Levi's jeans, and white tube socks. Without washing, he stepped into fresh jockey shorts and a clean T-shirt. He armed his way into a thin blue shirt.

Then he began to dress for the night.

Gershom was careful of the coveralls. They were a light gray. Last time, he'd had to work hard to get out the bloodstains. It might have been easier if he could have taken the work clothes to the cleaners, but that would have meant questions. Most of the blood had washed away in the shower. It disappeared down the drain, like his memory of the night. Only his dreams wouldn't let the memory go.

Tonight, he wouldn't dream. Tonight, he wouldn't sleep at all.

He zipped the loose cloth of the coveralls up the middle, crotch to neck, stopping at the name stitched in blue thread over the left breast pocket: Superintendent. He stuck an X-Acto knife and a wrench in one back pants pocket, a pair of needle-nose pliers, and a ball peen hammer in the other. In the deep pants pockets at the front of his coveralls, he slipped a roll of strapping tape and a length of wire.

There was little in the way of furniture in Gershom's

apartment. His bedroom held a twin bed, one chair, the wicker hamper, and a white-painted chest of drawers with nursery decals. There was no rug, no lamp, no end table or books to put on it. He had no phone, or painting on the wall, or even a family photograph. The room was strict and bare, like him.

Gershom knew the apartment building he would enter tonight. He'd seen the three children with their mother in the park, and followed them home. It was in an old brownstone, east of Central Park. He carried the address in his pocket: 308 Rotterdam Avenue, apartment 3-C. He'd followed them up the steps to the third landing, and watched as they entered the door. The mailbox said: E. Randolph. Not John Randolph, or Mr. and Mrs. John Randolph, but E. Randolph. E. for Eileen.

Tonight, he'd see the inside of the apartment.

He passed the mirror on his way out the door. His image stopped him. It wasn't the Gershom he recognized. It was someone else. Gershom never slicked his hair straight back. Gershom never wore a ring of jangling keys at his waist. And Gershom wasn't a murderer.

The reflection looked back at him from the mirror. He liked this man better.

The door banged shut as he left the cramped and stuffy apartment. Fresh air flooded into his lungs, filling his entire body with energy ... and excitement. He was going to live tonight. He was going to really live.

It was a five-block walk to 308 Rotterdam. He didn't mind. His heart was racing, and walking seemed to calm it. Over and over, he repeated the words he would say to the children. They would open the door. He was sure of that. They always did. The thought of the children made his heart race again, and he had to think of other things, trees, mailboxes, a dead-blue sky, to calm himself.

He was careful not to think of when he was a child. Little Gershom. The image made him tremble. Anger filled the cord at his neck with the hot pulse of blood, but he pressed the thoughts away. They would come later. Little Gershom could wait. He'd waited a very long time, until now. Tonight the waiting would be over ... again.

The brownstone had a black wrought-iron fence enclosing the ten steps of the entry and wide reddish stoop. There was no lock. He pulled back the wrought-iron closure, swung the gate open, and went inside the small front yard. There was no grass, an easy maintenance address. Gershom took the ten steps and opened the front door.

It was a nice building, well lit, recently painted, and quiet. He liked the buildings to be quiet. Silence let him think. When it was noisy, he couldn't remember the words. He'd tried a few places like that, noisy and harder sections of town. It wasn't as good. That rush when he said the words, when he saw how she looked ... he could never feel as good in a noisy place.

It was never noisy in his childhood. It had been so quiet, a silence that throbbed inside his head even now. Even now. No. It was too soon. He wouldn't let himself think of that yet. Some things were worth waiting for. He knew. Some things were bad—really, really bad— and worth waiting a lifetime for.

He walked up the stairs to the second-floor landing. No elevator. Other people rode elevators. He didn't want to see people. Or them to see him. His face was hot, and his brain felt swollen, engorged with blood. Ready.

He climbed the steps to the third-floor landing, turned left, and walked to the door marked 3-C. It was brown. Some people would have called it cream-colored, but it was brown. Gershom hated brown. The door made him feel exactly right; everything was unfolding just as it should. The brown door was a sign.

He knocked.

His pulse was pounding in his ears. He almost didn't hear the child's voice say, "Who is it?"

"Superintendent. I'm here to check the heater."

"Mommy!" the child called out. "Somebody wants to check the heater."

"The super," he reminded the child. Waiting. Waiting. God, oh, God, waiting.

"The super," the small voice repeated.

He couldn't hear the exchange of voices within the

apartment. The child had left the door for a moment. Who would open it? The mother? The child? Which face would he see first? Each question held a delicious mystery. He found himself fingering the blade on the knife in anticipation. Realizing, his arms dropped to his sides obediently, and he stood absolutely still. *Come on, bitch! Open the fucking door.*

"Let him in, Suzy. I'll be right there." He heard the words like bridges connecting the track for a roaring train in his mind. *Suzy*. Delicious.

"Suzy," he said.

The little girl was small, four or five years old, he guessed. He didn't think her pretty, but some people would have said she was cute. Not him. She had blond curls, a round face, and pink lips. He didn't look at her eyes. Not yet.

"Mommy," the little girl called again. Unsure. They never liked him, children. They knew. They saw right through him, through the coveralls that tricked their mothers, through the blue lettering above the pocket. They saw what he was, and knew.

"I told you to let him in," yelled the mother from somewhere deeper in the apartment. "Sorry," she shouted to the unseen super. "Come on inside. I'll be right with you."

You will, he thought, and stepped inside the apartment, closing the unclean brown door.

Suzy followed him, not coming near, keeping her distance like a wary animal. Her little feet treading behind his, marking the same path, watching. Would she watch it all? What color were Suzy's eyes? Brown?

"Hi, I'm Eileen Randolph." She extended her hand.

He took it in his, touched her for the first time. An excitement ran through him that he thought would show on his face, on his skin. Couldn't she see? But, they never did. They were blind to what was right in front of them, to what was touching their hand, and in the nest with their children. Blind.

"You've already met Suzy," she added, a laugh ready in her voice. A smile on her lips. The perfect mother.

Was she? How would she choose when it came time? Would she be a perfect mother then?

"Suzy's at that inquisitive age," Ellen Randolph explained. "I hope you don't mind if she follows you around. I can send her to her room with her brothers if she gets in the way."

He had to press back the scream that was bursting the walls of his throat to answer. *I'm gonna kill you! I'm gonna tear out your eyes and kill you, lady!* "No, it's all right. She won't distract me."

Eileen Randolph smiled a confused little grin. "You're here to check the heaters? Is that right?"

He nodded.

"They seem okay. I mean, we haven't had any trouble lately. Is there a problem? They're not leaking gas, or anything . . ."

He shook his head. "Building code maintenance check," he mumbled, moving deeper into the breeder's lair, the narrow hall leading to the bedrooms. Sanctum sanctorum.

There were pictures of the three children lining the walls of the dim hallway. Twenty or more, all sizes of frames. She was artistic, this one. She put her children's faces in square boxes and hung them on the walls. Eyes everywhere. Watching him. He saw their images, babies mostly, round blobs clutching a pink rabbit, a blue blanket, mother and son.

No eyes! They were empty sockets staring back at him. Mocking. Dark brown sockets . . . where the blood had dried.

"I guess you know where the heaters are," Eileen Randolph said to him. "You've probably been here lots of times. We're new to the building. Just moved in last month."

She was making conversation, he knew. Uncomfortable with his presence in the rooms she shared with her children. He made her feel threatened. Gershom turned and looked at Eileen Randolph's eyes.

They were brown.

The trembling began in the muscles of his face, spreading down from the heat of his brain. His body was in seizure with the force of it. Shook until his bones ached and his eyes felt swollen and hard as glass balls.

"Are you all right?" She was leaning close, staring at him with disgust. And fear. "My God! Do you want me to call a—"

His hand snaked out and caught her wrist. The trembling stopped. His grip was iron, a hunter's trap. She was the prey.

"What are you ... let go. Let *go*." She tried to pry her wrist loose with the fingers of her other hand. Nails tearing at him.

He grabbed that hand too, and held her ... facing him.

She knew. Now, she saw through the gray coveralls, behind the blue lettering and the word, Superintendent. He let her look at his eyes—*at his eyes*—and she saw the killer.

"Suzy, *run*," she shrieked. Her body bucked in his unyielding grip. "Get your brothers. Run. Suzy ..."

"Mommy," the child's voice cried.

He heard the fear in it. The sound of that fear fed him and made him strong.

"Mommy, Mommy, Mommy."

She was a fighter, this woman. She kicked at his legs and tried to knee him. He twisted the bones in her wrists, almost breaking them, and she crumpled to the floor in pain. Brown eyes looking up at him.

He said the words.

"Your children, or your eyes."

Those were the words the man who'd killed his mother had said. The very words, imprinted in his mind forever. He still saw her, cringing away, fighting desperately for her life. Brown eyes gaping wide and moving in frantic terror. Staring from the man's face to the locked door, to the tight fists cracking the bones of her wrists ... to the baby in the bassinet, and the little boy. Gershom.

"Take them," she screamed. His mother. "Don't kill me. God, oh, God. Take my children, but don't kill me. Please. No, no, no."

"No!" Eileen Randolph screamed. "No, no, no. Don't hurt me. Do what you want, but don't hurt me."

He threw her to the floor, knelt on her chest, and took his X-Acto knife from his back pocket. He pulled a pillow from the bed and threw it over her mouth, muffling the dry, terrible scream. One knee held the pillow in place. One crushed the air from her chest. She clawed at him as he cut a wide piece of strapping tape from the roll, knocked the pillow aside, and slapped it over her mouth, sealing in the screams.

He used the rest of the tape to strap together her wrists.

Only her eyes spoke. Wild, panicked eyes. They shouted to him, *Take my children. Let me live.*

He blinded her first, so she couldn't see what he was going to do. Couldn't see him being bad. Then he raped her. After, when the rage in him was over, and he felt small and frightened again, he killed her.

He felt nothing for the children. The little girl was the only one of the three who even knew what was happening. He killed her first. She had blue eyes. Then her little brother. And then the baby.

He didn't need to blind them. With children, he never did anything bad—nothing they couldn't see. He smothered the baby and the younger boy with a pillow, and cut the little girl's throat.

Finished, Gershom took off his bloody coveralls and put them into a plastic grocery bag. He put that bundle inside a larger, brown paper bag. He leaned over the kitchen sink and washed his hands, face, neck, and arms with a fat bar of Ivory soap, drying himself on Eileen Randolph's flowered dish towels. The last thing he did was stop before the mirror in her bedroom and comb his hair the way the real Gershom always combed his, neatly parted and to the side.

Feeling like himself again—free, and able to take long, deep breaths—he left the apartment as easily as he had entered it, and went home.

"Hey, Gershom," called Dominick Mancuso, the head gardener at the city park where both men worked. Dominick was sitting in the open driver's compartment of a converted mini truck. "How's your mother doing? You seen her lately?"

Gershom was bent over a bed of spring crocus, yellow and straight up as stakes in the ground. "She's okay. I went to see her over the weekend ... you know, in the home."

"Yeah? That's nice. I admire a man who does right by his mother." Dominick was distributing flats of pansy, dianthus, and portulaca to be planted as borders around the bulb beds. He wore thick work gloves and never got his hands dirty with the planting. That was for men like Gershom. He dropped three flats in front of the crocus bed and moved his mini truck a few feet away.

"It must be rough, her being blind and all. I mean, it must make it harder on you, thinking of your elderly mother at that place. I know how it would've torn me up, if my mother—God rest her soul—had been blind in her last years. Bet you wish you could bring her home, huh?"

Gershom stabbed the narrow spade into one of the flower stalks, deliberately breaking it at the base. He felt the fluid from the living green run onto his bare fingers. It calmed him.

"It can't be, Dominick. I had to accept that a long time ago. I've got to work here, and she's blind. You know? Can't leave her alone. Understand? There'd be nobody to take care of her when I was away. She accepts it."

Dominick reacted like he'd been caught by his parish priest, writing obscenities on the walls of the confessional. "Oh, man, I didn't mean to imply that she didn't. No, I think it's great that you go to see her so often, and that you keep her at such a nice place. I've heard it's a real nice place, that home you got her at. Really, Gershom,"—he was working hard at seeming sincere—"you're the kind of son every mother would want. I didn't mean nothin' else. Honest."

Gershom drove his spade into the soft earth again and rounded two narrow holes. They looked like dark brown eyes. He was caught up for a minute, staring at them.

"You okay?" asked Dominick. He had parked the mini truck and was standing beside Gershom, laying a comforting hand on his shoulder. "Christ, buddy. I know you're doing the best you can for your mother. Don't let nothing' I said upset you."

The hand touching his shoulder made Gershom snap out of the little trance he had going with the earth eyes. He stared instead into those brown cow orbs of Dominick's. The spaghetti-eater looked about ready to cry. "I didn't mean to cast no aspersions, or anything. I know you're doing everything you can for her. That's all right in my book."

"Thanks," said Gershom. He stuck a fat pansy plant with purple and blue heads on it into each of the sockets he'd cut out of the ground.

"Say hi to your mother for me next time you see her, will you?" Dominick got back into the cab of the mini truck. He leaned his head out the open side. "I know what it's like to love your mother. I miss mine everyday."

The truck moved on to the next garden plot, where the squeal of brakes announced more flats of annuals dropped to the paving stones with three loud thuds.

Gershom dug more holes, and watched the young mother and her two children walk along the garden path toward him. The woman was in her twenties, he guessed, wearing shorts, and thinly attractive. She was what ads in magazines said women should strive to be—well-defined facial bones, an ectomorph body, and blond, lion-mane hair.

He noticed her from a long way off . . . because of the children.

The little boy was about six; the girl, a year or two younger. They were well-behaved children, not tramping through the flower beds or yelling because they wanted something. They walked beside their mother without drawing any attention to themselves. Gershom selected them because they were so good.

And their mother didn't wear a wedding ring.

When they passed the garden plot where he was working, he bent lower to the ground, so they wouldn't see his face. They were close enough for him to reach out and touch. To grab.

He waited. When they had moved far enough away,

still within sight, Gershom rose from the empty sockets of the flower bed and followed them home.

Later that night, Gershom awoke from the dream. His sheets were twisted beneath him in the bed. He saw the players in the scene again, the young mother, the two children. His mind focused on the little boy.

Little Gershom had been about this other boy's age on the night his mother died. It was a time that stayed fresh in his mind, always. He could still smell the flowers of the room. His mother had liked fresh-cut flowers.

She had made a beautiful garden of their small backyard, and had begun that spring to teach Gershom how to care for the many roses, annuals, and bulbs. He was a willing pupil, his mother's son.

On the night of her death, his mother's room had smelled of blood and fear. It was a scent stronger than fragrance of the roses, a perfume of another sort—one he'd known a longing for ever since.

Now, so many years later, he could feel the need come to him, like heat building slowly in a kiln. He was the fired clay. He was lined with hair-width cracks, where the maker's glaze had not stuck, where life had scarred him. He was imperfect. And who's fault was that?

Who's fault, Mother?

The apartment was on Seventy-ninth street, number 14, on the fifth floor. He had waited two weeks, in case the woman or the children had noticed his face in the park. During that time he had thought of it, planned every instant, imagined the slow realization that would come into Mary Beth Wilson's eyes when she understood his question. When he said the words.

It was six o'clock in the evening when Gershom climbed the steps of the enclosed emergency staircases between each floor's landing. At each level he would open the fire door, walk to the sign marked EXIT-STAIRCASE, open that door, and climb again.

Before he opened the fifth-level fire door, he sat on the top step of the staircase until his heart slowed to a normal rhythm, and he caught his breath.

It was harder to calm the shuddering excitement at

the thought of what the night would bring. After tonight, the bad dreams would leave him . . . for a while. Nothing else mattered.

He opened the fire door, stepped out onto the landing, moved down the hall to apartment number 14, and rang the bell.

Jeremy Wilson opened the door. "My mom's cooking dinner," he said.

"Could I come inside? I'm the super."

The boy hesitated.

"There's something wrong with the toilet in the bathroom. I need to fix it."

Jeremy glanced toward the kitchen, where the rich smell of frying chicken fed into the air of the room. "I'm not s'posed to open the door. Wait a minute," he said, pushing the door almost shut, and heading for the kitchen, "I'll go get my mom."

Gershom gave the door a push, walked inside the apartment, and closed it after him. The room was wide and clean. Over the smell of chicken, there was a scent of roses.

"*Jeremy,* I told you not to let anybody inside unless I said it was okay," said Mary Beth Wilson. She stared first at Gershom, then back at her son.

"I didn't," said the boy.

"I'm sorry," she said to Gershom. "It's just that I don't like the idea of him letting strangers into the apartment. I don't mean you, exactly. It's just that . . . well, I want to be safe."

Gershom was having trouble keeping his hands in his pockets.

"You're the super?" she asked, reading the blue lettering on his coveralls. "I didn't call for any kind of repair. We're just eating dinner right now. It's not the most convenient time for us. Maybe you could come back tomorrow."

She wasn't making it easy. Kept looking at him funny, too.

"Have I ever seen you before?" she asked. "You're not the man who was here last time."

"I'm new."

"Uh-huh." There was a signal of wariness in her body language. She pushed the boy behind her and moved back a step. "Look, it's been a long day, and I'm not really up for this tonight. I think you'd better leave."

Her eyes were blue, and scared.

"I'm just going to look at the plumbing," he said and moved closer ... closer ... close enough. Twisting violently, he grabbed her arm.

Mary Beth Wilson was stronger than her thin-girl body had seemed. She fought him. Her fingernails raked his cheek, and she slammed the heal of her shoe into his kneecap. Somewhere in her life she'd learned a few self-defense moves. She got in one more good kick before he yanked her head back by her hair and pressed the blade point of the knife to her throat.

He could see her eyes staring up at him. "If you scream," he said, "I'll cut your throat."

She didn't make a sound, except for the rapid breathing that flared her nose and made her neck quiver.

It was time. He said the words.

"Your children, or your eyes."

"Don't hurt my children," she said. "Do what you want to me, but leave my children alone."

Gershom felt the muscles of his throat tighten. It was hard to swallow. Hard to breathe. Raging pain seized his chest and he wanted to cry, but he didn't.

"Let me put my children in their room," she asked of him. "Then I'll do what you say."

He let her stand upright, the knife still pressed hard at her jugular, and lead the boy into the room he shared with his sister. The boy's eyes never stopped staring at Gershom's face. He didn't cry, or try to run. He was silent and watching.

"Don't come out—no matter what you hear," she told them both, and pulled the door shut.

He took Mary Beth Wilson to the bedroom scented with the smell of roses. And there, he blinded, and killed her. Before he left her room, he leaned over her body and said, "Dominick says hi."

Gershom lingered for a moment outside the children's door, his hand resting on the knob. His bloodstained

coveralls, knife, and other tools, were in the shopping
bag under his arm. He thought of going into the room
and killing them; it would be a simple thing. But he had
made a bargain.

The woman had been a good mother.

Gershom released his grip on the doorknob and let
his arm drop to his side. Emotionally and physically exhausted, he left the apartment and descended the four
flights of interior fire escape stairs to the exit door
below.

Cold night air awakened his satiated, blood-drugged
senses, and he hurried home.

People crowded the garden pathways of the park in the
week before Easter. Families with their children, mothers with babies in carriages, lovers with their arms
wrapped around each other's waist. They had come out
of the city's skyscrapers and cave-like apartment com-
plexes to feel the sun on their faces, and to see the
beautiful spring flowers.

The child was about the right age. Gershom looked
up from where he knelt on the upturned earth, weeding
between the long-necked Iceland poppies. They were
still a good distance away, walking hand in hand, mother
and son. The mother wore a dress with a long skirt,
the kind young women favored now. The boy walked
obediently by her side.

It had been a long while since the last time. Weeks.
He felt a shiver of excitement draw through him as they
came nearer.

The woman's voice was animated, pointing out the
individual plots of iris, snapdragon, ranunculus, and
poppy. "That's sweet alyssum around the base of that
one," she said to the boy. "And over there's a bed of
pansies."

They walked closer. The mother kept talking, working
hard to draw the child into the conversation, but the boy
was silent.

Gershom felt their approach, that familiar rush of
adrenaline that flooded through him when he knew he'd
found another woman, another child. He didn't allow

himself the pleasure of looking up, mustn't let them see his face. He could feel a kind of shimmering building before his eyes, and saw his hands in that new light. They were radiant.

Closer. He could smell her perfume, see the black scrape marks on the toes of her white shoes, and the hem of her long skirt brushing against her leg just above the ankle. Closer. Closer. Right beside him.

Her left hand was visible at her side. No gold band.

"Come on, cheer up. It's a beautiful day. Can you smell the roses? Don't they make you feel good? This man has done wonderful work, hasn't he Jeremy?"

Don't look up. It's not him, not the same one. Gershom's neck began involuntarily to straighten, his head lifting, his eyes staring at the face of the child.

Jeremy Wilson stared back.

The woman in the long skirt wasn't the boy's mother. *That one's dead.* The little girl wasn't with them. But the boy was the one from that apartment, the same watchful eyes, staring at him. Knowing.

"Aunt Kerry," Jeremy leaned closer to the woman's arm . . .

He was going to tell her. Gershom could feel the child's words coming, building like the shimmering before his eyes. His head pounded, and the awful trembling scoured through him, relentless in its fury.

There were people all over the park. No place to hide, or run.

Should have killed him, Gershom thought. But no, he'd been honor bound by a bargain he'd made with a good mother.

"Aunt Kerry," Jeremy said again, more insistent now, and pulled her a few steps away, pulling at her arm to whisper something in her ear.

He's telling her. Gershom's arms felt leaden, heavy weights hanging from his shoulders, bearing him down. *The police will come.* He tried to rise, and couldn't. His legs weren't strong enough to lift him. The shimmering was worse. He couldn't see beyond the sparks, and the pounding in his head was terrible, much more terrible than the swelling he had felt in his brain each time before he killed. He couldn't make it stop.

They walked away. He heard their footsteps, the woman and boy, hurrying.

Desperate, he forced himself to stand on dead stalks of legs that would not hold him. *Run away. Run.* Like the little Gershom. Running away had saved his life. The man hadn't caught him, but now ...

The boy had seen him, told his aunt, and the police would come. There was no choice. He had to run away, or be caught.

He took one step, nearly fell, and then another. His head felt like the pressure of a potter's kiln. *I am the fired clay,* he thought. Another step. Another. But he was imperfect, the glazing uneven. And in the bare, unprotected spots, deep cracks appeared. There, the unmerciful heat entered, and the strength of the vessel shattered and burst into a thousand slivered pieces.

People crowded around the stricken man. "What happened? Somebody mug him?" someone asked. "It's gettin' so's you can't walk in the park without some nut case robbin' or killin' some poor innocent."

"It's a stroke," another voice said. "I've seen this before, with my dad."

Gershom couldn't speak. That part of him was already dead; the rest was dying. The shimmering was gone. It had exploded in a wash of crimson inside his brain. He was lying on his side, staring at the people's feet.

The white scuffed toes came close, and the child's brown shoes. "My God," said the woman. "We were standing right here a minute ago. We just left ... had to find a bathroom for Jeremy. Oh, that poor man. He was working on the garden. He seemed fine."

"Lady," someone said, "maybe you should take the little boy outta here. A kid shouldn't have to see things like this so young. Could warp his mind, you know?"

"Yes, it's terrible," the woman said. "I'll take him away. But it's all right," she whispered. "My nephew's blind—has been since birth."

The Instrumentalist
by William Relling Jr.
(For Wayne Allen Sallee)

Tequila

Words are sharp objects. Certain people should not be trusted with them. If you scrutinize words, examine them carefully, you discover that they are contradictory and unpredictable. All literature—the spoken, sung, or written word—is ambiguous and, therefore, meaningless. Words are beyond the control of anyone who attempts to use them.

Go back to the statement I made above—that certain people should not be trusted with words—and amend it to read: "*No* person should be trusted with them." Not even me. Especially not me. My words—like everyone's words—are invalid. *These* words are invalid.

But music is truth. Music has no ambiguity. Music, that is, without words.

The Happy Organ

The songs that I remember from my childhood are the songs without words. The songs of truth. Remember this: Music = Truth. That is the equation.

Sleep Walk

I haven't slept in years. When I go to bed—never before dawn—I lie awake listening to the music of the city.

The city has sound and rhythm. The city is music.

But the words are babble that overwhelm the music.

The words must be taken away. The music must be pure. The truth must be pure.

That was the realization I had come to. That is when I began to play.

Walk Don't Run

I am the instrument of purity and truth. I am a soloist. I perform alone.

My instrument: the knife.

I lived in the city. Therefore I worked in the city. Alone.

I was not caught because I was cautious. I worked on them one at a time. At night. Alone.

I took away their words. One at a time. With my instrument, my knife. Anyone whom I encountered in the city. Anyone who was alone.

I cut out their tongues.

Apache

How many tongues? A meaningless question, because it is composed of words. I will answer in equally meaningless words: dozens, hundreds, a thousand. Who counts? Numbers are not words.

I cut out the tongues, and I kept them beside my bed. In jars. The tongues were souvenirs of battle. I am a warrior on the side of truth.

The jars were taken away when I was taken away.

Pipeline

I lay in the bed, listening to the music of the city. Stacks and stacks of jars filled with tongues lay about my room.

Silence now, except for the music.

Until the tongues began to sing.

Wipe Out

I could not make them stop.

I begged, I cajoled, I pleaded. I grew angry. I threatened to smash them if they did not stop tormenting me with their *words*. Torment me.

And then I realized, in a flash of insight, how I could stop them. How.

I found a thick piece of wire. I took the knife. I sharpened the end of the wire.

End of the wire.

Tighten Up

My favorite of the songs without words.

Though there *were* words. I recalled the words.

Tighten up on the drums.

Drums. An instrument. Ear drums.

Tighten up.

I gouged the sharpened end of the wire into my ears. One at a time.

On the drums.

The words went away.

But not without pain. And someone heard me screaming.

And brought me here.

I've done as you've asked now: recorded my thoughts. I smile at the query you've written—you've written it, because you know I cannot hear what you say. I especially like the phrase: *Explain in your own words why you did what you did.* My thoughts, my words.

Thoughts are words. Therefore, thoughts have no meaning. That is why I can write what you've asked me to write, because it is meaningless. After this, I shall have no more thoughts. No more words. From this moment, there is only the music that plays inside my head. The music. Forever.

Isn't it beautiful?

Corpse Carnival
by Ray Bradbury

It was unthinkable! Raoul recoiled from it, but was forced to face its reality because convulsions were surging sympathetically through his nervous system. Over him the tall circus banners in red, blue, and yellow fluttered somber and high in the night wind; the fat woman, the skeleton man, the armless, legless horrors, staring down at him with the same fierce hatred and violence they expressed in real life. Raoul heard Roger tugging at the knife in his chest.

"Roger, don't die! Hold on, Roger!" Raoul screamed.

They lay side by side on the warm grass, a sprinkle of odorous sawdust under them. Through the wide flaps of the main tent, which flipped like the leathery wings of some prehistoric monster, Raoul could see the empty apparatus at the tent top where Deirdre, like a lovely bird, soared each night. Her name flashed in his mind. He didn't want to die. He only wanted Deirdre.

"Roger, can you hear me, Roger?"

Roger managed to nod, his face clenched into a shapeless ball by pain. Raoul looked at that face: the thin, sharp lines; the pallor; the arrogant handsomeness; the dark, deep-set eyes; the cynical lip; the high forehead; the long black hair—and seeing Roger was like gazing into a mirror at one's own death.

"Who did it?" Raoul struggled, got his frantically working lips to Roger's ear. "one of the other freaks? The Cyclops? Lal?"

"I—I—" sobbed Roger. "Didn't see. Dark. Dark. Something white, quick. Dark." He sucked in a rattling breath.

"Don't die, Roger!"

"Selfish!" hissed Roger. "Selfish!"

"How can I be any other way; you know how I feel! Selfish! How would any man feel with half his body, soul, and life cast off, a leg amputated, an arm yanked away! Selfish, Roger. Oh, God!"

The calliope ceased, the steam of it went on hissing, and Tiny Mathews, who had been practicing, came running through the summer grass, around the side of the tent.

"Roger, Raoul, what happened!"

"Get the doctor, quick, get the doctor!" gibbered Raoul. "Roger's hurt badly. He's been stabbed!"

The midget darted off, mouselike, shrilling. It seemed like an hour before he returned with the doctor, who bent down and ripped Roger's sequined blue shirt from his thin, wet chest.

Raoul shut his eyes tight. "Doctor! Is he dead?"

"Almost," said the doctor. "Nothing I can do."

"There is," whispered Raoul, reaching out, seizing the doctor's coat, clenching it as if to crush away his fear. "Use your scalpel!"

"No," replied the doctor. "There are no antiseptic conditions."

"Yes, yes, I beg of you, cut us apart! Cut us apart before it's too late! I've got to be free! I want to live! Please!"

The calliope steamed and hissed and chugged; the brutal roustabouts looked down. Tears squeezed from under Raoul's lids. "Please, there's no need of both of us dying!"

The doctor reached for his black bag. The roustabouts did not turn away as he ripped cloth and bared the thin spines of Raoul and Roger. A hypodermic load of sedative was injected efficiently.

Then the doctor set to work at the thin epidermal skin structure that had joined Raoul to Roger, one to the other, ever since the day of their birth twenty-seven years before.

Lying there Roger said nothing, but Raoul screamed.

Fever flooded him to the brim for days. Drenching the bed with sweat, crying out, he looked over his shoulder to talk with Roger but—*Roger wasn't there! Roger would never be there again!*

Roger *had* been there for twenty-seven years. They'd walked together, fallen together, liked and disliked together, one the echo of the other, one the mirror, slightly distorted by the other's perverse individuality. Back to back they had fought the surrounding world. Now Raoul felt himself a turtle unshelled, a snail irretrievably dehoused from its armor. He had no wall to back against for protection. The world circled behind him now, came rushing in to strike his back!

"Deirdre!"

He cried her name in his fever, and at last saw her leaning over his bed, her dark hair drawn tight to a gleaming knot behind her ears. In memory, too, he saw her whirling one hundred times over on her hempen rope at the top of the tent in her tight costume. I love you, Raoul. Roger's dead. The circus is going on to Seattle. When you're well, you can catch up with us, I love you, Raoul."

"Deirdre, don't you go away too!"

Weeks passed. Often he lay until dawn with the memory of Roger next to him in the old bondage. "Roger?" Silence. Long silence.

Then he would look behind himself and weep. A vacuum lived there now. He must learn never to look back. How many months he hung on the raw edge of life, he had no accounting of. Pain, fear, horror, pressured him and he was reborn again in silence, alone, one instead of two, and life had to start all over.

He tried to recall the murderer's face or figure, but could not. Twisting, he thought of the days before the murder—Roger's insults to the other freaks, his adamant refusal to get along with anyone, even his own twin. Raoul winced. The freaks hated Roger, even if Raoul gave them no irritation. They'd demanded that the circus get rid of the twins for once and all!

Well, the twins were gone now. One into the earth. The other into a bed. And Raoul lay planning, thinking of the day when he might return to the show, hunting the murderer, to live his life, to see Father Dan, the

circus owner, to kiss Deirdre again, to see the freaks and
search their faces to see which one had done this to him.
He would let no one know that he had *not* seen the
killer's face in the deep shadows that night. He would
let the killer simmer in his juices, wondering if Raoul
knew more than he had said!

It was a hot summer twilight. Animal odors sprang up
all around him in infinite acrid varieties. Raoul walked
across the tanbark uneasily, seeing the first evening star,
unused to this freedom, always peering behind himself
to make certain Roger wasn't lagging.

For the first time in his life Raoul realized he was
being ignored! The sight of him and Roger had gathered
crowds anywhere, anytime. And now the people looked
only at the lurid canvases, and Raoul noticed, with a
turn of his heart, that the canvas painting of himself and
Roger had been taken down. There was an empty space,
as if a tooth had been extracted from the midway. Raoul
resented this sudden neglect, but at the same time he
glowed with a new sensation of individuality.

He could run! He wouldn't have to tell Roger: "Turn
here!" or "Watch it, I'm falling!" And he wouldn't have
to put up with Roger's bitter comments: "Clumsy! No,
no, not *that* direction. I want to go this way. Come on!"

A red faced poked out of a tent. "What the hell?"
cried the man. "I'll be damned! Raoul!" He plunged
forward. "Raoul, you've come back! Didn't recognize
you because—" He glanced behind Raoul. "That is,
well, dammit, welcome home!"

"Hello, Father Dan!"

Sitting in Father Dan's tent they clinked glasses. Father Dan was a small, violently red-haired Irishman and
he shouted a lot. "God, boy, it's good to see you. Sorry
the show had to push on, leave you behind that way.
Lord! Deirdre's been a sick cow over you, waiting. Now,
now, don't fidget, you'll see her soon enough. Drink up
that brandy." Father Dan smacked his lips.

Raoul drank his down, burning. "I never thought I'd
come back. Legend says that if one Siamese twin dies,
so does the other. I guess Doc Christy did a good job

with his surgery. Did the police bother you much, Father Dan?"

"A coupla days. Didn't find a thing. They get after you?"

"I talked a whole day with them before coming west. They let me go. I didn't like talking to them anyway. This business is between Roger and me and the killer." Raoul leaned back. "And now—"

Father Dan swallowed thickly. "And now—" he muttered.

"I know what you're thinking," said Raoul.

"Me?" guffawed Father Dan too heartily, smacking Raoul's knee. "You know I never think!"

"The fact is, you know it, I know it, Papa Dan, that I'm no longer a Siamese twin," said Raoul. His hand trembled. "I'm just Raoul Charles DeCaines, unemployed, no abilities other than gin rummy, playing a poor saxophone, and telling a very few feeble quips. I can raise tents for you, Papa Dan, or sell tickets, or shovel manure, or I might leap from the highest trapeze some night without a net; you could charge five bucks a seat. You'd have to break in a new man for *that* act every night."

"Shut up!" cried Father Dan, his pink face getting pinker. "Damn you, feeling sorry for yourself! Tell you what you'll get from me, Raoul DeCaines—hard work! Damn right you'll heave elephant manure and camel dung, but—maybe later when you're strong, you can work the trapezes with the Condiellas."

"The Condiellas!" Raoul stared, not believing.

"Maybe, I said. Just maybe!" retorted F.D., snorting. "And I hope you break your scrawny neck, damn you! Here, drink up, boy, drink up!"

The canvas flap rattled, opened, a man with staring blind eyes set in a dark Hindu face felt his way inside. "Father Dan?"

"I'm here," said Father Dan. "Come in, Lal."

Lal hesitated, his thin nostrils drawing small. "Someone else here?" His body stiffened. "Ah." Blind eyes shone wetly. "They are back. I smell the double sweat of them."

"It's just me," said Raoul, feeling cold, his heart pumping.

"No," insisted Lal gently. "I smell the two of you." Lal groped forward in his own darkness, his delicate limbs moving in his old silks, the knife he used in his act gleaming at his waist.

"Let's forget the past, Lal."

"After Roger's insults?" cried Lal softly. "Ah, no. After the two of you stole the show from us, treated us like filth, so we went on strike against you? Forget?"

Lal's blind eyes narrowed to slits. "Raoul, you had better go away. If you remain you will not be happy. I will tell the police about the split canvas, and then you will not be happy."

"The split canvas?"

"The sideshow canvas painting of you and Roger in yellow and red and pink which hung on the runway with the printed words SIAMESE TWINS! on it. One night four weeks ago I heard a ripping sound in the dark. I ran forward and stumbled over the canvas. I showed it to the others. They told me it was the painting of you and Roger, ripped down the middle, separating you. If I tell the police of that, you will not be happy. I have kept the split canvas in my tent—"

"What has that to do with me?" demanded Raoul angrily.

"Only you can answer that," replied Lal quietly. "Perhaps I'm blackmailing you. If you go away, I will not tell who it was who ripped the canvas in half that night. If you stay I may be forced to explain to the police why you yourself sometimes wished Roger dead and gone from you."

"Get out!" roared Father Dan. "Get out of here! It's time for the show!"

The tent flaps rustled; Lal was gone.

The riot began just as they were finishing off the bottle, starting with the lions roaring and jolting their cages until the bars rattled like loose iron teeth. Elephants trumpeted, camels humped skyward in clouds of dust, the electric light system blacked out, attendants ran shouting, horses burst from their roped stalls and rattled around the menagerie, spreading tumult; the lions roared louder, splitting the night down the seams; Father Dan, cursing, smashed his bottle to the ground and flung himself outside, swearing, swinging his arms, catching attendants, roaring directions into their startled ears. Someone screamed, but the scream was lost in the incredible dinning, the confusion, the chaotic hoofing of animals. A swell and tide of terror sounded from the throats of the crowd waiting by the boxes to buy tickets; people scattered, children squealed!

Raoul grabbed a tent pole and hung on as a cluster of horses thundered past him.

A moment later the lights came on again; the attendants gathered the horses together in five minutes. The damage was estimated as minor by a sweating, pink-faced, foul-tongued Father Dan, and everything quieted down. Everybody was okay, except Lal, the Hindu. Lal was dead.

"Come see what the elephants did to him, Father Dan," someone said.

The elephants had walked on Lal as if he were a small dark carpet of woven grasses; his sharp face was crushed far down into the sawdust, very silent and crimson wet.

Raoul got sick to his stomach and had to turn away, gritting his teeth. In the confusion, he suddenly found himself standing outside the geeks' tent, the place where he and Roger had lived ten years of their odd nightmarish life. He hesitated, then poked through the flaps and walked in.

The tent smelled the same, full of memories. The canvas sagged like a melancholy gray belly from the blue poles. Beneath the stomaching canvas, in a rectangle, the flake-painted platforms, bearing their freak burdens of fat, thin, armless, legless, eyeless misery, stood ancient and stark under the naked electric light bulbs. The bulbs buzzed in the air, large fat Mazda beetles, shedding light on all the numbed, sullen faces of the queer humans.

The freaks forced their vague uneasy eyes on Raoul, then their eyes darted swiftly behind him, seeking Roger, not finding him. Raoul felt the scar, the empty livid stitching on his back take fire. Out of memory Roger came. Roger's remembered voice called the freaks by the acrid names Roger had thought up for them. "Hi, Blimp!" for the Fat Lady. "Hello, Popeye!" This for the Cyclops Man. "And you, Encyclopaedia Britannica!" That could only mean the Tattooed Man. "And you, Venus de Milo!" Raoul nodded at the armless blond woman. Even six feet of earth could not muffle Roger's insolent voice. "Shorty!" There sat the legless man on his crimson velvet pillow. "Hi, Shorty!" Raoul clapped his hand over his mouth. Had he said it *aloud*? Or was it just Roger's cynical voice in his brain?

Tattoo, with many heads painted on his body, seemed like a vast crowd milling forward. "Raoul!" he shouted happily. He flexed muscles proudly, making the tattoos cavort like a three-ring act. He held his shaved head high because the Eiffel Tower, indelible on his spine, must never sag. On each shoulder blade hung puffy blue clouds. Pushing shoulder blades together, laughing, he'd shout, "See! Storm clouds over the Eiffel! Ha!"

But the sly eyes of the other freaks were like so many sharp needles weaving a fabric of hate around him.

Raoul shook his head. "I can't understand you people! You hated both of us once for a reason; we outshone, outbilled, outsalaried you. But now—how can you still hate *me*?"

Tattoo made the eye around his navel almost wink. "I'll tell you," he said. "They hated you when you were more abnormal than they were." He chuckled. "Now they hate you even more because you're released from freakdom." Tattoo shrugged. "Me, I'm not jealous. I'm no freak." He shot a casual glance at them. "They never liked being what they are. They didn't plan their act; their glands did. Me, my mind did all this to me, these pink chest gunboats, my abdominal island ladies, my flower fingers! It's different—mine's ego. Theirs was a lousy accident of nature. Congratulations, Raoul, on escaping."

A sigh rose from the dozen platforms, angry, high, as if for the first time the freaks realized that Raoul would be the only one of their number ever to be free of the taint of geekdom and staring people.

"We'll strike!" complained the Cyclops. "You and Roger always caused trouble. Now Lal's dead. We'll strike and make Father Dan throw you out!"

Raoul heard his own voice burst out. "I came back because one of you killed Roger! Besides that, the circus was and *is* my life, and Deirdre is here. None of you can stop me from staying and finding my brother's murderer in my own time, in my own way."

"We were all in bed that night," whined Fat Lady.

"Yes, yes, we were, we were," they all said in unison.

"It's too late," said Skyscraper. "You'll never find anything!"

The armless lady kicked her legs, mocking. "I didn't kill him. I can't hold a knife except by lying on my back, using my feet!"

"I'm half blind!" said Cyclops.

"I'm too fat to move!" whined Fat Lady.

"Stop it, stop it!" Raoul couldn't stand it. Raging, he bolted from the tent, ran through darkness some ten feet. Then suddenly he saw her, standing in the shadows, waiting for him.

"Deirdre!"

She was the white thing of the upper spaces, a creature winging a canvas void each night, whirling propeller-wise one hundred times around to the enumeration of the strident ringmaster: "—eighty-eight!" A whirl. "Eighty-nine!" A curling. "Ninety!" Her strong right arm bedded with hard muscles, the fingers bony, grasping the hemp loop; the wrists, the elbow, the biceps drawing her torso, her tiny bird-wing feet on up, over, and down; on up, over, and down; with a boom of the brass kettle as she finished each roll.

Now, against the stars, her strong curved right arm raised to a guy wire, she poised forward, looking at Raoul in the half-light, her fingers clenching, relaxing, clenching.

"They've been at you, haven't they?" she asked, whispering, looking past him, inward to those tawdry platforms and their warped cargo, her eyes blazing. "Well,

I've got power too. I'm a big act. I've got pull with Papa
Dan. I'll have my say, darling."

At the word "darling" she relaxed. Her tight hand
fell. She stood, hands down, eyes half-closed, waiting for
Raoul to come and put this arms about her. "What a
homecoming we've given you," she sighed. "I'm so
sorry, Raoul." She was warmly alive against him. "Oh,
darling, these eight weeks have been ten years."

Warm, close, good, his arms bound her closer. And
for the first time in all his life, Roger was not muttering
at Raoul's back: "Oh, for God's sake, get it over with!"

They stood in the runway at nine o'clock. The fanfare.
Deirdre kissed his cheek. "Be back in a few minutes."
The ringmaster called her name. "Raoul, you must get
up, away from the freaks. Tomorrow you rehearse with
the Condiellas."

"Won't the freaks detest me for leaving them on the
ground? They killed Roger, now, if I outshine them
again, they'll get me!"

"To hell with the freaks, to hell with everything but
you and me," she declared, her iron fingers working,
testing a practice hemp floured with resin. She heard her
entrance music. Her eyes clouded. "Darling, did you
ever see a Tibetan monk's prayer wheel? Each time the
wheel revolves it's one prayer to heaven—*oom mani
padme hum.*" Raoul gazed at the high rope where she'd
swing in a moment. "Every night, Raoul, every time I
go around one revolution, it'll mean I love you, I love
you, I love you, like that—over and over."

The music towered. "One other thing," she added
quickly. "Promise you'll forget the past. Lal's dead, he
committed suicide. Father Dan's told the police another
story that doesn't implicate you, so let's forget the whole
sorry mess. As far as the police know Lal was blind and
in the confusion of the lights going off, when the animals
got free, he was killed."

"Lal didn't commit suicide, Deirdre. And it wasn't an
accident." Raoul couldn't hardly say it, look at her.
"When I returned, the real killer got panicky and
wanted a cover-up. Lal suspected the killer, too, so there

was a double motive. Lal was pushed under those elephants to make me think my search was over and done.
It's not. It's just beginning. Lal wasn't the kind to commit suicide."

"But he hated Roger."

"So did *all* the geeks. And then there's the matter of
Roger's picture and mine torn in two pieces."

Deirdre stood there. They called her name. "Raoul, if
you're right, then they'll kill you. If the killer was trying
to throw you off-trail, and you go on and on—" She had
to run then, off into the music, the applause, the noise.
She swung up, up, high, higher.

A large-petaled flower floated on the darkness and
came to rest on Raoul's shoulder. "Oh, it's you, Tattoo."

The Eiffel Tower was sagging. Twin flowers were
twitching at Tattoo's sides as in a high storm. "The
geeks," he muttered sullenly. "They've gone on hands
and knees to Father Dan!"

"What!"

"Yeah. The armless lady is gesturin' around with her
damn big feet, yellin'. The legless man waves his arms,
the midget walks the tabletop, the tall man thumps the
canvas ceiling! Oh, God, they're wild mad. Fat Lady'll
bust like a rotten melon, I swear! Thin Man'll fall like
a broken xylophone!

"They say you killed Lal and they're going to tell the
police. The police just got done talking with Father Dan
and he convinced them Lal's death was pure accident.
Now, the geeks say either Father Dan kicks you out or
they go on strike and tell the cops to boot. So Father
Dan says for you to hop on over to his tent, *tout de
suite*. Good luck, kid."

Father Dan sloshed his whiskey into a glass and glared
at it, then at Raoul. "It's not what you did or didn't do
that counts, it's what the geeks *believe*. They're boiling.
They say you killed Lal because he knew the truth about
you and your brother—"

"The truth!" cried Raoul. "What *is* the truth?"

Father Dan couldn't face him, he had to look away.
"That you were fed up, sick of being tied to Roger like
a horse to a tree, that you—that you killed your brother

to be free—that's what they say!" Father Dan sprang to his feet and paced the sawdust "I'm not believing it—yet."

"But," cried Raoul. "*But,* maybe it would've been worth risking, isn't that what you mean?"

"Look here, Raoul, it stands to reason, if one of the geeks killed Roger, why in hell are you alive? Why didn't he kill you? Would he chance having you catch up with him? Not on your busted tintype. Hell. None of the geeks killed Roger."

"Maybe he got scared. Maybe he wanted me to live and suffer. That would be real irony, don't you see?" pleaded Raoul, bewildered.

Father Dan closed his eyes. "I see that I've got my head way out *here*." He shoved out his hand. "And this business of the torn painting of you and Roger that Lal found. It points to the fact that someone wanted Roger dead and you alive, so maybe you paid one of the other geeks to do the job, maybe you didn't have the nerve yourself—" Father Dan paced swiftly. "And after the job was done, your murderer friend tore the picture triumphantly in two pieces!" Father Dan stopped for breath, looked at Raoul's numbed, beaten face. "All right," he shouted, "maybe I'm drunk. Maybe I'm crazy. So maybe you *didn't* kill him. You'll still have to pull out. I can't take a chance on you, Raoul, much as I like you. I can't lose my whole sideshow over you."

Raoul rose unsteadily. The tent tilted around him. His ears hammered crazily. He heard his own strange voice saying, "Give me two more days, Father Dan. That's all I ask. When I find the killer, things will quiet down, I promise. If I don't find him, I'll go away, I promise that too."

Father Dan stared morosely at his boot tip in the sawdust. Then he roused himself uneasily. "Two days, then. But that's all. Two days, and no more. You're a hard man to down, aren't you, number two twin?"

They rode on horseback down past the slumbering town, tethered up by a creek, and talked earnestly and kissed quietly. He told her about Father Dan, the split canvas, Lal, and the danger to his job. She held his face in her hands, looking up.

"Darling, let's go away. I don't want you hurt."

"Only two more days. If I find the murderer, we can stay."

"But there are other circuses, other places." Her gray eyes were tormented. "I'd give up my job to keep us safe." She seized his shoulders. "Is Roger that important to you?" Before he knew what she intended, she had whirled him in the dark, locked her elbows in his, and pressed her slender back to his scarred spine. Whispering softly, she said, "I have you now, for the first time, alone, don't go away from me." She released him slowly, and he turned and held her again. She said, so softly, "Don't go away from me, Raoul, I don't want anything to interfere again. . . ."

Instantly time flew backward. In Raoul's mind he heard Deirdre on another day, asking Roger why he and Raoul had never submitted themselves to the surgeon's scalpel. And Roger's cynic's face rose like driftwood from the tide pool of Raoul's memory, laughing curtly at Deirdre and retorting, "No, my dear Deirdre, no. It takes two to agree to an operation, I refuse."

Raoul kissed Deirdre, trying to forget Roger's bitter comment. He recalled his first kiss from Deirdre and Roger's abrupt voice: "Kiss her this way, Raoul! Here, let *me* show you! May I cut in? No, no, Raoul, you're unromantic! That's better. Mind if I fan myself?" Another chortle. "It's a bit warm."

"Shut up, shut up, shut up!" screamed Raoul. He shook violently, jolting himself back into the present—into Deirdre's arms—

He woke in the morning with an uncontrollable desire to run, get Deirdre, pack, catch a train, and get out now, get away from things forever. He paced his hotel room. To go away, he thought, to leave and never know anymore about the half of himself that was buried in a cemetery hundreds of miles away— But he *had* to know.

Noon bugle. The carnies, geeks, finkers, and palefaces, the shills and the shanties, lined the timber tables as

Raoul picked vaguely at his plated meat. There *was* a
way to find the murderer. A *sure* way.

"Tonight I'm turning the murderer over to the police," said Raoul, murmuring.

Tattoo almost dropped his fork. "You mean it?"

"Pass the white top tent," someone interrupted. Cake
was handed past Raoul's grim face as he said:

"I've been waiting—biding my time since I got back—
watching the killer. I saw his face the night he got Roger.
I didn't tell the police that. I didn't tell anybody that. I
been waiting—just waiting—for the right time and place
to even up the score. I didn't want the police doing my
work for me. I wanted to fix him in my own way."

"It wasn't Lal, then?"

"No."

"You let Lal be killed?"

"I didn't think he would be. He should have kept
quiet. I'm sorry about Lal. But the score'll be evened
tonight. I'll turn the killer's body over to the police personally. And it'll be in self-defense. They won't hold me,
I'll tell you that, painted man."

"What if he gets you first?"

"I'm half dead now. I'm ready." Raoul leaned forward
earnestly, holding Tattoo's blue wrist. "You won't tell
anyone about this, of course?"

"Who? Me? Ha, ha, not *me,* Raoul."

The choice news passed from Tattoo to Blimp to Skeleton to Armless to Cyclops to Shorty and on around.
Raoul could almost see it go. And he knew that now
the matter would be settled; either he'd get the killer or
the killer'd get him. Simple. Corner a rat and have it
out. But what if nothing happened?

He frequented all the dark places when the sun set.
He strolled under tall crimson wagons where buckets
might drop off and crush his head. None dropped. He
idled behind cat cages where a sprung door could release
fangs on his scarred spine. No cats leaped. He sprawled
under an ornate blue wagon wheel waiting for it to revolve, killing him. The wheel did not revolve, nor did
elephants trample him, nor tent poles collapse across

him, nor guns shoot him. Only the rhythmed music of the band blared out into the starry sky, and he grew more unhappy and solemn in his death-walking.

He began walking faster, whistling loudly against the thoughts in his mind. Roger had been killed for a purpose. Raoul was *purposely* left alive.

A wave of applause echoed from the big top. A lion snarled. Raoul put his hands to his head and closed his eyes. The geeks were innocent. He knew that now. If Lal or Tattoo or Fat Lady or Armless or Legless was guilty, they'd have killed both Roger and Raoul. There was only one solution. It was clear as a blast of a new trumpet.

He began walking toward the runway entrance, shuffling his feet. There'd be no flight, no blood spilled, no accusations or angers.

"I will live for a long time," he said to himself, wearily. "But what will there be to live for, after tonight?"

What good to stick with the show now, what good if the freaks did settle down to accepting him? What good to know the killer's name. No good—no damned good at all. In his frantic search for one thing he'd lost another. He was alive. His heart pounded hot and heavy in him, sweat poured from his armpits, down his back, on his brow, in his hands. Alive. And the very fact of his aliveness, his living, his heart pulsing, his feet moving, was proof of the killer's identity. It is not often, he thought grimly, that a killer is found through a live man being alive, usually it is through a dead man's being dead. I wish I were dead. I wish I were dead.

This was the last performance in the circus in his life. He found himself shuffling down the runway, heard the whirling din of music, the applause, the laughter as clowns tumbled and wrestled in the red rings.

Deirdre stood in the runway, looking like a miracle of stars and whiteness, pure and clean and birdlike. She turned as he came up, her face pale, small blue petals under each eye from sleepless nights; but beautiful. She watched the way Raoul walked with his head down.

The music held them. He raised his head and didn't look at her.

"Raoul," she said, "what's wrong?"

He said, "I've found the killer."

A cymbal crashed. Deirdre looked at him for a long time.

"Who is it?"

He didn't answer, but talked to himself, low, like a prayer, staring straight out at the rings and the people: "You get caught. No matter what you do, you're helpless. With Roger I was unhappy; without him I'm worse. When I had Roger I wanted you; now, with Roger gone, I can never have you. If I'd given up the hunt, I'd never have been happy. Now that the hunt is over, I'm even more miserable with what I've found."

"You're—you're going to turn the killer in, then?" she asked, finally, after a long time.

He just stood there, saying nothing, not able to think or see or talk. He felt the music rise, high. He heard, far off, the announcer giving Deirdre's name, he felt her hard fingers hold him for a moment, tightly, and her warm lips kiss him hard.

"Good-bye, darling."

Running lightly, the sequins all flashing and flittering like huge reflecting wings, Deirdre went over the tanbark, into the storm of applause, her face upward, staring at her ropes and her heaven, the music beating down on her like rain. The rope pulled her up, up, and up. The music cut. The trap drum pattered smoothly, monotonously. She began her loops.

A man walked out of the shadows when Raoul motioned to him, smoking a cigar, chewing it thoughtfully. He stopped beside Raoul and they were wordless for a time, staring upward.

There was Deirdre, caught high in the tent by a white beam of steady light. Grasping the slender rope strand, her legs swung up over her curved body in a great circle, over, up and down.

The ringmaster bawled out the revolutions one by one: "One—two—three—four—!"

Over and over went Deirdre, like a white moth spinning a cocoon. *Remember, Raoul, when I go around; the monk's prayer wheel.* Raoul's face fell apart. *Oom mani padme hum. I love, I love you, I love you.*

"She's pretty, ain't she?" said the detective at Raoul's side.

"Yes, and she's the one you want," said Raoul slowly, not believing the words he had to speak. "I'm alive tonight. That proves it. She killed Roger and ripped our canvas painting in half. She killed Lal." He passed a trembling hand over his eyes. "She'll be down in about five minutes, you can arrest her then."

They both stared upward together, as if they didn't quite believe she was there.

"Forty-one, forty-two, forty-three, forty-four, forty-five," counted the detective. "Hey, what're you crying about? Forty-six, forty-seven, forty- . . ."

The Book of Blood
by Clive Barker

The dead have highways.

They run, unerring lines of ghost-trains, of dream-carriages, across the wasteland behind our lives, bearing an endless traffic of departed souls. Their thrum and throb can be heard in the broken places of the world, through cracks made by acts of cruelty, violence and depravity. Their freight, the wandering dead, can be glimpsed when the heart is close to bursting, and sights that should be hidden come plainly into view.

They have sign-posts, these highways, and bridges and lay-bys. They have turnpikes and intersections.

It is at these intersections, where the crowds of dead mingle and cross, that this forbidden highway is most likely to spill through into our world. The traffic is heavy at the cross-roads, and the voices of the dead are at their most shrill. Here the barriers that separate one reality from the next are worn thin with the passage of innumerable feet.

Such an intersection on the highway of the dead was located at Number 65, Tollington Place. Just a brick-fronted, mock-Georgian detached house, Number 65 was unremarkable in every other way. An old, forgettable house, stripped of the cheap grandeur it had once laid claim to, it had stood empty for a decade or more.

It was not rising damp that drove tenants from Number 65. It was not the rot in the cellars, or the subsidence that had opened a crack in the front of the house that ran from doorstep to eaves, it was the noise of passage. In the upper storey the din of that traffic never ceased. It cracked the plaster on the walls and it warped the beams. It rattled the windows. It rattled the mind too.

Number 65, Tollington Place was a haunted house, and no one could possess it for long without insanity setting in.

At some time in its history a horror had been committed in that house. No one knew when, or what. But even to the untrained observer the oppressive atmosphere of the house, particularly the top story, was unmistakable. There was a memory and a promise of blood in the air of Number 65, a scent that lingered in the sinuses, and turned the strongest stomach. The building and its environs were shunned by vermin, by birds, even by flies. No woodlice crawled in its kitchen, no starling had nestled in its attic. Whatever violence had been done there, it had opened the house up, as surely as a knife slits a fish's belly; and through that cut, that wound in the world, the dead peered out and had their say.

That was the rumor anyway ...

It was the third week of the investigation at 65, Tollington Place. Three weeks of unprecedented success in the realm of the paranormal. Using a newcomer to the business, a twenty-year-old called Simon McNeal, as a medium, the Essex University Parapsychology Unit had recorded all but incontrovertible evidence of life after death.

In the top room of the house, a claustrophobic corridor of a room, the McNeal boy had apparently summoned the dead, and at his request they had left copious evidence of their visits, writing in a hundred different hands on the pale ochre walls. They wrote, it seemed, whatever came into their heads. Their names, of course, and their birth and death dates. Fragments of memories, and well-wishes to their living descendants, strange elliptical phrases that hinted at their present torments and mourned their lost joys. Some of the hands were square and ugly, some delicate and feminine. There were obscene drawings and half-finished jokes alongside lines of romantic poetry. A badly drawn rose. A game of noughts and crosses. A shopping list.

The famous had come to this wailing wall—Mussolini was there, Lennon and Janis Joplin—and nobodies too, forgotten people, had signed themselves beside the greats. It was a roll-call of the dead, and it was growing day by day, as though word of mouth was spreading amongst the lost tribes, and seducing them out of silence to sign this barren room with their sacred presence.

After a lifetime's work in the field of psychic research, Doctor Florescu was well accustomed to the hard facts of failure. It had been almost comfortable, settling back into a certainty that the evidence would never manifest itself. Now, faced with a sudden and spectacular success, she felt both elated and confused.

She sat, as she had sat for three incredible weeks, in the main room on the middle floor, one flight of stairs down from the writing room, and listened to the clamor of noises from upstairs with a sort of awe, scarcely daring to believe that she was allowed to be present at this miracle. There had been nibbles before, tantalizing hints of voices from another world, but this was the first time that province had insisted on being heard.

Upstairs, the noises stopped.

Mary looked at her watch: it was six-seventeen p.m.

For some reason best known to the visitors, the contact never lasted much after six. She'd wait 'till half-past then go up. What would it have been today? Who would have come to that sordid little room and left their mark?

"Shall I set up the cameras?" Reg Fuller, her assistant, asked.

"Please," she murmured, distracted by expectation.

"Wonder what we'll get today?"

"We'll leave him ten minutes."

"Sure."

Upstairs, McNeal slumped in the corner of the room, and watched the October sun through the tiny window. He felt a little shut in, all alone in that damn place, but he still smiled to himself, that wan, beatific smile that melted even the most academic heart. Especially Doctor Florescu's: oh yes, the woman was infatuated with his smile, his eyes, the lost look he put on for her . . .

It was a fine game.

Indeed, at first that was all it had been—a game. Now

Simon knew they were playing for bigger stakes; what had begun as a sort of lie-detection test had turned into a very serious contest: McNeal versus the Truth. The truth was simple: he was a cheat. He penned all his "ghost-writings" on the wall with tiny shards of lead he secreted under his tongue: he banged and thrashed and shouted without any provocation other than the sheer mischief of it: and the unknown names he wrote, ha, he laughed to think of it, the names he found in telephone directories.

Yes, it was indeed a fine game.

She promised him so much, she tempted him with fame, encouraging every lie that he invented. Promises of wealth, of applauded appearances on the television, of an adulation he'd never known before. As long as he produced the ghosts.

He smiled the smile again. She called him her Go-Between: an innocent carrier of messages. She'd be up the stairs soon—her eyes on his body, his voice close to tears with her pathetic excitement at another series of scrawled names and nonsense.

He liked it when she looked at his nakedness, or all but nakedness. All his sessions were carried out with him only dressed in a pair of briefs, to preclude any hidden aids. A ridiculous precaution. All he needed were the leads under his tongue, and enough energy to fling himself around for half an hour, bellowing his head off.

He was sweating. The groove of his breast-bone was slick with it, his hair plastered to his pale forehead. Today had been hard work: he was looking forward to getting out of the room, sluicing himself down, and basking in admiration awhile. The Go-Between put his hand down his briefs and played with himself, idly. Somewhere in the room a fly, or flies maybe, were trapped. It was late in the season for flies, but he could hear them somewhere close. They buzzed and fretted against the windows, or around the light bulb. He heard their tiny fly voices, but didn't question them, too engrossed in his thoughts of the game, and in the simple delight of stroking himself.

How they buzzed, these harmless insect voices, buzzed and sang and complained. How they complained.

Mary Florescu drummed the table with her fingers. Her wedding ring was loose today, she felt it moving with the rhythm of her tapping. Sometimes it was tight and sometimes loose: one of those small mysteries that she'd never analyzed properly but simply accepted. In fact today it was very loose: almost ready to fall off. She thought of Alan's face. Alan's dear face. She thought of it through a hole made of her wedding ring, as if down a tunnel. Was that what his death had been like: being carried away and yet further away down a tunnel to the dark? She thrust the ring deeper on to her hand. Through the tips of her index-finger and thumb she seemed almost to taste the sour metal as she touched it. It was a curious sensation, an illusion of some kind.

To wash the bitterness away she thought of the boy. His face came easily, so very easily, splashing into her consciousness with his smile and his unremarkable physique, still unmanly. Like a girl really—the roundness of him, the sweet clarity of his skin—the innocence.

Her fingers were still on the ring, and the sourness she had tasted grew. She looked up. Fuller was organizing the equipment. Around his balding head a nimbus of pale green light shimmered and wove—

She suddenly felt giddy.

Fuller saw nothing and heard nothing. His head was bowed to his business, engrossed. Mary stared at him still, seeing the halo on him, feeling new sensations waking in her, coursing through her. The air seemed suddenly alive; the very molecules of oxygen, hydrogen, nitrogen jostled against her in an intimate embrace. The nimbus around Fuller's head was spreading, finding fellow radiance in every object in the room. The unnatural sense in her fingertips was spreading too. She could see the color of her breath as she exhaled it; a pinky orange glamour in the bubbling air. She could hear, quite clearly, the voice of the desk she sat at: the low whine of its solid presence.

The world was opening up: throwing her senses into an ecstasy, coaxing them into a wild confusion of functions. She was capable, suddenly, of knowing the world as a system, not of politics or religions, but as a system of senses, a system that spread out from the living flesh to the inert wood of her desk, to the stale gold of her wedding ring.

And further. Beyond wood, beyond gold. The crack opened that led to the highway. In her head she heard voices that came from no living mouth.

She looked up, or rather some force thrust her head back violently and she found herself staring up at the ceiling. It was covered with worms. No. That was absurd! It *seemed* to be alive, though, maggoty with life—pulsing, dancing.

She could see the boy through the ceiling. He was sitting on the floor, with his jutting member in his hand. His head was thrown back, like hers. He was as lost in his ecstasy as she was. Her new sight saw the throbbing light in and around his body—traced the passion that was seated in his gut, and his head molten with pleasure.

It saw another sight, the lie in him, the absence of power where she'd thought there had been something wonderful. He had no talent to commune with a ghosts, nor had ever had, she saw this plainly. He was a little liar, a boy-liar, a sweet, white boy-liar without the compassion or the wisdom to understand what he had dared to do.

Now it was done. The lies were told, the tricks were played, and the people on the highway, sick beyond death of being misrepresented and mocked, were buzzing at the crack in the wall, and demanding satisfaction.

That crack *she* had opened: *she* had unknowingly fingered and fumbled at, unlocking it by slow degrees. Her desire for the boy had done that: her endless thoughts of him, her frustration, her heat and her disgust at her heat had pulled the crack wider. Of all the powers that made the system manifest, love, and its companion, passion, and their companion, loss, were the most potent. Here she was, an embodiment of all three. Loving, and wanting, and sensing acutely the impossibility of the former two. Wrapped up in an agony of feeling which she had denied herself, believing she loved the boy simply as her Go-Between.

It wasn't true! It wasn't true! She wanted him, wanted him *now,* deep, inside her. Except that now it was too late. The traffic could be denied no longer: it demanded, yes, it *demanded* access to the little trickster.

She was helpless to prevent it. All she could do was utter a tiny gasp of horror as she saw the highway open out before her, and understood that this was no common intersection they stood at.

Fuller heard the sound.

"Doctor?" He looked up from his tinkering and his face—washed with a blue light she could see from the corner of her eye—bore an expression of enquiry.

"Did you say something?" he asked.

She thought, with a fillup of her stomach, of how this was bound to end.

The ether-faces of the dead were quite clear in front of her. She could see the profundity of their suffering and she could sympathize with their ache to be heard.

She saw plainly that the highways that crossed at Tollington Place were not common thoroughfares. She was not staring at the happy, idling traffic of the ordinary dead. No, that house opened onto a route walked only by the victims and the perpetrators of violence. The men, the women, the children who had died enduring all the pains nerves had to wit to muster, with their minds branded by the circumstances of their deaths. Eloquent beyond words, their eyes spoke their agonies, their ghost bodies still bearing the wounds that had killed them. She could also see, mingling freely with the innocents, their slaughterers and tormentors. These monsters, frenzied, mush-minded blood-letters, peeked through into the world: nonesuch creatures, unspoken, forbidden miracles of our species, chattering and howling their Jabberwocky.

Now the boy above her sensed them. She saw him turn a little in the silent room, knowing that the voices he heard were not fly-voices, the complaints were not insect-complaints. He was aware, suddenly, that he had lived in a tiny corner of the world, and that the rest of it, the Third, Fourth and Fifth Worlds, were pressing at his lying back, hungry and irrevocable. The sight of his panic was also a smell and a taste to her. Yes, she tasted him as she had always longed to, but it was not a kiss that married their senses, it was his growing panic. It filled her up: her empathy was total. The fearful glance was hers as much as his—their dry throats rasped the same small word:

"Please—"

That the child learns.

"Please—"

That wins care and gifts.

"Please—"

That even the dead, surely, even the dead must know and obey.

"Please—"

Today there would be no such mercy given, she knew for certain. The ghosts had despaired on the highway a grieving age, bearing the wounds they had died with, and the insanities they had slaughtered with. They had endured his levity and insolence, his idiocies, the fabrications that had made a game of their ordeals. They wanted to speak the truth.

Fuller was peering at her more closely, his face now swimming in a sea of pulsing orange light. She felt his hands on her skin. They tasted of vinegar.

"Are you all right?" he said, his breath like iron.

She shook her head.

No, she was not all right, nothing was right.

The crack was gaping wider every second: through it she could see another sky, the slate heavens that loured over the highway. It overwhelmed the mere reality of the house.

"Please," she said, her eyes rolling up to the fading substance of the ceiling.

Wider. Wider—

The brittle world she inhabited was stretched to breaking point.

Suddenly, it broke, like a dam, and the black waters poured through, inundating the room.

Fuller knew something was amiss (it was in the color

of his aura, the sudden fear), but he didn't understand what was happening. She felt his spine ripple: she could see his brain whirl.

"What's going on?" he said. The pathos of the enquiry made her want to laugh.

Upstairs, the water-jug in the writing room shattered.

Fuller let her go and ran towards the door. It began to rattle and shake even as he approached it, as though all the inhabitants of hell were beating on the other side. The handle turned and turned and turned. The paint blistered. They key glowed red-hot.

Fuller looked back at the Doctor, who was still fixed in that grotesque position, head back, eyes wide.

He reached for the handle, but the door opened before he could touch it. The hallway beyond had disappeared altogether. Where the familiar interior had stood the vista of the highway stretched to the horizon. The sight killed Fuller in a moment. His mind had no strength to take the panorama in—it could not control the overload that ran through his every nerve. His heart stopped; a revolution overturned the order of his system; his bladder failed, his bowels failed, his limbs shook and collapsed. As he sank to the floor his face began to blister like the door, and his corpse rattle like the handle. He was inert stuff already: as fit for this indignity as wood or steel.

Somewhere to the East his soul joined the wounded highway, on its route to the intersection where a moment previously he had died.

Mary Florescu knew she was alone. Above her the marvellous boy, her beautiful, cheating child, was writhing and screeching as the dead set their vengeful hands on his fresh skin. She knew their intention: she could see it in their eyes—there was nothing new about it. Every history had this particular torment in its tradition. He was to be used to record their testaments. He was to be their page, their book, the vessel for their autobiographies. A book of blood. A book made of blood. A book written in blood. She thought of the grimoires that had been made of dead human skin: she'd seen them, touched them. She thought of the tattooes she'd seen:

freak show exhibits some of them, others just shirtless laborers in the street with a message to their mothers pricked across their backs. It was not unknown, to write a book of blood.

But on such skin, on such gleaming skin—oh God, that was the crime. He screamed as the torturing needles of broken jug-glass skipped against his flesh, ploughing it up. She felt his agonies as if they had been hers, and they were not so terrible ...

Yet he screamed. And fought, and poured obscenities out at his attackers. They took no notice. They swarmed around him, deaf to any plea or prayer, and worked on him with all the enthusiasm of creatures forced into silence for too long. Mary listened as his voice wearied with its complaints, and she fought against the weight of fear in her limbs. Somehow, she felt, she must get up to the room. It didn't matter what was beyond the door or on the stairs—he needed her, and that was enough.

She stood up and felt her hair swirl up from her head, flailing like the snake hair of the Gorgon Medusa. Reality swam—there was scarcely a floor to be seen beneath her. The boards of the house were ghost-wood, and beyond them a seething dark raged and yawned at her. She looked to the door, feeling all the time a lethargy that was so hard to fight off.

Clearly they didn't want her up there. Maybe, she thought, they even fear me a little. The idea gave her resolution; why else were they bothering to intimidate her unless her very presence, having once opened this hole in the world, was now a threat to them?

The blistered door was open. Beyond it the reality of the house had succumbed completely to the howling chaos of the highway. She stepped through, concentrating on the way her feet still touched solid floor even though her eyes could no longer see it. The sky above her was prussian-blue, the highway was wide and windy, the dead pressed on every side. She fought through them as through a crowd of living people, while their gawping, idiot faces looked at her and hated her invasion.

The "Please" was gone. Now she said nothing; just gritted her teeth and narrowed her eyes against the highway, kicking her feet forward to find the reality of the stairs that she knew were there. She tripped as she touched them, and a howl went up from the crowd. She couldn't tell if they were laughing at her clumsiness, or sounding a warning at how far she had got.

First step. Second step. Third step.

Though she was torn at from every side, she was winning against the crowd. Ahead she could see through the door of the room to where her little liar was sprawled, surrounded by his attackers. His briefs were around his ankles: the scene looked like a kind of rape. He screamed no longer, but his eyes were wild with terror and pain. At least he was still alive. The natural resilience of his young mind had half accepted the spectacle that had opened in front of him.

Suddenly his head jerked around and he looked straight through the door at her. In this extremity he had dredged up a true talent, a skill that was a fraction of Mary's, but enough to make contact with her. Their eyes met. In a sea of blue darkness, surrounded on every side with a civilization they neither knew nor understood, their living hearts met and married.

"I'm sorry," he said silently. It was infinitely pitiful. "I'm sorry. I'm sorry." He looked away, his gaze wrenched from hers.

She was certain she must be almost at the top of the stairs, her feet still treading air as far as her eyes could tell, the faces of the travellers above, below and on every side of her. But she could see, very faintly, the outline of the door, and the boards and beams of the room where Simon lay. He was one mass of blood now, from head to foot. She could see the marks, the hieroglyphics of agony on every inch of his torso, his face, his limbs. One moment he seemed a flash into a kind of focus, and she could see him in the empty room, with the sun through the window, and the shattered jug at his side. Then her concentration would falter and instead she'd see the invisible world made visible, and he'd be hanging in the air while they wrote on him from every side, plucking out the hair on his head and body to clear the page, writing in his armpits, writing on his eyelids, writing on his genitals, in the crease of his buttocks, on the soles of his feet.

Only the wounds were in common between the two sights. Whether she saw him beset with authors, or alone in the room, he was bleeding and bleeding.

She had reached the door now. Her trembling hand stretched to touch the solid reality of the handle, but even with all the concentration she could muster it would not come clear. There was barely a ghost-image for her to focus on, though it was sufficient. She grasped the handle, turned it, and flung the door of the writing room open.

He was there, in front of her. No more than two or three yards of possessed air separated them. Their eyes met again, and an eloquent look, common to the living and the dead worlds, passed between them. There was compassion in that look, and love. The fictions fell away, the lies were dust. In place of the boy's manipulative smiles was a true sweetness—answered in her face.

And the dead, fearful of this look, turned their heads away. Their faces tightened, as though the skin was being stretched over the bone, their flesh darkening to a bruise, their voices becoming wistful with the anticipation of defeat. She reached to touch him, no longer having to fight against the hordes of the dead; they were falling away from their quarry on every side, like dying flies dropping from a window.

She touched him, lightly, on the face. The touch was a benediction. Tears filled his eyes, and ran down his scarified cheek, mingling with the blood.

The dead had no voices now, nor even mouths. They were lost along the highway, their malice damned.

Plane by plane the room began to re-establish itself. The floorboards became visible under his sobbing body, every nail, every stained plank. The windows came clearly into view—and outside the twilight street was echoing with the clamor of children. The highway had disappeared from living human sight entirely. Its travellers had turned their faces to the dark and gone away into oblivion, leaving only their signs and their talismans in the concrete world.

On the middle landing of Number 65 the smoking, blistered body of Reg Fuller was casually trodden by the travellers' feet as they passed over the intersection. At length Fuller's own soul came by in the throng and glanced down at the flesh he had once occupied, before the crowd pressed him on towards his judgement.

Upstairs, in the darkening room, Mary Florescu knelt beside the McNeal boy and stroked his blood-plastered head. She didn't want to leave the house for assistance until she was certain his tormentors would not come back. There was no sound now but the whine of a jet finding its way through the stratosphere to morning. Even the boy's breathing was hushed and regular. No nimbus of light surrounded him. Every sense was in place. Sight. Sound. Touch.

Touch.

She touched him now as she had never previously dared, brushing her fingertips, oh so lightly, over his body, running her fingers across the raised skin like a blind woman reading braille. There were minute words on every millimeter of his body, written in a multitude of hands. Even through the blood she could discern the meticulous way that the words had harrowed into him. She could even read, by the dimming light, an occasional phrase. It was proof beyond any doubt, and she wished, oh God how she wished, that she had not come by it. And yet, after a lifetime of waiting, here it was: the revelation of life beyond flesh, written in flesh itself.

The boy would survive, that was clear. Already the blood was drying, and the myriad wounds healing. He was healthy and strong, after all: there would be no fundamental physical damage. His beauty was gone forever, of course. From now on he would be an object of curiosity at best, and at worst of repugnance and horror. But she would protect him, and he would learn, in time, how to know and trust her. Their hearts were inextricably tied together.

And after a time, when the words on his body were scabs and scars, she would read him. She would trace, with infinite love and patience, the stories the dead had told on him.

The tale on his abdomen, written in a fine, cursive style. The testimony in exquisite, elegant print that covered his face and scalp. The story on his back, and on his shin, on his hands.

She would read them all, report them all, every last syllable that glistened and seeped beneath her adoring fingers, so that the world would know the stories that the dead tell.

He was a Book of Blood, and she his sole translator.

As darkness fell, she left off her vigil and led him, naked, into the balmy night.

Here then are the stories written on the Book of Blood. Read, if it pleases you, and learn.

They are a map of that dark highway that leads out of life towards unknown destinations. Few will have to take it. Most will go peacefully along lamplit streets, ushered out of living with prayers and caresses. But for a few, a chosen few, the horrors will come, skipping to fetch them off to the highway of the damned.

So read. Read and learn.

It's best to be prepared for the worst, after all, and wise to learn to walk before breath runs out.